Buket Uzuner

The Long White Cloud

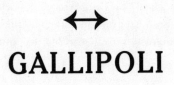

GALLIPOLI

Translated by: Pelin Thornhill Arıner

§

Fiction **30**

The Long White Cloud-Gallipoli
Buket Uzuner
www.buketuzuner.com
e-mail: buketuzuner@buketuzuner.com

The Original Title: Uzun Beyaz Bulut-Gelibolu
Translated by: Pelin Thornhill Arıner
Proofreading by: Bahar Yıldırım Çotur

Vignettes: Ali Murat Erkorkmaz
Back-cover photograph: Ömer Akçay

1. Edition: October 2004 (Everest)
ISBN: 975 - 289 - 173 - X

Printed by: Melisa Matbaacılık

EVEREST PUBLICATIONS
Ticarethane Sokak No: 53 Cağaloğlu/ISTANBUL
Phone: 90 (212) 513 34 20-21 Fax: 90 (212) 512 33 76
Distributed by: Alfa, Phone: 90 (212) 511 53 03 Fax: 90 (212) 519 33 00
e-mail: everest@alfakitap.com
www.everestyayinlari.com

Everest is a trademark of the Alfa Publishing Group.

In memory of
Lieutenant Ali Osman Bey,
Private Alistair John Taylor,
Ghazi Sergeant Alican
and all those who lost their lives
in the Battle of Gallipoli of World War I...

Thanks and Acknowledgements

In the course of writing this novel I received help from many readers, friends and associates. Readers who heard that I was going to write a novel on Gallipoli gave me valuable suggestions regarding resources.

Dozens of books and documents were packed and mailed to me from various locations throughout Turkey and the world. I am highly indebted to the contributions of all these valued readers, whose names would take pages to list.

I would also like to take this opportunity to offer my thanks to Sami Karaören, Prof. Emre Kongar, Prof. Talat Sait Halman, Orhan Koloğlu, Dr. Halit Özsüt, İzzeddin Çalışlar, Eser Eken, Kaan Erkorkmaz, Banu Gümüştüs, the Chanakkale University of March Eighteen, the Research Center for Ataturk Studies and the Battle of Gallipoli, the villagers and *Mukhtar* of the Küçük Anafartalar Village in Chanakkale, Emine and Hasan Helvacı, the New Zealand Consul in New York (1999) Jane Cunnlife, and the Turkish Second Consul in New York (1999) Muzaffer Özyıldız.

My sincere gratitude to my son Can, who showed a maturity beyond his years in tolerating my mental or physical journeys to Gallipoli during the four years of research, labor and writing that went into this book. An affectionate mention must go to Mürüvvet Fındık Sarman who spent long nights sitting next to me at the computer and giving me support in the final writing of the novel.

I would like to thank the personnel of Eceabat's "Down Under" Pension, my guide Anıl Mert who accompanied me on my arduous year-round treks on the ridges of Chanakkale and enthusiastically shared my writing excitement, and Fevzi Kılınçarslan and Gül Çalışkan, managers at Remzi Publishing, who stayed ever present by the telephone to assist me in solving technical problems.

In addition, I would like to thank the Office of the Chief of Staff – Hasan Tahsin Information Center, and the Office of Religious Affairs – Center for Date Calculation for their help.

Among the many books that I have used, I need to mention the following since I have employed some excerpts from them: *Cepheden Cepheye* (Münim Mustafa, Arma Pub.), *Kanlısırt Günlüğü* (Mehmet Fasih Bey, Arba Pub.), *On Yıllık Savaşın Günlüğü* (General İzzeddin Çalışlar, Yapı Kredi Pub.), *Gelibolu'nun İki Yakası* (Can Dündar, CD-ROM, Milliyet Pub.), *Gallipoli; The New Zealand Story* (Christopher Pugsley, Hodder & Stoughton), *Mustafa Kemal Çanakkale'yi Anlatıyor* (Ruşen Eşref, Akbank Pub.), *Ian Hamilton'un Çanakkale Savaşları Raporu* (University of March Eighteen Pub.), *Gelibolu, Yenilginin Destanı* (Steel & Hart, Sabah Pub.), *Gallipoli* (Alan Moorehead, Ballentine Books), *Voices of Gallipoli* (Maurice Shadbolt, Hodder & Stoughton), *Anzaklar'ın Kaleminden Mehmetçik* (A. Mete Tuncoku, Research Center for Ataturk Studies Pub.), *Reklamcılığımızın İlk Yüzyılı: 1840-1940* (Orhan Koloğlu, Reklamcılar Derneği Pub.), *İşgal Altında Istanbul* (Nur Bilge Criss, İletişim Pub.), *Gelibolu ve Yöresi* (Mehmet İrdesel, Geltur Pub.), *Çanakkale Savaşı Üzerine Bir Çalışma* (Selahattin Çetiner) and *Tarih Nasıl Yazılmalı, ya da Yazılmalı mı?* (Levent Yılmaz, Dost Pub.).

This novel is a work of fiction. Any similarities to reality must be coincidental.

"History is the most dangerous fruit of the human mind it has created so far"

Paul Valéry
(French thinker and poet-
Regards sur le monde actuel)

"Old World, New World, all the nations of the world
Seething, swarming, like a sandstorm is the crowd
Before you are the seven climates of the earth,
There, together with Australia is Canada!
Different the visages, the languages, the colors of the skin
The evenness of massacre is the one constant thing."

Mehmet Akif Ersoy
(*Epic of the Martyrs of the Dardanelles*)

"We had seized a fantastic opportunity but we failed to rob the Ottoman Bank."

General Ian Hamilton
(Commander of the British Army)

"In the end, the English and French withdrew from the Dardanelles. This was a successful withdrawal on their part."

Colonel Mustafa Kemal
(Anafartalar Group Commander)

"In reality, the great question remains: Who will control Constantinople?"

Napoleon Bonaparte
(French Commander and Emperor)

"The Battle of Gallipoli is the prologue for the New Turkey."

Fazıl Hüsnü Dağlarca
(*Epic of the Dardanelles*)

Granny Emine from the Küçük Anafartalar Village

büket k istanbul
an burya
çanakkaleye
kitap yazmaya
geldi helvacı
emine
27-2 2001.
2001*

THE LONG WHITE CLOUD ↔ GALLIPOLI

(AOTEAROA ↔ GALLIPOLI)

Winter is bitter in Gallipoli. It will get you, that ruthless chill.

Winter is mean in Gallipoli. It is much more wicked and merciless than one would expect from the Aegean region. The howling wind tells a sinister tale, it prowls around town, roughing up people on the street. The quiet drizzle of early spring rain sends a tremor across your heart as if it has fully understood the wind's sinister tale. This tale moves even those visitors that don't know it, or have never heard of it before, and leaves a trace of melancholy on them. Gallipoli's wind wears you down, leaves you lonesome. Gallipoli's winter is mean and chilly. Foreigners don't understand it, they cannot believe that winter so far in the Eastern Mediterranean can be so harsh. Only locals of the Dardanelles know of the winter's bitter cold. The Gallipoli Peninsula hits you hardest in early spring, when the cold is the meanest.

On a still dark March morning in the year 2000, a brand new model jeep was making its way through the Gallipoli National Park. A young tourist guide was taking a foreign tourist to the Ariburnu-Anzac Cove. Daybreak was near. Around them, everything except the clocks indicated night-time. The jeep stopped when it arrived at the Ariburnu Cove. Its two passengers sat for a while in silence and waited. The pitch black sky gradually gave way to a deep, smoky blue. It was dawn. The dim blue light revealed a calm sea meekly lapping against the shores of the Ariburnu Cove, and across from it the Ariburnu Cliff, in intimidating grandeur. The Ariburnu Cliff stood there, towering like a hostile, roaring head placed on a long neck and watched over the Cove. With its startling resemblance harking back to the Pyramids of Egypt, The Sphinx, as foreigners had deemed the Cliff, made its presence felt as the rightful owner of the cove.

As soon as shy pink clouds appeared in the sky, and the blue colors turned into shades of gray, the passenger door of the jeep flung open. Out stepped a young blonde woman, tall and slender. She wrapped herself tightly in her checkered wool-lined raincoat, threw the hood over her head and walked toward the cove. Her guide was to wait inside the jeep until her return.

When the woman reached the shore, she stopped and hiked her trousers up to her knees. Ignoring the damp, howling wind and drizzling chilly rain, she took off her boots and socks. She stuffed her socks in her boots. Then she waded into the sea, impervious to the sharp pebbles under her bare feet and the biting cold. She walked until she was knee-deep in the sea. There she stopped and turned to face the land, her back to the water. What she saw was a row of headstones was-hed clean with the rain, the graves of Anzac soldiers flanked by the foreboding Ariburnu Cliff. When the cool early rays of sunlight reached the woman's face, she began to bite her lips and blink rapidly. She might have been murmuring something to herself. Perhaps a prayer, or a song... It was as if she was just starting to feel the chill, but only her lips were cold. Ten minutes, maybe a bit more. She stood in the water, biting her lips, following some kind of ongoing activity at Chunuk Bair with a fixed gaze. Then she slowly walked back to the shore. She picked up a handful of pebbles from the beach, stroked them in her palm and began to weep. She wept without a sob, without a show, grieving deep inside, communing with some-one far away, perhaps riciting a prayer...

Every morning for the past week the woman had been co-ming to the Ariburnu Cove, which she kept calling the 'Anzac Cove', and had been going through the same course of acti-ons, as if part of a planned ritual, and had never succeeded in keeping herself from breaking down at the end.

Although the guide waiting for the foreign woman back at the jeep was used to all manners of 'weird' tourists coming to pay annual visits to their grandparents' graves at Gallipoli and to find their memories, he was nevertheless unsettled by this rather dramatic weeklong event. On the first morning he had run to her side, attempting to assist the 'damsel in distress', just as he was brought up to do. But when the damsel had ma-de it abundantly clear in a single sentence that she wanted to be left alone, he had returned to the jeep, somewhat offended. On the days that followed, though he tried to ignore her and mumbled "what do I care, she can do what she wants...", he continued to watch this image of a drenched woman crying in the dark chill of the morning with displeasure and a detached curiosity. Not only did he watch her, but also could not help trying to discern what the woman was looking at in the distance form the Ariburnu Cliff to Chunuk Bair, although he knew there was no-one up there.

Placing the pebbles in one pocket of her raincoat, the young woman produced a small towel from the other, dried her feet and put on her socks and boots. Meanwhile, the guide was marvelling at how she always managed to put these on and tie her shoelaces while standing on one leg, without losing her balance. He tried to do the same when he was alone but invariably ended up falling.

Then the woman straightened out her trouser legs, folded and tucked the wet towel into her pocket and marched briskly toward the jeep as if she bore no relation whatsoever to that other woman who just a minute ago was standing in the sea, crying. She opened the passenger door, settled into the seat and said, with a weary smile,

"Let's go Meh-met!"

She was a tall, fair-complexioned woman with a wide-brimmed nose which, in contrast to her delicate features, lent a distinctive quality to her face. Her anxious blue eyes produced a restless, 'forever foreign' impression. She seemed distant, even cold. Perhaps that's why her face had a mysterious charm. She did not smile often, or even much. When she did smile those around her could not help but feel elated. She was one of those people who seem to know a great deal but whose cool, enigmatic smiles betray no hint of that knowledge. She kept her long blonde hair in a loose bun or let it fall over her shoulders. She looked in her late twenties, spoke with a heavy British accent and had a becoming aura of mystery and cool detachment. And befitting this aura was the mild scent of fennel she bore.

Mehmet the Guide had accompanied many different kinds of tourists around the Dardanelles before, and therefore considered himself something of a 'character expert'. Although he felt a guarded interest in this woman who seemed to be slight-

6

ly older than him and whose story he thought he knew more or less, Mehmet found enigmatic women far too confusing and problematic. Therefore, he was taking care not to get involved in the woman's Gallipoli adventure.

Finally they returned to Eceabat, as they had done all week long. The woman rested until noon. Then she ate lunch at one of the restaurants by the beach, read a few pages from the novel she was carrying along, practiced a few sentences from her practical-Turkish dictionary, and jotted some notes in her small notebook. These were routine actions for most of the foreign tourists. In the afternoon they got back in the jeep and headed for the National Park. And, as in the previous days, they toured the grounds. Although he was originally from Izmir, Mehmet the Guide tried to please his customer by fervently reciting from memory all the facts he had learned about the area from history books and brochures. He inserted local and foreign anecdotes in the standard places, made her laugh and took her pictures where she wanted. For the last five years he had spent March and April working in Chanakkale and he believed he knew the area better than its natives. He was handsome and had had brief affairs with some tourist women. He worked in Gallipoli in the spring, and in the summers he headed for Cappadocia and Ephesus. Ultimately, he wanted to found his own travel agency and be its boss.

As night fell they returned to Eceabat once more. The foreign woman was staying at a little pension in town called 'Friendly Anzac'.

It was around ten a.m. when they arrived at the Eceyaylasi Village. Mehmet had called the *Mukhtar** of the village the day before and let him know that a foreign tourist woman wished to make an important announcement to the folks of Eceyaylasi.

The *Mukhtar* hedged at first, not being too keen on hearing important announcements. Then, presumably out of deference to Mehmet's boss, who was running a bus company, he extended a reluctant invitation,"Well, let's hear it then." He called the elders, and sent news for everyone else to assemble at the *kahveh*** early in the morning the next day.

---

*) *Mukhtar*: local governor
**) *Kahveh*: coffeehouse

"*Mari,* * some foreign tourist dame's in town. From some far land, what was it... England? No, no, a Zealender or somethin'... Anyway, *mari,* they say she brings some news, so come on to the *kahveh* early morn, *mari*... Let's see what she be sayin'."

When the brand new jeep pulled into the village at ten a.m. there were eight or ten villagers sitting outside the *kahveh*, sipping their tea and smoking. Mehmet the young guide, his long hair in a ponytail and wearing a single earring, stepped out of the jeep first, and was followed by the tall, thin blonde woman. The villagers stared at them as they did at anyone who did not look like themselves. They stared for a good long while. They inspected the newcomers with blank, motionless stares that betrayed no sign of life from the outside. Peasants in Turkey are extremely hospitable, humble and modest but they consider anyone who is not one of them to be a 'foreigner', and they never trust a foreigner. They also possess a special power that can freeze both time and their bodies. When applied, this power produces a shield of impenetrability over the peasant. That is how the villagers of Eceyaylasi eyed the two foreigners – with cool and unwavering stares. At that moment the only things that moved in the village were a lone white rooster strutting around the square and two preschool boys galloping around on horses made of tree branches.

Mehmet identified the village *Mukhtar* with a single glance, stepped toward him and shook his hand. After some small talk about the weather and the well-being of his boss, he introduced the foreign woman who was nervously smiling as she waited by his side. The *Mukhtar* shook her hand retiringly and gave a shy nod of greeting, not daring to establish eye contact.

"Good morning!" Mehmet called to the assembled group with his most affable smile.

---

*) *Mari*: a colloquial word used around Chanakkale to address any person

9

"Top of the mornin'! Bright and blessed it be! And to you too!" the villagers returned his greeting.

The elderly smiled and nodded, the young waited to hear the rest of his speech. Some were handling prayer beads, others held different spreads of a daily newspaper. They usually bought a single paper, distributed its pages amongst each other and passed these around. The younger ones wore caps, the older among them wore wool skullcaps or berets. All the villagers at the *kahveh* and the *Mukhtar* were male. Most of them had blue eyes.

Meanwhile the foreign woman, looking as anxious as when she waded into the Ariburnu Cove, spoke out to the villagers in a nervous voice,

"*Mar-ha-ba!*"*

"*Merhaba*, good day, welcome!" the villagers replied in chorus, taking care to avoid meeting her eyes. Then they all walked into the *kahveh*, sat around the tables and waited.

"This foreign lady wants to announce something today. Since she doesn't know Turkish, I'm going to translate for her. So, uncles, brothers, you'll excuse me as the messenger, I hope," Mehmet said in his most professional tone of voice. The villagers smiled and nodded. They resumed their attention in a most warm and friendly manner.

The woman turned to Mehmet and said something to him in English.

"She wants to know, what's the difference between New Zealand and yogurt?"

The place fell silent.

The villagers reacted the way they had for centuries to everything they found inappropriate; that is, they gave no reaction at all! They ignored it. They stared as if they hadn't heard a thing. The villagers of Turkey resisted this absurd ques-

---

*) *Merhaba*: hello

10

tion with their blankest and most transparent gaze, with an indifference honed much finer than any other peasantry's in the world. They stared long and listlessly at this foreigner who had come all the way from the ends of the earth and assembled them at the *kahveh* (not that they had anything else to do) in order to ask them this question. The ashes of their cigarettes lengthened, their teas grew cold, their prayer beads froze in their hands. They did not make the slightest move.

The woman took their lack of reaction as indifference and panicked. Mehmet the Guide, who had learned to read some of her body language from the early morning rituals at the Ariburnu-Anzac Cove, immediately came to her aid and repeated the question loudly, in the manner of a gameshow host,

"So, what do YOU think distinguishes New Zealand from yogurt?"

The woman nervously whispered something in Mehmet's ear... Not that there was anyone in the room who could've understood English anyway.

"Ha ha ha! Yogurt has culture!" Mehmet merrily declared the answer.

Once again, there was no reaction from the crowd. The woman, who had thought this subtle joke would be a big hit, wilted in the face of this desert of silence. A weary, hopeless expression covered her face.

"Uh... well, so the joke goes in her country..." Mehmet said, trying to recover the situation.

The villagers simply stared. Inside the Village *Kahveh*, which contained six or seven tables, a gas stovetop for tea and a small heating stove in one corner, the only sound that could be heard was the ticking of the clock. The villagers were feeling uncomfortable as well but in the interest of self-defense, they had been trained for generations not to reveal any such discomfort and were, by now, experts on the subject. They waited under the mask of a profound indifference that no na-

11

tive or foreigner who is unaccustomed to the history and traditions of this country can easily understand. The woman was biting her lips in desperation and impatience, searching for a way out of her predicament. This wait was so deeply disturbing that she found it difficult to breathe. Just then, she spotted a memorial to Ataturk, put up with amateurish meticulousness on the wall across from her. In a large wooden frame, a handsome, smiling portrait of Ataturk presided over the *kahveh*. The keen look in his eyes seemed to imply that he knew but pretended not to see all the mischief that went on below.

Ataturk, whose statues, paintings and busts familiarized him to every Western tourist after a day or two spent in Turkey. Even if the visitor who knew or had heard of His name had been taught at school and had come to believe that He is a dictator forced upon the population, when the very same person ran across His picture in barbers, travel agencies, taxi stops, internet cafés or beauty shops, the conclusion that this legend can only be kept alive through individual dedication became inevitable. This emotional bond, initially compared to the fame of movie stars or pop singers, could not at this point be understood by Westerners because in their culture the need for hero worship was only a phase of adolescence that became eventually dismantled. Western foreigners could no longer relate to the admiration and devotion an adult citizen of Turkey might feel for the values represented by a long dead figure. In their own right, they viewed this ardent devotion as childish and mock-heroic – something to be looked down upon. And yet they themselves could never again regain that feeling. Not through therapies, yoga, or little pink pills...

The picture of Ataturk was surrounded by dried flowers and a muslin headscarf with purple lace trim, and was flanked with photos of the Gallipoli War Memorial and some famous shots of Ataturk at the Anafartalar Front. Though it looked innocent enough to have been made by children, closer consideration of its presence and location could be construed as an indication of a civil initiative. Directly below the memorial hung the photograph of a gray-haired, blue-eyed, radiant-faced old peasant man wearing the Dardanelles medal of honor. The photo was captioned 'Battle of Gallipoli Hero *Ghazi** Sergeant Alican'. The foreign woman breathed a sigh of relief upon seeing the picture. Pointing towards it, she cried out in a broken Turkish:

"I am be-ing grand-daugh-ter of he, Al-ee John Taylor!"

This sentence had the impact of an explosion as though a bomb had gone off in the silent crowd. First, everyone sat up. Ashes that had long been dangling from cigarettes fell, the clicking of prayer beads fervently resumed. Sounds of bewilderment rose to a roaring tremor. The tremors bounced off the walls and jarred the small single-storey *kahveh*. The villagers were now arguing and gesticulating with a passion quite unlike their preceding silence. The *Mukhtar,* who had up till now been sitting among the men, leapt up from his seat and grabbed Mehmet the Guide by the arm. Mehmet could not hear what the *Mukhtar* was saying over the din but was trying, with forced smiles, to act amiable and placate everyone.

The foreign woman stood by herself and watched the villagers of Chanakkale who had once again forgotten her presence, this time owing to the heat of argument. She seemed rather perturbed. She wasn't that much upset because she had blurted out her final sentence right at the very beginning, but rather because her fabulous yogurt joke had gone unappreciated.

The villagers of Chanakkale had heard of New Zealand, even if they were unsure of its location. But the foreign woman had never heard that Turks, unlike New Zealanders, did not use culture to make yogurt, but simply mixed some yogurt with milk and left it to ferment.

---

*) *Ghazi*: veteran

13

Ghazi Sergeant Alican, one of the notabilities of Gallipoli, a veteran of the Battle of Gallipoli and a Turkish hero whose tales of bravery had spread well beyond the Gallipoli Peninsula, had died in 1985. His wife, Meryem, only survived him by one year.

He was the pride of the Eceyaylasi Village. It was said that Ataturk himself had laid one hand upon his shoulder and uttered the words *"A Homeland is the land for which one is willing to fight and upon which one wishes to live."* *Ghazi* Sergeant Alican was a villager who had gained the admiration of his fellow countrymen not only through his legendary courage during the war, but also through his efforts at developing the region in the peaceful years that followed.

Due to the incredible pain and torture he suffered in the Battle of Gallipoli, he was treated with utmost respect and tolerance for the rest of his life as a veteran. His considerable height had earned him the nickname 'tall', and since his wife Meryem often called him '*canim efendim*' or 'beloved sir', the word 'can' had stuck, causing his name to remain *Ghazi* Sergeant Alican.

The villagers of Gallipoli, who had lost their entire adult male population to the Ottoman Empire's campaigns on the Balkan, Tripoli, Suez, Sarikamish, Dardanelles and Anatolia Fronts during World War I, had regarded *Ghazi* Sergeant Alican's unharmed return to be 'a blessing of God' and him to be one of God's favored creatures. The 'women and children' of the Eceyaylasi Village, upon returning to their ravaged homes after the war, were overjoyed to discover *Ghazi* Sergeant Alican as the only young man with all his limbs intact. In extraordinary times, miracles and signs bear a much greater significance than usual. This was reason enough for the residents of the Eceyaylasi Village to sincerely embrace and protect young *Ghazi* Sergeant Alican as if he were a precious heirloom, a gift from the Almighty. And that was what they did.

The kind and generous *Ghazi* Sergeant Alican, when he was not suffering from ailments, was a peaceful, honest young man who ran to the aid of anyone in need. And so he remained to his dying day. Therefore, the outbursts and bouts of depression that frequently seized control of him and led to inexplicable situations in the wake of his long wartime captivity were often ignored and always treated with understanding by the village populace.

Ghazi Sergeant Alican had fallen captive to the British during the Battle of Gallipoli and, despite being subjected to all manners of awful 'British torture' which caused him immense psychological damage, he had stood firm and not betrayed a single secret about his country. It was this courageous resistance as much as his sound return from the front that made him a war hero, that caused his tales of bravery to spread by word of mouth from town to town. The British, once they had given up hope of extracting any information out of him, had noticed that he had a way with horses and used him as a groom for an English officer. Thus, when the Surname Law was passed, he had picked the name 'Taylar', meaning 'foals', for himself and his family. During his captivity, which he never liked to speak of, it was this love of horses that had kept him alive.

Also during his captivity, *Ghazi* Sergeant Alican had gained an elementary grasp of the English language. Some time after peace had been established and the Roman alphabet had been adopted nationwide, he employed this knowledge of his to read some foreign history books the family of his comrade in arms, Ali Osman *Bey** from Istanbul sent him and to pass what he had learned on to the villagers, and in the years to come, to train local tourist guides. However he used his English undoubtedly the most while educating his only daughter Beyaz, who had always been an eager student. But he himself had always refused to speak English to the foreign tourists who came to visit his village or the Gallipoli National Park. This decision, attributed as much to his staunch nationalism as his painful memories of captivity, had earned him further respect from his fellow villagers.

As a result of the pain of watching his beloved brothers and friends expire in his arms during the Battle of Gallipoli, which consumed the lives and futures of over 500,000 youths of various nationalities in eight and a half months, and his long as well as arduous captivity, *Ghazi* Sergeant Alican had acquired several ailments which were to plague him for the rest of his life. Naturally it was no fault of his that he had survived all

---

*) *Bey*: Mister (after the person's name)

16

his friends and relations, but he could never overcome the resulting feeling of guilt. This guilt, combined with the scars of torture his soul had incurred at the hands of the British, had made sudden fits of tremor, temporary partial paralyses, long term memory loss, stammering, violent headaches, insomnia and hallucinations a permanent part of his life starting at the age of twenty. For weeks on end he forgot his past, he shut himself away for days with headaches, he lost his capacity for speech and had to communicate in sign language, heavily depressed, he belted out foreign songs and marches, he burst out sobbing in front of children, he spent entire nights at Chunuk Bair, guzzling raki at the site where his brothers and friends were martyred although he was normally a devout Muslim. Until his dying breath at the age of eighty-eight, the villagers accepted the behavior of *Ghazi* Sergeant Alican, whom they had embraced with his friendly, magnanimous and brave personality, with a sorrowful compassion, regarding it as something of a price he had paid for the liberty they now enjoyed. For this favored soul, whose blue eyes were often shadowed with distant, dark clouds, served to remind them how difficult their past had been and how dearly their current freedom had been earned.

When he had first arrived in the village after the war, he had alternately stared at the mountains for hours in stony silence or thrashed about reliving nightmares in broad daylight. The women had initially been intimidated and the kids entertained by this behavior. But, with the exception of the elderly men, he was the only grown man living in town and they needed him. It was an extraordinary time and his fits were swiftly disguised. After a while folks only said 'there he goes again, poor thing', and eventually *Ghazi* Sergeant Alican's episodes became a matter of course. In fact, if he had ever recovered his memory, started speaking straight, and displayed two days of consistency, it would have convinced them of his ill health. After all, he was a war hero who had survived the torture of the infidel and this amount of strangeness was to be expected.

The women, upon seeing his suffering soul uneased through prayers from the Koran, offerings and sacrifice, decided that he needed to get married. "If he marries, he's bound to get better," they said. "Marriage will cure anything!" they proclaimed and tittered. When young peasant women talk of marriage amongst themselves they will invariable giggle and exchange meaningful glances. In contrast, the older ones will look grim and glum, their faces will settle into displeasure and they will not utter so much as a word. Women in all the villages of Turkey, across centuries, amongst themselves...

The one and only candidate that came to mind in the matter of marriage was Meryem. Indeed there were many other much lovelier and more appropriate girls of marrying age in the Eceyaylasi Village but Meryem was the one who had found *Ghazi* Sergeant Alican delirious, almost unconscious by the side of a fresh grave, and had brought him to the village. Yet besides the general unavailability of young men, the Sergeant's striking handsomeness had caused a great stir among the girls of the village. Nevermind his mild insanity, his slight oddness, all the girls were in line for this handsome youth. Yet Meryem, daughter of Hasan the Circumciser, whose own village of Ecebayiri had burned completely to the ground, had already developed a frightening passion for the Sergeant, and had become addicted to him when she brought him to the Eceyaylasi Village. And she remained devoted with the same intense love to him until her dying breath. Hers was an incurable love.

Nothing could stand in the way of Meryem's love; neither illness, nor foreign occupation, the heartrending poverty during the War of Independence, or the gossip that she was older and uglier than *Ghazi* Sergeant Alican. Meryem adored the Sergeant and devoted herself to him utterly, selflessly, as women at the pinnacle of love always do for their men. She cared for him with the feminine patience and tenderness that grows with unlimited self-sacrifice. She felt a great trust for this man, whom she regarded as separate from all others, but she was also very jealous of him.

At first, the villagers were much offended by the fact that Meryem was several years older than *Ghazi* Sergeant Alican, for they regarded the tradition of the younger wife as something akin to a divine ordinance. Some thought Meryem was three years older than her betrothed and some claimed it was thirteen, but in either case it was a grave impropriety if not an outright sin. But a 'spirit of unity and solidarity' was essential to stay alive in the postwar times of famine. At a period when young children suffered from the absence of their fathers, old couples from the loss of their sons, and the country reeled from scarcity and pains of recovery, events that would be construed scandals during peacetime lost their meaning and significance. Many things that were derided in times of peace could be tolerated in times of war. Not to mention that the love, tenderness and patience Meryem displayed toward the Sergeant in his times of crisis were no mean feat. It was with this self-sacrifice that Meryem made up for the impropriety of having a younger man as a husband.

When marriage, a few years after their hasty religious wedding, had not cured *Ghazi* Sergeant Alican of his woes, it was decided that children would do the trick. The women of the village strongly and firmly recommended that Meryem and the Sergeant should have many kids, and soon. This advice turned to pressure when it seemed the couple were taking their time. Meryem bore four children. Three of them survived. The firstborn, a boy named Ali after the Sergeant's beloved comrade in arms, died when he was a month old. Fearful that the death of this child would alienate her husband and leave her deserted, Meryem bore three more children. She was willing to do anything it took to keep her husband. Hers was a passion that far exceeded love itself. When Meryem was pregnant with her second child, her husband had a dream. In the dream, *Ghazi* Sergeant Alican had met His Holiness *Ghazi* Mustafa Kemal. Mustafa Kemal *Pasha** had put a hand on his shoulder and said, "You will have three children and name them Uzun (Long), Beyaz (White) and Bulut (Cloud), in that order. Just like the clouds of Gallipoli."

Meryem relayed this dream to the villagers. Shortly, *Ghazi* Sergeant Alican's dream was so frequently talked about between the townsfolk that each one was convinced he had seen it himself. This dream served to further prove and cement the Sergeant's repute as 'God's favored soul' among his compatriots. For the three children, who were named accordingly, did indeed live long and healthy lives.

The couple's two sons, Uzun and Bulut, were lively, affectionate and mischievious kids, but Beyaz was a sharp, cool, collected and forthright girl. She did not in the least resemble the other girls in the village, and she never grew to resemble them. No one could say she was 'like a man' either, because she was extremely beautiful. Beyaz was so lovely that those who took one look at her longed for another. Like all plain mothers who bear beautiful daughters, Meryem would sometimes stare at Beyaz in wonder. As for her father, he always kept Beyaz by his side, coddled and spoiled her to distraction. The villagers, who did not hold girls of equal worth as boys, were - once again - puzzled by this strange behavior, but managed to excuse and disregard his unreasonable love for a daughter, just as they did with his maladies through the reserve of tolerance they held solely for the Sergeant. It must be added that when Beyaz grew old enough to become friends with her father, there had been a decrease in *Ghazi* Sergeant Alican's trembling fits and hallucinations, and it was agreed that the girl had brought luck to her father.

---

*) *Pasha*: high rank officer

In those years the Sergeant also developed a particular interest in the clarinet, one of Gallipoli's traditional instruments. He taught himself how to play it, and was soon distributing hope to the villagers by playing merry tunes and songs. However, his musical mastery was somewhat less appreciated when he took it upon himself to give blaring concerts that roused the whole village from its slumber in the middle of the night.

Ghazi Sergeant Alican tried for months to teach English to his three children but his sons were not the least bit enthuiastic about his efforts. They liked the fields and the birds, they preferred to run around in the street, to play ball and fly kites. Beyaz, on the other hand, was a child hungry for knowledge, and she pressed her father for more. *Ghazi* Sergeant Alican had finally found the meaning and therapy of his life. He taught his daughter Beyaz as much English as he knew.

He taught his daughter with books in New Turkish and English, which he brought back from his annual fortnightly trips to Istanbul. He gave her unassuming gifts of pens and notebooks as could be obtained by the small means of the time. Beyaz never disappointed her father - she was always studious, inquisitive and quick to learn.

Meryem, who had supported her husband through thick and thin with love and passion, who strived to fulfill his every wish, and who had successfully maintained her predominance against all kinds of competition and threats, had now lost it to her own daughter; *Ghazi* Sergeant Alican had grown closer, more attentive and caring to this girl, whom she herself had brought into the world, than he was to anyone, including, of course, Meryem. She was unable to discern the similar characters and interests of her husband and daughter, and unwilling to acknowledge that special brand of compassion that exists between fathers and daughters, and mothers and sons. As a result, she waited helplessly and watched with increasing jealousy as her own daughter stole all of her beloved Sergeant's time and attention away from her. And when it came her turn to act, she said something that utterly shocked and saddened her husband, her husband whom she had never once disobeyed, whose willing slave she had been since the start. Only once in her life did Meryem say 'no' to *Ghazi* Sergeant Alican, only once did she refuse his wish. But that one refusal altered their whole life and never again were they as happy and close as before.

Meryem was not opposed to the idea that their daughter, spoiled, she thought, by her father, should attend the village school in exchange for a barrel of wheat. She herself was a literate woman and had learned the new alphabet immediately after the Language Reform had been adopted. In those years, rural elementary education was three years long. When at the end of that period the local teacher deemed Beyaz to be highly gifted and in need of further education, *Ghazi* Sergeant Alican was ecstatic. Right away, he began preparations to send Beyaz off to the all-girls Teachers' Boarding School in Edirne. Now it was Meryem's turn to act. One day, during dinner, she suddenly said "Girls don't go to school, they get married." As a matter of fact, Beyaz had in hand a big letter of recommendation from her teacher, which read "This girl will go far in life, she will study and become a successful professional."

On the morning that her father was to take Beyaz to Edirne, Meryem woke early, performed her ablutions and morning prayer, and wrapping herself in a white shroud, lay down before the doorway. There she waited. When dawn broke and *Ghazi* Sergeant Alican got up to take his daughter to the Teachers' School in Edirne, he found his wife lying on the threshold. And Meryem let loose a scream that was heard throughout the Gallipoli Peninsula.

"Over my body, this girl will only leave this house as a bride. Or I'll kill myself!"

Meryem's scream was so pitiful, so bitter that the pain it contained spread in waves across the Eceyaylasi Village, across the plains, through Chunuk Bair and over the Ariburnu Cove into the sea. When Meryem's shriek reached the water, the sea shook, the waves rose and the Aegean's waters were whipped into a vigorous, wrathful froth. Meryem's scream was far removed from a human voice. It was as sharp as giant metal shears, as terrifying as colliding icebergs. When he heard this sound echoing from the Anzac Cove, *Ghazi* Sergeant Alican stopped in his tracks. He looked at Meryem. Then he gazed at her some more and gave up on his decison to send Beyaz to school.

It is said that after that day, *Ghazi* Sergeant Alican never looked at Meryem's face again. It is said that from that day forth, the Sergeant never spoke directly to Meryem but only communicated with her through his daughter Beyaz. It is said that following that day, the Sergeant increased his drinking and often went out to Chunuk Bair to cry.

Even though, years later he was gratefully indebted to Semahat *Hanim*,* the mother of Lieutenant Ali Osman *Bey*, his beloved comrade in arms, for putting his youngest son Bulut through a Teachers' Boarding School in Istanbul, and personally assisting his upbringing as a young Istanbul gentleman, *Ghazi* Sergeant Alican could never get over the abortion of his daughter's education.

As for Beyaz; that morning she swore never to leave that house as a bride which she could not leave as a teacher to be.

Beyaz never left that house.

Beyaz never got married.

Beyaz remained by her father's side as his best friend, until the day he died.

Beyaz never forgot her mother's cry.

*) *Hanim:* Miss (after the person's name)

It is said that when *Ghazi* Sergeant Alican died in 1985, he had a beatific smile upon his face. Around him were his praying wife, his two surviving children, his five grandchildren and seven great-grandchildren. It is said that as he went on his final voyage, in one hand he held the hand of his daughter Beyaz and in the other, the hand of one of his son Bulut's grandsons, the lawyer who was living in Istanbul. It is also said that Meryem wept and read from the Koran but kept her eyes averted from her husband's, even on his deathbed.

Ghazi Sergeant Alican had asked to be buried in the modest cemetery of the Eceyaylasi Village, beside his beloved comrade in arms from the Battle of Gallipoli, Lieutenant Ali Osman *Bey*. But his will also contains the request that a jar full of soil brought from the Anzac Cove be poured every year over both of their graves. His small, austere headstone, also dictated by his will, reads:

GHAZI SERGEANT
ALICAN TAYLAR
1897-1985

LONG-WHITE-CLOUD
↔

GALLIPOLI
FOUGHT IN
GALLIPOLI AND DIED
IN GALLIPOLI
MAY HE REST IN PEACE

"That's what New Zealand is called: the Long White Cloud!" the foreign woman cried excitedly. "The natives call it *Aotearoa* and that word translates as Long White Cloud!"

Frustrated and angry at not being understood, she was scolding Mehmet in her heavy British accent. The young guide was not sure what he had done to deserve this strong reaction, so he repeated his translation to the villagers. But he stumbled while trying to pronounce the native Maori word 'aotearoa' for New Zealand:

"Aotearoa!" the woman groaned. "A-o-te-a-ro-a!"

Mehmet tried once more and failed. The word was incompatible with Turkish phonetics, it strained his capabilities, his tongue seemed to swell within his mouth and however much he tried, he could only sound out some vague approximation.

"You see, the New Zeland Islands resemble a long white cloud and the Maori, who were its original settlers, named it accordingly. They still call New Zealand 'Land of the Long White Cloud!'

The villagers would have been less surprised if a UFO had landed at the Eceyaylasi Village and its passengers had announced that they were actually from Gallipoli. As it stood, a foreign woman claiming, eighty-five years after the Battle of Gallipoli, to be the granddaugher of a beloved Turkish hero, a righteous, pious, trustworthy, respected, and long-dead *Ghazi*, whose life had been tough with the ailments that remained after the war, was queerer than an UFO, even less believable than a space alien.

The greatest sin that could be committed against the memory of a decorated Moslem Turkish hero, who had remained an exemplary citizen despite deep psychic wounds, was to slander him by saying that he had fathered a foreign, not to mention non-Moslem, granddaughter. And to claim that he was the grandfather of an offspring of the occupying forces, the very people against whom he had defended his country!

To smear the good name of *Ghazi* Sergeant Alican, who, save for his annual fortnightly trips to Istanbul, had never in all his life left the Gallipoli Peninsula or, at most, the borders of the Chanakkale province, this blessed Sergeant who had valued his family, his honor and his virtue above all else... Well now, was that any kind of thing to do? What was the meaning of coming to Gallipoli all the way from the ends of the earth to commit such slander?

It had taken exactly ten minutes for the hubbub raging within the *kahveh* to spread to the center of town and then across the whole village. At 10:40 a.m. the entire village was talking about how a foreign tourist lady had besmirched the good name of *Ghazi* Sergeant Alican, God rest his soul. In an hour's time the news had reached the entire Gallipoli Peninsula.

26

The villagers first gaped at the news. When they recovered from the initial shock, they started talking all at once; slapping their knees, giving out short shrieks, objecting vehemently, and absolutely refusing to listen to one another. Their tirades were mostly centered on what an honest, generous, kind and devout Moslem *Ghazi* Sergeant Alican had been. The elders among them listed off the entire bloodline of the *Ghazi* and showered praises on his lineage. Everyone in town was immensely hurt and offended.

The *Mukhtar* was the first to regain his composure. He grabbed Mehmet the Guide by the arm and pulled him to a relatively empty corner of the *kahveh*.

"Mehmet, son, whatch'ou say was the name of this tourist miss?"

"Her name is Victoria but she likes to be called Vicki for short, Uncle *Mukhtar*," Mehmet replied anxiously. He too seemed extremely ill at ease to find himself in this unexpected situation.

"Fine. Where exactly is she from, this Vicki *Hanim*, *mari*?"

"From New Zealand. See... last Christmas she makes an online reservation at our travel agency. So the boss calls me and says 'Mehmet we have a private tour, you take this one'... And so I... I mean, I don't know her at all other than that... Just business...."

"So how does she know our *Ghazi* Sergeant Alican?" asked the *Mukhtar*, who had been listening closely.

"I really have no idea, Uncle *Mukhtar*. She never mentioned it before. I heard his name here for the first time, same as you did, I swear... I would say maybe her own Anzac grandpa told her about him but then... I mean, how would he know, right? No, no, that can't be... You know, these foreigners never go anywhere without doing some research on the place first. They read a ton of books, look through websites and stuff like that... Maybe that's where she saw his name."

27

The *Mukhtar* sighed as he had learned nothing substantial enough to calm the unsettled crowd. Mehmet, meanwhile, brooded over how a tourist matter had become so serious. He was trying his best to remain outside the situation but he was quite baffled as to what he should do next.

"Who could have known?... She seemed like such a good person..." he mumbled.

"You don't say?" the *Mukhtar* replied, absently scratching the stubble that had grown on his face despite his morning shave.

"I mean... She's been here for a week, and I've taken her to the National Park every day, but she just wants to go see the same places over and over. For example, every morning we go to the Ariburnu-Anzac Cove... She prays... I don't know, she just seems like a good person. She's generous to me. Yesterday, out of the blue, she says to me "Call the Eceyaylasi Village, I have something important to tell them." I thought maybe she had brought some kind of present or some note of gratitude from her country. You know, how these Anzacs are so fond of these parts because their grandfathers died here..."

"But this is outrageous, *mari*!" muttered the *Mukhtar*, upset that he had not gathered the clues he expected from Mehmet the Guide.

"Now, how'd this foreign lady come up with this tale? Must be crazy or something, *mari*. Comes here all the way from Zealand to say nonsense! Ain't these folks got nothin' better to do? Course, they don't have inflation or unemployment over there so they prob'ly get bored... They don't have crops, base prices for their produces or interest to be paid to the State Bank of Agriculture, nor a government that can't pay its farmer or no such thing. What they got over there's social security for the farmer, or that's what I'd heard from another tourist guide friend, he was a real mature fella - no better than you, of course."

This last sentence bothered Mehmet. So he pretended not to have heard it, as he did with every other bothersome detail. Meanwhile, the villagers had slowly closed in around Mehmet and the *Mukhtar*, hoping to hear some sensible explanation. Now one of them turned to another and said,

"Farmers got social insurance over in Zealand, the *Mukhtar* said, didja hear?"

"Right sure they do, human life got some value over there," remarked someone else.

The men clicked their tongues in unison. The dissatisfaction and discontent registering on their faces was not so much about their living conditions, which by now they were used to, but rather the matter of *Ghazi* Sergeant Alican.

"Oh, and... How should I say, Vicki did do something kind of strange," murmured Mehmet. He seemed relieved to be sharing his story.

"Strange, what do you mean strange?" the *Mukhtar* seized on this comment. Not that he had any burning political ambitions, but then again, one never knew. It was of utmost importance that he catch the first clue.

"Well, how should I explain? See, every morning for the past week, Vicki goes into the sea at dawn and gathers stones from the beach."

"Heaven forbid! Don't tell me she goes around half-naked in this weather?" asked the *Mukhtar*. "I reckon these foreigners never get cold."

"Then she starts crying..." Mehmet continued in a sad voice, "She stands there, in the waters of the Ariburnu-Anzac Cove just as the sun begins to rise and she gazes way up there towards Chunuk Bair and this Vicki just starts to cry."

The grief in Mehmet's voice suddenly spread over the villagers; the voice that had brought them the sorrow inherent in Vicki's tears had moved them all.

"So she was crying. The tourist woman was crying at Ari-

29

burnu every morning," the villagers whispered to one another. They pictured this foreign woman crying as she stood in the water directly below the hills where they had played as children, sometimes discovering human bones and skulls among the mixed graves of Ottoman and British, Turkish and Anzac, French and Indian soldiers. Then their feelings of animosity towards this woman who had slandered their very own *Ghazi* Sergeant Alican swiftly receded to be replaced by a sense of pity and protection. They looked at each other thoughtfully. Shaking their heads sadly, they said,

"The poor thing was crying... All by her lonesome, the foreign lady was crying... Well, how about that, *mari*."

Through their eyes, which still looked vacant to outsiders, they shared a wish, incomprehensible to any foreigner, to 'solve the foreign woman's troubles'.

Mehmet, thinking it was time he said something, added,

"It's against the rules too ask any personal questions in our line of work. Something of a gentlemen's agreement, Uncle *Mukhtar*. So we never question our clients about their private lives."

The *Mukhtar* liked the word 'gentleman'.

"*Ghazi* Sergeant Alican was a gentleman, a real noble sort, may he rest in everlasting peace."

"Amen, amen," echoed the villagers.

Tired of being left out of the conversation, Vicki approached Mehmet and asked him some questions. The *Mukhtar*, who now eyed the foreign lady with more calm and interest, sighed,

"Well I never heard of such a thing... Who ever heard of such a thing?"

"Uncle *Mukhtar*, Vicki says she'd like to meet *Ghazi* Sergeant Alican's closest living relative, if at all possible."

A chorus of foreboding noises issued from the villagers. They eyed each other nervously and tilted their heads up, eyebrows raised, as if to say 'no good will come of this'.

"*Ghazi* Sergeant Alican's daughter, Auntie Beyaz is still alive but no! Absolutely not!" said the *Mukhtar*.

He paused, thought for a while, then repeated,

"No, there ain't a chance in heaven!"

"Or in hell!"

"She'll kick us straight out!"

"She'll do us in!" the villagers muttered warily and clicked their tongues again.

The *Mukhtar* sighed deeply and explained to the bewildered Mehmet, "This Auntie Beyaz of ours is an old timer. She's probably about eighty, isn't that so?"

"That's right, eighty or so," the crowd agreed.

"Auntie Beyaz ain't left her house in years. Remember that big fire that happened? Since that fire she's quit us and the whole rest of the world. Oh, and she's nothing like her late father. How should I say, *mari*? Well... she's a downright grouch, so don't say I didn't tell you! Isn't that so?" he asked.

The villagers cried in unison, "It's a fact!"

"See here now, I don't want to be unfair either. Auntie Beyaz knows much, been through it all, talks straight, tells no lies and is capable and virtuous besides. Isn't that right?"

"Sure is!" the villagers once again agreed in chorus.

"She's a decent woman!"

"Even though she's a woman she's a wise person!"

"In deed and fact... She's just and skillful, besides!"

"Sound and able!"

"She's knowledgeable like her father, practically a walking library!"

"And she's as nationalistic as her father too!"

"She's a valuable elder!"

"So she is, but Auntie Beyaz is also ill-tempered, an odd sort. If she don't want to do something, you can't never make her do it. She flat-out refused to get married, just to spite her mother."

31

"Indeed, she did... So that's it in a nutshell, Mehmet *Bey*, my son," the *Mukhtar* remarked to wrap it up. "What we're saying is, she'll never in a million years take Vicki *Hanim* into her house... Might even say something mean. It'd embarrass us in front of Vicki *Hanim*... After all, she's a guest here... Wouldn't be right."

Mehmet translated everything the *Mukhtar* and the villagers said, strongly emphasizing the impossibility of the visit but he was unable to convince Vicki. The *Mukhtar* and the villagers pleaded with Vicki as though she could understand Turkish, but it was no use.

"Me want Auntie Be-yaz!"

The *Mukhtar* finally gave up, saying,

"This Vicki *Hanim* is just as stubborn as Auntie Beyaz!"

They walked collectively through the village to Auntie Beyaz's house. As they passed by, women who had not gone to work at the fields that day leaned out of their windows to watch Vicki and exchange dozens of fictional stories about this foreign woman, about whom they knew nothing except the fact that she claimed to be the granddaughter of *Ghazi* Sergeant Alican.

They came to a halt in a narrow street filled with stone, brick and concrete houses. They were standing in front of a two-storey stone house painted all white except for its door and windows, which were blue. There were geraniums potted in oil cans on the window-sills.

"Auntie Beyaz don't like me one bit. Ain't no way I'm knocking on that door! Maybe you ought to give it a try Mehmet *Bey*, my son," the *Mukhtar* hummed and hawed.

The rest of the villagers had similarly stepped back, their eyebrows raised. So Mehmet the Guide was stuck with the task of knocking on the door of an old lady who instilled considerable fear into the hearts of the village men. Mehmet could have quit his beloved profession right then and there, so displeased was he to be standing alone at the doorstep of an old woman whom he imagined was mean, grumpy, rude and (God knows why) ugly. But he sighed, drew in a deep breath and, gathering up all his courage, gave a knock on the blue wooden door.

"Gwon, git outta here!" cried a resonant voice from inside.

"Auntie Beyaz, my name is Mehmet!" called the young guide in his sweetest tone. "See, there's a tourist *hanim* here. She came to Gallipoli all the way from New Zealand, from the ends of the earth. She wants to talk to you about Grandpa *Ghazi* Alican," he continued with artificial sweetness, as if talking to a child.

"Gwon, I said... Git outta here, *mari*!" Auntie Beyaz yelled even louder.

"I told you as much," said the *Mukhtar* shaking his head knowingly. "For years, the only people allowed to enter her house have been her brother's grand and great-grandchildren. And that only to deliver her meals and necessary goods. Oh and there's the lawyer, the grandson of her brother who settled in Istanbul. She likes him well. She talks to him. And that's it. She's turned her back on us. Hasn't left her house in years. Though... if we have some kinda trouble we'll ask her advice, though she hasn't been giving us that in the last few years either..."

"You said this granny was patriotic, right Uncle *Mukhtar*?"

"Sure is, a strong patriot just like her father."

Then Mehmet tried his luck one more time, calling out in a victorious voice,

"Auntie Beyaz, see this tourist *hanim* is practically a guest here. What happened to Turkish hospitality, then?"

"Go on, I told you all to git out!" scolded the same voice.

"That's it! I give up," said Mehmet, turning his palms up in defeat.

"Well, that's what I figured," said the *Mukhtar*. The villagers, who had gathered around the door in curiosity, now shook their heads. Mehmet sighed and turning to Vicki, said,

"Let's go, Vicki!" But Vicki pushed Mehmet aside, walked up to the door and shouted:

"I am Alistair John Taylor's great-granddaughter. My name is Victoria Taylor. I came to talk to you from a very long way up to Gallipoli. Please let me talk to you. Please?"

Vicki's voice was trembling. What followed was a brief moment where time seemed to stand still. It felt as though a miracle was going to happen; the foreign woman's quavering English words were going to create a magic power and the blue wooden door of the white stone house was suddenly going to creak open. The villagers held their breath, awaiting a small miracle. They waited. And waited. And it really happened. First, they heard footsteps and then the blue door was quietly pulled ajar. Vicki immediately slipped inside. Mehmet tried to follow but the door shut in his face.

"Well?" asked Mehmet, peeved. "How are they supposed to communicate without me?"

The *Mukhtar* had not even heard his question. He was gazing at Auntie Beyaz's door in thoughtful silence. Remembering Mehmet, he turned to him with a troubled expression.

"Now what did this Vicki *Hanim* say to Auntie Beyaz?"

Mehmet repeated her words. The villagers grumbled amongst themselves and, with no apparent intention to leave Auntie Beyaz's door, stared at the *Mukhtar* for an explanation. The crowd kept getting bigger.

"Mehmet *Bey*, son, you happen to have some kind of identification for this Vicki *Hanim*?" asked the *Mukhtar*.

Mehmet, unsure about what he should do in the middle of this increasingly strange and convoluted tourist story, hurriedly produced some papers from his pocket. The *Mukhtar* and the villagers huddled around him in curiosity. The *Mukhtar* began to read:

Name: Victoria Taylor
Place of Birth: Wellington, New Zealand

Date of Birth: 25.03.1970

Occupation: Clinical Psychologist

"Oh, that explains it then," said the *Mukhtar*, breathing a sigh of relief. "It don't got nothing to do with it, *mari*. Our late *Ghazi* Sergeant Alican's last name was Taylar. This lady's name is Taylor, *mari*. Come on boys, tea's on me..." So saying, he led Mehmet and the villagers to the *kahveh*. They all seemed relieved. Only Mehmet walked uncertainly, as though his head was screwed on backwards, and only he was still concerned for his client Vicki.

"My father was a hero! My father was a great wise man!" said Auntie Beyaz with a thick British accent.

They were on the second floor, sitting on sofas facing each other in a plainly decorated living room, which was dimmed by white lace curtains. Vicki was as pale as if she were about to faint. The pace of her breathing betrayed great excitement. Sitting cross-legged on the sofa across from her was an old Turkish peasant woman. This old, blue-eyed woman wore her long snow-white hair in a single braid wrapped into a bun at her neck, and had a face so white it seemed powdered a thousand times over and lovingly embroidered with hundreds of deep wrinkles. She was thin enough to be called skinny, old enough to be a hundred, and agile as a youth. She wore a handknit vest over her flower-print flannel *shalvar** and a blouse made of the same fabric. A scarf with leaf designs rested on her shoulders, ready to cover her head. She had handknit wool socks on her feet. The socks were stitched with tulip shapes. In her hand was a string of agate prayer beads, which she was slowly counting.

Vicki could not for the life of her believe that this old lady, who intimidated even the men of the village, had accepted her into her house. The woman, who had led her upstairs without so much as a word, spoke fluent English with a thick accent and a vocabulary strictly limited to words of the past century. She was comprehensible, despite her soon to become apparent habit of inserting Turkish words such as *'mari'*, *'hele'*, *'hech'*, *'yani'*, *'Mashallah'* and *'Inshallah'*** into her speech. Vicki was positively drinking in the sight of the old woman. Secretly terrified to be finally experiencing this moment which she had longed for years to reach, she felt physically crushed by the excitement. Her immense interest in 'great-grandpa's secret', had turned it into the primary goal or even issue of her life, and the feelings of anxiety and nervousness that she had so far suppressed by curiousity were now manifesting here in this Gallipoli house as a physical burden upon her. She had begun to feel very, very tired.

"Nobody can ever smear my father's memory, no matter what their excuse! I won't allow it, *mari!*" Auntie Beyaz said all of a sudden, while still counting her prayer beads.

She did not look at Vicki while speaking. In contrast to the severity of her words she seemed extremely calm, and softly mouthed prayers in Arabic, which Vicki assumed were in Turkish. Meanwhile she was uttering resolute sentences in English. This old woman was certainly an unflappable character.

---

*) *Shalvar*: baggy trousers
**) *Hele; hech; yani; mashallah*; inshallah: now; never/not at all; that is; 'Praise God'; and 'If God willing' respectively.

It was one of those moments when people who have a lot to say are at a loss to begin speaking. Vicki thought that no sound would come out if she opened her mouth. Yet it was her who for years had dreamed of just such a meeting. And like all dreams that one secretly fears will become a reality, this was scary. Here she was in Gallipoli, in the Eceyaylasi Village, in a completely foreign environment, sitting across from a foreign old lady in a foreign house. Yes, she was finally here. So she was... So... But instead of feeling relief in the situation she was growing more and more uneasy.

"What if everything I have thought is true, if all the 'ifs' are true?" she wondered. As soon as the thought crossed her mind she felt a surging bolt of pain in her stomach. She emitted a small cry and jumped up from her seat. Hearing this, Auntie Beyaz stopped counting her prayer beads and looked up. Then she saw the young woman trembling as though struck by electricity and staring through nervous blue eyes. The two women stared at each other for a while. Vicki could not detect anger in Auntie Beyaz's talisman blue eyes. Her gaze did not contain grief or anticipation either. Was she nervous? No. This old woman was extremely collected. Extremely. Her snow-white face, marked like an elaborate map with countless lines, seemed illuminated by a special light. There was a glow about her face that seemed separate from the paleness of her skin. Or perhaps that's just how it seemed to Vicki. But she liked it. Auntie Beyaz's glow felt good to Vicki. She felt a little calmer in the presence of this glowing face and unaccusing gaze.

"I was expecting it, *mari*," said Auntie Beyaz, pulling her gaze away from Vicki and resuming her prayer beads. "I was expecting someone to show up from New Zealand and ask about him."

She sighed and handled her beads. Five minutes later she stopped again:

"I always expected it, *mari*."

Vicki opened her mouth to say "me too" but decided against it. Instead, she repositioned herself cross-legged on the sofa, the same way as Auntie Beyaz. Before coming to Turkey she had learned from guidebooks that it was necessary to leave one's shoes at the door of traditional Turkish households. Now, sitting cross-legged on the sofa, she suddenly felt like a Tibetan monk in meditation, but she was in Gallipoli, sitting perhaps across from her great-aunt.

"We could be relatives," Vicki timidly whispered, her voice trembling with excitement.

Auntie Beyaz, calm and determined, without interrupting her prayer beads, muttered:

"My father never did anything dishonorable. He was an honorable man. He lived with his honor and died with his honor."

That same day, Mehmet the Guide, the *Mukhtar* and the residents of the Eceyaylasi Village waited for hours for Vicki to emerge from Auntie Beyaz's house. They waited at the *kahveh*, in front of Auntie Beyaz's house, pacing the village streets. They rung the doorbell and called the house occasionally but all their efforts were in vain. Once, Vicki stuck her head out of a window on the upper floor and told Mehmet, who was pounding on the door, that she was all right. "I'm OK, Mehmet, everything's fine."

The village women were gathered around Auntie Beyaz's door, whispering amongst themselves and awaiting the outcome of this odd meeting. They were all intrigued that Auntie Beyaz had allowed this foreign lady into her house when the only other people she received were her late brother's granddaughter Havva and her children, so they could bring her food. None of the villagers thought well of the foreigner's claims, let alone believe them, but people were still naturally curious.

Hours went by and slowly the sheep and cows returned to their stables, the chickens and roosters strutted back to their coops, and the kids went inside their houses. Daylight dimmed and the weather grew cool. Evening fell. That was when a small shadow appeared in a blue window of the house that Vicki had entered hours earlier and shouted in an authoritative voice:

"*Mukhtaaaar*, get over here quick, *hele*. This tourist lady up and fainted here, *mari*."

Mehmet ran to the door before the *Mukhtar* and, upon finding it locked, began to bang on it and yell:

"Open the door, you old hag! You're gonna be sorry if anything happens to Vicki! I'm sick and tired of your attitude! Open this door, I said!"

The *Mukhtar* grabbed Mehmet's arm and tried to calm him down:

"Now hold on, Mehmet *Bey*, son, don't get so edgy, nothing bad happens to a person who's with Auntie Beyaz."

"And why's that? Is she a doctor by any chance, this Auntie Beyaz? Look Uncle *Mukhtar*, this woman's a foreigner, if anything were to happen to her, it'd be a diplomatic scandal and then even I can't save the day."

The *Mukhtar* laughed and said:

"You don't know Auntie Beyaz, son, nothing's going to happen to your foreigner when she's with her."

Just then the door opened and Vicki stepped out, looking wan and exhausted. As soon as she was outside, the door was shut and locked behind her. Mehmet made a big show of taking her arm and consoling her like a baby.

"I'm fine, Mehmet. I got a litle dizzy but Auntie Beyaz gave me some sugar water and I'm fine now. Don't worry."

"Yeah, great, sugar water," Mehmet grumbled. "You wait here Vicki, I'll bring the jeep," he offered, but Vicki insisted on slowly accompanying him. She leaned on Mehmet's arm and started walking.

A little girl came up to Vicki and smiled coyly:

"Auntie Beyaz happens to be my great-aunt!" she announ-

40

ced. Then, seeing Vicki's ashen face she called, "Mo-om, this tourist lady's sick, lookee her face's all white!"

"Let her be, Meryem. They say she slandered grandpa. Let Auntie Beyaz take care of her."

Although she could not understand what was being said, Vicki did sense that the young woman was not being entirely friendly as she dragged away the little girl.

"Let's go, Mehmet," she moaned.

She looked truly ill and reached the jeep with difficulty. When she got to Eceabat, she went directly to her room at the Friendly Anzac Pension and spent the next two days and nights in fever. Mehmet the Guide and the owner of the pension hurriedly found a doctor and secured medicine.

"She has a serious cold and is possibly suffering from exhaustion and change of climate," pronounced the doctor. "If her fever does not subside in the next twenty-four hours, we will take her to the Chanakkale Hospital."

Mehmet, who was torn with guilt at not having taken proper care of his client and at having delivered her into the hands of Auntie Beyaz, whom he had already branded a murderer, was angry:

"Vicki has an extensive travel insurance. We can take her immediately to the best private hospital in Istanbul. Her insurance even covers a helicopter, Doctor *Bey*. I mean, since these people are from New Zealand, it's even possible to have her taken to England for treatment."

"Now, now, don't get so carried away, my boy," the doctor tried to reassure him. "She'll get over it by tomorrow. Foreigners don't know about these parts of the world. Winter is bitter in Gallipoli. It will get you, that ruthless chill. It's easy to be fooled by the sunshine here. Also, it could be something she ate. Their countries are awfully sterile, whereas here we're terribly immune to all kinds of things. So, what happens? Our food hits them hard right away."

41

"I tried to warn her but she wouldn't listen... She walks into the sea in the morning chill, stands around soaking at Ariburnu. Now, of course, there's hell to pay," Mehmet muttered
dejectedly.

"Then of course, there are some heavy historical associations here. After all, they have lost their relatives on this soil. It
wears them out emotionally, as well," the doctor told the young guide, whom he judged to be a novice.

"No, no, it was that mean old woman who made her sick!"
Mehmet realized once again. "That old hag they call Auntie Beyaz. See here, if Vicki doesn't get better soon, I'm going to go
and have a few words with that devil!"

The doctor and the proprietor of the pension exchanged
glances and chuckled. They were old enough to smile at youth.

"You don't know Auntie Beyaz," said the proprietor, pat-
ting Mehmet's shoulder.

"And I hope I never do!" Mehmet retorted.

Vicki's fever did not subside the next day. The doctor was
determined to have her hospitalized that afternoon. Mehmet,
who was sitting by her bedside with a fear and tenderness
that seemed odd even to himself, could occasionally hear her
talking in her sleep but could not make out the words no matter how hard he tried. Unable to stand it any longer, he finally
called the receptionist girl upstairs to ask her what she could
make out. The young woman was a native of Gallipoli, who studied at the University of March Eighteen and worked part-time
at the Friendly Anzac Pension.

"Seems like this lady keeps saying 'Auntie Beyaz' over and
over again," she said, smiling.

During the twenty-four hours that Vicki lay in bed, journalists and television crews from Ankara and Istanbul had started appearing in Gallipoli's Eceabat township, in search of a
woman from New Zealand. The Friendly Anzac Pension was
besieged by e-mails, faxes and telephone calls all posing the

same question: "It seems there's a woman from New Zealand staying at your place who claims to be the granddaughter of a veteran of the Battle of Gallipoli. Could we please talk to her?"

Two days later the matter had been crudely analyzed and resolved by a number of newspapers and TV stations that specialized in sensationalist fare:

'Here's a new addition to the horde of foreign women seeking fame by claiming to be the granddaughters of figures such as Haidar *Pasha* or the last Ottoman Princes: Now an Anzac Daughter says that she is the progeny of an honorable Dardanelles *Ghazi*!'

'Don't, for the love of God, Anzac Daughter!'

'We won't let our heroes and *ghazis* be smeared! Better watch out, Anzac Daughter!'

In no time at all the media was flocking to Gallipoli, cameras, recorders and microphones in hand, spinning and drawing out the issue without any research.

Mehmet the Guide, who could not figure out how a conversation that took place between a handful of people in a tiny village could possibly reach the press, suspected that the 'media spy' might be the *Mukhtar* of the Eceyaylasi Village. He might have had designs to make his village famous. Maybe he wanted to appear on TV, to gain recognition. Mehmet now added the village *Mukhtar* to his list of accusees, after Auntie Beyaz. And yet, after returning to Eceabat and securing a doctor for Vicki, it was he who had called the Istanbul headquarters of his travel agency and told them the story.

One day, Auntie Beyaz, who had not left her house for years, who spoke to no one except one grandnephew in Istanbul and one grandniece in the village, put on a long black handmade coat called a *terlik* in the Gallipoli villages, wrapped her wool shawl around her shoulders, slipped on her imitation leather shoes, boarded Mehmet's jeep and headed off to Eceabat. The residents of the Eceyaylasi Village had never been more surprised than on that day.

As it happens, Mehmet had gone to Auntie Beyaz's house to ask her what devilish things she had said to poor Vicki who was to be hospitalized that day. He had parked his jeep in the village square, waved away the greeting of the men at the *kahveh,* and had literally run to Auntie Beyaz's house.

"Auntie Beyaz, open the door!" he had yelled and pounded the blue door. "Open the door and tell me what you did to that poor tourist woman! It's high time we learned what you said to her, don't you think?"

As Mehmet shouted and banged on Auntie Beyaz's door, the puzzled villagers began to gather around the house. First, a male tourist guide with long hair and an earring had shown up with a tourist woman to interrupt their quiet little village life, then she had insulted the memory of a beloved figure, a Dardanelles *Ghazi*, and then the village had been invaded by dozens of TV and newspaper crews who had never even heard its name before. And now, the most important and respected living elder was practically being attacked.

"Don't even bother, Mehmet *Bey*, son. There were two 'papermen and one cameraman here yesterday and she didn't even answer them," chuckled the *Mukhtar*, who had materialized by Mehmet's side.

"Some of them offered tons of money and Auntie Beyaz didn't even give 'em the time of day!" added a peasant woman, proudly.

The other women in the crowd giggled at this last statement. Auntie Beyaz was the only village woman they knew who could not be pushed around or disdained by men, whose words were valued and whose opinion mattered. It was true, she had never gotten married or become a mother (poor thing), but that was probably the price of avoiding men's disdain... Maybe... But there it was, she was a woman who had cityfolk, newspapermen and the *Mukhtar* lining up at her door, afraid of her every word.

"Quit this charismatic attitude, Auntie Beyaz!" Mehmet yelled.

"You better not yell at my Auntie Beyaz that way, mister! You'll lose your fortune, you'll lose your luck and you'll be separated from your loved ones, I'm not lying!"

Startled, Mehmet swerved around to see little Meryem,

who had told Vicki the day before that Auntie Beyaz happened to be her own great-aunt. That was when he regained his senses and noticed the *Mukhtar* and the villagers gathered around him. He took a deep breath. The air was clean, the sky bright blue, but it was cold, very cold. It was a bitter cold. Winter was truly bitter in Gallipoli. Little Meryem was rocking back and forth, smiling sweetly at Mehmet and eyeing him up and down, particularly his earring. Mehmet wished that her friendly gaze could be enough to quell his anger, but his heart, seeking the responsible party for Vicki's continuous fever of the last two days, always seemed to lead him to the blue door of this house. Besides, Vicki was a good person. Sure she was mysterious, did strange things, told meaningless jokes and made outrageous claims but she was a guest here after all. She was also an attractive woman and...

"That foreign woman who came here two days ago," he called out again to Auntie Beyaz. This time his voice was more controlled and bore the tone of a messenger rather than that of an accuser. "Vicki. She's now lying in a fever in Eceabat. She has neither her family nor her relatives by her side! Whatever you told her, whatever you said, it made her ill. Good for you Auntie Beyaz! Well done! I guess you're happy now!"

"Hush sonny, don't you talk to Auntie Beyaz that way, it's a sin!" warned the *Mukhtar*.

"What now, the tourist lady is sick? A pity, the poor woman!" the village women sympathized.

"Did you hear, the poor thing don't even have anyone to take care of her, not a one!"

"What do you think she's doing all by herself in some strange land?"

"Serves her right!" cried Havva, little Meryem's mother. "What business does she have coming all the way from Zealand or whatever to insult my great-grandpa? Slandering is a sin."

"Hush girl, didn't you hear she's sick! God forgive us."

Sick of the conversations, Mehmet decided to try his luck one last time:

"Poor Vicki, she only says your name, she just keeps saying Auntie Beyaz in her sleep. You know, they're taking her to a hospital in Chanakkale today. What did you say, what did you tell the girl Auntie Beyaz, tell me for the love of God!"

"Hear that, the poor wretch keeps saying Auntie Beyaz's name."

"Mm-hmm... 'Tis a pity. She's God's guest after all."

That was when the door swung open and Auntie Beyaz appeared, ready and dressed to leave. Upon seeing her everyone fell silent. They all took a step back without even realizing it. Everyone, including the *Mukhtar*, was agape. They were seeing her face for the first time in years. It seemed to Mehmet that at that moment even the kids, who ran happily around on the streets and the chickens, roosters, and dogs that wandered freely about, fell silent. It was impossible to remain unimpressed by this exquisite scene of shock. And Mehmet was duly impressed.

Auntie Beyaz stood in the doorway, blinking at the sunlight. She sought and found Mehmet among the crowd. She looked at him carefully. Mehmet was amazed to realize what a beautiful old woman Auntie Beyaz in fact was. He had never thought that an old, a very old woman could look this lovely. Besides, whoever thought of old women anyway? He had never even really looked in the faces of women who seemed old...

He stood transfixed by the old woman's face. The more he stared the more he felt filled with a joyful wonder. 'She must be one of those 'kind old ladies' they talk about in fairytales,' thought Mehmet. Her eyebrows, her eyelashes and the hair visible under her woolen shawl were all snow-white. Her blue eyes were so youthful, so incandescent that they seemed lit from within like blue beads. There was such an enchanting loveliness to her face that one felt a deep sense of peace just looking at her. This pure white face, embroidered with delicate wrink-

47

les, owed its beauty to having preserved its innocence despite remaining so long upon this earth. Only a baby's face could compare to its beauty, could remind a person of such purity and goodness. Hers must have been the only visage in the world that depicted light and innocence, kindness and pride in such a masterful way. Contrary to expectation, the lovely old woman's face did not portray kindness and meekness side by side. The goodness in that face made it abundantly clear to even the most evil of doers that it could exist without being necessarily meek or sweet. No, there was no tender, sugary softness in this face. On the contrary, it held a steady, proud expression. This woman, who in contrast to her small shrivelled frame met one's eye with a firm, lively gaze, perhaps owed her striking beauty to a combination of clear, reliable goodness and indomitability of spirit.

"Well, come on then, take me there, *mari*!" she said in a thin but authoritative voice. She held out her hand.

Mehmet was hypnotized. He could not take his eyes off Auntie Beyaz's face, he could not get enough of looking at her. He absently took the wrinkled little hand that was held out to him. It was soft and warm as can be. Although it looked like a child's hand Mehmet regarded it as that of a benevolent sage. He stared at the hand and suddenly found it difficult not to kiss it and raise it to his forehead. And yet it had been years since he had kissed an elder's hand. Particularly since that mean grandmother of his had forced him to kiss her hand every day he had sworn never to do it again. Mehmet had hated the tradition ever since his cruel grandmother had earned him many a good thrashing by complaining to his father. But now he was a little boy again and his shrewish grandmother, who had never loved him or never showed her love, had been transformed as if by a magic wand into Auntie Beyaz, with the soft, warm hands. Now, at a most unexpected moment, his old, much suppressed longing for a grandmot-

48

her's love had come crashing back. And the same magic wand had turned him into the lovable, obedient little boy who was stopped on the street by women wanting to pick his chubby cheeks.

Mehmet and Auntie Beyaz walked up to the jeep hand in hand. More accurately, Mehmet led Auntie Beyaz to the jeep with care and awe, as though he were holding in his hands a priceless gem. He opened the passenger door and helped her settle into the seat. He fastened her seat-belt, made sure it did not chafe her neck, then got in the driver's seat and started the car. Auntie Beyaz uttered '*Bismillah*' and they drove off to Eceabat.

The *Mukhtar* and the villagers, who had followed them to the jeep, were left to stare after them.

They did not speak the whole way since Mehmet could not gather up the courage to say anything. Hands folded on her lap, Auntie Beyaz watched with interest the blooming trees and the tourists, both foreign and domestic, who had come to tour the National Park. Despite their lack of conversation, the silence within the jeep was in no way uneasy, cold or odorless. On the contrary, the fifteen minute silence was gentle, soft and comforting. And when Mehmet delightedly detected a familiar scent of fennel, it was the scent of this silence.

They parked in front of the Friendly Anzac Pension, and as Mehmet helped her get out of the jeep, Auntie Beyaz asked:

"Do you keep that hair of yours clean, then?"

"I wash it with good quality shampoo at least twice a week," Mehmet replied. His voice contained not so much the anxiousness of a private answering his commander as that of a child trying to please his mother.

"Good for you. You have fine hair, *mari*. Looks good on you, too. Fine as a lion, *Mashallah*!"

Mehmet was positively overjoyed; not even the praises his girlfriends had given him about his hair had made him this glad.

"Thank you, Auntie, you're too kind," he said, grinning from ear to ear.

"Well, so where's this Vicki *Hanim*, then?" Auntie Beyaz scolded.

It was lunchtime when they entered the pension and there weren't many journalists or camera crews in sight. The young receptionist recognized Auntie Beyaz, ran up to her and kissed her hand. Auntie Beyaz looked at her briefly, stroked her hair and walked on without so much as a word or a smile. Besides, Mehmet had already adopted the role of her personal bodyguard and was busily clearing the way from a non-existent crowd as they walked.

They took the elevator to Vicki's room on the second floor. The room was dim. Despite a faint smell of illness and eau-de-cologne, it was still possible to detect Vicki's own particular fennel scent in the room. Mehmet led Auntie Beyaz, who had started moving her lips in silent prayer as soon as they had entered, to a chair by the head of the bed. Then, with a host's reflex, he tried to offer her lemon cologne. Auntie Beyaz, who was accompanying her prayers with a string of prayer beads she had produced from her pocket, pushed away Mehmet's hand without looking at him. Then, after Mehmet had stood around for a while not knowing what to do, she nodded towards the door, without raising her head.

As Mehmet, who obeyed her wishes with the meekness of a lamb and with pleasure, left the room, he saw Auntie Beyaz put a hand on Vicki's forehead and say, with a thick British accent:

"Time to wake up, clever young Miss Taylor."

He closed the door behind him, puzzling not so much about the fact that an old village grandma spoke a foreign language but over how she managed to have such a thick British accent.

Once he had left, Auntie Beyaz asked Vicki in a whisper:

"You didn't go and get sick before properly hiding away those letters you read me, did you, Vicki *Hanim*?"

50

Tuesday, January 19, 1915
Zeytun Military Camp, Egypt

Dearest Mother and Father, Darling Helen and Little Stuart,

We've received the Christmas package along with your letters. Every sentence and package we get from you feels like it has been sent from heaven.

I would never have believed, even in my dreams, that I was going to spend a Christmas in the desert. Well, I probably wouldn't have dreamt of a desert since I'd never seen one before. (Oh, all right, I know you're not terribly fond of my jokes!). But there you have it, we spent Christmas of 1914 in the desert. Can you believe it? We will have tons of desert stories to tell next Christmas when we're back home. I hope we'll also have stories of celebrating Easter in France.

I hope I didn't bore you with my last letter, the one where I described our exhausting sea voyage in detail. I know I don't write home as frequently as the other boys do. The main reason I've been lazy is because I know my brother Will(iam) has been writing to you often and in detail. But I don't want you to think that

I've forgotten you or New Zealand. I already miss a lot of things and a lot of people. I miss things I used to find boring and complain about like rugby games, playing hockey, rowing and even our life that I found a bit too rural and tedious. Sure, I miss it all, but I don't fancy writing as much as Will. I'm not as patient as him either, as you all know. Also, Will's got nice handwriting, his spelling is better, and he writes fluidly. After all, big brother is (was) studying at the seminary and he's four years older than me.

The trip to Egypt was awfully long and tiring. You know I don't get seasick but it's different on warships. The whole way here was like a nightmare, and for the first time in my life I found out what a curse seasickness really is. But it was exciting to get to Egypt. Because Egypt was a very important step in reaching our final destination. Our destination: Europe! You know how much I've been dreaming of it. Now that we're in Egypt, it means we're one step closer to Europe. Ah Europe! The main reason I joined this journey, sorry, I mean campaign, was so that I could see Europe. Now I see that many of the boys are after the same thing here, it's as if the war is a bit of an excuse. Well, is it so odd for us lads to fancy a bit of Europe, a bit of civilization, adventure, excitement, when there's not even the tiniest shred of adventure back home in sleepy old New Zealand?

Dearest Mum and Dad, please don't get me wrong. Things were certainly very different when you were my age. As you say, there was a pioneering spirit back then. You came to New Zealand from England, Scotland, Ireland and Holland with sacred goals like spreading civilization to the 'ends of the earth', and lived glorious adventures, you settled into a new land and built a new country. But it's different for my generation. We, and I especially, want to see the world, and I most of all want to go discover Europe, the center of the world. Europe! Grand civilization!

Nobody can doubt my loyalty to England our homeland, and to the King. Naturally, like every New Zealander, I am devoted to England and the King, but I also have dreams of my own.

There's a boy here with us from Auckland. His name is Russell. He's a history teacher, and he's seven years older than me. He's quite good friends with Will, and the three of us hang around together. He often tells us how proud he is to be a part of the Great British Empire. Sometimes he gets so carried away telling us about British history that it seems he was there among the blood and sweat of the great battles, as though he'd seen it with his very own eyes. Sometimes he gets most affected by his own tales and his eyes well up and his voice starts to tremble. I think the reason his voice trembles is not because of personal ardor but due to his spirit that burns with the fire of nationalistic pride. To be honest, I have a hard time understanding Russell because the fire in me kindles a different passion. I want to travel far, to explore, to get to know European civilization better, and to have adventures. Russell's nationalism is surely something to be proud of but, how should I put this, I sense a violence in his enthusiasm. When he talks about devotion to the Motherland and to the King, I see a deathly gleam in his eyes. That gleam is powerful enough to make him lose his head and, I'm afraid, even to take control of him. It seems dangerous to me. Will is nationalistic as well, but as you know, my brother's religious and romantic. His nationalism is pastoral. New Zealand's countryside, its plains, mountains, woods, ocean and birds... His love of the country is peaceful, like romantic love. Will also keeps reminding us how important it is that we are participating actively in an international event as New Zealanders for the first time in our history. He says it was becaus we needed this significance that we all raced each other to sign up for the army. That's his sense of nationalism.

As for my nationalism, of course we ought to pay our debt to Great Britain and teach those damn German pigs a lesson. Pardon my language, I've picked up quite a bit of it around these parts!

Meanwhile, I cannot help but notice a strange situation here. Here in Egypt, the Arabs think of us as English but to the English we seem to be distant, provincial people - not one of their own.

You may be very surprised to hear this, but the English don't consider us to be one of them. Will disagrees with me on this point. A while ago they teamed us up as the Australia–New Zealand Army Corps, calling it ANZAC for short. Thus we're now completely segregated from the Canadians, the Indians and the English who are here. But if you ask me, even the Australians look down on us; they accuse us of being undisciplined and stubborn. If you could just see their arrogance, as though they too were English and we were the only country bumpkins. But when there's trouble, it's not the English who come to their aid but us New Zealanders. Isn't it odd how a person discovers some truths only when he is away from his country?

I want to tell you a bit about Egypt. Egypt is our first experience of the 'Orient'. And we're all convinced that 'Orientals' are nothing like us. For one thing, Orientals are extremely romantic people. The two cities we have seen so far, Cairo and Alexandria, are large, complex and highly colorful places. For instance, if we were to pile together all the cities in old New Zealand, they would not amount to one Cairo. On the other hand, you would not be able to find a single town, village or house that could contain the disorder, the mystery, the thievery, the crookery and the filthiness of Cairo alone. There's a contradiction for you. My response to this Oriental culture, which is briefly entertaining as a foreigner and visitor, is: Thanks, but I've had enough. No thanks!

The Arabs are truly poor. They say the wealthy among them live in pleasure and comfort but we haven't seen any. Children go barefoot on the street, they don't even have shoes. The men wear red, cylindrical hats called 'fez', which look like buckets, and long gowns called 'potur'. The women have to be completely covered up. They walk around like round black figures, carelessly swaddled in black cloth. I would like to voice a protest here. It seems that the Arabs have enslaved their own women. Arab women are not free. When I think about the girls back in New Zealand, I sincerely feel sorry for the ones here. Meanwhile, some Arab women I have seen carry such indecent, lewd expressions in their eyes that it gives a man the impression they are completely naked, despite being covered in black cloth. I don't know how they do it. But you'll forgive me if I say that our women could never manage such sensual glances. I don't understand their language but I hear them use their voices in a most incredibly coy, seductive manner. Will says that oppressed people may develop different skills. Maybe he's right.

Will purchased a little antique figurine to take back home as a present. But it turned out that the Arab antique vendor had sold him a fake, for there's quite a few of the 'unique masterpiece' handed around among the boys. One of the duped Aussie soldiers says he'll kill the Arab merchant if he gets his hands on him. I don't know if this incident is enough to prove the Arabs a deceitful lot but it's safe to say that the prejudice has firmly settled among us ANZACs. Will says it's a sin to think this way but everyone laughs him off. They may be cheats because they're poor but I haven't been able to figure out why they are so dirty. The Arabs eat with their hands, yes, they use their hands instead of knives, forks and spoons, which are available, and then they wipe their hands on their clothes. The boys have nicknamed the Arabs 'Abdul', and there's no end to the Abdul jokes and caricatures in sight. Will says it's easier to bicker with others than bicker with yourself.

Of course, our daily life in Egypt is not all trips and obervations. Every day they make us march twenty-four miles, fully equipped. I don't think there will be any among us who has fond memories of Zeytun Military Camp in the future.

Two days before Christmas, our cavalry units organized a glorious procession on the streets of Cairo. We all marched down the street as sons of England, clean-shaved and impeccably dressed. Mum and Dad, if you had seen the parade, you would have been proud of us and of New Zealand.

I don't think Helen or Little Stuart should read what I'm about to say now, because it's not very appropriate material for them.

In fact, Mum and Dad may be a little shocked as well, but I'm going to relate a striking example of how things that would not even cross our minds in New Zealand are considered daily fare in Egypt. (Hope Will doesn't find out, or he'll kill me!)

Forgive me for what I'm about to tell you, but 'those houses' are legal here. I mean those houses of ill repute. I am not joking, believe me. There's even a neighborhood of such houses in Cairo, called the Wazzir. Can you imagine? The police know all about it, in fact, it's said that they gather taxes from it. Don't get the wrong idea, Will and I only went to the Wazzir because of Russell's curiosity. Otherwise, we would not even think of it... Anyway, since there began a mention of contagious diseases, those who used to frequent them have become more cautious. And yet, ir a country where such an ugly trade is legal and tolerated by the police, that same police is allowed to whip anyone they fancy right out on the street. No one can do a thing about it. The Arab police is allowed to beat anyone they please. Think of it, such things happen in the world, even in the year 1915!

There are also plenty of shops that sell alcohol in the Wazzir. You can imagine how crowded the place gets on leave days. The three of us sometimes go walking around there for lack of anything better to do. Street brawls often erupt between our boys and the Aussies or the Arabs. Sometimes the shops that sell alcohol are even looted. It's disgraceful, of course. There was a huge fire the other day. The girls working in those particular houses threw themselves off the roof in fear. There were some dead, some injured. People taking the opportunity to loot, fighting on the street, screaming... Then the Australians and, I regret to say, some of our boys, overturned a fire engine that came to put out the fire and caused a shameful scene. There was such an uproar that finally the English came and started shooting, and then things settled down. Unfortunately, there were soldiers who died in this tumult. It was all terribly savage and embarrassing. A kind-hearted Arab merchant gave us refuge in his shop when the madness erupted, and the things we witnessed were truly disheartening. I suppose the extreme heat, the foreign culture, and most of all that awful sense of uncertainty as to where and when we will be sent, has gone to all of our heads. The innocent and idealistic youths who left New Zealand have been changed. We seem to have grown coarse and violent without even having experienced war... Or did a violence awaken, which was always within us? Here's another thing I wonder: Will the English tell the families of the boys who were accidentally shot during the hubbub, that their sons died in combat? Or would a single New Zealander believe that the English had killed their own sons in arms?

I want to end my letter with a somewhat cheerful anecdote. This way, you will see that we are also having some fun here and will not worry too much. The story I'm about to tell is not a dream, we were all there and had a blast. One night, the three of us were strolling about aimlessly in front of Sheperd's Hotel, one of Cairo's renowned hotels, when we came upon a fortune-teller. Seeing a fortune-teller on the street might sound odd to you but it's quite common here. In Egypt, there are many fortune-tellers on every street corner. But the one we met that night was much poorer and older than the rest, and quite 'stoned', if you see what I mean. There's a considerable number of drug users here... The fortune-teller wore a rough, hooded burlap robe but it seemed that both the robe and the hood were empty. He only consisted of two eye sockets bored into a dark face. Two dark and deep holes. Frightening, mysterious and striking. It was a hot night and we were so tired of idleness and our gapingly uncertain future that we decided on a lark to have our fortunes told. You know our religious Will, he immediately objected. But Russell and I were so insistent that it was only a game that he finally gave in. The fortune-teller first read Russell's future: "You will soon fight in a war," he says. We were cracking up in laughter. We're soldiers, mate, we're her to fight for Great Britain and the King, the whole world knows that! And he's supposed to be telling our fortunes. "You will be badly wounded in the war but you will not die. You will return to your country at last," he says. We kept on laughing.

When it was my turn he really outdid himself. "You too will go to war," he says. Our bellies were aching from laughter. "Your wound shall be bloodless, you will not die. But you will not return to your country," he says. "So, where'm I headed then, Mr. Fortune-teller?" I asked, cheerfully. Then he gives me this awful glare! Would you believe it?

Will was upset at what the fortune-teller told me. He gave him a mean stare and told him he didn't want his fortune read. Of course, the teller was quick to take his revenge. "I would not be able to read your fortune anyway, son. I cannot do it. Your fortune can't be read!" he cried. By this point Russell and I were rather silly with laughter, I don't think I've ever laughed that much in my life. As we were laughing, Will for some reason grew sullen. Meanwhile, the fortune-teller had disappeared into Cairo's dark streets. He hadn't even asked us for money, unlike the other tellers. He seemed to have vaporized. Just vanished into thin air, like Aladdin's genie... Well, these are the sort of things that happen in the 'Orient', and they're considered quite natural.

Now, my hand needs some rest. Anyhow, it's almost time for maneuvers. I'll end my letter here. On the whole, we are fine except for the heat and the damned uncertainty. They say we are to be transferred to the French front. I truly hope that that will be the case. Because France is Europe. And Europe...

I trust Will's longer and more detailed letters are keeping you updated on our daily life. His presence here is a comfort to myself and many others. His common sense and simple humanity works like a balm on our restless spirits. I don't know what I would do without him.

Don't worry about us. We're here because our country needs us. When we return, you will find men who have had their share of adventure. Then, I'm planning on setting up a business in the city instead of working at dad's sheep farm, where we only receive the paper once a week and it's a long trek to the post office. You know how ever since I was a kid people said I had a knack for carpentry, well, maybe I'll open up a little workshop and then expand it. I have some progressive ideas on the subject. But let us go win this war first.

I miss all of you. Mum dear, pray for us, will you? Little Stuart, you can use my fishing gear if you promise to take good care of it. Dad, you're keeping track of rugby scores for me, aren't you? God bless us all.

Your loving son,
Alistair John Taylor

Private N.B. for my sister Helen:
Helen, I haven't received any news from Keri. Please give her my regards. Don't forget, now, ok?

Vicki looked tired when she ended reading the letter. She turned toward Auntie Beyaz:

"That was one of the letters I inherited from my great-grandfather, Alistair John Taylor," she said.

Auntie Beyaz was calmly counting her prayer beads and moving her jaw that had dentures on it as if sucking something. She seemed not to have heard or understood the letter that Vicki just read. Not a leaf stirred on her face.

"My great-grandfather's older brother, William, died at Gallipoli. Their friend Russell returned to New Zealand as a disabled veteran who had lost one of his legs at Gallipoli. The Arab fortune-teller had guessed their fate. Only my great-grandfather Alistair John Taylor was missing. No news was received of him. And his body was never found. Ever. His name was among the list of the missing, and there it always stayed. But my great-grandfather was alive. He was living here, in Gallipoli. The Arab fortune-teller had been right on that count as well. I don't have any definite proof, Auntie Beyaz, but ever since the day I first heard the story and ever since I read these letters as a young girl, I have been convinced of this fact: My great-grandfather did not die at Gallipoli." Auntie Beyaz was gazing out the window, looking completely serene as she moved her lips and handled her prayer beads. Vicki added, in a weary voice:

"As for Keri. She was a New Zealand native, that is, a Maori. At the time, she was also pregnant with Alistair John Taylor's illegitimate child. And that baby was later to become my grandfather."

Auntie Beyaz suddenly got the hiccups.

Esteemed Mother, Cherished Brother Salih,

I have received your letter, filled with kindness and advice. I kissed it a thousand times and held it to my forehead. The letter smelled of Istanbul, our house, your kind self, and my brother. It relieved my soul. May God shed his mercy on you, Mother dearest.

I hope this letter finds you in good health and humor. Though you have thoughtfully neglected to mention the fact, the state of our country and nation is evident. Nevertheless, I pray to God that He might keep us from further evils and confer brighter days upon our people. You express concern for my wellbeing. I beg of you not to trouble yourself. When a Turkish youth is called upon to defend his country, his spirit is, and shall ever be, fully prepared for the task. I fully assure you that your son is alive and well at the head of his sacred mission. The virtues which I owe to the lofty upbringing of yourself and my beloved late father, light my way whenever I falter in the face of fate's surprises. Although I have not yet entered the twentieth year of my life, I am acutely aware of being part of a hallowed duty.

---

*) Friday, January 8, 1915

Time flows like water. It has been almost three months since I parted from your good company, from our house and from my fair city of Istanbul. To be able to perceive at this young an age the fragility, briefness and divine generosity of human life, I believe is yet another act of His mercy. I know not whether you will share this opinion, but your humble Ali Osman, who is now a Turkish officer, looks upon last year's image of himself, studying at the Law School, as though it were a separate, inexperienced boy he were seeing and smiles compassionately. Is it right to mature thus in the course of a year? I do not know the answer but life will show it. However, dear Mother, it has come to my understanding that the being we call man is in fact far more weak, inept and alone than I had thought before.

With your permission, I would like to relate here a memory of mine. As you know, my beloved father used to take me for walks at Beylerbeyi, whenever he could find time to spare from his duties at the Gumushsuyu Hospital. On one of our final strolls, he had told me the following:

"Son, I believe there will soon erupt a great war in Europe. It is highly probable that this war will be fought on a larger scale. I fervently hope that this general war, which will bring ruin upon humanity, will not force you to abandon your studies."

During this conversation, while puffing on the pipe he had brought from Paris (which I now smoke with the tenderest of care), my dear father had indicated that in the future the (Ottoman) Empire would diminish considerably and become transformed by educated Turkish youth into a civilized and scientific government. In the course of these strolls and conversations I would carefully observe dear father, looking at his powerful hands which had saved so many lives, and committing to memory his every gesture and expression, as though I had sensed his untimely departure. I admired, and always will, his progressive ideas, common sense and magnificent learning.

As I witness dear father's sage concerns become manifest one by one, I pray that God will also prove correct his more favorable predictions regarding our nation.

Mother dear, I continue to diligently inscribe for you my impressions regarding our trying but sacred campaign, yet I cannot be certain of whether or not you have received all of my previous letters. Thus, if you should encounter some repetition in my narrative, it is only due to the fact that I am doubtful of the fate of my previous correspondences.

Do you recall the day mobilization was declared? The kiss you bestowed upon my forehead, the mournful tears you tried to hide when you heard of my intention to cut short my education and enlist in the army as a reserve officer candidate... And the amazing scene I discovered, when with winged step I made my way to the Military Academy! I still remember the incredible crowd of intellectual Turkish youth that had gathered to enlist in front of the Academy. I must admit that even now, it gives me goosebumps to recall the thrill I felt upon beholding that sight. Yet, even though I cannot quite decribe it, there was a kind of savage exuberance to the crowd, the likes of which I had not seen before. We made such a ruckus, like children who scream all the louder to avoid discovering the source of their exuberance. We were cheering but had forgotten why. If we had noticed the reason for our joy, we would have been wrecked with sorrow, we would have died of grief. In order to hold back the anxiety and sadness deep down, we disguised the excitement on the surface with noise. That is all. It is my opinion that that savage joy was in fact an unconscious attempt to suppress a tragedy. For we were shaken. And what a violent jolt it was, dear Mother. My spirit was tossed from shore to shore by a strong southerly wind, and sustained deep injuries each time she hit. On one shore was a soul ready to be sacrificed for its country, on the other, Mother dear, was youth, a life to be lived, hopes and dreams...

I know that, try as I may, I can never hope to describe my feelings with as much brilliance as yourself. You, Her Grace the Lady Semahat, daughter of Husnu *Pasha*, who grew up with both French and Russian nannies, you who know by heart the great literature of the two languages and who are schooled in the Eastern Canon due to her Sheikh ul-Islam lineage, I ask your forgiveness for my insufficient prose. Your high culture, your social graces, and your legendary beauty have always been subject to the admiration of not only my late father but also our entire circle. You will recall, better than I, how even as a young child I used to envy your admirers, how I would sulk among society, feeling a mixture of awe and resentment.

To continue with my topic, another important incident I remember from that first day at the Academy was the personal visit His Highness Enver *Pasha*, the Minister of War paid to the site, thus inciting our excitement to even greater levels. He was not as tall and imposing a figure as I had imagined, but he was extremely handsome and exuded an aura of authority. His posture contained an impressive grandeur, and his gaze a confidence-inspiring spark. He must have been aware of it, for he walked with great dignity and self-assurance. With the subsequent start of the holy month of Ramadan during our training period at Maslak and Kagithane, we were advised not to fast. Though we were assured by our officers and hodjas that we were exept from our sacred obligation as we would be considered 'travelers', I admit to you now that some of us continued to fast in secret for longer durations than normal because we did not have time to eat due to the exercises. All through our training period in Istanbul I experienced the bitter-sweet joy of meeting hundreds of educated youths of various professions; lawyers, engineers, men of science, poets and students such as myself. Despite the strict discipline during maneuvers, we kept ourselves occupied with wry laughter, sharp jokes and making various plans and rendezvous for when we returned. Has there ever been an army in the world that consisted entirely of the university-educated? Ours was, for one. At the time, a jest became popular among us that stated our army could only be considered an 'Army of Knowledge', and I must say it rather pleased us. God forbid if something were to happen to this division, can you imagine the future of our country? Upon my word, there would not be any educated folk left in the country! I pray that God does not allow such a possibility, *inshallah*!

As reserve officer candidates, while we marched every day from the Academy to Maslak, singing military marches, what a tremendous effect the dreamy gazes of the young girls lining the windows of Shishli Avenue, had on us, dear Mother! The love of country that filled our young hearts would suddenly become muddled with the worldly excitation of the young girls' dreamy, admiring stares, and we would arrive at Maslak, tense and perspiring from a most peculiar mix of emotions. Add to that the exultation of the public that lined the streets and waited to especially show us their support, and you can see how we were spiritually exhausted before the day's training even began. At that time, the Empire had not yet entered the war and we still bore favorable hopes regarding the future.

Then, receiving word that we were to be transferred into the command of our army in Damascus, and you, beloved mother, you paying a visit to the Bekiraga Division... The way I clutched the bag of clothes and 'necessary items' you gave me, as though it contained your very soul. And finally that word, the word that was to become the most common in my life:

Dispatch!

"Gentlemen, we are off to dispatch!"

Dispatch meant separation. Dispatch meant facing reality, it meant the hard slap of truth upon our faces. The time had come to leave behind the romantic effect of our female admirers' gaze, and the flood of love that poured from the hearts of our people, it was time to part.

Dispatch!

We were leaving behind, for now, our family hearths, our loved ones, and our professional and personal dreams regarding the future. We were parting from one another. We were leaving this incomparable Istanbul. We were leaving behind everything we liked to do, every gift that we had heretofore taken for granted. We were parting with clean clothes, hot meals and the silhouette of Istanbul. Yes, we were parting... And even... we were even parting with our arms, our legs, our eyes, and perhaps even with the world itself.

To leave the mansion in Fatih, which came alive with your piano performances of Dede Efendi and Chopin in the afternoons, to leave behind the delectable cup of Turkish coffee Atifet *Kalfa** made in the evenings, to abandon our lovely horserides with Salih, to give up the pleasure boat cruises we made from the seaside mansion at Beylerbeyi! No more hours reclining with friends at the Zeuve Beerhouse near the Tunnel, sipping scotch and soda from a lemonade straw and perusing the French, German and English newspapers, no more staying up til dawn under the pine trees at Buyuk Ada, farewell to the gorgeous library at the Fatih mansion... Oh mother, why does a person only realize the good things he has when he comes to lose them?

"Gentlemen! We're off to dispatch!"

With the predawn call of the morning bugle, we set off on the journey that was to take us from Istanbul to Damascus, and will soon lead us to the (Suez) Canal Front.

First we went to Sirkeci and there we took trailers to the Haidar Pasha Train Station. As we boarded the train, we took our leave of our commanding officer. "Gentlemen, Godspeed to you all!" were his parting words. We had come to love him as a father, despite his young age. The bitter wail of the whistle at the station, the hands and kerchiefs waving goodbye amidst sobs... It must have been to restrain ourselves from weeping collectively that we all sang marches and tried to rid ourselves of the searing spiritual anguish. After passing Kiziltoprak, Goztepe and Kartal, we arri-

---

*) *Kalfa*: maid

66

ved at Pozanti on the third morning. Then the Toros Mountains, which came upon us in the dead of night, towering in darkness, with frightening animal cries carried on the wind. At dawn we began scaling the mountain range, on foot, of course. The railroad was spent!

The Toros Mountains possess a frightening splendor which you must absolutely behold. Mist, snow, cliffs and ridges - take what you please. Our struggle to make headway on our uncertain path that was shrouded in mist... But when we reached the summit, we were rewarded with so excellent a view as to make all our toil worthwhile. A gorgeous, thrilling view that inspires jealousy within the viewer. Enthralling! Darling mother, I shall most certainly take you there someday. The sight of this miracle of nature could inspire tears in a person. C'est magnifique!

In Tarsus, the public met and hosted us. We were greeted with sincere warmth and interest. Yet the road that followed was even more treacherous. We walked for days. Both nature and the weather cruelly reminded us of the fact that we were now far south. We strode on, in hunger and thirst, battling our way through mud, rocks and thorns. On the way we sometimes came upon skeletons and, perhaps owing to our fear, we took up the march with renewed ardor. I will give short shrift to these sections so that I might not weigh down your spirit. But I must say this much: The eastern and southern regions of the Empire are in a much graver state than you might imagine. The unbearable poverty and ignorance we saw in these parts plunged us educated youth into deep despair. The people are suffering here. Most of the administrators are indifferent and government rule is poor. Ignorance and backwardness, which are the true enemies, are not being addressed. Not only is the people's Turkish incomprehensible, very few here can understand Istanbul Turkish.

Mother dear, the sorrow that passed across your visage when, after your European voyages you described our beloved Istanbul's shortcomings in comparison to Paris and Berlin, is somewhat similar to the pain I felt upon seeing the southern and eastern regions of the Empire.

I must mention here the kind assistance shown to us by the *Kaimakam* Effendi*** of Islahiye. Our goal was Damascus but as soon as we arrived there we learned that the Empire had entered the war. It was expected news, yet we were depressed nonetheless. Not because we feared war, but probably because war has rarely been known to bring any good to mankind. War must only be resorted to when a nation's sovereignty is in question. For if a nation is invaded, there is but one choice left: to hurry and send the invaders back to from whence they came.

About seventy of us enlightened youth were anxiously waiting in Damascus to find out where we would be appointed to next. Our journey had lasted a mere three weeks but we had lived through such difficult, private moments together that we felt we had known each other all our lives. In the course of this short but fateful journey it was our personal courage that bound us inseparably. But when our appointments were disclosed, we all parted ways. God only knows if we will ever be able to see one another again.

I was appointed to leave for Amman. I was in charge of the administration at Amman. There were Bedouin and Circassian villages nearby. The area is desert as far as the eye can see and its residents have been left in bitter ignorance, Mother dear. They have not so much as heard of the existence of a device called the telephone. I built a telephone system for them. Oh Mother, if you could have only seen the joy and surprise on their faces. They regarded me as a genius, a saint. I swear to you, I do not jest. Ah mother dear, what a cruel foe is ignorance to leave man so naive, crippled and needy even at an advanced age, to reduce humans to wretchedness. He who lives side by side with ignorance has no fate other than slavery. And that, I'm afraid, is no fate at all.

Ever since the telephone system, the villagers have been greeting me with 'Stamboul gentleman, ya salaam!' and demonstra-

---

*) *Kaimakam*: district governor
**) *Effendi*: mister (very formal)

ting respect by bowing down to the ground. Yet what they perceive as a spiritual power is a result of science and physics, a product of the human intellect. If, God willing, I should return alive from this war, Mother dear, I plan to dedicate the rest of my life to battling ignorance and superstition – the greatest enemy of my country and people. As one who sincerely believes in our empire's superior record of humanism compared to the other great empires in history, I regard ignorance and superstition to be the cause of all the ills that have befallen the Ottoman Empire and its people. This is the cause I shall pursue, and if I should be martyred, then other sons of Turkey will SURELY battle this curse. A bright and comfortable future for our country will cease to be a dream when, and only when, every single individual believes that knowledge and science will triumph over any twist of fate.

Now, allow me to relate some more cheerful articles. For instance, I learned in the provinces of Amman that a camel is called 'hedjin'. I wonder if you can picture me giving commands atop a 'hedjin' during a conflict between the gendarmery and Bedouin rebels. Had I the time, I would have enjoyed myself but it was not to be. Also around Amman, the public would mistake my *calpac** for a hat, and whisper to each other that I was in fact European. But the gendarme who brought up the rear would call out to them "He happens to be a Turkish officer!" It may also please you to hear that the Mayor of Amman lavished upon me a most kind regard and attention.

When it was decreed that Jerusalem was my next post of duty, I set off once again with the gendarmes and camels in my command. A host of absurd and humorous incidents followed one another on the way. Our passage through the Valley of Sharia and the Bahr-i Lut was filled with adventures. Although our concern for our water supply prevented us from fully appreciating the loveliness of Lake Lut, we did make a note of it in our minds. Perhaps some other time...

On the way, the mule convoys carrying oranges from Jaffa saved our lives by presenting us with generous amounts of this de-

*) *Calpac*: fur cap

69

licious fruit. If you think of the gusto with which our parched lips welcomed the oranges, you can imagine why the fruit has become to us holy as dates. Thank goodness we finally arrived in the fair city of Jerusalem, which is surrounded with lemon, date, banana and orange trees. But upon my word, dear Mother, what a wealthy and magnificent place this Jerusalem is! It is a city out of a fairytale. Its views, its spick-and-span buildings and avenues left all the more powerful an impression on us after our arduous journey. Jerusalem is not only beautiful, it is also a civilized city. The town, which is connected to Jaffa by train, boasts a degree of civility that allows men and women to stroll side by side in the evenings. The happy events in Jerusalem are too numerous to recount but the first thing that springs to mind is undoubtedly our fierce enjoyment of the *hamam**, where we washed and bathed and freshened up to our hearts' content.

I also visited the Masjid of Aksa and the Hacer-i Musalla and prayed for the memory of my beloved father, for the wellbeing of yourself and Salih, and for the good of our country. May God accept my prayers.

So, my darling Mother and beloved brother Salih, I am still in the fine city of Jerusalem, but rumor has it that we will soon receive orders to move to the (Suez) Canal. By the time you receive this letter the matter will be long decided.

An older officer whose acquaintance I have recently made, has taken me under his wing, and his knowledge and manners have already inspired my devotion. This officer, known as Iskender of Skopje, possesses all the qualities of a leader and has aroused interest not only with his progressive and nationalistic opinions, but also with the courage and boldness of his character. While all the other officers vie to gain his favor, he devotes most of his attention to the author of these lines, causing me the greatest elation.

The foreign papers we receive, however outdated, announce that the British have enlisted youth from their colonies to enter the war. We hear that Ostralia, from far off in the Pacific, Canada,

*) *Hamam*: Turkish bath

70

India and Zealand, whose name we have only recently heard of, are among these colonies. Wouldn't you know it, a world of Christian nations is once again declaring war on us. Well, then we shall defend our country. They would have done the same.

With your permission, here I must end this letter, which I have been inscribing for hours. Our new destination is the Canal Front. The rest is a mystery. At this point it is not the address that matters, but rather our country and our freedom.

Mother dear, I bestow my kisses on your blessed hands and on Salih's cheeks. Please give my respects to Atifet *Kalfa* and to Auntie Mueyyet. I do not need any new clothes. My money remains unspent. Do write to me often. And do pray for me and for our nation. May God bless you all.

Your Son,
Reserve Officer
Ali Osman

Auntie Beyaz read the long letter through, pausing only to push back her spectacles with trembling hands, and exhibiting a heroic disregard for the hindrance caused by her dentures that made her splutter continuously. Though her exhaustion was readily apparent, she did not seem to pay it any mind. She held her spectacles gingerly, as though they had been designer glasses, when in fact the frame was held together by scotch tape. The letter she read was a photocopy in which the pages were divided into three vertical columns. Each page contained three versions of the letter; the original Ottoman script on the right, the modern Turkish translation in the middle and the English version on the left. The Turkish part of the text looked like a page full of musical notation because of the Turkish equivalents given in brackets for dozens of Ottoman words. Auntie Beyaz read the letter in English, occasionally checking some of the words against the Turkish, and by the end she looked tired but proud. She slowly drank the glass of water that had been waiting on a little end-table by her seat, patted her mouth dry with a handkerchief she produced from her handknit vest, and folding the letter with utmost care, placed it back in its envelope as though it were a holy manuscript. She picked up the Koran that was waiting in the window ledge, tucked the envelope into its pages with a prayer and put the Koran back in its place.

The emotional impact of the letter had shaken her tiny old frame a few times during the reading and her blue eyes, surrounded by snow-white lashes, had filled up with tears but she had not cried. It was Vicki who cried. It was Vicki whose head ached, whose body temperature rose as though with fever, who felt sick. The old woman called Auntie Beyaz was solid as a rock, cold as ice, stubborn as a mule and tranquil as a cat. She looked tired but sat bolt upright on the sofa, alternating her crossed legs and frequently replacing her dentures which had a tendency to slip. Vicki, meanwhile, was suffering from shock and having trouble regaining her composure.

"My father had lost his mind when they found him," Auntie Beyaz said suddenly. "Poor soul, he'd suffered a heap when he fell captive to the Brits, *mari*. He'd fled torture and gone days without food or water. He was only twenty years old. A babe in arms! His eyes were all rollin' back in his head, his hands were shaking, and the poor wretch had forgotten how to talk when they found him. My ma, Meryem, used to tell us that when she first saw him she thought 'his mind's done gone, up there with the angels.'"

Vicki, wincing from the throbbing headache, spoke in a barely audible voice:

"It is a known fact that veterans of World War I, who were subjected to extended periods of stress, developed symptoms such as temporary blindness, paralysis, and loss of speech and memory that allowed them temporary relief from the fighting conditions. References say that the symptoms are not organically based. But they are temporary and not lifelong."

"I wouldn't know about anyone else, I only know about my dad, *mari*," dismissed Auntie Beyaz. "Them three letters was all my father had on him. The one I read you was the first letter. 'Twas afterwards we switched to the Turkish alphabet. All us folks learned to read and write, thanks to Ataturk, God rest his soul... Back then, schools was only three years long but even them in the villages who saw not a day further schooling still read the papers at seventy. Indeed they do... Anyhow. What was I saying, *mari*? When my dad got better, he translated them letters into the new alphabet first, and then to the language he learned from the British. Used to teach me their language, he would. See now, teaching me really did help my father get better."

It was clear to Vicki that the letter concerned an Ottoman intellectual, as well as his wealthy and noble bourgeois family, but she was having difficulty understanding how the same person could be provincial Auntie Beyaz's father. The letter was signed

73

"Reserve Officer Ali Osman" but the villagers insisted on calling the man Sergeant Alican. Could it be that Auntie Beyaz was confusing names, events and letters owing to her old age? She could well be suffering from Alzheimer's. Or did the language barrier cause a misunderstanding between them? Alternately, Auntie Beyaz might have been teaching a lesson to the foreigner who, in her eyes, had come all the way to her doorstep in Gallipoli in order to meddle with the memory of her father. But then... Why were there no gaps of reason in Auntie Beyaz's words, no slips of time or logic in her narrative? As for her English, like all languages acquired during early childhood, it was remarkably fluent and intelligible. The only thing different about it was Auntie Beyaz's antiquated accent, her use of archaic words and various Turkish colloquialisms (such as *mari*, *hele*, *felan*** and of course, the obligatory *mashallah and inshallah*, 'Thanks God's and 'God forbid's that Turks use a lot which only helped to further her mystery and charm. At the same time, this old woman was so similar to all other Turkish peasant women she had seen that despite her blue eyes, she could not be called a Levantine, as other Westerners who had settled in the East.

Under normal circumstances, Vicki would have been preoccupied with finding out how on earth the sensitive and aristocratic Turkish youth in the letter had ended up spending the rest of his life in this village. Yet Vicki was in a completely different state of mind. She felt as cheated as a thieving pirate who spends years searching for a treasure chest only to discover that it is empty. Thieving, because she was trying to steal someone else's father, and in the process causing grief to the innocent villagers and to an aged woman, however cold and stubborn. She felt crestfallen for having made a fool of herself and for having pursued a cause that boasted no supporters from the beginning.

---

*) *felan*: etc.

For years, she had nursed her 'Gallipoli or Bust' obsession; the sharp instincts that she had inherited from her Maori ancestors and every new sign had fed her growing curiosity. Was she to find now that it was all a fanciful dream? Had her great-grandfather, Alistair John Taylor, really died on the Gallipoli battlefield, like thousands of other Anzac soldiers? Did the Gallipoli hero, *Ghazi* Sergeant Alican truly have nothing whatsoever to do with her great-grandfather? Who was Ali Osman, this intellectual officer from Istanbul, and what an intriguing woman was his mother, Semahat *Hanim*, if that in fact was her name?

"Come and have some of this, *hele!*" bade Auntie Beyaz.

It was still a mystery what this old woman, whose sweetest tone of voice bore a trace of regal command, felt towards Vicki. Here, in provincial 20th century Turkey, where women can not share a cup of coffee or a backgammon game with the men at the *kahveh*, this wise woman who had established dominion over all the villagers including the *Mukhtar*, had suddenly been confronted by a foreigner who threatened her rule, and who was attempting to undermine the very source of her power. Auntie Beyaz was an intelligent woman and it went without saying that she would play her cards expertly well. Perhaps savoring every move, with the victorious expression of those who know that they have won the game from the very beginning...

"Here, take this lemon cologne, *hele*. Pour yourself a good handful, wipe it on your face, inhale it. You look pale as a ghost, *mari!*"

Vicki did as she was told, and wouldn't you know it, for the first time the sharp Turkish cologne that was offered literally everywhere, from buses to public lavatories, did not strike her as offensive. Strange to say but here, in Auntie Beyaz's house, the scent even seemed pleasant. She felt refreshed. Maybe it was because she wanted to believe that Auntie Beyaz had supernatural powers.

"You know how to make coffee, then?" asked Auntie Beyaz, somewhat condescendingly.

"Coffee? Who doesn't?"

"I mean Turkish coffee!" snapped Auntie Beyaz.

Then, without waiting for a response, she got up from the sofa with a prayer. She straightened out her vest and *shalvar* and waddled toward the kitchen. But she stopped midway and turned to give Vicki a glance indicating that she should follow. She seemed certain that her commands would always be carried out. Vicki also rose and followed her into the kitchen. Meanwhile, Auntie Beyaz was muttering to herself in her archaic vocabulary, with a heavy British accent, and loud enough for Vicki to hear:

"So her great-granddad didn't die in the war and could my dad be her granddad and so on... blah blah blah... you come all the way here from the ends of the earth and you don't even know how to make Turkish coffee! Lord give me patience. Can you fathom, *mari*? Was her granddad a Zealander or a Turk? Who cares? What's it to me? *And whoever heard of the same man being a hero in two countries? Think of that, the same man a hero in both countries*, mari... What kind of daydreams does this lass have? Besides, wherever a person's grandmother and grandfather are from, that's where she's from. Best to let the dead be. That's right. But to come all the way out here and don't know a thing about making coffee! Well, I'll be darned."

Vicki realized that she had been listening to her with a smile and guiltily snapped back to attention. Upon entering the kitchen, she was surprised to discover a top of the line refrigerator and turbo oven in this modest village house.

"My youngest grandson from Istanbul, my brother Bulut's grandson bought these for me. He studied well and made a name for himself. Now he's an important lawyer," Auntie Beyaz proudly explained. "Here, take this *jezveh*."

Vicki inspected the contraption that Auntie Beyaz had somewhat roughly thrust in her hands. It looked like a cross between a miniature frying pan and a milk jug.

"*Jez...veh*," she repeated, indicating her desire to learn.

"Here's the cups, let's see you pour in two cups of water."

"*Jez-veh*!" Vicki repeated once again. She was convinced that if she managed to wear down Auntie Beyaz's anger there would emerge some milk of human kindness. After all, this woman was not made of stone! Furthermore, there could well be the reluctance of a jealous child unwilling to share her father lying beneath her brash, angry manner toward Vicki. If, as they said, this woman was as strong as a Turk, then she herself was as patient and diplomatic as an Englishman and as strong-willed as a Maori.

Just then the doorbell rang and there came a pounding on the door downstairs. Mehmet could be heard yelling in an anxious and irate voice:

"Vicki, hey Vicki! Are you all right? Do you feel okay? Are you going to stay in there much longer? Vickiii!"

"Go hush up that rascal and be quick!" Auntie Beyaz scolded Vicki.

Vicki called out to Mehmet from the kitchen window:

"I'm fine. Everything's fine, Mehmet. I am OK."

Mehmet reluctantly went back to the village *kahveh*.

"See here, in this jar, this is finely ground Turkish coffee. Let me see, what was it called? Arabica, I think. Me late father had told me once that the *giaours** called it Arabica. Anyways, whatever."

"The *giaours*? Who're they?"

"Don't you worry about the *giaours* now, you add two teaspoons full of coffee for every cup but mind you Vicki *Hanim*, our teaspoons are wee little things, don't mix them up with dessert spoons or somethin!"

---

*) *Giaour:* non-muslim

Vicki *Hanim*?

This was good. Auntie Beyaz had not called her Ms. Vicki or added the Turkish equivalent 'Bayan' to the beginning of her name as Turks did with foreigners. No, she had addressed her the way Turks spoke to one another, called her *Hanim*. Vicki *Hanim*. Yes, this was a good sign.

"The coffee's got to be slightly sweet. Now, add half a teaspoon of sugar for each cup. How many does it make for two cups? One teaspoon. There you go. Give it a little stir in the *jezveh*. No, no, not fast like that. You've got to stir it slow. Won't work otherwise. You don't make Turkish coffee in a hurry. Got to be over a low flame, patiently, lowly. Here, light that stove now."

Vicki had trouble with the task since she was accustomed to electric stoves.

"Vicki *Hanim*, you press that button there and it lights right up. See what a modern stove this is? No more matches and lighters like before. My youngest grandson bought this for me, my youngest from Istanbul, yes he did," she proudly mentioned that clearly favorite grandson once again.

"Good for you, you're learning Vicki *Hanim*. That's the ticket. It's very important that you be patient. In this country, every single thing takes patience. You wouldn't understand. That's the way things go around here. Even coffee takes patience. When the coffee foams you gently fill half the cups then put it back on the flame. Once the rest starts boiling, you top off the cups, gently. There, you go. Good job."

With held breath and rapt attention, Vicki had finally completed her course on making the legendary Turkish coffee. The kitchen had been sanctified with the miraculous scent of the coffee. The smell made Vicki long for home, for New Zealand, for the first time in days.

"Now, carry the coffee slowly to the room, without spilling a drop. Careful now, if you spill the foam, you'll be an old maid! You won't find a husband, I warn you! You got a husband or fiancé back in Zealand?"

Although she had no idea what relation coffee had to husband-seeking, Vicki, treading as cautiously as a tightrope walker with a coffee cup in each hand, gave a chuckle at the absurdity of the concept. When she laughed, the foam spilled from one of the coffee cups. Vicki suddenly felt scared. Scared as though she had committed a crime. That's when she realized that Auntie Beyaz intimidated her.

"Here, I'll drink that one. Anyway, I ain't likely to find a husband at this age," Auntie Beyaz said, without a hint of humor in her voice.

Soon they were sitting across from each other, drinking coffee. Actually, Auntie Beyaz was smacking her lips and sipping her coffee with an almost ritual zest while Vicki pretended, for the sake of appearances, to be enjoying the beverage that was far too strong and bitter for her taste. She wished that she had put more sugar in her own coffee. Or that she had filtered out the bitter sediment at the bottom and managed as though it had been an espresso.

Auntie Beyaz, who had noticed Vicki's distaste and apparently anticipated this outcome with great pleasure, asked proudly:

"You seem to find this coffee here too bitter but my father, *Ghazi* Sergeant Alican used to take his coffee black. No sugar at all. That was my father's taste. What about you, how did your Anzac great-grandpa like his coffee, Vicki *Hanim*?"

Dear Mother, Father, Helen and Little Stuart,

Our dreams are over. Our plans to see France or motherland England have been shattered. As you can tell from the top right hand of this letter, I am writing you these lines from Gallipoli, with deep disappointment and under difficult conditions. It is a mystery why they have sent us here instead of France but the fact is, we're in Gallipoli!

They piled us all on board and sent us not westward but toward the Eastern Mediterranean; those of us who were selfishly looking to gain a 'Taste of Europe' in France, along with those of us who were bored with the monotony of life in Egypt and declared "C'mon boys, enough show, let's do some manly work, let's see some action!" We have been here for nine days.

Only a fortnight ago Russell and I were thinking of fleeing to Marseilles through Alexandria to fight the Germans there. We were ready for anything, come what may, just as long as we did not have to spend another minute in that desert. Also, if you remember how eager we were to serve the lofty interests of Britain, you can imagine the direness of our situation. We had all grown restless and aggressive, not just because of the monotony of the desert but also because of that damned uncertainty. We had turned into people who get upset and fight over mere trifles. All except the Maoris. The Maori soldiers among us ANZACs did not have any complaints about being in Egypt, and some of them even enjoyed the hot, sticky and stifling desert climate. Even our boys took this as a surprise but I think I understand the Maoris. After all, they have not left New Zealand for centuries and in that light Egypt certainly has a fascinating culture. What surprised the English commanders was the easygoing, soft-hearted nature of the Maoris, in contrast to their strong, imposing physique. When they realized that the Maoris' burly appearance did not contain soldiers of steel, the English commanders began to fret that "They'll die on the way to the battlefield."

As for us, if you were to calculate the distance we have traveled since we left New Zealand, you would see that no other army in history has gone this far to fight in a war. The distance was so far that some, like Russell, were worried that the war would be long over before we ever reached the battlefield. But they did not have to worry. No, we had not missed the war. As a matter of fact, they had delayed it just long enough to give us the lead roles in its heaviest, bloodiest scenes...

Dear Mother and Father, Helen, whose stubbornness I have always admired, and clever little Stuart, here on the Gallipoli Front, I am faced with an utterly new and bitter side of life, and one that is making me discover all sorts of unknown things about myself. I am trying to view and understand the causes of events from different perspectives. I wouldn't have known that I had the capacity or patience for such a task. I mean, the difficult conditions we have been thrust into, unprepared, is causing all of us some strange discoveries about ourselves. How would you like it if I told you that it seems a person gets to know himself much better during times of danger and strife?

And yet, until April 10, when we saw hundreds of ships lined along the Port of Alexandria, it all seemed like a joke and we were no different than boyscouts in short pants out for a picnic. Though we did not want to say it, seeing those ships occupying the Port of Alexandria in intimidating grandeur, made us too afraid to even look at one another. Can you imagine hundreds of ships ready for battle packed in a port? Can you? The moment when it is time to board one of these ships and sail off to war? That moment. That dangerous moment when, tired of the nightmare, you wish to wake up but realize that you are not dreaming. It was like that... I think it was like that. Then we were loaded on one of those ships. But even as we slept on the deck of the ships, we were not aware of our destination. That is to say, thousands of us young lads were sailing in a warship without knowing where we were headed. It is hard to comprehend. Very hard. Perhaps it is one of those situations that you must experience in order to understand. You would best not even try. But even then we kept right on with the jokes and the jabs: "I say, thank goodness we're out of Egypt!" Wherever we were going, it was to be North and West of Egypt. Hurrah!

Some said we were headed for Palestine or Gallipoli but, save for some exotic images, these names did not give us any sense of reality. Palestine was one thing but what on earth was Gallipoli? We only knew from the map that it was a peninsula in Europe, between Greece and Asia Minor. Oh, and that it belonged to the Turks, who were allied with the Germans that we were dying to fight with...

The English have trouble understanding why us New Zealanders and Aussies are so keen on going North or West. They do not try to conceal their bafflement either. To be perfectly honest, I am surprised that the English are so foreign to us. I would never have thought, before this trip, sorry, I mean campaign, that there would be any differences in culture and understanding between and Englishman and a New Zealander. Back home, the King and the Motherland were as close to our hearts as could be. The King: King of Great Britain, the Motherland: England. Naturally, the same goes for Australia. But there is another side to the story. That is, the English think nothing of looking down on us as hicks. And it makes us all the more uneasy when we hear rumors that they consider the ANZACs to be an undisciplined, unruly bunch.

I remember as though it were yesterday the article in our New Zealand School Newspaper: "When the Empire needs your help, it is counting on you to assume responsibility and hardships." Then there was the editorial in the *New Zealand Herald*: "We've never been a military society, we are navy men. For 400 years we have depended on our navy for defense and security." Well, who is the WE in question? Is it we New Zealanders or we English? Or is it a collective WE, as I had thought? I am not sure anymore. I rather doubt that New Zealanders are included among the men whom they say 'are navy men'. Navy men? Us? The only New Zealanders who will believe that are those like Russell, whose hearts have been deafened and blinded by nationalism or like my brother Will who have devoted all their minds to God without a thought to themselves. As for me, the things I have seen since embarking on this trip, I mean 'campaign', lead me to think that the editors at the New Zealand Herald regard New Zealand as just another overseas branch of Great Britain. This attitude is just as imperialist as claiming that it is New Zealander women's greatest purpose to provide healthier babies for the Empire. As you know we were already told this, but isn't it ironic that I should start realizing such things only when I am on the battlefield, miles away from 'home'?

Granted, New Zealand has small cities and few factories. We still live on farms, you might call us peasants. We love forests and fields. And in return, our greatest ideal in life is to make New Zealand into a large, productive farm to feed old England. I beg your pardon, but is that not the truth? Is it a lie? After what I have lived through in the nine days, which seem more like nine years to me, that I have been at this place called Gallipoli, these thoughts loom before me like the remains of a shipwreck that have suddenly surfaced from their long wait at the bottom of the sea. Even if I don't do anything, my experiences force me to see the wreck. And these thoughts pain my soul. Will says that praying will put my heart at ease. Russell believes that for a New Zealander to question his loyalty to England and the King is depravity and moral dissolution, and gives me fiery lectures to keep me from straying from the path. "You'll feel better if you kill a few Turks," he says. I wish he was right. These reflections remind me of novelist Anthony Trollope's words, which used to irk me (and us) as being too adversarial and proud. But I wonder if he was wrong to say: "We New Zealanders regard ourselves as the cream of the British Empire, and think we are more English than the English themselves." Dad, didn't you tell us that at the turn of the century we allowed all New Zealand men aged 14 to 30 to receive compulsory military training? Then, when anti-war pacifists were sentenced to prison, there was still no social reaction. Even England did not have a strict military system at the time, so weren't we obviously trying to prove something with our efforts?

And yet I was still an innocent New Zealander when they brought us to the Island of Lemnos. Fifty miles from the Dardanelles Strait, the Aegean Sea and this Greek island were a most pleasant change after the desert climate and the monotony of our days in Egypt. There were not a lot of trees but the rain-fed soil was covered with green shrubbery and red and yellow flowers. Instead of autumn, April means spring on the Northern Hemisphere, but we had no trouble getting accustomed to it. The nature and climate at Lemnos helped us recover morale. Will told us that in ancient times the soil of Lemnos was used to cure snake bites and the plague. Also, these Aegean islands and Troy, which is somewhere near Gallipoli, are apparently the origins of mythology, the motherland of Odysseus and Aphrodite. We smiled, thinking that we are now in the land of ancient gods and goddesses and like them, we are going to war. We had not yet been to Gallipoli, so we smiled...

Russell helped increase our morale by telling us that among the Allies at Lemnos were negroes from the French colonies in Africa, mercenary Gurkhas and Sikhs brought by the English from India and volunteer Zionist divisons from Palestine. In Egypt we had heard that the British Government was unwilling to use the native population from the colonies to fight in Europe. But the truth was different. On that lovely Aegean island there were Indian Sikhs and Gurkhas, who were going to fight alongside us against the Germans and the Turks in the name of England. It gives me a strange feeling to think that there are Moslems among these Indians. It must be sad for the Turks that in Egypt, which was Ottoman territory until recently, the Moslem Arabs greeted us with open arms on our way to battle the Turks... It seems just as illogical and unsettling a situation as if we were to one day assist a Moslem army that was waging war against England.

On the evening of April 24th, the ships began to depart Lemnos, to the tune of bugles and bands, as if headed for a festival. We watched them leave from our own deck. As one English battleship cruised past, we saw a sign painted in big letters on its side: "FIRST TO CONSTANTINOPLE AND THEN TO THE HAREMS!" Naturally, it almost tickled us to death. We laughed so much our sides hurt. But now I wonder, is that what the English really want, to conquer Constantinople? Is that why we are here now, in this hellish Gallipoli?

The Australians left Lemnos under cover of night, we left at 6 a.m. Would we ever see the place again? The thought ate away at all our hearts. The first few hours of our journey were unforgettably lovely. Although cannon shots and a vague din could be heard from 8 o'clock onwards, we were all spellbound by the view of the Aegean. The color of the Aegean Sea is a very special mix of blue and green. Its color... how should I say, it possesses a joyful gleam. This praise, coming from one who knows the gorgeous play of light on our own ocean, goes to show that the Aegean deserves all those mythological tales. The Aegean Sea has a soothing and positive effect on the human spirit.

After a while our attention was wrested by the mighty sounds of the cannon fire coming from our fleet and the dust clouds that rose above the newly visible hills of Gallipoli. Seeing this view, we assumed that the Turkish army was already on the wane and that there would not be much work left for us to do. Our seaplanes and sentry balloons were flying overhead, the battleships were guarding the destroyers with cannon fire. We felt secure and strong. We were calm. We were still calm. In fact, some boys were stretched out on deck, reading. Some read novels and some, like Will, read the Bible.

At breakfast the commanders showed unusual attention to the adequacy of our rations, and while their compassionate concern made me uneasy, I kept it from both Will and Russell. As our ship approached Gallipoli, the smoke on the hills grew denser and the sound of machine gun fire louder. But I will never, ever forget the scene that I beheld when we drew closer to shore. I was struck frozen. There were barges ahead, filled with Australians heading straight for the Gallipoli shore under cruel fire from the Turks. The soldiers in the barge were belting "Australia Shall Be There" in chorus. Even though it later seemed impossible that I should hear this from that far away, among all that noise, I swear to you I did. As the barges advanced, some of the soldiers were hit by Turkish bullets and fell one after another into the sea. The soldiers, that is, our ANZACs were being shot dead. There, on the shores of Gallipoli. And the shore... Good Lord, there were hundreds of corpses floating on the shore! I felt chilled to the bone. I was frightened. Terribly frightened. I felt as cold as if it had been snowing.

As our ship sailed on, I saw a beach flanked by precipitous cliffs and steep, sparsely covered hills. Was this Gallipoli? Shortly ahead, the Australians who were trying to scale the hills were falling like flies under the merciless hail of Turkish gunfire, but those who survived were heroically continuing their climb. Some of those advancing were mistakenly being shot in the back by their friends.

We had heard that the Turks were monstrously cruel and lazier than flies. The *Egyptian Gazette* frequently ran articles reporting the Turkish tortures of all Christians in Anatolia (which is apsent to the Australian soldiers parently their territory in Asia). I heard that the newspaper *Argus* sent to the Australian soldiers said Turks were a murderous lot who enjoyed maiming and torturing people. And those were the Turks who fired upon the Australians on the forbidding Gallipoli shores. But why in heaven were they landing us in that particular cove against these Turks? I could not understand why we were landing at this rocky spot when there were many other far suitable beaches on the shore. Since it can't have been a mistake, it must be a matter of military strategy that is beyond our grasp. Even I, a private, could tell that the Turks would pick us off like hot potatoes from their hideout behind the hills, and yet... The awful notion did cross my mind that we might be paying for a general's misguided decision with our lives but I quickly brushed it aside. For, in no time, we were to board the barges to head for that shore. Not that any of us had the will to fight. We had finally understood that this was not mere exercise, that it was no longer a rehearsal. This was war. Yes, this before us was war! It was no game or joke; war was to kill or be killed. It was ugly, unsensible and primitive. It was stupid to die in this lovely weather, on this lovely Aegean Sea, at our lovely young age, in a stranger's land. It was bloody stupid. I turned to look at Will. He looked calm but his face was white as a sheet. I looked at Russell who, a few hours earlier, was roaring: "Today will be the greatest day of my life!" His chest was heaving fast, his jowls were trembling. His hands were balled into fists and he was shaking his head in outrage.

Then we too were ordered into the barges and we started heading for the Gallipoli shores, under gunfire. I glanced at my watch; it was 9:30 a.m. local time. It must be 7:30 p.m. in New Ze-

aland, I thought, long past tea time. I don't know if my calculati-
ons were correct, but we had been told that Gallipoli was in the
same time zone as Egypt. Anyway, what difference does it make?
The important thing at that moment was not what you were actually doing but that I was thinking about you, and I wanted to imagine you drinking tea and eating biscuits. I really truly wanted
that. Because meanwhile we were approaching the Gallipoli shore in the barges, defenseless, like target practice for the Turks.
Bullets were raining down from every direction and, as though
impervious to them, we were advancing onward. We sat frozen.
Our fate was sealed. There were many among us who had a burning desire to get on shore and teach the enemy a lesson but I'm
afraid they too were beyond questioning why we were here and
simply wanted to get back at whoever was shooting at us and put
a stop to it. Frankly, it was too late to ask questions. The Aegean
Sea, which shortly before had mesmerized us with dreams and
brought mercy upon our souls, was now covered with bodies, her
stunning blue green waters had turned scarlet. In fact, in the end
the bodies formed a landing between the barge and the shore. No,
I did not miswrite that; the bodies floating on the water had piled
up so as to form a landing. The sea was frothing with shrapnel
from the bombs that the Turks rained on us. The Aegean, which
had offered us her beauty only a little while ago, was mad with rage at Gallipoli, she had turned bright red and seemed to be rejec-
ting us. As for us, we were like committing collective suicide. It
was not the Turks who were butchering us, it was whoever had
ordered that faulty landing. It was a state so bizarre and maddeningly painful that all of a sudden I went deaf. All the gunfire, cannons and screaming stopped. And my vacated ears were at once
filled with the strains of that hymn, the Ave Maria. Ave Maria... Someone, a woman was singing and it was positively beautiful. I felt
lighter and could breathe a little. Just as a tranquil smile spread
over my tensed face, I noticed Will tugging at my arm and shouting. I could not hear him but I could tell from the movement of

his mouth that he was shouting. I simply smiled at him. For I was grateful to whoever was singing that hymn for me at that moment. And I will remain grateful until the end of my life. God bless her. When our craft shook with a violent jolt, I turned around to look behind me and only then saw four soldiers lying dead in the barge. I was splattered with blood, the other boys in the barge moved and opened their mouths but no scream or sound came from them. My ears did not pick up the sounds around me. My ears only rang with a soaring, gorgeous soprano voice singing the Ave Maria. The ringing made me dizzy. I watched the events around me as though they were happening to someone else. Then we jumped on shore over the pier of corpses, formed by the freshly dead. I never knew that blood smelled so strong. The hymn stopped as soon as my feet touched land. Once again, I began to hear the sound of war. The hymn stopped and the war began. By the time we stepped on the Gallipoli shore, all of my innocence had sunk to the depths of the Aegean Sea. All of my innocence.

We have been here for nine days, and we are still alive through some miracle of God. Our only order has been to "Dig in, boys, keep digging!" That is all. They say it is General Hamilton, anchored out there in his ship, who gave the order to dig but that his real boss is a Mister Churchill, First Lord of the Admiralty, who is comfortably sipping his tea in London. I can't quite say that the First Lord is well loved around here. Also, we have still not been told why the mighty British Navy, with its proud 400-year history, decided to launch an attack from this inhospitable a shore. This place can justly be called the Cliffs of Hell. Our landing here can only be a mistake of the navy. For we are utterly exposed here. Who knows, maybe we shall go down in history as the victims of a great naval gaffe. But until that history is written, we must stay alive and dig. For nine days we have had no thought other than to dig trenches and protect ourselves against the Turks' counter-attacks. Thinking is a very dangerous act here. We pray that the day should end as quickly as possible, since there is a greater chance of survival at night-time. As for our nightly gunfire against the enemy searchlights, it seems to me we might as well be shooting at the moon.

The rumor mill has it that over seven hundred New Zealanders died on the first seven days. If that number is correct, the Australian losses must be two or three times as much. Strange, isn't it, the Turks were described to us as lazy, incompetent, short on arms and practically disbanded, whereas they have been fighting aggressively, bravely and efficiently for days. Is someone constantly playing dirty jokes on us? Our morale is not at its highest point. We are practically trapped in this cove. I imagine we look like insects writhing at the skirts of these cliffs. Grains of sand and the taste of soil in our mouths. Russell has turned into a powder keg, he swears almost nonstop. Will, on the other hand, has shut down completely. He's been assigned to carrying the wounded to the field hospital. He's a stretcher-bearer. Sometimes he carries the dead. Sometimes, when he looks at me, I doubt that he sees me at all. Another odd thing is that although there are so many people dying, there is not a single Turk to be seen. We don't even know which way to shoot. There could be a Turk anywhere, behind every hill and bush. They fire on us when we least expect it, as though they are mocking us. No enemy in sight but plenty dead. Have these Turks summoned all the mystery of the Orient at their service? Or are they just ghosts? The fact is, the mountains of Gallipoli are giving birth to Turks! Furthermore, we have begun to think these Turks are hardy fighters who are not about to give up anytime soon. At the moment, they possess a strength which we are lacking. For the Turks are defending their own country.

Russell says the Turks don't understand our language and curses at them. He says the Turks don't have any commanders of their own and that they've relinquished their armies to the German generals. When I counter, "Well, English generals are commanding our army," he grows furious with me and claims that it is not the same thing. We end up quarreling whenever the subject is brought up. But in the end, we all hate the Germans. That's who we came here to fight.

As if to spite all the chaos and restlessness surrounding us, the whole place is spread with red poppies. A carpet of poppies covers the interior and exterior of our tents, its red sheen reminding us of the beauty of life and of long forgotten love. I will press one to send with this letter. Don't be fooled by the burgundy color, though; that's the color of dead poppies. You ought to see it here, alive in Gallipoli, here on its own soil, blooming bright as a drop of blood amidst the green grass. The poppies of Gallipoli bring me a pained joy with their beauty. It's like thinking that there are lads my age in other parts of the world who, at this very moment are drinking beer and walking hand in hand with their sweethearts... Yes, the poppies of Gallipoli give me that sort of feeling.

I share a tent with Will and Russell. There're two rugby players from Auckland in the adjacent tent. Nick and Vic. They're both red-headed, I think they're cousins. Jolly boys, they laugh at almost everything. When they count the number of Turks they've killed in a day it seems like they're talking about how many sheep they've killed. The other day they showed me a cartoon hastily scrawled by a soldier named Norman Lindsay. The paper was creased and tattered from being passed around. In the cartoon, each country fighting here is represented by an animal. As you can guess, a Kiwi bird, with his hat and rugby ball, represents us. In the first panel the Kiwi bird and a Koala with Australia labelled on his hat are playing rugby. The score is Australia:3, New Zealand:20, and the Koala is telling the kiwi "If only you knew cricket instead!" In the next picture the Kiwi bird has donned a gun and military cap and is setting off with the words "Seems we are going to fight a Turkey." The third panel has an armed Koala joining a beat-up Kiwi bird, saying "Well, this is US." The Kiwi agrees "That's how it should be." Meanwhile there's a giant Turkey waiting for them ahead. The Koala turns to the Kiwi and says "Hey Kiwi, I thought you was an armless bird." The Kiwi stammers "Yeah, well... but you got to have arms to fight a war," and then the two of them set to thrashing the Turkey. For some reason this cartoon, which saddens me, has them all in stitches. Actually, I san say that everyone except me has reacted with guffaws at this comic strip.

This morning, upon seeing no sign of Nick or Vic, I asked Will where they were. He averted his eyes and said "God knows where they are, John." These words can only mean one thing in Gallipoli, and that is death. Funny isn't it, we have gotten accustomed to it in a short time. Otherwise one would go mad. Or have we gone mad? I asked "How?" and my brother was silent. I too fell silent. I wanted to cry. But I couldn't. Not a single feeling stirred inside me. That's it. That's all there is to it. Those two boys are no more. That's all. It's that simple.

There is a ridge here that I want very much to describe to you. It seems insufficient to call it a ridge or a rock because ever since I first laid eyes on it I have thought of it as a living entity. There is a sharp rock that juts out like a roaring head toward us from the highest point of the hill, across from the cove where we landed. We call it the Sphinx because it looks just like that Egyptian figure of the lion with a human head. This mass of rock sits proud atop the mountain, as though keeping watch over the cove and protecting it from strangers. Or, I don't know, like a sentry carved by human hands and placed directly above us. It watches us. You can't get away from it. It is always watching us. No, that's not it either, this Sphinx is threatening us. Will learned in Egypt that according to Ancient Egyptian mythology, the Sphinx is a symbol erected to safeguard the Pyramids from evil forces. As soon as he told me, I understood the significance of there being a natural Sphinx right across from the cove where we landed. Could it be a coincidence? It seemed to me that we were the foreign

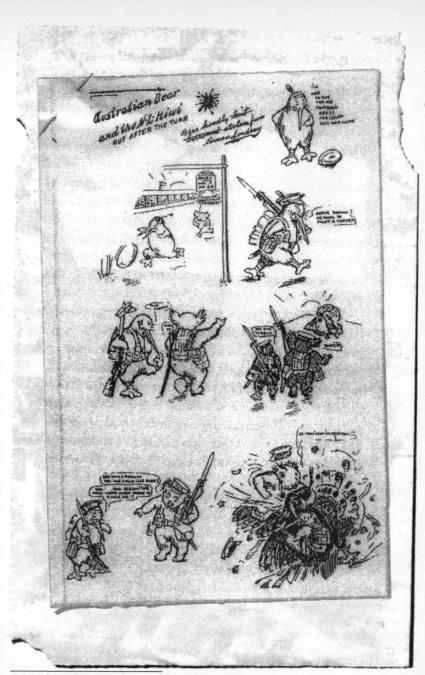

93

and evil forces here, that we were unwanted on this soil. Russell finds this explanation ridiculous and grows cross with me. But whenever I raise my head that Sphinx rock is there, staring at me. It invades my dreams during my brief periods of sleep, where it roars some words from its proud and mighty head. I don't know what the Turks call this cove but we named it Anzac Cove because of our landing. Anzac Cove strikes me as a rather romantic but artificial name. I think this spot should go down in history as the Bloody Gallipoli Cove.

Now I am going to get some sleep. Forgive me for the lines and thoughts you will find disrespectful and arrogant in this letter. Perhaps you would prefer me to write more frequent and optimistic letters like Will, but unfortunately, that would not be keeping with the truth. The directness of my manner is an outcome of the conditions. Otherwise, I have no doubts whatsoever regarding my devotion to you and to my country, New Zealand, I never have and never will. Think of me and pray for me. Rest assured that I will not die in this war.

I send my fondest love to all of you from the Gallipoli inferno.

Your son and brother,
Alistair John Taylor

PS: Helen, I wrote several letters to Keri but did not receive any replies. I hope she is all right. Please find her and tell her that I think of her often and that I will most certainly come out of here alive.

Vicki did not raise her red, swollen eyes from the pages in her hand when she was done reading the letter. Her manner was so devotional, so washed with pain that it seemed she could have spent the rest of her life in that posture, if allowed. She looked perfectly sincere, perhaps even secretly enjoyed the pain. The letter she read from was also a photocopy.

This letter, penned eighty-five years ago in that very geographic proximity, had descended like an almost visible cloud of fog between the two women who listened to its contents. The two women remained silent for a long time, one counting her prayer beads, the other hiding in the pages of the letter. Who knows what dark alleys of their minds they were pacing in. The furniture had lost its density in that yawning vacuum that results from a prolonged silence between people, and just when it seemed about to start levitating, Vicki murmured, as if to herself:

"My great-grandfather, Alistair John Taylor, did not die in the Battle of Gallipoli. Three women held a lifelong conviction that he was alive and those women always waited for him: his mother Victoria, his sister Helen, and his sweetheart Keri."

She fell silent. They were both silent. They maintained a resolute silence, each knowing very well what she expected.

In time, Vicki spoke up once again:

"Keri was a Maori, and at the time society frowned upon marriage between Maoris and whites. I mean, those things just did not happen back then, people were not ready for it. Nowadays, cross-cultural marriage and adoption is run of the mill in New Zealand but it was different back then... Keri was pregnant when this letter was written, a fact Alistair John Taylor was not aware of. Keri believed for the rest of her life that the father of her child was going to return from Gallipoli, and she waited for him. Her strong Maori intuition and spells told her that John was still alive after the war. But sadly, her own life did not last long. After Keri's premature death, it was Aunt Helen who raised her son. Like Keri, Aunt Helen believed that her brother was alive and well somewhere. Unlike the neighbors and some family members, Aunt Helen had embraced young John as her own nephew. These letters were passed on from Aunt Helen to John Jr. and then to his son William. William donated the original copies to the Museum of Elizabeth II. He was also convinced that his grandfather, Alistair John Taylor did not die at Gallipoli, and to this extent, he gathered all the possible clues. In the end the letters were passed down to me from William. William is my father."

Auntie Beyaz listened as dispassionately as to a conversation on the weather, counted her prayer beads and waited. Then she looked up and eyed Keri carefully.

"You hungry, *mari*?"

"What?" started Keri. "What did you say?"

"I said, are you hungry, it's been hours since you ate anything, *mari*."

Vicki was annoyed at this unexpected talk of food, which wrenched her from her dreams and reminded her of where she was. For she had felt removed to another dimension, far from any worldly needs such as food, water or sleep. It would be a while until she even noticed her headache. She was still in a trance. She was on her great-grandfather's track, in legendary Gallipoli, the place she had dreamed about since childhood. All her sleuthing led her to believe that the shroud of mystery that covered her great-grandfather, whose grave had never been found, lay right here, under her hand. Here was an eighty-five year-old curtain of gauze that covered the secrets within her hand's reach. If she just reached out and touched it the curtain would fall and... But whenever she extended her hand, this old woman stepped in the way and shattered all the roads, bridges and dreams Vicki had constructed. A calm, aloof, thick-headed and stubborn old woman! A strong, patient, resilient and intelligent old woman! Auntie Beyaz. Vicki wanted to beat her at her own game, to act like she did not care and to argue her case more strongly but all of her attempts were foiled by the vast knowledge and technical mastery of her opponent. Here she was, utterly unfazed, having listened to this sensitive and important document as if it were a fictional letter extracted from a novel, and now she wanted to know if Vicki was hungry. Though it was all part of the game, these things affected Vicki and, of course, vindicated Auntie Beyaz.

"No, I am not hungry, thirsty or tired!" Vicki snapped. The anger in her voice came as a surprise to herself too.

"Fine then," said Auntie Beyaz, with a nonchalant shrug.

Just then, the phone rang. It rang eight or nine times, then stopped.

"No, that's not him. He rings three times," said Auntie Beyaz.

Vicki did not feel any curiosity as to who that might be. She knew perfectly well that the caller was Mehmet, and that he was dying to know what was happening.

"He was a smart man," said Auntie Beyaz with a nod. "I mean this Zealander great-grandfather of yours, sounds like he was a smart man. I like what he says, may he rest in peace."

Vicki held her breath for a moment.

"However, he was my father's enemy, he'd come here to enslave my father and take away his country, and he held the gun that shot at my father."

For a moment Vicki had fallen for Auntie Beyaz's trick, and she froze with a bitter smile on her face. Even if she forced herself to like this old woman, the old woman would not let her.

"It's impossible to change the facts, Vicki *Hanim*. But it's capital that one should learn them, you know what I mean?"

Once again, Vicki smiled with yellow bitterness.

Without paying her any attention, Auntie Beyaz said a prayer and picked up the Koran that waited in an embroidered cloth cover in the window ledge. She took out an envelope with great care and opened it with her trembling hands. In order to read the second letter, she put on her nearsighted glasses with the scotch-taped frame, shifted her jaw to secure her dentures and with a *"Bismillah"*, began to read. Vicki likened herself to an amateur and romantic youth of the past, who is engaged in a duel to death with a masterful and experienced knight. That was when she noticed a splitting headache.

23 July 1915, Friday
Chanakkale
Number:16

Beloved Mother, Cherished Brother Salih,

I write this letter from the skirts of Kodja Chimen Tepe. It's afternoon, the weather is exceedingly warm. I am in heavenly Chanakkale, on the Gallipoli Peninsula where the sunsets display a most exquisite charm. On one side I have the Aegean Sea, stretched vast beneath towering hills, its turqoise waters an ideal marriage of blue and green, and on the other side I behold the fertile plains of Chanakkale. When one considers the bloody battles occurring amidst this miracle of nature, one either violently rebels or becomes swept with melancholia. There is no moderate response possible between the two: Rebellion or melancholia!

Mother darling, the beauty of this place puts words to shame. Even the cruellest, the most barbaric person on earth could not but feel humanism budding in his soul when confronted by nature's unparallelled harmony hereabouts. So resplendent is Mother Nature in Chanakkale, that her generosity rattles the human spirit by holding a mirror to its own miserliness. To war in such a paradise as this, where scores of birds, insects, snakes, rodents and hundreds of herbs, vegetables and fruits of a stupendous savor all exist peacefully side by side, can only be a weakness, a misfortune, and a fault particular to the creature called man.

Mother dear, when, with God's will, we emerge victorious from this war, my greatest wish is to bring you here and show you this heavenly locale with our mortal eyes. I am quite certain that you shall be most impressed with the surroundings. You, an honored Turkish mother, who has born a soldier for the defense of this nation, will doubtless get to see these grounds as a humble gift from your devoted son. May God grant us that day.

In order to properly describe the setting allow me to paint you an idyll, rife with olive trees, those symbols of peace, with delicious almonds, which are locally considered to bring good luck, with laurels which so handsomely crowned the heads of mythological heroes, figs of a fragrance sweet enough to not only bewitch Mother Eve and Father Adam but their progeny as well, and walnuts which our country's children encounter at their first game of marbles. But do not think that I have forgotten to add sound to this picture. The voice of Chanakkale is, without a doubt, the nightingale. Since my arrival I have come to understand that never before had I heard a sweeter sounding creature. The nightingales that sing here at dawn seem each to be a troubadour, well-trained in the art of music. I mourn that it took me so long to discover what powerful throats these tiny birds possess. When I return to our beloved Istanbul, I intend to purchase a nightingale for our home. It is said that these birds can only be caged while young, otherwise they will die. This, then, is the true view of the place, dear Mother, despite the wreckage it has incurred by the war. And the act of war in such an Eden as this, shakes the very foundations of my spirit.

When my reflections embroil me in this tangle of rage, despair and meaninglessness, I cannot help but think that God intentionally placed humanity as a demonic seed within the heaven of His creation. We are the ones who make a hell of this earth and a wreck of our lives. We are our own enemy, dear Mother. That most intelligent creature called man is unfortunately crueller than the devil, worse than the vulture and more merciless than the executioner.

I realize that it is a military weakness to harbor such thoughts on the battlefield, as I scurry hither and thither conveying communiques in a hail of bullets and a storm of grenades. However, I cannot help it. I had chosen to become a lawyer, not a soldier, but when it comes to defending the country we are all soldiers. Alas, this seems to be the extent of my soldiership. Of course, it is entirely another matter of discussion whether one is born a human or a man foremost... Therefore, it drives me to the brink of sanity to witness the blood gushing forth from fellow, nay, even enemy soldiers, in such sharp contrast to Chanakkale's celestial beauty. Meanwhile, it is blood which tests our sacred duty of defense at this most trying hour. For we have been receiving most depressing news: the Russians have occupied Mus, Van and Agri, we have lost at the Caucasus Front and been defeated by the British in Iraq; the British have invaded Mesopotamia, the Armenians have revolted in Van and orders have been given for them to migrate. The mighty Empire is going up in flames. These are only the news available to the Dardanelles Front of the 5th Army. Who knows what other items may have come to your attention. When I am thus beseiged with news from all over the country in the midst of the battle and unable to distinguish between what is rational and what is irrational, Iskender of Skopje, who is now my blood brother, comes to my rescue with the mature views he formulates out of his vast experience and superb intelligence. May God bless his soul. What a stroke of fortune that I should meet him in such unfortunate circumstances.

In order to assist your memory, I should like to remind you that Iskender of Skopje is the young officer who accompanied me last spring, when I paid my respects to you at the mansion in Beylerbeyi on my return from the (Palestine-Suez) Canal Front. It was to my eternal delight that your succeeding letters should mention, albeit briefly, your approval of him. Iskender is an extremely realistic and patriotic intellectual and you correctly guess that he is several years my senior.

In my opinion, his older brothers have exercised considerable influence over the development of Iskender's ideas. His brothers were previously, members of the Committee of the Homeland, then joined the Committee of Union and Progress, and they belong to a Turkish family from Thrace. Iskender's views regarding the Unionists, though in essence similar to my late father's views, are ultimately sharper and more revolutionary. As you know, my late father was a most self-possessed and moderate person. In contrast, Iskender of Skopje is a bold and daring youth. Therefore, serious inconsistencies exist between my late father's and Iskender's accounts of the Unionists.

Iskender of Skopje argues that the Unionists were initially motivated with patriotic notions and emotions but that their characters have since been weakened by fantasies of heroism and personal glory. Intoxicated by the victory of coming into power, each Unionist dreamer has turned into a despot, and consequently Iskender does not spare them his sharp criticism. I would like to repeat for you the pithy quote which Iskender often declaims and which never fails to move me, though I know not its source: "Every revolution replaces the tyrants which it has sought to destroy with revolutionaries of their own." If this is not fact, is it then caution, dear Mother? Do individuals who fight for liberty indeed become despots in the end? After all, didn't the French Revolution, which we studied with such ardor and interest, yield the same results?

Iskender believes it is because of the Unionists' reckless character that we have entered this great war allied with Germany. It is a tragedy to entrust the Germans with our army and all its secrets instead of working towards its improvement and the general wellbeing of our country and people! That this tragedy is a result of Unionist foolhardiness infuriates me at first, then saddens me to no end. Furthermore, if Iskender is correct in his view that the Minister of Defense, Enver *Pasha*, the Minister of the Interior, Talat *Bey*, and the Prime Minister, Sait Halim *Pasha* sit in their gilded salons devising grandiose plans which wreak misery upon the nation, then this must be recorded in our history to prevent future generations from repeating the same folly. If indeed Iskender is correct, it is inevitable that a poet will one day declaim: "Enver *Pasha* has murdered Enver *Bey*, the champion of liberty."*

While I suffer such contemplations, rumors circulate that thousands of this nation's sons have frozen and perished at Sarikamish, once more due to Enver *Pasha*'s arrogance and inexperience. My outrage pales in comparison to Iskender's fury. Yet, however correct it may be to heap the responsibility of all these mistakes and follies on a single person, is it not just as misguided to make a hero out of such a character?

Meanwhile, Iskender is not altogether lacking in favorable news. For instance, I was not aware that young Balkan Turkish intellectuals secretly read and discussed the works of Voltaire, Rousseau, Hobbes and John Stuart Mill, which had been banned during the reign of the despot Sultan Abdul Hamit, who was nicknamed 'Red Fox'. Upon being thus informed by Iskender, I harked back to the happy strolls my late father and I conducted through Gumushsuyu, whence we discussed Rousseau's Social Contract. I now understand how abstract our ruminations on the concepts of self- and social determination were when compared with our brethren in Salonika.

In order to accurately portray my blood brother Iskender's character, I need to add that his determined wrath is not only reserved for the Crusader's mentality that dares label the Empire a 'sick man', but also for the incompetency and inefficiency of our sultan** and for the hodjas who decree profanity in every progressive idea from their perches at the mosques and lodges which drain the very blood of this nation with superstition. However, if

*) Poet Süleyman Nazif
**) Sultan Mehmet Reşat V

you ask me, he is most exasperated by the Unionists because their conservativeness and passivity serve to betray all the hopes resting upon their shoulders.

Although Iskender and I hold many a fiery debate during our brief breaks to share a cigarette or coffee amidst this calamity, we wholeheartedly agree on one common conclusion. We believe that the Turkish nation will overcome all internal and external spectres through its own will, and by determining definitive goals instead of indulging in ostentatious dreams of glory. To that end, we need distinguished leaders and teams of enlightened revolutionaries to assist them. Naturally, one need not be a soothsayer to predict that after our victory, the officers serving here at the Dardanelles Front will be entrusted with duties of the highest importance pertaining to the nation's future. What counts is how many intellectual youth will survive this violent battle. May God help us. For only intelligent and competent nations give rise to leaders of greatness.

Esteemed Mother, please forgive me if I have tried your patience with these long-winded contemplations. Most likely I have written these lines to inform you that educated Turkish youth are not only ready and willing to sacrifice their lives for the defense of their country but that they are also aware of the responsibilities conferred upon them by their education. To further illustrate this point, I would like to say a few words about another notable officer who is serving here at the Northern Dardanelles Front, one whose name is always mentioned with awe and excitement. The heroic tales circulating about this brave and daring officer, who by the way is an acquaintance of Iskender's brother from Salonika, helps buoy each and every one of our spirits. The person in question is an educated commander by the name of Colonel Mustafa Kemal *Effendi* and it is said that he knows Gallipoli like the back of his hand, owing to his previous experience here during the Balkan War. When the name Colonel Mustafa Kemal is mentioned at the Northern Front, we are filled with the warmth of blessed and joyful tidings.

Mother dear, since I am aware that unlike my late father you give credence to the effects of celestial movements upon our spirits, before I end my letter I would like to note, in the hope that it may render your opinion of him more favorable, that my blood brother, Iskender of Skopje, was born under the house of Leo. Perhaps that is why this most handsome, tall, patriotic and well-learned young man, one of God's blessed souls, roars like a lion at the mention of any injustice. And it may simply be a coincidence that yours truly, who is not quick to anger, who is calm yet determined and, in your words, 'discreetly stubborn', was born under the sign of Cancer.

Cherished Mother,

Please excuse me as I was forced to interrupt my letter for a few days. The weather is extremely hot here and it is impossible to foresee developments at the Front. Our conditions are so dire and vital that many of the concepts we have previously known to be true have become invalid. Principal among these are the concepts of time and speed. In the course of my past year at the fronts, I have come to bitterly comprehend that absolutely dissimilar concepts of time and speed are being experienced in the various reaches of the Empire. Time and speed, which are tracked with clocks and calendars in the Capital, are measured according to wholly different criteria in the southern and eastern regions. In the South-East, patience and resignation are substituted for clocks and calendars. I believe this disparity in the concepts of time and speed within the same empire to be chiefly responsible for the grave and deplorable situation in which we now find ourselves.

As for the front, at the front time is equal to staying alive and speed is equal to saving lives. The only difference between day and night are the comparative advantages of staying alive in the dark or in daylight. Speed has lost its relation to time and amount of distance covered and has become a separate entity. If the notion of time presents such diversity in different locations and situations, then is it not correct to consider it entirely relative, Mother dear? If such is the case, the idea of speed is also one that requires redefinition. It should come as no surprise if the future brings specialists and engineers on the subject of time itself.

Due to the time and velocity difference between us, I have been delayed in conveying to you the following glad item of news. Upon my transfer to the Dardanelles Front from the Canal Front, I had been promoted to the rank of army officer from my previous rank of reserve officer. In the course of the past five days, whence I was forced to interrupt this correspondence, some new promotions were issued as a result of the extraordinary acts of bravery and sacrifice displayed by everyone from privates to commanders. And yours truly was promoted yesterday to the rank of lieutenant.

I wonder how my late father would have reacted, opposed as he was to my becoming a soldier, if he were informed that I held the position of lieutenant officer without ever having attended the Military Academy. I recall my father, who was a distinguished physician and a patriot, frequently saying: "The military is the only profession that is different between times of war and peace." When the defense of the nation is at stake, especially at present where the Christian race seeks to violate our country, each citizen is forced to become a soldier. Meanwhile, according to Iskender's sources, the British have brought Moslems from their colonies to the Dardenelles to fight against their own Moslem brothers. This news has yet to be confirmed but it is certain that our Moslem Arab brothers in Egypt have welcomed the British into their midst, thus providing direct assistance to the bloodshed of Moslem Turks. In that case, the worldwide union of the Moslem Community, which we have been brought up for centuries to believe, must either be a figment of the imagination or a lie. Moslems, just like Christians, find sanctions for killing and violating one another. It appears that religion is not powerful enough to forge a bond of solidarity between people of different nations. It appears that a Moslem is slaughtering a fellow Moslem. And yet there are still those among us who imagine that after the Final Victory our Arab brethren will oust the British and rejoin the Ottomans. It can thus be said that common ideals can only be shared between people of the same nation. Must this significant point necessarily be illustrated by an example so gruesome? However, did not our history courses at the Galatasaray Lycée teach us that some Europeans of the same nationality massacred one another for thirty years over differences in the Christian sects? Therefore, in the new world order only nations that can ensure the equal liberty and welfare of the public residing within its borders will be able to forge a fraternity which transcends the ideals of religion and race. This, dear Mother, is what will come to pass, in my humble opinion.

As for the historians, I cannot say how they will record this war in the future, but it is abundantly clear that the battles in Gallipoli are not only a struggle for Turkish autonomy but also a brutal parable demonstrating that Turks should no longer choose their brothers based solely on the associations of Islam. I only wish that the future youth of Turkey will take stock of the sufferings of this nation, and that the battles fought under terrible hardships here in Gallipoli, will serve them as an example. Otherwise, it will be a pity! A great pity.

As you know, it is the sacred month of Ramadan. Though it is time to fast, the climate here is infernally hot. Be it the hodjas and *imams** at the front, or us educated officers, we frequently remind the recruits that there is no place for coercion in our holy religion and that they are not obligated to fast or perform prayers, since our national duty renders us exempt. While a few men continue to fast, the number is not large.

---

*) *Imam*: religious leader   107

When we hundreds of civilians from Istanbul first arrived at the Dardanelles Front, the recruits mocked us and called us 'lily-livered', particularly those such as myself who speak foreign languages and grew up in lordly circumstances with nannies, *kalfa*s and finicky palates as children of *Pasha*s. However, all that is now in the past and we have all become fierce comrades. Anyhow, there is no longer a distinction between reserve and active duty in our division. We have become bosom mates in the course of this honorable struggle, for which we are gladly willing to lay down our lives. I have learned to love the rosy-cheeked *Efe*s of Izmir, whom we rather dismissed back in Istanbul but whose *zeibek* dances have delighted me to no end. I have grown to appreciate the valiant *Segmen*s of Ankara whose own *misket* airs rouse a man's very soul; I have gotten close enough to know and love the *Ushak*s, *Dadash*s, Kurds, *Djan-Khurban*s*, and all the other brave men who left behind hearth and home and came flooding from all over Anatolia to aid the Dardanelles. The sons of this nation share the same ideal. This country is ours and we shall defend it together.

Mother darling, in almost every page of your last letter you reproach me for omitting mention of life at the front, and you express a powerful interest in the matter. Doubtless, you are entitled to some idea of your son's life but I had deliberately excluded my daily life at the front so as to spare you any grief. However, since you insist so fervently, I will briefly summarize for you the grim routine of the trenches, though I fear it will cause you more anxiety than relief.

Our time here in the narrow maze of trenches and shelters, which we dug together with the privates, is none too pleasing. The shelters are underground holes of critical value positioned behind the battlefield. Since the shelters are devoid of air circulation, these humid pits make for most effective dungeons, which cause a man to perspire incessantly and feel as though he were a mole. The fact that my promotion has rescued me from these

---

*) *Ushak, Dadash, Djan-Khurban*: how men from the Black Sea region, Erzurum and Eastern Anatolia respectively call themselves

shelters does nothing to alter the fact that tens of thousands of my fellows continue to suffer in them. Not that we need shelters to sweat. Never would we have imagined that we would encounter at the Dardanelles the same insufferable heat that plagued us in the deserts of Arabia.

Last night at 4 a.m. there occurred a lengthy cannon duel. Our trenches were hit with shrapnel and our sandbags were completely ruined. Cannonballs were pummeling the right flank with extraordinary force, and it was not yet dawn. We took refuge in the sewer. But then an enemy torpedo exploded the sewer. A mighty tremor went up. The enemy has taught us this torturous strategy of blowing up sewage. When an existent sewer is exploded beneath the enemy trenches, it emits a most fearsome stench of gas. If one manages to save himself from being poisoned to death, he escapes in a fit of coughing, blackened as though by soot. Then the enemy, who has been lying in wait, showers us with sniper and machine gun fire. Thus they ensure the outcome.

Rest assured that we did not suffer any losses but you will concede that one cannot be very cheerful when bullets are swarming like locusts above one's head. Later, I was informed that two privates were wounded and one martyred while relieving themselves out in the open. I warned the recruits about relieving themselves outside the trenches. I expect they will be more cautious in the wake of this regrettable incident. Not long afterwards, we were subjected to an airplane attack. Oh if only we were not so poor in ammunition, and the enemy so rich; then we would really show them! I brood over when the Turkish people will find liberation from this poverty, dear Mother. It is not only ammunition that we lack; doctors, nurses, medicine and rations are also pitifully low in supply. Oh, were the sacrifices made by the populace here ever to be recorded, it would make for one of the greatest legends in history!

The day was dawning gradually. The enemy had fallen silent. Just then, the nightingales, which I so love, had begun singing and my soul was once again replenished with a deep love and tranquility. God willing, when after the Final Victory you and I come to visit these grounds, we will listen to these nightingales in peace, Mother dear. We had not drunk tea that morning. Taking advantage of the enemy's silence, we consumed a modest breakfast of dates, raisins and hard biscuit. My blood brother Iskender of Skopje, who has now earned the rank of deputy divisional commander, was paying me a visit. Using this as an excuse, I had some coal brought over for the grill. We enjoyed a good puff, Iskender on a *nargileh** and I on my pipe. In hard times such as this, one learns the true character of his friends and of oneself. I believe that people who can endure and support each other through challenging periods will remain genuine comrades in the future. Iskender of Skopje, with his brave, consistent, proud and resilient character, has become a deputy commander whom all the recruits trust and admire. My esteem for him grows with each passing day, and his existence illuminates my soul in these dark hours. Although he is something of a father, a brother and a mentor, most of all he is my greatest friend in the world, my soul mate.

At lunch the division shared a cauldron meal. I was served canned soup. I consumed it with relish. But do not assume that our circumstances are always this reduced. Last week, for instance, we were served stuffed eggplants in olive oil. Occasionally, the peasants of Gallipoli curb their own rations to bring us milk. What a godsend is fresh milk. The milk in Chanakkale especially, has a savor of its own. Thank goodness, we have enough food here. The two items we most lack are sugar and vinegar.

Yesterday I received a typhoid inoculation. It caused a great deal of trembling and afflicted me through the night. But now I am much better. Believe me, Mother dear, I am well recovered.

But this just will not do... You will be wracked with worry and grief when you read some of the details I have described. *It will not be wise of me to tell you about this life in the trenches. No, de-*

---

*) *Nargileh*: waterpipe

ar Mother, no, I ought not do it. I must send you more heartening news. For instance, I must tell you that while I was initially housed in a tent at army headquarters, I now live in relative luxury in my small nook at the front. Keeping in mind that privates use their overcoats as beds, I am sure you will see my straw pillow, my *kilim** bed, my crystal oil lamp, my coffee set and my tin grill as the lavish accoutrements they truly are. I could not ask for anything more. Praise God for these blessings!

Naturally, you must be nothing short of stunned to hear me heap praises on such conditions, when you know how meticulous and picky I am that my butter should be pure, my *gullach*** many-layered, my coffee frothy and my lamb stews scrupulously prepared. You are right, dear Mother. Your son, who only a year prior would not deign to sit at a table without starched white tablecloths, spotless silverware and Bohemian porcelain, has fast relinquished many a taste and habit for the sake of such sacred a task as national defense.

Huseyin, my mail clerk, occupies the nook adjacent to mine. He is an Aegean peasant, good-willed and obedient, and every time he finds me penning you a letter, he sends his respect and regards. It is incredible that so many fine and smart young men as he should be illiterate. The ignorance of this nation grieves us officers just as much as the tyranny of war itself. All of this nation's children, whether boy or girl, urban or rural, must be educated. They must be educated at once. Oh, there is no enemy greater than ignorance!

However, at present we are under such grave circumstances that ignorance can only be confronted after the Final Victory. For the most part we live here as a band of tired men, with unshaved beards and long hair, our faces darkened with lack of sleep and weighed down with a heavy sense of responsibility. The worst part is, we smell awful. And yet we are between two seas. On each side we have crystal clear water that we cannot bathe in. We have become quite filthy. The reason for this is the lack of water and

---

*) *kilim*: rug
**) *gullach*: a dessert made of pastry and milk   111

transportation at the front. Though this is the age of machine and industry, we are still living in the era of picks and shovels. We try to obtain drinking water through such primitive methods as digging the earth with picks and shovels. There is concern that infectious diseases will increase due to this lack of hygiene. Not to mention the nightmare of lice!

Strapping young men have fallen thin and weak due to malnutrition. Ah, if only my late father were alive, he would have sent us bottles of Hasan Power Syrup from the Hasan Pharmacy at Bahcekapi! These concoctions would have cured the anemia, fatigue and ill temper, which are so prevalent here. Unfortunately, at the price of 18-20 centimes per bottle, there is no money to spare for such potions at present.

We officers make a point of shaving every day in order to keep up the privates' morale. Your son, who can manage the challenges of thirst, hunger and squalor, is not, as you can guess, very resistant to the natural disaster of sleeplessness. I frequently tour the trenches, occupy myself by conversing with the recruits, drink coffee and smoke any kind of cigarette, *nargileh* or pipe tobacco that I might find; all in order to stay awake. In fact, I read the same newspapers many times over. Still, sleep proves victorious and draws me to itself. I cannot stand this lack of sleep. I fantasize that if I should return home alive, I shall slumber for days on comfortable beds. Speaking of newspapers, though it is not possible to find them regularly at the front, we do receive belated copies of the *Tanin, Ikdam* and *Turan*.

Last week we distributed salaries to the recruits. I had two and a half liras left over. With your permission, I am enclosing it here. It may be useful in a time of need. Mother dear, Huseyin my mail clerk just stopped in to inform me that the uproar outside is from cannon bombardment. I must leave immediately.

Mother dear, just as I was about to complete my letter, I was once again interrupted by the news from my clerk. I mounted my horse and rode right over to the battlefield. The valley, once home to vineyards which produced the world's sweetest grapes and which were a source of fortune and beauty, was covered in a thick cloud of dust. However, the scene I beheld upon my arrival was infinitely more terrifying than the demolition of these famed vineyards. I have witnessed many a harrowing and sorrowful spectacle during the war, but none so dreadful as this last one at Kanlisirt. May God spare others the sight. A scene so gruesome as to make one's hair forever stand on end, and render it impossible to ever feel unadulterated joy. First, one feels staggered by the sight of so vast an area covered with human flesh and dismembered limbs, by the smell of burning flesh and by the sound of screams and moans. Then, one's ears start to ring and one's vision grows dim. One stands frozen. One loses consciousness. And when one revives, he feels ashamed to be human. And he has no recollection of what elapsed in the meantime. Next, one feels consumed by flames of vengeance. The blaze is powerful enough to drive a man insane, and concrete enough to cause him violent trembling. The flames of vengeance wreak intense pain, dear Mother. One waits on the verge of a breakdown, crying deep inside. At that moment, one is as alone as at the moment of his birth and death. After that, he either breaks down or recovers. For at the moment he witnesses this greatest of human cruelties, his heart expires. It is the moment when hope dies. And after beholding this spectacle, one becomes bitterly aware that he can never again be the same person.

How could I describe the scene, Mother, oh dearest Mother! A panorama of the apocalypse. Young bodies fallen on bullet riddled overcoats, dazed youth yet unaware of their missing limbs... There is only one color on the field: Red! Those who remain alive gaze at their lost limbs and regret having survived. Those who are uninjured wander about like sleepwalkers, weary and in stupor, blood dripping from their bayonets... Corporals clutching bloody rifles, tattered portable tents, sheepskins that the privates used as beds now soaked in blood, pages from letters scattered about... It is inevitable, this hill shall forever be known as Kanlisirt!*

Detachments were employed to clear the trenches, which were filled to the brim with corpses. The enemy continued to fire even on the privates who were taking out the corpses. It is hot, terribly hot, and the situation is critical. What kind of a man is this enemy, who would threaten our lives with shrapnel fire in the course of such a vital clean up? Is he a man or a devil? I was stunned... Directly at my feet lay a young lad slain while clutching a barely used bayonet, obviously just arrived at the front, still wearing his brand new boots. Looking at him, I did not care the slightest bit how likely I was to suffer the same fate. I had become fearless, not out of courage or heroism, but because my mind was too numbed to protect me. One loses his mind when he sees tender young arms and legs are raining from the sky. Instead, his head becomes filled with a great vengeful desire to tear the arms and legs off of his enemy. Once a man tastes such a lust for revenge he can no longer maintain his innocence. I began to shake violently, as in a fit of malaria. I was trembling like a leaf in that heat. I felt ill, terribly ill, and could not, perhaps would not, do anything to improve my condition. But a miracle occurred. I heard a voice. An old voice, filled with affection. I recognized the voice immediately. It was my grandmother. She was singing. I listened carefully. My grandmother was singing a hymn. My grandmother was singing me a hymn there at the front. My trembling ceased. I was soaked with sweat but had begun to breathe regularly. The hymns that my grandmother used to sing to me instead of lullabi-

---

*) *Kanlisirt*: Bloody ridge

114

es suddenly calmed and stilled my body, which vengeance had struck like a bolt of lightning. I would have laughed off the notion if I had not personally experienced it, but I now sincerely believe that small miracles only come to those who have faith. Mother dear, grandmother's hymns kept me from committing an act of insanity at Kanlisirt. My grandmother sought and found me at the front in order to sing hymns in my ear, the way she did when we were children and, unlike my brother Salih, I had difficulty falling asleep. The poems of Yunus* that she sang in my ear worked like a balm upon my enflamed body, which shook like a tree in a storm, and brought a brief but much needed measure of peace to my soul: 'Your love has taken me from me/ All I need is you, you/ Each day burns me through and through/ All I need is you, you'. Mother darling, would you do me the favor of visiting my grandmother's tomb and having the *Fatiha*** recited for her soul? She must have wanted the *Fatiha* for her soul if she guarded my sanity at the front with her hymns. May she rest in heavenly peace.

After today's battle, the enemy continued to bombard Merkeztepe and unfortunately succeeded in occupying Kanlisirt.

Esteemed Mother, I do not think it is right of me to tell you these things. No, Mother dear, no, I should not do it, I should not send you this letter. More and more, this letter resembles a grisly journal of war, and I shall either destroy it or keep it for myself, as I have done with previous letters that I have written and have been too hesitant to send. For I would prefer that you await my return with romantic dreams of heroism, instead of lamenting over the miserable and appallingly brutal tales of war. Therefore, I must not send you this letter. For there are no heroes in true war stories. Heroism can only be found in history books and novels. Perhaps we shall read these lines together, after the Final Victory… Who knows…

Nonetheless, life here is not completely without its quirky experiences.

For instance, the enemy does not always attack us with bombs. He appears to have some other interesting and highly

---

*) *Yunus Emre*: a 13th-century Sufi dervish from Anatolia
**) *Fatiha*: the first chapter of the Koran.

imaginative techniques. Sometimes the enemy tosses over cans of sardines or jam into our trenches, which are but ten body lengths apart. Our boys respond in kind by throwing cigarette packets. Has anyone ever heard of such banter among enemies, especially on an active front?

We now know that this jokey enemy is not English or French, but instead a group culled from the colonies on the Ocean; a division called ANZAC, which consists of Australian, Zealander and even Canadian youth. It is my opinion that these nations have adopted English as their native language due to their colonialisation by the British. But Iskender of Skopje claims that they are people of English, Scottish, and Irish descent who were not wanted in England and fled to settle on distant shores. I must admit my knowledge of the world's nations is not as extensive as his. Iskender, God bless him, is practically a walking library! All I can boast is a few insignificant languages. Though my English is weak when compared to my French and German, I am the only person who can make some sense of their language. Occasionally I try to decipher their notes by comparing some of the words to their French counterparts. Nevertheless, it is very satisfying to be of some use.

There are other jokes as well. Sometimes the ANZACs raise puppets made of paper and cloth on long sticks above the trenches and make them dance from side to side. Our boys watch in delight, clapping and laughing along. If I didn't know better, I would think there was an international festival being held in Chanakkale. These diversions, which Iskender of Skopje pours scorn on as tomfoolery, take place during rare periods of peace, when both sides are eating meals. There are no personal enmities between these youths, and if allowed, they would be most eager to carouse together. Having dispelled with such odd amusements the gloom of battling away the springtime of their lives in the infernal heat of this heavenly setting, they resume their banter, but this time with rifles and cannons. Shooting off bombs instead of sardine cans, jam tins and cigarette packets... The war depresses me, like all grave situations that bear no logic or explanation. As the war and the heat continue, anger and violence escalate. Violence makes a person more savage.

Iskender's mail clerk, Hasan *Effendi*, was martyred in yesterday's clash. Only a few days ago, his cousin had been shot down. May God rest both their souls. We all loved Hasan *Effendi*, he was a handsome fellow from the Black Sea Region and one who fervently loved his country. When they carried away his corpse, his lips were pursed as though in a deep sleep. But there was blood dripping from the stretcher. We had become inured to the scene, which would have been heartrending under normal conditions. It is a dangerous thing to become inured, Mother dear. For once a person's heart becomes calloused, once his skin grows thickened, he abandons his humanity and may fall prey to all sorts of calamity. Iskender's eyes were bloodshot with the tears he could not shed over the death of his beloved mail clerk, Hasan *Effendi*. His jaw trembled, he clenched his teeth, and the expression of grief on his face grew sterner. This beloved subject of God, this knowledgeable man, this dashing figure, this patriot and devotee of enlightenment was wasting away before my eyes and I could not even summon the voice to console him. And it was he who put a hand on my shoulder to give me comfort. Then he whispered in my ear: "The poor soul had a babe only three years old." At that moment I was racked with the desire to embrace Iskender, my blood brother on this world and in afterlife as well, to burst into sobs and damn to hell all the instigators of war all over the world. My nerves were rattled. I felt my constitution weakening. I might have shattered into a thousand pieces at the slightest touch. Iskender must have perceived my vulnerability for he gave my shoulder such a squeeze that it made me wince. But with this gesture some of the strength and faith in his body flowed into me from his arm, as from a circuit, and restored life to my flagging spirit and waning frame. Then he spoke to me in his sonorous voice, loud enough for the disheartened officers and privates to hear: "Man is the only creature on earth who possesses will power, Lieutenant!" His voice was so strong, so determined and so promising that all the men fell to rapt attention. Iskender then continued: "That will power which belongs only to man is God's greatest gift to us, Lieutenant. That is why the creature called man is resilient. For he can show patience, forbearance and perseverance in order to reach his goals. This war shall continue until every single enemy is ousted from the Turkish soil that he attempts to violate, and if necessary, until we are all martyred to this cause, like Hasan *Effendi*. Let no one doubt it! We shall only be free to shed tears of joy, to dance the *halay*, and to resume our individual lives with humane feelings on the day that the Turk proves victorious and his invaders prove defeated. To lose hope or to yield even an hour before that is a sin!"

These words had a tremendous effect on the soldiers. Iskender's words worked as powerfully as my grandmother's Yunus hymns, but whereas her song instilled a sense of peace, his words renewed our resolve for struggle. Our hearts, which were crushed under the weight of defeat, death and poverty, were filled with hope and we were unexpectedly restored. Iskender of Skopje, like all born leaders, knows where and how to speak successfully, and he exerts a great deal of influence. Sometimes he exudes such a sense of awe and strength that I can almost see it with my eyes and touch it with my hands, and this frightens me. From time to time I am truly startled by my devotion to and extreme admiration for Iskender, probably because I know I have never felt this close to anyone outside my own family. I am convinced that due to our extraordinary circumstances we are all more susceptible to exaggerate, and that this heightened sensitivity is the reason I have come to regard Iskender as something like a superhuman. Perhaps his stable and trustworthy character fills some of the void left in me after my father's untimely death... I cannot say....

I shot him a look of gratitude after the short but powerful speech he gave to the soldiers on the battlefield. I looked, and saw him in actuality. I saw how sad and alone he was behind that cheerful and robust visage, how fragile he was beneath his hard shell. I believe I saw this only because he let me. I realized that I would not be able to commiserate with him there in public, so I mounted my steed to head back to my division. Then he approached me and said: "Are we not sworn brothers after all, Lieutenant Ali Osman *Effendi*? If not in this world, we will commiserate in the hereafter, brother." I smiled before I rode away. My smile froze on my face. Then, with a sudden shudder, I left.

Oh Mother dear, but oh! It will be a great mistake for me to send you this letter. No, no, I cannot do it. I will keep this correspondence. I will keep it along with the other letters, which would be unwise to mail in a time of war.

Beloved Mother,

I just received your latest letter. I reread it many times, savoring your distinguished script. Your eloquent description of details, with all the skill of a poetess, made me long for the civilization that I have long since forgotten. I inhaled your letter in the vain hope of filling my lungs with Istanbul's superior air. It is nighttime here. The weather is dreadfully hot. Things have been quiet for the past few hours. I write to you by the light of an oil lamp. There is an exquisite crescent in the sky.

Please do not go to the trouble of sending me the undergarments that you mention. Although I understand that two for 88 centimes at the Karlman Arcade is not a financial burden, I still ask that you keep them. My brother Salih can make use of them. Under the present conditions, I have no need for undergarments or other goods.

By the way, I was very glad to hear that Salih has been listening to Viennese waltzes on the gramophone we purchased from Kemani Aga. He is still tender of age. He must remain a stranger to war and hopelessness. I was also happy to hear that you are rereading the novel, *Taashuk-i Talat ve Fitnat*.* Whereas, I last remember you enjoying your way through the novel *Eylül*.** And of course, your perennial favorite, *Mai ve Siyah****... I can almost see you praising the masterful way in which Halit Ziya *Bey* described the hero, Ahmet Cemil's despair as he departs Istanbul on a dark night. These musings remind me that your reading bench always includes a copy of *La Dame aux Camelias*. I greatly miss reading novels here. When I return, I would also like to reread Shemsettin Sami *Bey*'s novel, *Taashuk-i Talat ve Fitnat.* Do I recall correctly that this work criticizes the forced marriage of youths to undesired partners? However, these days I am chiefly preoccupied with the story of Robinson, who lives alone on a desert island. I seem to recall that it was Shemsettin Sami *Bey* who translated the novel *Robinson Crusoe*. Am I mistaken? Perhaps it is because I read this novel during the happiest days of my childhood that I now think mostly of Robinson. Or perhaps it is his loneliness on that desert island which chills my mind, perhaps it is the longing for civilization which sets my heart trembling... Who knows, who could possibly guess...

If, God willing, I should return home safely, I not only want to read novels but also pay a visit together to that exceptional craftsman, Nurettin *Bey* the Tailor, at his shop on the Cadde-i Kebir, across from the Russian Embassy. There, I imagine having fine costumes of silk and wool designed for my person, and suits tailored for your self. Afterwards, as in the old days, we can make our way to the Salonika marketplace, which my late father regarded as the only Moslem institution in its field. I would much like to purchase a particular accordioned camera, which caught my fancy there some time ago. At this point, Mother dearest, with your permission I would like to embellish my fantasy a little furt-

---

*) The Love Story of Talat and Fitnat
**) September
***) Blue and Black

her. I can see you smiling. So be it, madam! Once we are done shopping, we say "Onward!" and head for Auntie Mueyyet's seaside mansion at Goksu. First we rent a horse carriage, then, we take a boat and finally we board another carriage to reach our destination. On the way you take a cup of *salep** if it is wintertime, or a glass of sherbet if it is summer. Auntie Mueyyet receives us with fondness, wines and dines us, and of course relates those childhood stories for the thousandth time. You and I exchange tolerant glances and chuckle discreetly, but we continue to listen without protest. At one point we gaze at the crystal clear waters of the Goksu stream through the binoculars that Auntie Mueyyet inherited from my late father. Presently we once again take to the road and proceed to the waterfront mansion at Beylerbeyi if it is summer, or to the mansion in Fatih if the season is winter. If it is summertime, we rest in the salon of the waterfront mansion while Atifet *Kalfa* serves us coffee, which you take sweetened and I take black. Next, you seat yourself at the piano and sound out your divine renditions of Dede Efendi or Chopin. I rejoice in the beauty of the Bosporus, which seems renewed daily, and I deeply inhale the atmosphere of domestic peace, which is compounded by your lovely scent. Then you stop and look at me. Ah that glance, ah those affectionate mother-son glances that I recall here so fondly... The unique strength that brims in a mother's gaze toward her child, that is born of love, tolerance, and a willingness for any sacrifice. It is so unparalleled that even the bravest, mightiest, and most experienced soldier in the world cannot match a mother's strength. No, there are two areas where men cannot compete with women, and one of them is the supernatural strength that a mother reserves only for her child, for the sake of whom she will undertake any challenge. (I do not possess much experience in the other female domain but every boy realizes the existence and extent of such a power, when at a young age he discovers his own maleness.)

---

*) *Salep*: a starchy hot drink prepared from the dried tubers of certain orchids

Mother dear, your olive-colored eyes, which every day I recall with a deeper longing, shower me with love in that very glance. And I smile back, with the greedy uneasiness of knowing that no matter what my age, I shall never again find the same generosity of love in another woman's gaze. Perhaps you remember my late father as you gaze upon my visage, which they say resembles him more the older I grow, and you pray for my longevity even as he lies blessed in his tomb. And I pretend ignorance.

Ah, I hope I am not boring you? Do allow me to continue with my fantasies, since they provide a comfort and a haven away from my present hell.

Soon, evening falls. As Istanbul bathes in the wondrous colors of sunset, we commit the view to the depths of our memory, enriching our souls like maharajahs whose treasuries are filled with gold. Then there is a knock on the door and He appears. Iskender of Skopje, handsomely blond and of proud carriage, dawns almost like a sun in our abode. Despite being a man of modest background, he has educated himself and understands music enough to recognize that it is Chopin you are playing on the piano. He has brought a French novel for Salih, possibly a Hugo. He will present you with Gala Peter or Nestlé milk chocolate bonbons, Atifet *Kalfa* with lavender cologne, and me with Kibar Ali brand cigarette paper. Before dinner, you attempt to offer Iskender of Skopje the *Perfeksiyon* whisky that for years my late father tricked you into drinking by telling you it was a liqueur beneficial to the stomach, nerves, and all the organs in general. However, Iskender informs you that he would prefer a glass of raki with ice. Salih will have fizzy lemonade, I will drink *Olympos* beer and you and Atifet *Kalfa* will sip homemade raspberry liqueur.

Since the country is completely liberated, we will all enter into a deep discussion of the educational and economic reforms that are imperative for the good of the nation and the state. For after a most arduous and bloody struggle, after the Final Victory, which naturally included the Dardanelles, it has become clear that the progress of the Turkish nation lies only in the path of science, insight and knowledge.

Mother darling, while I sat recording these blissful fantasies, as happy as if you were sitting across from me, bombs have once again begun exploding outside. So as to avoid another interruption, I shall end here this long and painful letter, which I have been writing for days. My dear, darling Mother, your vision always watches over me, and I long to once again inhale your scent and kiss your sacred hands. Please give Salih a warm embrace for me.

Forever your devoted son
Lieutenant Ali Osman
Dardanelles Front

PS: Although I hesitate to send you this letter, I will fold it as though it were to be mailed immediately, and carry it close to my heart.

Auntie Beyaz was tired. She had recited most of the letter from memory, pausing often to adjust her dentures and scotch-taped spectacles, taking sips from a glass of water, which she refilled from a handy pitcher, and occasionally wiping the beads of perspiration on her forehead with a cloth handkerchief. However, as her audience, Vicki appeared much more drained. She felt crushed by Ali Osman *Bey*'s emotionally laden letter. Until now, the picture of Gallipoli had consisted solely of her own countrymen's tales of suffering and woe, but for the first time a firsthand account of 'the other side' had been added to the frame. And the Ottoman soldier in question was of a sort she had never encountered in the Anzac and English histories of Gallipoli. Here was a soldier who was more modern and intellectual than most (or all?) of the hundreds of New Zealander and Australian veterans whose memoirs she had read. Was it a twist of fate that produced such a figure in the midst of her great-grandfather's trail, from among the ranks of the Turks, who were generally described as good and honest fighters but a poor and ignorant lot? Could it be a sign that she should relinquish her obsessive search for her great-grandfather? Vicki was not sure, but her heart was heavy with mixed guilt and love for this young Turkish soldier. Ali Osman *Bey*'s innocence and youthful ardor also inspired a certain degree of maternal protectiveness in her.

But it was the extraordinary bond between mother and son that staggered Vicki, that caused her to feel an inordinate empathy for complete strangers. She cringed, perhaps because her own mother had passed away when she was too young to remember. She had always shown a moody indifference toward the idea of motherhood, mostly because she could not recall a single glance or smile that belonged to her own mother, and it made for an abstract longing. However, the filial love so evident in the letter caused her to reconsider the possibility of maternal joy. She thought of what a great pleasure, what a thrilling experience and terrifying adventure it would be to lovingly raise a child, to contribute to his daily growth and change. The thought shot through her like a flame. Lately, it had been appearing more frequently and though she wanted to dismiss the idea now, she closed her eyes with an unfamiliar sense of anticipation.

While listening to the letter, she had wanted to ask Auntie Beyaz to clarify some culturally foreign concepts, but had held back so as not to interrupt the flow. In fact she had barely moved, so keen was she to maintain the overall sense and impression that the letter had left upon her. Auntie Beyaz, who obviously had long committed the letter to memory, looked so calm that she might as well have been reading a chapter from a work of fiction. What had been most taxing for her was the effort to translate the letter's flowery Ottoman Turkish into plain English. Vicki felt somewhat slighted by Auntie Beyaz's stolid rendition of her father's letter, which was poignant enough to effect total strangers. Slighted because she felt a pressing urge to prove that 'Auntie Beyaz was born with the typical trait of English composure', and it was tiring. For each letter that Auntie Beyaz read weakened Vicki's thesis and posed a smirking counterthesis of its own.

Vicki was hesitant to dwell too long on this counterthesis. She had only one letter left to read. In fact, at this point, it did not seem very necessary for her to read her great-grandfather Alistair John Taylor's final letter, since her own thesis was considerably weakened. Nevertheless, it was still a mystery why Auntie Beyaz's father, who signed his letters Ali Osman, would come from an aristocratic Istanbul family to this village and spend the rest of his life under a different name as a villager. But it was one of those questions you felt afraid to ask. There was something here she could not quite grasp, either because of cultural differences or because Auntie Beyaz was playing an intentional ruse. Weary, disheartened and her head

125

and stomach aching, Vicky took out the final letter from her great grandfather but she was unable to start reading. Auntie Beyaz had fallen asleep while sitting there on the sofa.

'She's old, a very old woman,' thought Vicki. 'Did I have the right to come out here and cause her distress, to unearth the sorrows that lay deep in her heart? What am I doing? Honestly, what is it that I'm after?... Do I want to correct a historic error or do I want to rewrite history?' She scolded herself. "I'm making a mistake," she murmured. "I am doing wrong! Wrong!"

She rose from her seat. But she could not move. Her whole body was asleep. She froze, constricted with a sharp pain, and waited. Finally her muscles relaxed and she stretched. Having stretched, she started to worry that she might fall ill in this rural house where she had been shut in for hours. Both her stomach and her head ached tremendously. Nonetheless, she went over and covered the old lady with the cotton spread that was lying on the sofa. She was not going to leave this house or Gallipoli before reading the final letter. Vicki was going to read the final letter. She was going to read it, whatever the cost. Even if she was going to fall ill, she would wait until she read the last letter and then acquiesce to the illness. Then she could leisurely mourn her defeat. That was when she spotted the pipe. It was an antique pipe, lying next to Ali Osman *Bey*'s letter; a pipe that had seen and experienced the war. Vicki cautiously reached out her hand, as though she were about to touch a miracle. She picked up the pipe and inspected it with wonder. An affectionate smile spread across her face. She felt like she was touching Ali Osman *Bey*.

"My father's pipe!" muttered Auntie Beyaz, in a drowsy voice. "It was in his pocket when they found him."

Vicki nervously dropped the pipe, as if she were caught red-handed. "I must have dozed off. Old age. Did I sleep a long time, *mari*?"

"No Auntie Beyaz, you didn't fall asleep at all. You just finished reading the letter."

"Fie, you're just lying!" Auntie Beyaz retorted. "I saw a dream, *mari*, a very long dream!"

"But you just…"

"Hush then, *hele*! Are you supposed to know that I dreamt or I? We may be old but not that old, *hele*."

Vicki fell timidly silent.

"I saw you in my dream. You brought a green, egg-shaped flower to my father's grave. When you sliced it open there were seeds inside. A fuzzy flower, brownish on the outside. You placed it on the grave and said a prayer."

"That's a kiwifruit!" Vicki cried elatedly. "The kiwifruit's not a flower but a fruit."

"What do I care what it is, *mari*!" snapped Auntie Beyaz.

"But you can't possibly dream of a kiwifruit if you've never seen or heard of it before… I'm a psychologist, Auntie Beyaz, and I know a little about these things."

Auntie Beyaz was not listening. She was sitting up, completely awake and alert, handling her prayer beads.

'There, you finally slipped up, Auntie Beyaz. Your kiwifruit dream gave you away,' thought Vicki jubilantly. Just as she was about to phrase this thought more tactfully, "Well come on, read that last letter and be done with it, so you ease your mind and push off back home," Auntie Beyaz rebuked her.

"What do you call that thing, a kiwifruit? I didn't like that hairy thing one bit. Tasted something sour but even salt didn't do it any good, *mari*! My brother Bulut's grandson brought me some from Istanbul but I couldn't stomach it. Tastes real sour to me, but that little rascal is fond of them things - he peeled and ate them by the spoonful. You eat those things?"

"Yes, Auntie Beyaz, I do!" said Vicki, with a deep sigh. "I do."

August 10, 1915
Gallipoli

My Dear and Once Happy Family,

Greetings from the Hell called Gallipoli!

I suppose you have received all the awful news and you know of our state. But a piece of news is just a hollow result and, unfortunately, it does not reflect the experience that leads to that result. That's why every item of news that leaves Gallipoli is dry, stupid and meaningless by the time it reaches you. News is nothing but filth. Only idiots listen to the news. For news is empty. Don't listen to the news. Don't believe the news. The only news that reaches you from here is the number of dead and wounded. Just meaningless numbers. That's all.

I did not intend to write you this letter. In fact, I'm not sure if I ever want to talk to, or see, anyone again. I think I don't want anything anymore. But, of course, there's no need to be so gloomy. Save for the stink of corpses, blood and sewage; the plague of flies, lice and dysentery; the lack of sleep; food that's only canned; the heat that beats Egypt's deserts, the thirst, the sense of being crammed into narrow hillsides forever, and the disease of monotony, Gallipoli's a lovely place! Oh yes, sure! The beach where we landed must be splendid under normal conditions. Under normal conditions! But you see, by naming this beach from the start we changed the normal conditions. We called it Anzac Cove, though the Turks probably have some name for it in their own language. This reminds me of something Keri once said: "This place already had a name before you named it New Zealand. This is Aotearoa: the Long White Cloud, because New Zealand resembles a long white cloud." That's what Keri once said. Keri said that once to me.

Anyway, don't listen to me when I say this place is hell. In fact, you'd better not pay me any mind at all. This is a truly beautiful place. The plentiful olive trees, before they got covered in dust and grime, the cheerful red poppies that bloom everywhere oblivious to war, the heartbreaking sunsets that paint the peninsula crimson at eventide, and those Gallipoli nightingales... Good Lord, is it anything short of a miracle that I can still see these things? But the nightingales are the reason. If I still have a shred of soul left unannihilated at Gallipoli, I owe it to the nightingales. It's as if they are striving to keep me alive, to save me from perishing as a number. Perhaps they are the only ones...

The nightingales of Gallipoli are indescribably skilled musicians. Their feathers are dull in color and their flight is awkward, so you only notice them when they start to sing. But once you do, they become more fascinating and delightful than any other showy bird. I wake at sunrise to the song of the nightingales. That is, if there are no guns or cannons being fired and if I've managed to wrest one of those very rare moments of sleep. They really do have a lovely song. Sometimes I find myself doubting whether they are birds at all. I imagine they are not birds but flautists playing a lament for distant sweethearts who inflame their souls with longing. These master flautists are also the composers of the breathtaking lament. There is one among the nightingales of Gallipoli who weeps with his song, who fervently rails against an in-

129

justice. An injustice against love and life. What else could be subjected to injustice anyway? I don't know... This nightingale is different from all the others, and I can now tell its voice apart. Yes, I can actually recognize its voice. Of course, this is a very strange and sad situation. The nightingale cannot tell me apart from the other soldiers at Gallipoli and it presumably despises the whole lot of us for turning this once happy and peaceful peninsula, its home, into a nightmare. I have named it The Nightingale of Anzac (TNA). I don't know why. To give a name of our own to every place we go and everything we see, to believe we are bringing civilization to that place, is this an affliction particular to us or do other nations share it as well? I don't know that either. But I swear that I did not name this nightingale to possess it; I just wanted to make it more personal and find a companion for my loneliness.

There are even instances when TNA and I meet as though arranged. At dawn, I climb up to the hill where it comes to sing with its friends, and I wait. If it is there, I seek out and find it in the trees. I wonder if it is really him that I find. I wonder if I pick a different nightingale each time. But he looks back at me. Maybe he even recognizes me - or am I going mad? Is it possible? After all, I am only one of a thousand soldiers here - see, we're back to numbers.

And he's just a bird. But what a bird! When I listen carefully to TNA, I can distinguish almost twenty different pitches in his song. Is there any bird with a voice so rich? Speaking of birds, I am reminded of the colorful parakeets, the bright-hued parrots and the adorable Kiwi birds that live in our forests, but it is none of those. Not even remotely. Gallipoli's nightingales are something else, and TNA is something else entirely. When it sings, or more accurately when it wrenches my heart with its song, I manage to accomplish something that has eluded me for months: I cry. It is impossible to put into words the sense of gratitude I feel for this nightingale as those salty teardrops relieve me. The many months of brutal violence, which I have had to witness and engender, and pain, which history will doubtless fail to convey, have turned my soul to ice. It only thaws and comes to life with the aid of a Gallipoli nightingale, with TNA's song. And that's the only time I can cry properly. Thanks to TNA, I cry feeling once again like a human being, and it makes me glad. I have come to realize here that crying is a gift and emotion an indication of humanity. Whether this is a fortune or a misfortune, again, I do not know.

And the sunsets... If we are not busy killing or being killed by Turks, we sit on an occupied hill and watch Gallipoli's fantastic sunset. It is painful to think that the sun that is sinking into the Aegean Sea is just beginning to rise over the Pacific Ocean and illuminating New Zealand. To watch the same sun on the same earth under utterly different conditions! So knowledge can be painful after all... But the sting lasts only briefly. Then I grow numb again. I do not feel or sense anything for hours at a time. I simply stare, hide, shoot, attach bayonets, kill enemies, pick lice, eat the dry biscuits, crackers and pieces of meat that are supposed to be our rations, lie down if there is time and sleep, very rarely. I am simply an Anzac soldier now. That is all that's left of Alistair John Taylor. I no longer have favorite songs, foods, people that I love, or dreams... I am a number now. A living number. If I die, I'll still be a number. A number who 'died heroically for his country'. Heroically and for his country! Heroism? Come on... Heroism can't be imposed. As for country... This country belongs to the Turks, and this is not our war. We are just 'eager boys', as the English now say blankly and arrogantly to our faces. It's the Turks who are heroes. For the Turks are resisting us under very difficult conditions, in order to defend their country. We used to call them 'Abdul' like the Arabs in Egypt but now we call them 'Johnny Turks'. And they are the real ones that die heroically for their country.

Last week a ceasefire was declared to bury the dead, and that was the first time we saw the Turks alive and up close. The ceasefire resembled a tragic spoof of halftime in a rugby game. That's

when we saw the Turks. They did not seem much like the mons-
ters that we had heard about. They were also young people whose eyes showed worry and grief. Just like us, they looked tired
and weary. They also had anguished families, aged parents, wives, and maybe sweethearts waiting for them back home. They
too bled and suffered when they were wounded, and left behind
youthful dreams when they died. The Turks were human beings
too... Upon closer inspection, the Turks we saw during the ceasefire appeared to be strong, solid, farmer-like soldiers. They wore
odd triangular caps called *Enver* hats. None of them spoke our
language but some understood French. They smiled and called us
'Johnny'. Two Turks offered me cigarettes and I tried to recipro-
cate by giving them bully beef but they refused. We had learned
in Egypt that Moslems do not eat pork. I tried to tell them that it
was beef but they did not understand. So I mimed a pair of horns
and lowed like a bull. They laughed. "English meat," they said.
"I'm not English, I'm from New Zealand!" I explained. They laughed again and so did I. There we were, enemies on the battlefield,
surrounded by the corpses of soldiers, and we were laughing at
one another. Never before had I experienced anything more absurd, meaningless and terrible, and I vowed then to never do so
in the future.

One of the Turks who offered me cigarettes asked in surprise:
"You no English?" "I'm not English," I repeated. "I-am-a-New-Zea-
land-er." Like breaking it up into syllables would help. "Ah, Zealander!" said the Turk but I'm not sure he understood. Then he
held out his hand. "Me Turk," he said. So I took his hand and replied knowing how they called us: "And I am Johnny Turk." We stood there and shook hands on one of Gallipoli's bloodiest battlefields. The Turk had strong hands. He gave me a warm handshake.
How could I be enemies with this man any longer? Why was I this
man's enemy? My foe had now become a 'friend Turk'.

As I smoked the cigarette he gave me, I tried to say something
friendly: "Maybe after the war we'll see each other in Constanti-

nople and have Turkish coffee," I said. But I realized before I'd even closed my mouth what a gaffe I'd made. I bowed my head and shook it in regret. The Turk smiled bitterly. He might not have known English but he knew well what Constantinople meant.

Then we began the task of burying the dead. God damn such a task! The dead were spread out all over. Their bodies were bloated, blackened and riddled with holes. What all the living shared was only a wish to vomit and a feeling of sorrow. No, there was not a single Anzac or Turkish soldier there who felt rage, despair or revenge. We were all filled with sorrow. We were all on the verge of vomiting from the fearful smell of the corpses, and some of us did vomit. On the ground I saw a Turkish soldier who was cut in half and I realized that the sight would never leave my mind. We met two German and one Turkish doctor among the Turks. Then a few of their officers arrived. The Turkish officers were very polite, gentlemanly, European types. They spoke French and German with ease. One of them was tall, blond and blue-eyed. He was handsome and had a strong, proud gaze. I could tell that the soldiers bustling around him thought a great deal of him. The Turkish officer observed us carefully, nodded in greeting and inquired after us in French. His voice was deep and proud. He and the other Turkish officers treated with great kindness those soldiers who carried Red Crescent and white flags by their side. We were unable to conceal our surprise upon seeing them. Had anything they taught us about the Turks not been proven false? How were we going to fight them after this day of ceasefire?

But the next day we resumed shooting as though nothing had happened. We attacked, we killed, we fired, we were fired upon, and we were killed. Like we were all slaves and were killing because of our master's orders. A soldier has no will of his own. We had abandoned our will to the commanders when we volunteered to join the war. Gnawed by lice and heat, we toiled to keep our bodies alive a little while longer in those narrow trenches. I promise you that if their mothers could see their New Zealander sons who died in the trenches, the war would end that instant. That same instant! But we were each a number, numbers who had to perish in order to become heroes. The worst thing about a war is the destruction, not so much of life, but of the hopes of the living. This war has extinguished our hopes. I've come to understand that the massacre will continue until every single one of us is slain. There is no escape. Or maybe death is the only escape!

Now that our failure and injustice in Gallipoli are so evident, why don't we withdraw? Why don't we just tell the Turks: "Pardon us, Johnny Turk, we seem to have misperceived you and misunderstood the reason for this war. Terribly sorry!" and go back home? But wait a minute. Did I say go back home? How silly! The war makes people say silly things like that. Go back home? And what if we did? Do you think for a moment that life in New Zealand will take us back? How could people who have suffered this madness, whose friends have been blown to bits right next to them, who have lived with death as part of everyday routine, return to normal life? Besides, what could we who lost our dreams, limbs, friends, relatives and innocence to Gallipoli, to the Aegean Sea, possibly have left in common with the normal people over there, who cannot fathom this violence and horror? What kind of common life could we share from now on? No, I don't believe such a thing is possible. I don't believe it. No. In fact, I don't believe anything anymore. Because I'm aware. Because I have seen deceit, treachery and death. I've already seen them.

Even if I were to make it back to New Zealand in one piece, I am aware that I will never again be a happy, peaceful and well-adjusted human being. I'm not even sure whether or not I can be considered a human being with my soul so calloused from blood and violence… How can I live in the same neighborhood, the same farm, the same country where I used to live with my old innocence and my cheerful and hopeful spirit? No, no, absolutely not! The thought does not even cross my mind. I don't even think about it. I cannot even imagine the merry, mischievous Alistair John

Taylor who used to joke around with girls, who loved his family, who dreamed of having a carpenter's shop and a family of his own, walking around the streets of Wellington or riding horses on his father's farm. I've lost my own image. He's gone. I've lost him, the way a person loses the image and dreams of someone who has long been dead. Him. Myself. Thus, it is easier to imagine getting out of the hellhole called Gallipoli alive and in one piece than to imagine myself back in my old life. It's easier... But the other... To return and try living there all alone among people who have not experienced this war... I'm not good for anything any longer! No, I cannot come back, it is out of the question. I don't dare to.

I must come to that goddamned subject no matter how much I beat about the bush. I can't avoid it any longer. Anyway, you must have received the news. About Will. I mean the news of Will. He didn't suffer at all. It all happened in a matter of minutes. He was right next to me. And we buried him right away. That is, other people buried him and I just watched. I did not shed a single tear. I just stood there staring. Just staring. That's all. It was like something I had been fearing for months, and it had finally happened. I suppose they sent you that letter that goes out to all the families of those soldiers who are killed. The condolence letter that informs you that your son, William Andrew Taylor, died heroically, in the name of his country, liberty and victory. A standard letter for you to keep at home in Will's stead. Thousands of families receive that letter every day. Will is now a dead number. Will now sleeps under a wooden cross in Gallipoli, like many other Anzac and British soldiers. Sleeps eternally.

The next day it was Russell's turn. He didn't die, but worse. Russell lost both his feet. They sent him back as a youthful cripple. Eternally unable to walk.

Both were gone. Will and Russell had both vanished, with one day between them. But new people immediately filled their vacated spots in the trenches. Whose turn was it now? Maybe it was mine. Well, as soon as I saw the soldier who had replaced Will in the trenches two days later, I made up my mind: I was not going to die in this war. I refuse to die in this war! This is not my war! But I don't have the will to live either. May God forgive my sins. I neither want to live nor die!

Dear Mother and Father, darling Helen and little pal Stuart, do not grieve if you should cease receiving word from me after this letter, and if you should fail to find my grave after the war is over. Know that I did not die. I refuse everything I have been taught until now. I swear upon the nightingales, the olives, the sunsets and the daunting lion-headed Sphinx that I will not die in this war. I don't say this to console you if you should stop receiving news of me, and I certainly do not say it because I have lost my marbles, but only because I am determined.

I love you all.

Tell Keri I will always love her.

Yours forever,

Your son
Alistair John Taylor
Gallipoli, 1915

PS: Aotearoa-Gallipoli

Vicki fell silent. She looked exhausted. Her face was flushed and her body temperature had risen. She had a violent headache. It seemed she had contracted a sudden fever.

"My great-grandfather, Alistair John Taylor, was never heard from again. Despite all the research done after the war, his grave could not be located."

She was quiet again. There was a deep silence. Auntie Beyaz sat placidly counting her prayer beads, as though she had not heard or understood the letter that had just been read. Maybe she was dozing off.

"Now you go on into that kitchen, pour yourself some salty *ayran** from the refrigerator and drink a good bit. I don't like the looks of you, Vicki *Hanim*," she said suddenly.

"Ay-rahn? That yogurt drink? No, no, I wasn't very fond of that beverage!" said Vicki, gesturing away with her hand.

"Did I ask if you liked it, *mari*? Go and have some, it'll do you good!" Auntie Beyaz scolded. "Oh and by the way... You're young still so you wouldn't know. But my advice to you is, never believe every word a man writes from the service, especially from the battlefield! You mark my words, Vicki *Hanim*!"

---

*) *Ayran*: a salty yogurt-water mix

12 August 1915
Chanakkale
Number:19

Treasured and Most Revered Mother, Beloved Brother Salih,

I have received the letters you penned with your blessed hands. Please forgive the tardiness of my reply. Do not be concerned, I am sound of health and still posted in Chanakkale, on the Northern Front. Though it is yet midmorning the weather is fearfully hot. Lately we have had difficulty sparing a moment for our most basic needs, let alone finding the time to write. Especially since the occupation of Kanlisirt, the Chunuk Bair offensive and the Anafartalar battle have been raging forth. We are under the most strenuous and demanding of conditions. We are extremely busy. Either we shall liberate the country or we shall, every one of us, be crushed beneath the enemy's heel. Yet it is disheartening that we should be required to slay and be slain with such vehemence to this purpose. It is a tragic fact that your son, who used to pity the rams slaughtered for the Feast of the Sacrifice, now mercilessly kills, bayonets and slits the throats of every man wearing an enemy uniform for the defense of his liberty and his country. But the truly severe fact is the reality of war itself, Mother dear. It is a dreadful experience that teaches a person harsh and merciless lessons. You learn well, in the course of war, that if you do not slit their throat, they will slit yours. Your throat, in your own country...

Terror, confusion and panic reminiscent of the Judgement Day reign on the battlefields, which echo with cries of 'Allah Allah!' and 'Hurrah Hurrah!'. It is as though Armageddon is upon us and both sides are only concerned with vanquishing the monster labeled 'enemy'. And do we have a choice? He who kills stays alive, this much is apparent. Nevertheless, we are in no way on equal terms. What makes our circumstance direr than the enemy's is that we have our back to the wall; not only our lives but also our country and our liberty are in danger of extermination. Fire, blood and sweat, heat, smoke and humidity... Between these and the lingering stench of death I constantly suffer from headaches. The unrelenting heat is enough to quell even the enemy. As you can surmise, staying alive at the front under these conditions inspires more a sense of astonishment than gladness. Indeed I am alive, however I suffer from constant headaches and a maddeningly clear consciousness. This clarity addles me with pain. If I could only lose this constantly alert and awake consciousness, which seems always ready to destroy me, if only for a moment I could relinquish it... But it does not come to pass. The awareness is perpetually present; while I sleep, when I am awake, when I am killing, when I am about to be killed, when my friends are dying and most of all during the brief moments of peace... Always. It is utterly exhausting to live with the crushing burden of a sharp and clear consciousness. There is a single miracle that keeps me alive, despite the constant anguish of my soul, the viselike grip of the headaches and the maddening command of my consciousness. One single miracle. A ray of hope! Only that ray of hope, which flashes briefly from time to time, gives me a reason to live. Mother dearest, this hope dawns like a heavenly light amidst the human sorrow, destitution, and longing, and it warms my soul. This light pertains to liberty, freedom and independence, and every Turk who is willing to die for his country here feels its presence more strongly than the sun itself. If we did not have hope of the Final Victory, we would not be able to last an hour against the allied world army, whose guns and cannons, tools and implements, and medicine and food are far superior to ours. As for how we maintain this hope in the face of such desperate conditions, that, dear Mother, is a miracle that the creature called man possesses against injustice, poverty, despotism and invasion. What gives me the power to struggle under these dreadful conditions is my spirit's resistance against injustice. It is a hope drawn from righteousness. Like love, the ideal of a free and prosperous Turkish State refreshes my soul. These words may sound like a jest to those who are foreign to the feeling. Yet I do not have the strength to jest or utter fabrications under present conditions. Everything is excessively real here.

Isn't it strange? Just look at the things I write from such a divine setting of nature. You will recall that you and I could not fathom a sky more ravishing than Istanbul's own heavens. In fact, we had observed the skies over Paris, Nice and Vienna on our voyage to Europe three years ago, and compared these to Istanbul. You will also recall that we had preferred Istanbul's skies to all of these. And how unfortunate it is, Mother dear, that I should be inscribing you such ominous lines under the infinite blue of Chanakkale's sky, which almost approaches Istanbul's in its beauty. But such is the case.

A few days ago the enemy carried out a violent attack on Kanlisirt, then began to advance in waves upon Chunuk Bair and the Anafartalar plains. After three days of bombardment our emplacements were ruined. Bedlam broke loose, and the ground was bespattered with human flesh and blood as far as the eye could see. This bombardment, which lasted for days, has been the bloodiest of my time at the front, and the most hellish and maddening of my days on earth. If I survive and return to Istanbul after the Final Victory, you can be certain that I shall never ever forget the Chanakkale summer of 1915. And I assure you, dear Mother, that it is not death that frightens us here. If it is so writ, we shall die for our country. The subject bears no discussion among any of us, be it a private or a commander. We are not, in the end, the instigators of this war and we are here to defend our country. And have faith that we will indeed win this war, Mother dear. Yes, we will triumph but what if the Germans, to whom we have entrusted our army, celebrate our victory as a German victory, what if the history books describe the Dardanelles as a victory for the Germans? Then will we not die of our shame? Though the commander-in-chief of our army may appear to be Enver *Pasha*, it is Liman (von Sanders) *Pasha*, a fatherly fellow about whom we have heard nothing unfavorable, who is our leader at the Dardanelles.

I stated that no one here is afraid of death. Do not say "How can one not be afraid of death?" Death seems different to us than it did during civilian times, perhaps because ever since it became a part of our daily life here in Chanakkale, our sense of fear has been subdued. However, the thing that is difficult, Mother dear, the thing that is most difficult, is to see the dying, even if they are the enemy, to hear their expiring cries and moans, to hear men call in every language the names of their mothers or sweethearts with their final breath, wishing they could see them one last time, to hear the death rattles issuing from their throats, and to witness them calling and praying to God in every language, uttering their faith. Nay, it does not seem as hard anymore to bear the deafening detonations of howitzers, the bayonet battles and the knowledge that we might die at any given moment.

So far we have lost thousands of privates and commanders, particularly in the latest battles. Corpses are everywhere. You cannot possibly imagine how heavy and disheartening the stench of corpses is. There are times when we find it difficult to breathe. Even though I have strained to make my situation appear brighter than it is, as my mother, you have most certainly detected the extent of my misery. Then why try to conceal from you the fact that sometimes I feel ashamed at having remained alive, and that I am conscious of having lost a great deal of my humanity and sensitivity? I might as well admit it; there are times I envy those who have been martyred, when I wish I were in stead, freed from all this wretchedness.

Yet it is cruel of me to burden you with this much despair, Mother dearest. Either I shall add this letter to all the other unsent ones I carry near my heart, or I shall speak of gladder tidings. You are not aware of it but there are several letters that I have written and not sent you. These are, for the most part, letters in which I have poured out my soul and described the stark reality, without fear of causing you distress. Therefore, I hesitate to send them to you and instead keep them near my heart. But wait, I must inform you of a blessed news. In fact, you must already have heard it in Istanbul, but I will repeat it here regardless. The most auspicious, joyous news on the Dardanelles Front has to do with Colonel Mustafa Kemal *Bey*, commander of the 19th Division, of whom I have spoken to you numerous times in my previous letters. Mustafa Kemal *Bey* is a mighty commander whose name has already become legend in Chanakkale, and for whom I feel an especial affinity, seeing as he is a family friend of Iskender's, from Salonika. Mustafa Kemal *Bey* was promoted to the position of Commander of Anafartalar on the night of August 8th, and there are many tales of valor being told about him. However, the most important of these is the great victory with which he concluded the Battle of Anafartalar; the battle that took place at Chunuk Bair, which the enemy had occupied after a concerted attack. The Commander of Anafartalar led the counter-attacks personally, whip in hand, and news of his *sui generis* personal insight, competence, soldiership, courage, determination and true leadership have been circulating wildly. The legends that have formed around the name of Colonel Mustafa Kemal *Bey*, and the victories gained under his command, work like a balm upon our spirits, which are weighed down by the desert he-

142

at, the unfavorable conditions, the loss of thousands of men, and the defeats on the Balkan, Palestine and Caucasus Fronts. It is as though God has delivered him to us. There is a great spiritual need here for someone of our own, with true courage and leadership skills, at the head of the Turkish troops. We, the sons of the centuries-old Ottoman Civilization, deserve this much, Mother dear. Our successes here at the Northern Front have helped boost the morale of our fellows at the Southern Front, for we have received some favorable tidings from there as well.

I have not yet had the opportunity to see Colonel Mustafa Kemal *Bey* in person, but those who have seen him report that he is very handsome and possesses a most effective gaze. An overwhelming number of them say that his gaze is as piercing as a blade. It is natural to encounter such exaggerations at a time of war but it must not be coincidental that many months ago Iskender of Skopje had told me of the striking gaze of this venerable commander, and friend of his brothers in Salonika.

A new story going around the officers in Chanakkale has it that a few days ago Colonel Mustafa Kemal *Bey* was saved from death by the help of his pocket watch. Not having been there, I cannot attest to whether or not it really was the watch, which miraculously prevented enemy shrapnel from piercing his heart, however, if this already legendary tale is correct, then God has truly spared this man to the Turkish nation and given us an opportunity to be rescued from the myopic, incompetent and egotistical leaders who have for years degraded our honor. This land is fertile enough to produce leaders of honesty and integrity, Mother dear. In regards to the tale of Colonel Mustafa Kemal's miraculous watch, at this moment in time and place, its truth or falsity is of no import whatsoever. The story has served its historical purpose. The rest will be up to future historians.

It is not easy to keep track of the news here, but the other day I saw a few officers gathered around a recent *Tasvir-i Efkar* newspaper, talking and laughing, so I approached them to find out more. I am not sure if I understood their meaning correctly, since I have been suffering from ceaseless headaches, fatigue and absent-mindedness. But I thought I heard my fellow officers say that the English commander, Hamilton *Pasha*, was going to concede defeat and quietly withdraw, with the words "There could be very few bad things worse for us," meaning Mustafa Kemal. I do hope that this fantasy of theirs soon comes to pass and that the bloodshed of both our and the enemy's men is brought to a halt.

Speaking of the enemy, during the last offensive they captured but could not keep our trenches, and as a result we have quite a few prisoners of war who, being wounded, failed to escape. This morning I met a red-faced English youth with no eyelashes, whom our reconnaissance patrol had found wounded. They had bandaged his wounds and were about to send him back to division headquarters when he started saying something to them insistently, but no one could understand him. Thus my mail clerk Huseyin came and fetched me, saying: "Commander, you'll know what he's trying to say. Poor infidel's got some kind of trouble."

I looked at this red-faced soldier, who was presumably the same age as myself and who, being a prisoner, stared back at me in absolute terror. As you know, my English is not on a par with my French, Persian, Arabic and German, but it was enough to have a brief conversation with that American writer we met in Paris three years ago. I asked the captive soldier his name. "What is your name, soldier?" The Brit went pale with fear. He did not reply. So in order to put him at ease, I prompted: "Johnny?" He seemed even more alarmed. The color left his face. "Do not worry, you are our captive from now on. You will not be harmed," I said. I made him sit down so he could rest. "Sit down, please," I said. Then he studied me carefully but he was still fearful. I told him: "You should fear Turks during war but we are kind to prisoners and those in need!" Upon hearing this he moaned: "Some water." The poor man had apparently been asking for water all this time. I had a cup of water brought in. He asked me to drink first. Then he drank. "More please," he moaned. This time I had water brought in a mug. I watched him as he drank. If he weren't so red-faced, how would he be any different from our own boys? What a queer thing was enmity that it did not give us a chance to get to know each other at all. Just then the captive soldier told me that he was not English but Irish. At first I thought he was Australian. That is, an Anzac soldier. But he insisted that he was Irish. I offered him food but he refused, he wanted to sleep as soon as possible. I let him sleep for about three hours but I could not keep him at the front any longer than that. I awoke him. He was pleased to have rested. This time he smiled at me. Then he gave me a salute. I returned it. As he was being accompanied to headquarters by the privates, he turned around suddenly and began running toward me. The privates were afraid that he would do me harm but he pulled out a picture from his pocket and held it out to me. "My fiancée," he said. I looked and saw that his fiancée was a skinny, blonde young girl. I nodded. He gave me another salute and said "Thank you, sir." I smiled. That was when I realized that I have no pictures of Iskender.

As the captive Irish prisoner was being taken away, bullets were flying past over his head. I don't know if he realized it but he was now in danger of being killed not by Turkish bullets, but by his own friends' fire.

My darling Mother, time is flying, the sun is high in the sky, and I might need to end my letter at any moment. Mother dear, however much I try to delay it, whatever I do to prolong my narrative, I must in the end inform you of that great catastrophe. There is no medicine, no treatment or consolation available for this deep wound. I shall always carry its pain in my heart and nothing I do, no place I go will ever save me of its effect. I am now a handicapped person; I have lost a part of myself forever. I lost it here, in Chanakkale, dear Mother... I did not want to tell you at first, but with whom else can I share this mighty grief? With whom?

How to begin? I don't know how to say it, I do not know the words one uses to express such anguish. Just yesterday, at dawn, that celebrated, strapping young lad who shared every instant of my pain and joy since the Palestine-Canal Front, who watched over me, whom the soldiers, commanders and I loved so dearly, but whose name I cannot bring myself to pronounce in such a manner... that invaluable soul... Iskender of Skopje is no longer with us. Ah but I cannot... I cannot state that Iskender of Skopje was among the soldiers martyred yesterday without going mad... I endeavor to accept the idea, in vain. Even the possibility that it might be true is enough to freeze my blood. Furthermore, I truly do not know how to convey the vast sense of emptiness and destitution that he has left behind. How do I speak today of someone who perished in my arms yesterday at dawn, how do I use verbs of the past tense to describe him? My knowledge, my experiences, the things I have been taught are of no use. No use at all! I am in an utterly foreign, listless state. I am despondent, inconsolable and heavily injured. Even the nightingales of Chanakkale have gone silent, and refuse to sing. The only thing near to my heart is that famous folksong, which I have made the men sing hundreds of times, and which they sing dolefully each time. Oh how that song expresses my pain, how it declares my condition, Mother dear! That song, Chanakkale's anthem, voices all of our pain, and has made a deeper place than any Dede Efendi or Chopin in my heart; it has become entirely my own. Allow me to write you the words, in case you do not know them, dear mother:

"There is a mirrored market in Chanakkale/Mother, I am going to fight the enemy/Ah pity my youth! They shot me in Chanakkale/They buried me before I died/Ah my youth, pity my youth!" Ah pity us, indeed!...

Oh that magnificent lad, the apple of my eye, my brother, my mentor, my blood brother, my soul mate... A distinguished man, an inimitable soldier, a close friend who defied death even as he expired in my arms, who illuminated his surroundings with the light of his mind and spirit... Oh Iskender, oh blood brother, o precious soul, how could you leave me... My mind floats away like a handful of clouds, my body throbs with fever, Mother dear, yet I cannot reconcile myself to the fact that Iskender will not return.

Iskender's loss has left our country bereft of his mind's light, his soul's compassion and the benefit of his ideas. Do not be fooled by my resilience, as my heart has turned to stone. After his death, I cried so long on the battlefield that my tears ran dry. Huseyin, my mail clerk, was there, weeping alongside me, but in the end even he, who has never once disobeyed my orders, cried out in protest: "That's enough, commander, don't cry no more - have mercy on yourself!" Thus, I have no tears left to shed. And I have ceased to feel the pain. All that is left is emptiness, continuous headaches, and a constriction in my chest, as though a large piece of quince were lodged in there. If I could only doze off, sleep a little, if I could only forget... But it is impossible. Just as my mind has gone and left me, my cruel consciousness has taken material form and turned into my worst enemy. My own consciousness has become a gnawing, destructive foe. Can you believe it, dear Mother? Or do you think I am going mad? Observe, even as I write you these lines, my own consciousness stands starkly before me, eyeing me with a mocking expression, questioning my soul, tearing my spirit to pieces. I have become a prisoner of my own consciousness. This war, this torrent of human blood that has stained the entire landscape, this year, 1915, has ruined me. What's more, Iskender of Skopje, is no longer; he who used to proclaim "We shall be happy and content in the future, dear boy!" I am tired. I am restless. My heart is leaden...

I was not with him when they found Iskender heavily wounded at the Anafartalar Front. After the messenger ran wildly to inform me of the news, I do not have the slightest recollection of how I reached the battlefield. When I arrived, he was lying on the ground, having been dragged to the back of the trenches. Even at dawn, the weather was extremely, inordinately hot. I ran up to him and cradled his head in my arms. Tears gushed from my eyes as I stroked his blond hair, matted with blood. That's when he opened his eyes. The light had expired in his fiery blue eyes. He recognized me. He forced himself to smile, with obvious effort. There was camaraderie, there was love, there was confidence in his gaze. He was dying, we knew that, and I was closest to him at that moment. He lay dying and I could only watch, unable to help. This is an experience so excruciating that I would not wish it upon my enemy!

As I sat there crying like a fool, he strained to move his lips, and said: "Ali Osman, my brother... our blood... our blood shall not be wasted, dear boy." Damn me, for I was weeping even at that moment when fortitude was required of me, and Iskender was consoling me when it was I who ought to have been consoling him. He sometimes used to tell me: "You were not made to be a soldier, Ali Osman *Bey*, my brother. You are a man of ideas, knowledge and art. God willing, you will serve our country with your superior education, standing in salons, schools and conferences, giving lectures in all your fluent foreign tongues and in our beautiful Turkish! After the Final Victory, we will have great need for young men who possess a refinement of thought, feeling, and speech, such as yourself. But know that you will not make a good soldier!" We would laugh together. He was right. I did not have the same scope of vision as Iskender, I was too emotionally inclined to make decisions of life and death at the necessary moments. And once again I had proven him correct by obliging him to console me even as he lay dying on the battlefield. Seeing this bright Turkish son expire before my eyes, I felt as though I were losing my late father for the second time. I was also bidding farewell to the older brother I never had, to a mysterious distant lover, and to my youth. He squeezed my arm with his final strength and whispered: "Live, live so you may remember me when this country is content and free." Then he shut his eyes. "Brother, please, don't go, don't leave me here... for God's sake Iskender, don't!" I whimpered. He murmured, eyes still closed: "Reason is God's greatest gift to man... If there were a religion greater than reason, God would have granted that instead... This country needs reason... reason..." Those were his last words. He then fell silent and never spoke again. But as I sobbed fitfully, he opened his eyes and smiled at me. I swear upon my soul that he did, Mother dear. He smiled. I saw it. I swear upon everything I hold sacred that Iskender gave me one last smile before he went. He went to heaven, leaving me alone at Anafartalar. He left behind his handsome, magnificent frame in blood, and went. He left. He is gone.

Huseyin, my mail clerk, was reciting prayers with tears streaming from his eyes. "Did you hear that Huseyin? Did you hear what he willed me?" Huseyin looked at me and sniffled. "I swear I ain't heard nothing, commander," he said. How is it possible? We were right next to each other, and Huseyin must have heard everything that I heard. He said: "Commander Iskender confessed his faith and other than that I ain't heard nothing else, commander. May God rest his soul and bless your own. May our turn come next, sir!"

Iskender believed in God but he was not a religious man. He would often say, "God's creed is reason! Why else would he create us with this devil in our head?" I suspect that my mail clerk heard this but was scared. He too will understand one day and he will cease fearing his own reason. Then the light of reason will shine forth and illuminate us all. Dear God, spare me my reason! It is my only hope, and Iskender's will to me.

Precious Mother, Salih, my bright-eyed brother, I am not afraid of death. I swear to you that I am not. Particularly since Iskender's passing, death does not cause me fear. I do not know if this is a favorable sign or not. I have no idea. *What I do know is that I shall not send you this letter. No, Mother darling, I cannot send you this letter drenched in blood and tears. I suppose this too will remain atop my heart, here at the front.* I will write a shorter, more hopeful letter to send to you. I will write and send it immediately.

Mother dear, today is the holy Feast of Ramadan. I wish you a blessed holiday and send you and Salih my most respectful and fondest greetings.

Your son
Lieutenant Ali Osman

When the final letter was finished, Auntie Beyaz adjusted her dentures, thirstily drank a glass of water and smacked her lips at length. She looked tired. But she was still holding out. It was almost evening. Mehmet's voice could be heard outside, talking angrily with the *Mukhtar*.

Auntie Beyaz gave Vicki a triumphant look.

"Ali Osman *Bey* was martyred three days after he wrote this letter," she said.

Vicki, whose eyes were red from crying, did not understand what she heard. She stared in amazement.

"What do you mean, Auntie Beyaz? If he died… then?"

"Ali Osman *Bey* was killed around August 15, 1915 at the Anafartalar Front. God rest his soul!" dismissed Auntie Beyaz.

Vicki's stomach sank. This was too much. This was really too much. She grew dizzy. Had things become hopelessly muddled or exceedingly clear? She could not decide. But she was certain of being utterly lost. She felt an urge to get up and flee immediately this house and this enigmatic old woman. She felt a terrifying desire to get far away from this stubborn and resistant woman who read her conspiring letters in order to confuse her, to never see her again. She moved to get up from her seat but failed. She tried once more, but fell back on the sofa. At that point Auntie Beyaz flung open the window and called:

"*Mukhtar*, hurry up and come here *hele*, hurry, *mari*! This Zealander tourist woman fainted!"

151

"Open your eyes, Vicki *Hanim*. Come on, I've got something to tell you, *mari!*"

Vicki was dumbfounded to discover that Auntie Beyaz had materialized in her room at the Friendly Anzac Pension, where she had been lying ill for three days. She was so surprised that she sat bolt upright as if stung with a needle, when in fact she had not had the strength to roll over in the uncomfortable single bed.

"You came all the way out here, Auntie Beyaz? You came out here for me?" she asked, with a shy, crooked smile.

"Of course I came, *mari*, we Turks are a hospitable lot!" replied Auntie Beyaz, smiling serenely. "Actually, I came to fetch you. I need to have a word with you."

"A word?" echoed a surprised Vicki.

"You're coming to stay with me. I know why you're ill. Go on then, up, up, get up, stop wasting time and let's go. I'm going to make you creamy *tarhana** soup with me own hands. Once you take a sip, you'll be fit as a fiddle, *mari*!"

Vicki sat on the bed looking tired, wan and defeated, and she studied Auntie Beyaz with tentative admiration and what she thought was concealed spite. This old woman definitely had to be seen to be believed. For one thing, her memory would put young people to shame. Her English, though old-fashioned and flowery, was nonetheless lucid and eloquent. In terms of concepts, her vocabulary far surpassed that of a professional guide. Her perception was startlingly swift. It was apparent that Auntie Beyaz had received a considerable amount of education, however unofficial. Because this modest Eastern-Mediterranean village did not in the least resemble a fairytale setting.

By now, Vicki was convinced that this old woman was far too odd, knowledgeable and obstinate to be compared to any other peasant grandmother in the world. Auntie Beyaz was a genuine character. It was impossible not to be impressed once you met her. As for feeling admiration... The only obstacle to this was Auntie Beyaz's ruthlessness and stubbornness. She was so ruthless that she had been playing a game of cat and mouse with Vicki since the very beginning. If the Ottoman officer Ali Osman *Bey*, whose letters she had read, had died in the war, then who was *Ghazi* Sergeant Alican, who had lived until the ripe old age of eighty as a war hero in the Eceyaylasi Village and in the end, died of natural causes? If her father was *Ghazi* Sergeant Alican, then who on earth was Ali Osman *Bey*? Why did Auntie Beyaz insist on telling lies and obscuring her already complicated personal history? Could it be that the truth lay hid-

---

*) *Tarhana*: a soup made of a dried yogurt-dough mix

den in a much more awful and dangerous corner, waiting to harm not only its discoverer but also those around her?

Besides, could hospitality alone explain why Auntie Beyaz, who was rumored not to have left her house or her village for years, would come all the way to Eceabat for the sake of a foreing woman who was trying to alter her father's heroic past? No, it could not. There were other explanations, there had to be other things involved... Vicki felt like a character in a detective novel. She shuddered. She was only seeking a lost person, not a suspect. Well then, why had she thought of a detective novel and not a mystery, or fantasy novel? Was she in fact searching for a suspect? No, no... That was not possible? Of course not... But... but what if it was? Vicki postponed the question until some other time and felt a little better. But she could not entirely cease wondering about the real reason for Auntie Beyaz's unusual visit. Not only did she wonder, but she wished strongly that this old woman's visit had something to do with her great-grandfather. There had to be a significant reason why this remarkable woman, who was much more than an obstinate peasant grandmother, would come all the way here. There was a reason. There had to be one.

"What else do you have besides soup, Auntie Beyaz?" she asked.

Her voice contained the manic dare of a gambler who has risked everything and saved all her fortune for the final round. Auntie Beyaz sat by Vicki's bedside, handling her prayer beads, reciting prayers and blowing them in Vicki's direction to facilitate her speedy recovery. And of course, she seemed to have barely noticed Vicki's 'rogue hand'. As she blew another breath full of prayer toward Vicki, she opened her eyes and for the first time gave her what could be considered an affectionate glance.

"We got a lot of stubborn people in our family, but nobody appreciates stubbornness in womankind. Menfolk like their women tame as sheep, naïve as children and dumb as the village idiot. You seem headed down the wrong path, Vicki *Hanim*. Looks like you got stubborn women in your family as well…"

Vicki laughed. Despite this old woman's meanness and cruelty, she felt a kind of… well, a kind of affection for her… or wanted to. Affection? How absurd! But if this was not affection, then what was it? Admiration? Maybe the feeling stemmed from the possibility that this woman could be her own great-aunt. Not that possibilities and 'maybes' mattered much at this point. Auntie Beyaz was the second person she felt close to in this completely foreign and Eastern culture, which she had inhabited for two weeks, second only to Mehmet, her guide, whom she found compassionate and trustworthy despite being too childish and naïve.

"Are you better now, *mari*?"

Vicki laughed out loud in response. For three days she had been lying in a fever, and this old woman thought she could cure her with a couple of prayers, a few breaths and a promise of creamy whatever it was called soup? Did this lady think she was a shaman or some sort of voodoo priestess? Anyhow, Vicki regarded such metaphysical beliefs as mere elements of folklore and held that recovery was only possible through medicine.

Auntie Beyaz slowly sat up in her uncomfortable chair and reached toward Vicki, who was still sitting up in bed. She placed her little, snow-white hand, etched with the magnificent geometric patterns of a million wrinkles, upon Vicki's forehead.

"There, *mashallah*, my words and prayers have worked on *kizcagizim**. Your fever's gone down. Come on then, get dressed, I'm taking you to my house, *mari*. Besides, only God and I know the real solution to your woe!"

Had she said *kizcagizim*? Yes, Vicki knew what *kizim* meant. It meant 'my girl'. It was an embracement. And it had a positive meaning in Turkish culture. So, was *kizcagizim* an even

---

*) *Kizcagizim*: my poor/little girl

more familiar way of saying *kizim*? Why had Auntie Beyaz referred to her in this manner, out of the blue? Vicki was puzzled. Then suddenly she sensed that her fever had subsided. She put a hand on her forehead and it truly did feel cooler. She was tired and weak but also extremely hungry. Hunger? She had not felt hungry for days. Suddenly she noticed that she felt better. Tired, weak, but better.

"This woman's a witch! Yes, she's a witch!" she thought angrily.

She was not quite sure why she was enraged. She got up slowly and began to get dressed, muttering:

"Mean, cruel, grumpy witch!"

Auntie Beyaz waited for her to get dressed with her eyes closed, wearing a peaceful expression, fingering her prayer beads and calmly reciting prayers, her lips moving fast. At least that's how she appeared to the outside observer.

It was afternoon when Mehmet the Guide took them back to the Eceyaylasi Village. As the two women walked through the blue door of Auntie Beyaz's house, the villagers looked on in silent and respectful curiosity. Throughout the day, Havva and her relatives brought creamy *tarhana* soup, *bulghur pilaf* * with vegetables, chicken stew and pear compote to Auntie Beyaz's house. The villagers talked and laughed about the foreign woman's appetite and knocked on wood to keep it safe from the evil eye. More importantly, the farmers interpreted it as an auspicious sign that Auntie Beyaz had left her house after so many years, and took heart.

The next day, Mehmet paid Vicki's bill at the Friendly Anzac Pension, packed all of her belongings into her backpack and took it to Auntie Beyaz's house. Having met Auntie Beyaz, Mehmet was not very surprised to see Vicki move into her house. What did surprise him, though, was the question that Vicki had been asking him frequently for the last few days:

---

*) *Bulghur pilaf*: coarsely ground wheat rice

156

"Mehmet, what religion did the Turks have before Islam? Did the Turks have shamanic beliefs before they became Moslems?"

"How am I supposed to know? Shaman, shmaman... Besides, what's it to me?"

"It was precisely the twelfth of August…" said Auntie Beyaz. "You know that famous cloud of Gallipoli? Well, on August
12, 1915, a unit of soldiers disappeared in that cloud."

Vicki had moved into Auntie Beyaz's house and recovered
completely. It was in this house that she finally got rid of the
awful nightmare that had plagued her like a curse since childhood. For the first time, here at Auntie Beyaz's house, she ac-
hieved what doctors call 'quality sleep'. Until now, no amount
of therapy had helped keep her great-grandfather from penet-
rating her dreams with his entreaties, but for the past week he
had left her alone. He had appeared in her dreams for years,
writhing bloodied on the Gallipoli shore, extending a hand to-

ward her and pleading: "You're the one who will find me Vicki, you're the one who will come in search of me…" Vicki, who had come to accept waking in a sweat from this dream as almost a health condition, was well aware that she had slept soundly for a week. Her face seemed relieved of its insomniac tension, and enlivened with the healthy complexion of sound sleepers.

She had been fed organic cheese, homemade bread and jam, free-range eggs, creamy *tarhana* soup and vegetable *bulghur pilaf*, which she loved, and had apparently adapted well if she could drink dozens of cups of Turkish tea, provided it was black, in one sitting like the Turks themselves. She was wearing one of Auntie Beyaz's *shalvar*s, which she found extremely comfortable and aesthetic. The *shalvar* fit her like a pair of bermuda shorts, and as a top she wore a terribly mismatched t-shirt. Her travel agency had given her the t-shirt as a gift on her first day in Eceabat. It was printed with the words: *Lest We Forget - Anzac Day - Gallipoli 2000*. She sat cross-legged on the sofa, her long hair twisted into a bun with the aid of a pencil, her face calm with the repose of domestic languor and regular sleep, and in her hand an umpteenth glass of tea, which she had finally learned to hold without burning her fingers. She could easily have been mistaken for a peasant girl who had left the Eceyaylasi Village to attend school in the big city and, upon graduating, had returned home. Easily.

"On the morning of August 12, 1915, there were seven or eight clouds, looked like them loaves of bread, right above the Suvla Bay," said Auntie Beyaz.

She sounded as confident as though she had personally been there and seen the clouds on August 12, 1915. She looked up at the ceiling while she was describing them, as though gazing at the sky and searching for the clouds even now.

"Day was dawning. The southerly wind was blowing mighty strong, but the clouds didn't seem to move an inch. There was

159

a separate cluster of clouds beneath the one in the sky, this one near touching the ground itself. It didn't look like a cloud of fog, it looked hewed out of some rough cloth. This thick cloud, which looked almost about to fall down to earth, had simply appeared near the British at the Suvla Bay. What can I say, an act of God. See, that cloud, which is still a bit of a mystery, was soon to swallow the British soldiers. Yes, indeed. You know that famous British unit, they marched straight into that cloud that day and never made it out, *mari*! They say more than two hundred soldiers walked into that cloud, but they were never seen again, dead or alive!"

"Oh yeah, that's the story about the famous Royal Norfolk Unit, Auntie Beyaz," Vicki concurred. "Everyone knows that story where I come from. The Norfolk were an inexperienced unit formed for non-military purposes. In fact, the British used to jokingly refer to them as 'weekend soldiers'. But they sent them off to war anyway. When the war was over, the Brits asked the Turks for the return of this lost unit but received no reply. So, they figured that the 267 missing soldiers..." here she leaned over and whispered to Auntie Beyaz, "that the 267 missing soldiers were killed by the Turks..."

She stopped speaking, sipped her tea and suddenly wondered if she had hurt Auntie Beyaz's feelings. Auntie Beyaz, however, was still watching the clouds on the ceiling.

"Last year, the BBC, I mean... you know that English TV station? Well, it made a documentary on the subject. I think it was called *All the King's Men*. It claimed that the unit that vanished at Gallipoli was massacred by the Turks; a kind of genocide... Actually, my dad quipped that the Turks now had a 'Gallipoli Express' in addition to their *Midnight Express*. I never told him this but my dad was a pretty funny man, ha ha ha!"

When Vicki laughed, Auntie Beyaz took her eyes off the clouds on the ceiling and looked straight at her. In light of the stare, Vicki pursed her lips like a child who has done something wrong. A joke that was amusing to one person could be disturbing to another. Whatever degree of amusement a joke provided one person, it could cause the same amount of pain to someone else. And maybe it had... A laugh and a sigh had been released simultaneously into the same atmosphere. Vicki felt a sting of remorse. She was torn as to how she could compensate for her truly unintentional blunder.

"The Turks fought fair and honest at Gallipoli, Vicki *Hanim*. They were dying to preserve their country and their liberty. Ah, indeed... May God spare us the knowledge, but there are many different reasons to die, *mari*!" she said sadly. Then she swallowed and went on in her usual determined, defiant voice: "Invaders are unjust. Whoever they are, wherever it is, invaders are unjust. Makes no difference whether they are English, Turkish, Zealander or Australian... And the unjust are always cursed."

Auntie Beyaz was angry. Her aged chest heaved fast and she fingered her prayer beads disgustedly, as though she were touching something dirty. Vicki was mad at herself for being inconsiderate and kept silent, guessing that whatever she said would make matters worse. Auntie Beyaz raised her head and took another look at the clouds she had tucked away on the ceiling.

"But what do you figure happened afterwards? The English could not enter Chanakkale with their guns so they signed a pact or a treaty or whatever it's called and came and settled that way. Well, around that time they found a few... what's it called... goes on the lapel. You know, has a pin? Tell me what's the word. I can't remember."

"Badge," offered Vicki.

"Yes, that. The English found a couple of badges with those soldiers' signs. What was their name? Norfolk or something. A bit later one of our villagers found some bodies at a farm up a ways. When they heard this, the English swarmed in and dug like there was no tomorrow. They dug up the ground

161

relentlessly. Finally they found about one hundred bodies. They marked and measured, and said these bodies are far from the Turkish Front. What possibility does that leave? Hmm? Only that these English were killed on the farm, right, *mari*? Fine, but… Then where are the rest?"

"Really? I hadn't heard this part of the story Auntie Beyaz… Then there would be… about one hundred and fifty bodies unaccounted for… How odd!"

"Yes, I see, you know what you want to know and don't know the rest, is that it? That just won't do… You come all the way out here, you've read all the books and seen all the movies. But you don't know the rest of the story. No, it just won't do. My advice to you is don't believe everything you see and hear. Or else you'll get fooled like this, *mari*. You go tell that to your funny dad. He can come and be my guest, drink my tea, have creamy *tarhana* soup, but let him come see for himself, *mari*."

Vicki laughed. There it was again, the cure-all creamy *tarhana* soup. Then she thought, 'Why not? After all, not many family members are left who haven't been to Gallipoli…'

"So, Vicki *Hanim*, that's the situation. The poor soldiers vanished. Who was that handsome English *Pasha*, supposed to be the commander of the whole enemy army, you'd know his name. Supposed to have been a poet besides. They say he was a real sharp fellow but didn't have an ounce of military skill… What's the name of that *pasha*, *mari*?"

"You mean Sir Ian Hamilton?" asked a surprised Vicki. "But he was a general."

"Yes, that's the one. Well, that Hamilton *Pasha* said…"

Vicki could not help laughing. She was amused to hear a tall, blond, noble English general dubbed a 'pasha', with all the word's associations of an 'Oriental' soldier, fezzed, mustachioed, swarthy, leisurely and semi-dictatorial. When her laughter expanded into a sincere belly laugh, Auntie Beyaz shot her a defiant look.

"And what're you laughing at? What difference does it make if he were a *pasha* or a general? The important thing is whether he was a good commander, my girl! May God rest his soul, you see that *Pasha* over there? Ah, my girl… now, he was a mighty good commander. The soldiers, the people, they all loved him. He was a blessed man. May he sleep in peace!"

At first Vicki was not sure to whom Auntie Beyaz was referring, but following her glance moist with longing she saw a picture above the TV set of that one man, this time sitting on a swing with cheerful, childish eyes. This picture was very different from the one she saw at the village *kahveh*, where he wore a *calpac* and a most severe expression.

"You know that Hamilton *Pasha* of yours, well they say he reported to the King even back then that the English soldiers had disappeared into a cloud. Smart man, he was. Besides, look here, if those soldiers had died in battle, instead of going off and vanishing, nobody would have worried their heads, *mari*! They would have become heroes. But the fact is these soldiers are still missing and, how do you say, a soul can't rest until he's found dead or alive. So you see, it's still a matter of question… A pity for those poor blameless boys, my girl…"

Vicki wondered if she truly felt sorry for those enemy English soldiers. She inspected her face closely. Indeed, she looked sorry.

"After the war, when we were just babes, we'd play in these here fields, ignorant of any lost English soldiers. Sometimes we would find skulls, bones or empty cartridges, and we'd run and deliver these to the grownups, as if we'd found gold. The English would inspect those heads and they could tell right away whose they were. But we never came across no missing soldiers' skulls. If there were any, they'd have been found in no time. Back then, it was normal to discover such things; the ground gushed humans if you so much as scratched it, my girl. You mark my words, though, no death remains a secret forever, *mari*!"

163

What? What did this old woman just say? That no death would remain a secret forever? Now, why did she go and say that? What does she mean? She's clearly implying something. She's back to her cruel tricks.

"They boarded the cloud and left."

"Excuse me? Boarded the cloud?"

"Yes, indeed. The English soldiers boarded the cloud and went away."

"You must be joking, Auntie Beyaz."

"Why should I be? See here, do you know that big old men and women from Istanbul and Ankara came all the way out to these parts, *hele*? What's it called, people from the sky, from space have those round planes, OFFI or something?"

"UFOs," said Vicki, confused as to the subject.

"Yes, those. These people came here, part of some UFO Union. They talked long and serious about how those UFOs carried off the English soldiers. Then it appeared in the newspapers and everything."

"Oh come on... That's ridiculous!" protested Vicki, a little put off.

"You come on! See here, everybody has his own story. Your English send young boys here to kill the Turks and take away their country, then they claim that the Turks annihilated these soldiers, the UFO people say they got on round planes and flew to the moon, or to Venus or whatever, and I say they boarded the cloud. What of it? Anyhow, once a rumor starts, it won't end anytime soon."

Vicki took the opportunity to refill her tea and went into the kitchen to hide her annoyance.

"Your great-grandfather, Anzac private Alistair John Taylor was also at the Suvla Bay on August 12, Vicki *Hanim*."

Vicki thought she misheard from the kitchen and ran wildly into the living room, to Auntie Beyaz's side.

"What? What did you just say, Auntie Beyaz? What did you say?"

164

"I said that your great-grandfather was there, at the Suvla Bay, as the famous cloud was descending to the ground."

She gazed up at the ceiling once again, at the cloud that was visible only to her, and began narrating as surely as if she had personally witnessed the story:

"Private Alistair John Taylor was running like a madman. He did not know where, but he was fleeing the Battle of Gallipoli, which was not his own. His mind had deserted him. He didn't have a thing left that he wanted out of life. Poor wretch had grown old. He'd grown old at the age of twenty-one. He ran and ran and ran. Maybe he wanted to be killed by a Turkish sniper. He had lost his head, lost the strength to regain his bearing. He was convinced that no one could help him anymore. He was left all without hope. God only knows how far he ran, how long he went without bread and water, and where he lay down to sleep. Because he himself didn't know. Poor man's mind had flown up to the Gallipoli skies, and it would only return occasionally afterwards. Just then he saw the cloud and the English soldiers approaching it, and he stopped. There were three other Zealander soldiers there with your great-grandfather. When these three soldiers returned to their country, oh, right, that'd be your country, they went with heavy consciences to a notary and signed a paper."

Vicki swallowed and perched on a chair across from Auntie Beyaz, trying to calm herself. She felt dizzy, and she was having trouble following the narrative, as she could only hear disjointed fragments.

"Wait, wait, don't sit down. Open that stand under the TV set there and hand me my black folder."

"Your what?"

"Go on and open the stand first… There, see that black folder on top, hand that one over, *hele*."

Upon opening the door of the TV stand, Vicki found a number of tattered folders, a few books and a photo album stacked together. She picked up the black dossier on top and meekly

165

handed it to Auntie Beyaz. She had learned not to rush anything with Auntie Beyaz. Or she might completely sever the string that she dangled before her.

"Now, hand me my glasses as well, *mari*."

She put on the scotch-taped glasses, licked the index finger of her right hand, uttered a prayer and began rifling through the folder's contents. Vicki held her breath, sensing a powerful anxiety that she was about to find out something important, whether it was good or bad.

"Ah, here it is, *hele*."

It was a typewritten text.

"But this is in Turkish," said Vicki with disappointment.

"Look on the back, it was English originally, they must have had it translated."

"Private F. Reichardt, Private R. Revnes and Private J. L. Newman do solemnly swear that the 4th Norfolk Unit entered a cloud of fog and disappeared."

"Oh wow, I know this document. I came across it when I was researching my great-grandfather at the Waiouru Military Museum," Vicki remarked with renewed interest.

In truth, she was dying to know whether the story about her great-grandfather was being told allegorically, but she was obliged to trust the intuition of this old, stubborn, difficult yet smart woman, who had opened up her house and now her private archives to her, and in whose fairness she by now believed. She had already begun to trust her... Besides, the old woman held the key to the lock.

"See here, there's their addresses on that document the soldiers signed. This is no joke... Tell that to the BBC! This is a Turkish granny saying these words, not some fancy filmmaker who reads history books at his table!"

"Looks like one of them lived at Matata in the Bay of Plenty, the other one in Cambridge, and Newman lived in Tauranga."

"What kind of addresses are those, *mari*?"

"Most of them are in the Maori language, Auntie Beyaz. We preserved many of the place names that the native Maori had given before we came to New Zealand," Vicki explained proudly.

"We?" muttered Auntie Beyaz, adjusting her dentures. "Your great-grandmother, the one your great-grandfather kept sending his regards to at the end of his letters, what was her name? Wasn't she of native origin? Or did I miss something?"

"Keri... Um, of course..." Vicki blushed. "Of course, I am one-sixth Maori."

"Oh... I thought you forgot there for a second..."

"What a witch...," grumbled Vicki to herself. "But if I can prove she's half New Zealand, then I'll show her!"

"So you say, Vicki *Hanim*, but your boys turned our centuries old Ariburnu Cove into Anzac Cove in one night. Besides, didn't your great-grandfather, may he rest in peace... May God forgive his sins... didn't he say so in his letter?"

They became silent. The atmosphere between them had grown heavy. Trounced, Vicki waited for a counter-attack and swallowed back the words on the tip of her tongue. She was irritated, but she would hold on.

"Now, you might say was it the New Zealanders who changed Constantinople's name? You'd be right. But remember what I told you? Hmm? Think back a minute... Didn't I say that there was no such thing as a good invader? See, my late father, may he rest in peace, used to say: 'Daughter, being fair is the greatest torture in the world. But once you succeed, the curtain is lifted from your eyes, your soul is cured of blindness, and you become liberated, but from then on you are forced to see all the impostors naked.' You understand the meaning of these words, *hele*?"

This was what made Auntie Beyaz different. This was where her appeal lay. She had all the qualities of a guru. She was a spiritual teacher purified of personal ambition, fair, worthy of respect, and possessing a keen insight. Like all gurus, she was special and had followers. Vicki smiled. She had not forgotten the way the villagers spoke of her. She had most probably spent a solitary childhood, like all gurus. In the end, it did not matter anymore whether she was her great-aunt or a Turkish villager with no relation to her whatsoever. She had begun to feel an extreme fondness for this old woman, whom she conceded was a guru, and who was teaching her a lesson about life. She wanted to return the gesture:

"I once read a novel satirizing how Dr. Livingstone discovered a waterfall and named it Victoria. That was the first time I started thinking about political correctness and ethics."

"I don't know any such doctor... Are you going to give me another cup of tea then, *mari*?"

Soon they were sipping their tea and looking at one another with the renewed confidence of two sailors who have weathered a storm together.

"Do you know, Vicki *Hanim*, why those three Zealander privates waited fifty years before giving testimony about the soldiers who disappeared into the cloud?"

No, Vicki did not know. As a matter of fact, she had not calculated that there was a fifty-year lapse between the time the three soldiers returned from Gallipoli and the time they testified to this mystical event.

"They were afraid, *mari*. One of them was a field officer, though you should check that writing, I don't understand these things... I think he was a mechanic, poor thing. They were afraid, *mari*, they were afraid of being mocked, Vicki *Hanim*. People will laugh at you, my girl, if you say that two hundred something soldiers boarded a cloud and left! But there were three of them and three men cannot have the same dream at the same time!"

Vicki reinspected the article that was clipped from an English language newspaper and read aloud:

168

"Engineer private F. Reichardt, ID No. 41165, was transferred to Gallipoli on April 12, 1915 as a member of the 1st Battalion, 3rd Company."

"Yea, fine, whatever. Come on, get up, I'm hungry all of a sudden. Let's go find us something to eat until granddaughter Havva brings us our meal."

On their way to the kitchen, Auntie Beyaz leaned on her cane; something she rarely did. Vicki followed close behind.

"Now, open the door of that mister refrigerator and let's see. If only those foolish journalists would leave, then we could open our front door as well... They're all crowded here when the country needs a million things taken care of, *mari!*"

"There's some feta cheese, black and green olives, and some *bulghur* from yesterday," said Vicki, listing the contents of the fridge.

"Let's make an omelet. You liked the eggs here. What do you say to that, *hele?*"

"Free-range eggs, Auntie Beyaz. They are very valuable. Delicious and organic!"

"God have mercy... You talk like my grandson from Istanbul, Vicki *Hanim.*"

"What can you do, Auntie Beyaz, everything is synthetic, everything is artificial... Whatever the chicken eats, thus becomes the egg!"

"All right, enough talk, you get cooking on that omelet Vicki *Hanim*. And I'll just sit here on this chair, *hele.*"

"You know that great-grandfather of yours? He ran through that cloud of fog and just kept on running. At that point he had crossed over to the Turkish front but as I said, his mind was long gone. Just as a bullet was flying toward him, just as it was about to enter his brain, well, there but for the grace of God Almighty... your great-grandfather tripped on something and fell. When he fell, the soldier who had aimed at him thought that he was dead and decided not to take another shot. The

169

thing your great-grandfather tripped on was the wounded Turkish officer Ali Osman *Bey*, and he had saved your great-grandfather's life."

The egg that Vicki had cracked for the omelet fell to the floor. It splashed bright yellow, oozed and congealed on the rug.

As though it were an age-old habit, Mehmet the Guide went to the Eceyaylasi Village every day to visit Vicki and Auntie Beyaz, who was by now the granny of his dreams. These visits lasted for about an hour, during which he had tea or coffee, sometimes ate fresh *gozleme*s*, and divulged news from the outside world. He was elated to see the two women so compatible, as though they had been living together for years, and strangely enough, he could not help but take some amount of credit for their success. Afterwards, he returned to Eceabat. These visits produced in him the warm feeling of having just left a well-lo-

*) *Gozleme*: very thin pancakes, mainly with cheese or minced meat

ved relative's house with several days' worth of pampering. Also, since these were technically considered work hours, he did not receive any flack from the travel agency.

As he was returning to Eceabat from one such visit, wearing the satisfied and ageless smirk of affectionate coddling, he saw someone waiting in front of the agency office. At first, he did not pay any attention. It was twilight, almost evening. He parked the jeep and headed towards the office.

"Hey you over there!"

The man waiting in front of the office was short and stocky, with a weightlifter's build, short hair, mustache and brown hair. He looked about thirty.

"Are you talking to me?"

"Yeah, you!"

Mehmet glanced around him. The street seemed to have suddenly emptied out, leaving him alone with this questionable character. He felt a shudder.

The man approached Mehmet. He took his arm in a single swooping motion, and pulled him close. Despite being shorter than Mehmet, he was extremely strong.

"Look buddy!" he said, practically dragging Mehmet along. "Now, you're gonna listen carefully to what I say. I don't like to repeat myself. You know that client of yours, that foreign lady? Yup, that's the one! You tell her to act like a lady and shut her trap. Tell her to stop saying funny stuff all over town! You got that, buddy?"

"Just a minute, why are you dragging me like this? What are you trying to say?"

"Look, dear brother, if a bird croaks out of turn and out of tune, you know what happens!"

As he said this, the man grabbed an imaginary bird with his spare hand and wrung its neck in one swift motion. The mime was so successful that Mehmet cringed as though he had seen a real bird get killed.

172

"Not to mention people who enter risky tangoes with national feelings! They don't come to a bit of good, is all I'm saying. Got that? This country is not without its owners!"

"What on earth are you talking about? And who are you anyways?" Mehmet bristled.

But the man squeezed his arm with such force that Mehmet winced.

"Look brother, I'll explain this more clearly since you're a man. I guard the name and honor of these here parts. You don't see or hear of me much, but you feel my presence all right. I don't poke my nose in people's business and I don't mess with anyone's honor. I just wait. I'm a patient man, and I can be real tolerant and democratic when necessary. But when the chickens come home to roost, I take a stand! This foreign broad of yours went around telling absurd stories, tried to stir up the place and I waited, I didn't get involved. Then she went and bothered Auntie Beyaz, but I still kept quiet. We have infinite respect for Auntie Beyaz in particular. That blessed lady is the purest symbol of Turkish motherhood. You follow? But then she goes and settles in the house of that blessed lady, who never even receives anyone in her home. No, that did not go over well. That was an unwise move. It drew attention. It caused rumors. We do not approve!"

"But who are you? And what do you care?"

"Look bud, you still don't get it, do you? Either you're a little slow on the uptake or you got some other condition. I'm going to explain this for the last time. This foreign woman, your client, claims that a great Turkish hero, a revered *ghazi*, is not actually Turkish. Does she claim that? Yes, she does! Now, hold it right there and add a full stop! No way! If they said the world was not round, then you might say maybe, but if they mess with a Turkish soldier's honor, then you say hold it right there! You think we'd let such treachery stand?"

"Oh come on, don't tell me you took that seriously? Gee, and I thought something was really the matter. Poor thing must have heard a few things and then made up this story so her grandfather could have a gravesite. She's a real nice lady, just trying to get by. What's so offensive about that?" said Mehmet, letting go a deep breath.

Upon hearing this, the man relaxed and let go of Mehmet's arm.

"See here, pal, you seem like an upright Turkish youth. Allow me to introduce myself. The name's Tahsin. They call me Tahsin the Body. If you get into any kind of trouble, just send word and, by God, we'll take care of it! I was born and raised on this blessed soil. I can't allow some no good woman coming around here and disturbing the peace, we won't allow it!"

Mehmet prickled up again, encouraged by the man's slackening mood.

"And who might you be? Some kind of peacekeeping force? I thought the police took care of these things."

Tahsin, irritated at Mehmet's defiance, once more took up his arm and led him toward the back streets. Mehmet was startled. It had gotten dark by now, and the streets were completely empty.

"Look Mehmet, brother, I'm saying this for the last time. That foreign client of yours will go back to her country as soon as possible, safe and sound. It'd be a pity if anything happened to her, our tourist industry would suffer a great blow and we'd be very sorry..."

He stopped. He gave Mehmet the once-over, and let go of his arm. He reached out and grabbed Mehmet's ponytail, then pulled it hard. Mehmet flinched and took a step back.

"Got some nice hair on you!" said Tahsin in a threatening sneer. Then he walked away slowly, shoulders hung high in the air, with a bouncing strut.

It was the first time in his life that Mehmet, who had so far paid attention not to get into trouble, had been seriously threatened, and the first time he had so violently tasted the pain of being slighted and humiliated. He felt the piercing and unforgettable smart of verbal abuse down to his very bones. Then suddenly it occurred to him that 'Vicki's great-grandfather tale', which he had laughed off until then, might possibly be true. Could Vicki's great-grandfather really be a Turkish *ghazi*? Maybe Vicki was not a bored young woman from a prosperous nation, who came to fulfill a historical fantasy, but had instead come here with a desire to solve a genuine mystery. Maybe Vicki's story was true? Could it be true? Mehmet stopped in the narrow and empty street where Tahsin had dragged him, and for the first time considered the possibility. For the first time.

He revived slowly, and walked toward the travel agency office, through the pedestrians who seemed to have waited for the episode to blow over before materializing on the street. Just as he was about to enter the office, he saw it. He felt a sting in his heart. Someone had keyed the hood of the company jeep deep enough to reveal the undercoat. The jeep seemed shrunken, humiliated, stripped naked in public. It seemed shrunken.

Was there something more serious to Vicki's story than he had suspected? Did Vicki's story contain a great secret that he was unaware of? Why had the scene suddenly grown so grim?

Mehmet shuddered. He entered the office quietly.

"In the August of 1915, at the Dardanelles Front of the Great World War, Turkish Lieutenant Ali Osman *Bey* and Anzac Private Alistair John Taylor spent two days and two nights together. They were both twenty years of age.

"These two days were the last days of Ali Osman *Bey*'s life. They were also the end of Alistair John Taylor's twenty-year-long life.

"Meanwhile, around this time, Meryem of the Eceyaylasi Village, daughter of Hasan the Circumciser, was busy looking for her six-year-old brother Isa, who had disappeared hours ago. The Ottoman government had resettled Chanakkale's peasants to the relative safety of far away villages. The women and children of the Eceyaylasi Village had been sent to the Kadhi Village, which is now called Evreshe. They got along right well with the Greeks who already lived there. It was flat out crazy for little Isa to run away from the haven of the village, which was itself not altogether safe during the war. But what can you do, Isa was still just a babe. Meryem ran around wildly looking for her brother, and though the women cautioned her not to leave the village, she paid them no mind.

"Meryem was stubborn as a mule, a defiant girl whom even her father, Hasan the Circumciser, could not bring to heel. Even as a little brat she would secretly watch her father's circumcisions and smoke her older brothers' cigarettes. She was skillful, handy, strong and resilient. Was she smart as they come or just plain crazy? Can't say. Only God knows... Finally Hasan the Circumciser, what could the poor man do, *mari*, put Meryem on the back of his saddle and took her along to jobs in other villages. So, as her peers worked at home and on the fields, as they put together their trousseaus, this girl Meryem grew up in precisely this manner...

"At first, the people were shocked. Here was a girl eight or nine years old, wandering around from village to village with her circumciser father, cleaning the equipment, handling the business, collecting the money or grain or provisions that the villagers gave as payment, and generally running the show. Soon, though, the people got used to Meryem. But there was one little thing they couldn't get used to. Meryem watched the circumcisions, come hell or high water. All the advice, all the beatings that her dad gave her didn't do one bit of good. Little Meryem went and hid and watched her dad's circumcisions the way women these days watch films on TV. She wasn't afraid one bit.

177

"Years passed, Meryem grew up but she didn't want to marry nobody. Anyway, she didn't have too many suitors because of this circumcision thing, *mari*. Hasan the Circumciser and his two sons went to fight in the war. The sons froze to death at the Sarikamish Front, and Hasan never returned from the Palestine-Canal Front. As for Meryem's mother, she died soon afterwards, unable to stand the loss. So there was Meryem, left an orphan with no one but her little brother Isa in the whole wide world. If she hadn't been a girl, they would have let her perform circumcisions, but the poor thing had been born a girl, *mari*. Nowadays they got woman circumcisers as well but no way that was going to happen back then. So Meryem girl had only one relative left living in the world when the two of them moved to the Kadhi Village along with the women and children of the Eceyaylasi Village, and he had run off to the front to play.

"Meryem knew Gallipoli like the back of her hand, from wandering around from town to town with her dad. While she was skulking about looking for her brother, she came across a young Turkish soldier who was keeping vigil at the site of a fresh grave. At first she grew shy, and hid behind some trees. She watched the soldier for a long time. The young man was emitting strange noises, crying and laughing right afterwards. His blue eyes were swollen, he kept looking into the distance, lamenting and singing in a foreign tongue. Whoever lay in that fresh grave was obviously a close friend, for he would not leave its side, he kept stroking the ground. His clothes were ragged, his uniform shrunken, leaving the cuffs of his pants and jacket too short. His blond hair and beard were unkempt, he looked tired and mighty ill. Meryem had seen plenty of disabled veterans who had lost an arm or a leg, but this was the first time she was seeing one who had lost his mind, *mari*. She was puzzled, intimidated but not scared. Meryem was never scared. So, young Meryem forgot all about her brother Isa and remained rooted to the spot. She could not take her eyes off this young soldier. For the youth was handsome enough to drive any girl crazy, he was one of those lucky souls whom God created painstakingly in His spare time. Now, I'm not joking when I say he was as handsome as they come. Handsome enough to make any girl swoon. And that's what Meryem did.

"Meryem must have been about twenty-two years old when she discovered this Turkish soldier, who was keeping a half-crazed vigil by the fresh grave… Yea, I suppose she was getting on in her years… Right then and there, her soul flew straight out of her body. That day, Meryem fell so completely head over heels in love with the soldier that she would never again have eyes for anybody else, she would never give her heart to anyone else, and she would never say a kind word to anyone except him. Around here, they call the disease 'lovesickness'. There ain't no cure available. Once you catch it, you're ill forever. Meryem had become lovesick, and every hour, every moment of her life would from then on be devoted to this man. She was to become his wife, his mother, his grandmother, his slave, his subject, his everything. That is, until she gave birth to a baby girl…

"My mother Meryem did not love her children, her brother, her grandchildren or her great-grandchildren. She did not love the three of us who lived, or the one who died a few months after he was born, my older brother Ali, may he rest in peace, or my Uncle Isa, who frequently ran away to play at the front. My mother Meryem did not love any of us. She could not. Her heart did not belong to her after she met *Ghazi* Sergeant Alican and became lovesick for him in August 1915, at the site of the fresh grave. Her will had left her body. There's a thing called black magic, a most terrible thing. It is so terrible that the Koran forbids it. Yes! That's exactly what it was like. Meryem's lovesickness was just like black magic. She was cursed. And she remained cursed until the day she died.

179

"My mother Meryem was besotted, infatuated, obsessed. Her soul was blinded with love. From the day that she met him, *Ghazi* Sergeant Alican became her everything. He was her only light, her man. Even if she wanted, she would not have been able to show compassion or kindness to anyone except my father, *Ghazi* Sergeant Alican. And she didn't. My mother had neither the time nor the strength to love anyone other than my father. Therefore, my mother Meryem never loved, kissed, or caressed us. She barely even saw us. She saw us simply as unseemly, what's the word, obstacles, yes, as unseemly obstacles between herself and her beloved. My mother always resented our presence. And mine most of all, *mari*...

"Some nights, when I was a wee little girl, I'd wonder what my mother would do if my dad did not love us, if he did not care for us? Hmm? The thought always scared me half to death. I'd cry in fear and early the next morning I would run up and hug my dad. 'My little girl had another nightmare,' my father would say. I thought that if he were to die, my mother would throw us all out. I thought she was only taking care of us for the sake of our father. And I never found out the answer to this question... My mother was an old dame by the time my father died. I was the one who took care of her. Anyhow, took her no more than a year before she hurried after her beloved.

"She wasn't wrong altogether, though... In villages like this one, especially back then, menfolk couldn't coddle and spoil their kids. Wasn't proper. That was the tradition. Especially girls, they were not even considered children. Even today, boys are considered more important than girls in villages. Because the girls are bound to leave. They go off as brides to some other household, to serve, to make and take care of babies, to work on the fields, in the homes and in beds. Just until recently, village men could not hold and caress their babies in front of their fathers, *mari*. But my father, *Ghazi* Sergeant Alican was entirely different... May God bless him in heaven, may he rest in abundant peace... Ah, my dad, what a grand man he was... Even back in those days he didn't care a whit what people said, he loved and fussed over us all, me especially. He would play with us for hours, he would teach us English games and songs, which he learned when he fell captive to the British. My older brother Uzun and my younger brother Bulut, he was a wee little lad back then, would tire quickly of the rhymes and songs but I never grew bored for a moment. Just so long as I was with father, just as long as I kept learning. The more I learned, the greater father's affection grew for me; he would stroke my hair with sparkling eyes and say "My clever little girl!"

"One day he and I were busy playing games – I must have been about seven or eight years old – and mom came and stood over us, and we didn't notice her at all. She just waited there in the corner and watched us for hours. When we did see her, her face was set like stone. I can never forget my mother's stony face staring at us. The jealousy in her stare, her petrified skin, the fear in her eyes, the tautness in her frame, ready to bolt like an arrow from its bow... I still have nightmares of my mother's stony face. It scares me to this day.

"Mother never talked with the neighbor women, or with us. Truth be told, mother never spoke, period. She was always quiet, always observing. I never saw her yammering away with the village women by the fountain side. There was great poverty back then. It was a time of war, scarcity, need... It was hard times, mighty hard, *mari*. May God never show us those days again. May the Almighty spare my enemy from hunger's lessons, *hele*... My mother used to work as a maid on the wealthy farms. She would come home with almost three pounds of barley flour, set to cleaning and cooking, work and toil endlessly so she could provide a hot meal for my father, even in that time of need. Every house had an animal or two, which the kids tended. Back in those days, they sold a flask of milk

181

for one Ottoman coin. No matter how busy she was, mother always made sure that father had a clean robe to wear, even if it was patched. She took better care of him than us, she doted over him like he was a babe in arms. Father treated us like a mother, and mother treated him like a mother and wife... At the time there was no other able young man at the Eceyaylasi Village besides my father. Everybody had been killed in the war, and the veterans were all disabled. The youngest men after my father were boys no bigger than eight years old, *mari*. Therefore, his presence was very important to the villagers, very important...

"Some nights I would secretly watch my mother and father, the same way mother used to sneak peeks at my grandfather, Hasan the Circumciser, as he went about performing circumcisions on little boys. You know how kids are... I would not believe the things I saw, my jaw would drop open. My mother Meryem would turn into a whole different woman when she was left alone with my father, *mari*! That stone-faced, tight-lipped, hard-hearted Meryem, Hasan the Circumciser's mule-stubborn daughter, the mother who never once stroked my hair, would turn into some other honey-tongued, bright-eyed, love-filled, playful woman, *mari*! I wouldn't have believed it in my dreams but when I saw it happen I would almost faint in disbelief. Meryem would embrace my father, kiss his face and eyes, sit on his lap and do all kinds of indecent things. My father would just laugh along. My father was like a little boy. He couldn't resist mother's charms and he would start to fool around as well. Then father would kiss her on the mouth. Now that's what shocked me most of all. I could never imagine anybody kissing anybody else on the mouth, *hele*... Next they would take off their clothes. At that point I would cover my eyes because I couldn't bear to see any more. I was jealous of my mother over the same man. That man was my father, he loved me dearly, but still my heart trembled, *mari*. It trembled like a leaf, for fear that my mother would steal my father away from me. My one and only wish was to keep his love. At any cost. Any cost at all... But I could not do the things that mother did. Besides, I was still a kid. And I wasn't too eager to grow up to be a woman. Especially not to get married and leave the house and go live with some man other than my father... God forbid... I was happy enough just being my father's daughter. Being the apple of my father's eye brought me such a field of joy that no other tree would be enough for me. It couldn't be. I would grow heartsick and scared. I would wait, holding my breath, until they fell asleep and then return to my own bed.

"Father was expert in keeping us two women enamored of him. In the end, I suppose I was also lovesick for my father... Because father was different from all the rest, he didn't have an equal in the world... My father... God bless his soul, he was a good man, a mighty good man, a man with a great heart... my father was a hero... My father... Oh, my dear old father..."

Suddenly Auntie Beyaz stopped talking and torrents of tears began streaming down her face. There was no change in her appearance. In fact, the tears running down her cheeks were the only sign that she was crying. She had been sitting and narrating peacefully, as though the tale were someone else's fascinating life story, or the plot of an adventure movie. Then she had abruptly felt a great longing for her father and begun to cry. But it seemed that only her eyes were crying.

Vicki, who had been listening for a while with keen interest, held breath and enormous enthusiasm, felt her heart sink when she saw Auntie Beyaz's tears. She immediately ran up to her and attempted to comfort Auntie Beyaz with a hug but the old woman pushed her away. At that moment Vicki seemed to glimpse Meryem, Hasan the Circumciser's mule-stubborn daughter. Although Auntie Beyaz adamantly claimed "I am my father's daughter," she was perhaps more like her mother Meryem, and too afraid to admit it. Vicki grasped the fact at that

183

instant and knew that she would make Auntie Beyaz happier by keeping her distance. Just like Meryem, there was something wild about Auntie Beyaz as well, and as a result she had only been able to get close to a few people throughout her life. Maybe just one person. The thought frightened Vicki. For these characteristics could describe herself just as well. Yes, herself. She paused, took a deep breath, and swallowed. From here on she would bear witness to the old woman's tears without intervening and without feeling guilty, but with a dangerous curiosity snowballing inside her. She tried. She waited silently and patiently. She sealed her lips and refrained from asking that crucial question, which she was dying to ask. As Vicki sat there silently Auntie Beyaz turned inward, shrunk, diminished and fell asleep sitting up, with a strange smile on her face.

The sudden naps of the elderly are nature's small death rehearsals. These short episodes prepare them for the real item, the long sleep. Vicki panicked when Auntie Beyaz suddenly dozed off.

What if she was dying right now, what if she died in a few minutes? What if she was going to die just as she was revealing the truth? What if the last remaining witness subsided into history with all her secrets? Then how would Vicki find out who the man was whom Meryem discovered at the site of the fresh grave, wearing a Turkish uniform? Was that man, Auntie Beyaz's father, Ali Osman *Bey*, or was it her own great-grandfather Alistair John Taylor? How would Vicki be able to tell if the soldier who survived was an Anzac or a Turk when half the villagers of Gallipoli were blue-eyed? What if the officer called Ali Osman had killed and buried her great-grandfather? After all, war was still raging on at the time and her great-grandfather was an Anzac soldier who had come to invade the Turkish officer's country. Yes, Lieutenant Ali Osman could well have killed Private Alistair John Taylor. Then he could have lost his memory owing to emotional trauma and settled in this village under the name *Ghazi* Sergeant Alican until the end of his days. Why not? That would defeat her theory and leave her looking like a fool once again. But... but what if not? Oh the irresistible appeal of infinitesmal possibilities lodged within those 'buts' and 'what ifs'! Oh the confusion of feelings that holds us captive as we are swept in the seductive glimmer of possibilities! Oh the high costs of journeys we take in pursuit of 'what ifs', the journeys we sometimes recall with pangs of regret. But, what if not? There was a chance, however slight, that her great-grandfather was the soldier who survived. Yes, there was! Thus, Auntie Beyaz could not die. Not now. Vicki had to see this thing through to the end, even if the truth hurt, for she had come too far and spent too much patience in its pursuit. She had to do it. It was now or never.

"Auntie Beyaz?" Vicki called in a trembling, anxious voice. "Auntie Beyaz, you're sleeping, right?"

"What is it, *hele*?" grumbled Auntie Beyaz, opening her eyes. "I just dozed off for a minute, *mari*, what's wrong with that?"

"Can I get you some tea, Auntie Beyaz?" asked Vicki, breathing a sigh of relief.

"I feel like having some nice plum compote, Vicki *Hanim*. Maybe we ought to call granddaughter Havva and have her make us some compote. And some *lokma** too, fresh and piping hot, with lots of sherbet. Aren't you hungry, *hele*? Look at you, skinny as a reed. Granddaughter Havva will fix some cheese *halvah*** for you, it'll do you good, put some meat on your bones, bring out your fairness."

"You are hungry, Auntie Beyaz," laughed Vicki.

Although she did not understand their names, she gathered that Auntie Beyaz was talking about food, from the way she smacked her lips. Vicki was already familiar with the

---

*) *Lokma*: deep-fried lumps of dough
**) *Halvah*: Turkish sweetmeat

words for compote, rice, sweetmeat, bread, water and soup. She had begun to appreciate the local cuisine, both because of its tastiness and its organic pedigree. She picked up the phone and dialed by heart the number of Havva, Auntie Beyaz's older brother's great-granddaughter, who lived next door.

"Hello Havva *Hanim*, me Vicki. Auntie Beyaz speak," she said in broken Turkish, and handed the receiver to Auntie Beyaz.

In the beginning Havva had not taken very warmly to Vicki, but after she saw the foreign woman wearing a *shalvar* like the rest of them, praising the dishes she cooked and eating them with relish, and learning Turkish swiftly from her little phrasebook, she had changed her mind and become friendlier. The villagers heard through Havva that Vicki was picking up some Turkish and they held her in favor especially because she was providing companionship for the lately reclusive but blessed Auntie Beyaz. Guests are favored in this land. Perhaps it is because they will ultimately go back home, but guests are favored nonetheless. It has been this way for centuries. The legendary Turkish hospitality is not a myth, and it begins with the assumption that everyone is a guest who sets foot peacefully upon this soil. Everyone who has lived or been a guest in this country is well aware of this fact.

Vicki's 'Anzac great-grandfather' tale had not bothered the peasantry of the Gallipoli Peninsula, because they never for a moment doubted the Turkish identity of the Gallipoli veteran *Ghazi* Sergeant Alican. None of the villagers felt an enmity toward Vicki. Anyhow, the reason Auntie Beyaz and Vicki remained cloistered in the house was not because of the Gallipoli populace, but rather because of the press, secret police and politicians who arrived from the big cities.

An hour later Havva knocked on the door, bearing a tray laden with plum compote, delicious cheese *halvah* made with Edirne cheese, salt bonito with plenty of lemon and olive oil, chicken dumplings and the inevitable vegetable *bulghur pilaf*.

They let Havva in, barely fighting off the reporters who tried to enter alongside her and who clamored to snap pictures of Vicki through the door crack.

Havva began the lessons as soon as she stepped through the door. Teaching Vicki a few new words had become the highlight of her day. She enjoyed it immensely. Vicki, for her part, played along.

"Sevda: sev-dah, means heart, soul, love... Auntie Beyaz, lookee here, this Vicki's really starting to get the hang of Turkish, *mari*! Yes, uh-huh, sev-dah. Hah, hah, ha... You're too funny Vicki... God bless your soul!"

Vicki had put a hand to her heart and was making faces and mouthing "sev-dah!" in order to amuse Havva. It seemed that in the process she was amusing herself as well.

"Come on, quit it you crazy fools. I'm hungry. A body can't feed on no *sevda*. Bah! *Sevda* indeed! Give me my food first."

After the meal was over, Havva picked up the empty plates and left, emitting happy sounds. On her way out, they again had trouble keeping away the reporters. Next, it was time for Turkish coffee, which Vicki had by now learned how to make. Auntie Beyaz looked happy slurping away at her coffee and embellishing each sip with the praise "Good for you, Vicki *Hanim*." They watched TV for a short while. Auntie Beyaz surfed through ten different channels, glanced at the news, grew angry at what she heard and cursed in Turkish.

"These nincompoops, they don't give a damn about the country, all they care about is themselves!" she grumbled. Then she switched off the TV.

"Who?" asked Vicki.

"Who do you think, *mari*, the politicians, of course. See here, *hele*, what are yours like? Do they love their country or their pockets, hmm?" she questioned.

Vicki chuckled. This Auntie Beyaz was something else. Lively, curious, and interested...

187

"You're amazing, Auntie Beyaz," she laughed.

"I feel sleepy all of a sudden. I'm off to bed, Vicki *Hanim*. But first, let me prepare your bed, *hele*. Here we go, *bismillah*!"

Every night, despite all of Vicki's protests, Auntie Beyaz resolutely spread out a bedsheet on one of the living room sofas, brought out a pillow and a blanket and prepared Vicki's bed. "Guests don't make their own beds!" she had declared. Since she was raised in a culture where everyone took care of their own tasks starting at an early age, it was extremely unsettling for Vicki to sit idly by as an old woman made her bed. However, she knew by now that Auntie Beyaz could not be contradicted. She fell silent, sighed, and waited. She took out a book from her bag. She planned to stretch out in bed and read the absorbing stories of Katherine Mansfield, whom she had neglected since early youth. But she never got around to it. Instead of going to sleep in her own room, Auntie Beyaz, who had just claimed extreme drowsiness, settled cross-legged on the bed she had just made for Vicki and abruptly began to speak:

"Anzac Private Alistair John Taylor had been running madly in no particular direction when he narrowly missed being hit in the head by a Turkish bullet. He was dazed when he fell to the ground. At first, he thought he fell because he was wounded. He lay sprawled out for a while. Then he raised a hand to his head and found nothing amiss. But when he touched his stomach his hands came away drenched in blood. He figured he was about to die. But he wasn't sorry. He accepted it. The people he loved had all gone and died anyway, *mari*. He was also going to be freed of this misery. He did not rejoice either. He was still so young. He thought of Keri. His girl Keri, who was waiting for him back in his country, far away. He lay on the ground for a long time. But he was still not dead. Maybe this is what dying is like, he thought, God forgive him! But he did, the poor thing. Then he heard a moan that was not coming from him. That was when he finally noticed the soldier who was lying beneath him, the one he had tripped over. He was terrified. He lay still, not knowing what to do, but the Turkish soldier was moaning and bleeding. Without further thought, maybe out of some human instinct, who knows... he quickly dragged the Turkish soldier towards the nearby olive trees. It was an odd moment of silence. Two enemy soldiers were lying next to each other under the olive trees. The Turk, whom they had been introduced to as Abdul, was a handsome, fresh-faced young man. He was a man, even if his name was Abdul. Alistair John was nervous. He was bewildered. He took his hat and propped it under Ali Osman's head. Ali Osman opened his eyes and the two men stared at each other for the first time.

"'Bonjour!' said Ali Osman. Mind you, bonjour means *marhaba*, hello in French! Alistair John said 'Good Day!' The Turkish officer said 'I speak little English' and asked for a little bit of water. Alistair John gave Ali Osman a drink of water from his flask. They were silent. After a little while, Ali Osman began pointing to his pocket. Alistair John emptied the contents of the indicated pocket. What came out were three letters and some money.

"The Turk looked at the letters and, with a wistful smile, whispered: 'My mother.' The other understood.

"'I am Ali Osman. Turk. Constantinople,' groaned Ali Osman.

"'I'm Alistair John Taylor, from New Zealand, Wellington,' replied the Anzac, and shook his hand. Soon Ali Osman fainted.

"In the hours that followed, whenever Ali Osman revived, the poor things tried to communicate in a hodge-podge of English, French and Turkish, *mari*. The Turk knew better French than English but the Anzac didn't know any foreign languages. Nonetheless, the Turk managed to convey that he had studied to become a lawyer and that he had a mother and brother waiting for him back in Istanbul. In return, the Anzac related his life story to the Turk with great excitement and enthusiasm. But he had no idea how much of it the Turk understood. The Anzac shared his remaining biscuits and tinned beef with the Turk but the Turk had no appetite. Toward daybreak, the Turk began to emit long moans. Alistair John held his hand and prayed for him to survive. He felt as sad as if a close friend were about to die. As dawn broke the Turk grabbed the Anzac and pulled him close with a strength that was not to be expected from a wounded fellow. He was pointing to his clothes and saying something, but it was all in Turkish. The Anzac did not understand a single thing. The Turk pointed for a long time. He kept pointing to his uniform and talking. Finally he became quiet. When he stopped, Alistair John began to tell him of his own farm and of his girl Keri. He talked for hours. Then he felt hungry so he stopped and turned toward Ali Osman to share with him his last piece of biscuit but the Turk had gone to meet his Maker, he had expired. Yet Alistair John did not realize it, or who knows, maybe he refused to accept it, *mari*. Only God knows for sure, I would not be able to tell you. He flung the Turk over his shoulder and started running once more. Maybe he was looking for someone to save him. Who can say? He himself didn't know anymore. His mind had flown away. The poor wretch's mind had flown away, never again to return completely... He ran for hours, carrying the lifeless frame of the Turk on his back. He had traveled a long way north. It's a mystery why no one saw him, shot him or took him captive. No one knows. It's not for us to question God's ways, to reason out His miracles.

"Only when Ali Osman's body began to smell did Alistair John believe that he was dead. All of Alistair John's ties to life had been severed now that the last man he had spoken to had also died. The poor wretch was suspended in a kind of vacuum. He kept falling and falling but he simply did not hit the bottom and die. It was then that he lovingly made a grave for the Turk. He cried as he dug the grave. The poor man had not been able to cry the way he wanted to when they buried his older brother Will, but now he was sobbing to his heart's content. Just as he was about to lay the Turk in the grave, it dawned on him what the Turk meant by pointing to his uniform. He immediately stripped the Turk, ripped off his insignia and changed into his uniform. The outfit was a little short on him but he didn't even notice. He buried the Turk with his underclothes and insignia, and kept the three letters from his pocket. Was this what the Turk had meant, no one knows, but what did it matter anyway, *mari*? It had already happened, the arrow had been released from its bow... Alistair John then bloodied his hands using his penknife to whittle a crescent out of wood, set it at the head of the fresh grave, sat down beside the grave and began to pray and sing hymns. He knew that he had buried his past along with his own uniform. He had made up his mind. He could never relive any of the things that he had lived before. Not anymore! He had lost his will to live, anyhow. He was hungry, thirsty, alone and in freefall. He did not feel like doing anything. His mind had flown away, together with his will to live.

"That was when Meryem, Hasan the Circumciser's daughter, found him. It was God's will... See here, it bears no questioning. They met at the site of Ali Osman *Bey*'s fresh grave. Alistair John was startled to come across a woman for the first time in a long while. He took her for an angel. He approached Meryem, who was gazing at him shyly but curiously, as an angel, and kissed her hands. Meryem savvied that he was a harmless and mighty handsome young lad, and she also made up her mind. This soldier was going to be her man. The soldier looked at Meryem, then pointed to his uniform and said: 'Ali Osman.' Then he pointed to himself and said 'Alistair John.'

He didn't realize it but he had pointed to himself both times. Meryem took a good long look and she understood. 'You're Alican. *Ghazi* Sergeant Alican,' she said. The other smiled and nodded. In the days that followed he would smile and nod to practically everything that Meryem said.

"Meryem took him to the Kadhi Village. 'He's from around our parts. I saw him once when dad and I went to a circumcision. His name's *Ghazi* Sergeant Alican. The English took him captive. He was tortured, he's a mighty brave soldier but his mind's a bit gone, poor thing,' she said. The peasants embraced this unfortunate young veteran and no one ever asked anything further. They fed him and just as they were about to bathe him, Meryem objected. 'He's got wounds, let them heal first, then you can bathe him,' she said. In those days, circumcisers were something of a doctor in the villages, you know. So, the daughter of the circumciser was also practically a doctor. That night Meryem circumcised Anzac Private Alistair John Taylor. They did not bathe him until a week later. The same day, Meryem's brother Isa was found and brought in from a neighboring village. Meryem took it as an auspicious sign.

"After the English, the French and the Anzacs were defeated and quietly fled the Dardanelles, Meryem took Sergeant Alican and Isa back to the Eceyaylasi Village. One year later they had their first baby, and named him Ali. Six or seven years later I was born. They named me Beyaz."

Vicki had listened to the story tearfully, biting her hand to keep herself from screaming, and now her body convulsed with quiet sobs. She could not find anything to say. What was there left to say? She got up and approached Auntie Beyaz; she wanted to embrace her own great-aunt, to rest her head on her breast, to touch her. That's what she wanted. That's what she wanted more than anything. But Auntie Beyaz had suddenly fallen asleep on the guest bed that she had prepared for Vicki. Exhausted by her narrative, she had curled up, shrunk, shriveled, and fallen sound asleep. She slept just like a baby. This time Vicki was not scared. She was not scared that this sleep was a rehearsal for death. She daubed her eyes with her hands, wiped her nose on her sleeve, curled up like a fetus next to Auntie Beyaz and there fell asleep. There they both slept. There slept two women, both with a faint scent of fennel. Auntie Beyaz and Vicki slept soundly.

What bothered them was the media horde that had descended upon their village and proceeded to act as heedlessly as though they were a group of foreigners who had stepped on Turkish soil for the first time. The villagers of Eceyaylasi were otherwise unperturbed by either Vicki or her tale of 'the Anzac great-grandfather who later became a Turk'. No, after the initial shock, the villagers had laughed at and even enjoyed the story. To think that a beloved late veteran, a religious Gallipoli hero, a compatriot who had suffered months of 'various infidel tortures' at the hands of the British without betraying a single military secret, could in fact be a non-Moslem, a foreigner, and especially an Anzac who had come to invade this very land was just plain craziness. There are some things that are beyond doubt. These things are accepted without question, preserved and left untouched. And the greatest disappointments and depressions in life come when these 'born truths' are demolished. But there exists something beyond dogma in this claim. For, according to Ottoman tradition, which itself was comprised of diverse backgrounds, once a person is accepted as a Turk on this soil, he remains thus. This tradition has survived for centuries. That is why, once they had recovered from the initial shock, the villagers of Eceyaylasi did not give a second thought to Vicki's story. In fact, they would not entertain the slightest doubt as to *Ghazi* Sergeant Alican's Turkishness, even if someday the opposite were to be proven one hundred percent.

The villagers of Eceyaylasi actually liked Vicki for having successfully been received at Auntie Beyaz's house and for keeping company to that blessed soul, who had secluded herself for years, and who was their last link to the late *Ghazi* Sergeant Alican. In the end, Vicki was a polite and respectful person but most important of all, she was a guest. Hospitality toward guests was a cultural heritage, which the villagers of Eceyaylasi had inherited from their forefathers.

What disturbed them was the noisy herd of media employees that ambled through their village in obvious disregard. A media army had invaded the village; men and women holding aloft cigarettes and soda cans, chewing gum, poking their noses into everything and barging in everywhere without asking for permission. With few exceptions, these youngsters thought that working for the media alone gave them a right to do anything and considered it a feat to infiltrate every occasion. Thus the villagers of Eceyaylasi, who had a very low tolerance for insolence and impertinence, treated the members of the media with coldness and indifference, and waited patiently for their turn to come.

195

At first the villagers enjoyed seeing their relatives and neighbors on television and hearing the name of their town pronounced, but these strangers who set up camp at Eceyaylasi and frequently haggled Auntie Beyaz's house, who were willing to do anything to talk to Auntie Beyaz and Vicki, could doubtless not be considered guests. They seemed more like invaders, and they vexed the villagers.

It was not that the villagers were entirely pleased with the perfunctory Gallipoli Victory ceremonies that took place once a year on March eighteenth. If thousands of Anzac grandchildren did not travel thousands of miles every year to Chanakkale to pay tribute to the souls of their forefathers, despite their defeat in the war, perhaps the villagers would have been less troubled. Naturally, the villagers of Chanakkale, whose emotions had been shell-shocked due to many years of war, did not expect a large and ostentatious celebration at the site of so much pain and suffering. However, it added a wrinkle to their centuries-old wistful smile that their once 'heroic enemies', the Anzacs, treasured the memory of the Battle of Gallipoli as a matter of national culture while the Turks themselves did not pay much heed to this bloody and difficult victory. The Gallipoli Victory was gained against all odds, through the massive sacrifices of Ottomans of every age, ilk and gender, but the urban media youth who now stormed the village had not come all this way to laud this significant achievement or inquire about its meaning. They did not seem very concerned with reassessing history or the Battle of Gallipoli. Their real concern seemed to be pursuing the ratings that could be gained from the scandalous headline: 'New Zealander woman's great-grandfather'. And how they pursued it! However, there was one thing they failed to comprehend: that *Ghazi* Sergeant Alican, who was a son of this land, would always remain thus. Though everyone noticed it changing slowly, though some scorned and some praised it, this land had such rules of its own. The villagers sensed these contradictions and although they enjoyed seeing their neighbors, relatives and surroundings on television and in newspapers, they were deeply unsettled by the event.

It was the village elders who first awoke from the hypnotizing stupor of newspaper and TV coverage. Thus the glamour of overnight fame, which the *Mukthar* and the younger folk had allowed for advertising purposes, began to fade. For the journalists had picked Auntie Beyaz as a target and zeroed in on her house as the key address to the '*historic scandal of the century*', which they magnified with intense relish. Since the newspaper and TV crews did not go to the trouble of investigating how deeply Auntie Beyaz was loved and respected in the area, they caricaturized her, portrayed her as a nasty old lady suspected of possessing supernatural powers, and practically reduced her to a sort of witch. They had succeeded in turning the story into a spy drama in which a reclusive old peasant woman with strange talents harbored a foreign (and inevitably) gorgeous woman in her house.

'Another case of Haidar *Pasha*'s bride! Foreign women choose to slander Ottoman History to gain fame!'

'Anzac woman's incredible tale!'

'How dare a questionable foreigner disparage a great Turkish hero?'

The topic had started out as an amusing and ridiculous news item, but its coverage eventually grew vulgar and aggressive thanks to the efforts of certain news producers who pushed it into the national limelight and forced the public to respond. Not so much forced as pushed and shoved.

Historians, conservative politicians and retired diplomats specializing in the Gallipoli issue began appearing on prime time news where the matter was discussed incessantly. The prospect of live coverage made these people, whose professional successes had gone largely unnoticed until then, rush to the studios with a bitter-sweet thrill that came from years of being neglected. The Battle of Gallipoli, the Dardanelles Victory, and the Anzacs were thrashed about for days. The Turkish media had finally rediscovered the Battle of Gallipoli.

'Our national pride and honor have been smeared by the shadow of an enemy soldier forced upon a valiant Dardanelles hero!' was repeated endlessly in a tone that would make every citizen of Turkey cringe or become sick to his stomach. Forums were held to discuss the 'traitorous motives' behind this conspiracy, rather than the illogic of how *a man can be a hero in two countries for the same war.*

The issue was so exaggerated and overblown that it inevitably became the first item on the national agenda. Political party spokesmen, the Ministry of Foreign Affairs, the History Association and the Office of the Chief of Staff were compelled to make statements addressing the negative press.

Announcements were aired that the Turks, throughout history, have been extremely sensitive about their veterans and war heroes, that the Turkish people would take offense at any disrespect foreigners showed on the subject and that meddling with our spiritual values might yield unfavorable circumstances.

Following these announcements, the New Zealand Embassy was forced to hold a press conference. It was stated that "every New Zealand citizen is free and independent in his thought," and that "Turkey and New Zealand possess a close friendship born of historical bonds and it will not benefit any parties to distort history through certain romantic and fictional tales." It was added that "New Zealand does not condone the vilification of soldiers who were able to refer to one another as 'my heroic enemy' at Gallipoli in the year 1915."

Upon hearing New Zealand's public declaration, the Australian Embassy also felt the need to hold a press conference. It emphasized the importance of Australian soldiers who fought bravely at the Dardanelles in World War I, and proclaimed that "the venerable soldiers of Gallipoli must be allowed to sleep in peace".

After both Australia and New Zealand had made their official statements, the British Embassy thought it necessary to weigh in. The English sufficed to say that "Great Britain shall ascribe no import to such tabloid spectacles and their proponents".

A pudgy news impresario, well known for his ruthless and unscrupulous exposes of scandals and private lives, held a live broadcast of his Cool-Shock News program from the Gallipoli National Park. As much as the program itself, the exorbitant costs of providing lighting for the National Park were discussed for days afterwards.

The merciless and insensitive producer and announcer of the Cool-Shock News embellished his broadcast with marches and epic poems, kneeled on the ground at the Ariburnu-Anzac Cove, picked up a handful of soil and declared: "Fie, dear viewers, on the lovely Anzac lady who dares insult our national pride for the sake of fame and fortune! The Turkish people have said 'there's no passing the Dardanelles!' and made it clear to those who, like her, disdain history, veterans and noble heroes. We cannot help but wonder how certain grannies who shelter her and her kind, will be able to look their martyred fathers in the eye when they reach the next world!" Then he slowly raised the fistful of soil up to his nose and inhaled it deeply. As he smelled the soil, the camera followed previous instructions and began zooming in on the anchor. Displaying his expert skill, the famous newsman burst into tears as the camera dove in for the final close-up. Quoting the national anthem, he cried: "Martyrs shall spring forth, Anzac lady, if you so much as wring this soil!" and with this, collapsed in a fit of sobs. The camera then froze and the closing credits rolled. In the background you could hear the song *They Shot Me in Cha-*

nakkale' being played. The viewers were very moved. The show got fabulous ratings but its famous anchor suffered a depression immediately afterwards, leaving his assistant to host the program on the following night. Viewers who believed the story about his depression took it as a sign of sincerity and the Cool-Shock News further increased its ratings. It was now officially registered that the issue of *'the New Zealander woman who came to Chanakkale to seek her great-grandfather at a Turkish hero's grave'* was the most important item on Turkey's agenda.

When it became clear that the first journalist or reporter to speak with Vicki or Auntie Beyaz would become a hero, albeit for a short time, things reached their breaking point. There were those journalists who called Auntie Beyaz's house continuously and harassed her when she answered the phone, there was the reporter who got stuck while trying to sneak down the chimney, and there were a few newsmen who threw rocks at her windows. When these attempts proved unfruitful, seductive offers were made to the villagers of Eceyaylasi. The villager who could provide a brief interview with Auntie Beyaz was promised a job in Istanbul or Ankara, tuition for his children, credit from the banks and an audience with ministers of state and members of parliament. These offers were seductive enough to sway almost any citizen of Turkey in the year 2000. But they were all refused with the same answer: "No, brother, I can't do anything to hurt Auntie Beyaz!" This reply left some of the reporters and journalists gaping in amazement. "Such people in this day and age!" Yet it was not out of principles or material wealth that the villagers flat out refused their offers. What the reporters and journalists failed to grasp, what they made no effort to grasp, was just how extraordinary a woman Auntie Beyaz was, and just what values her character represented.

Auntie Beyaz was a highly intelligent, insightful, disciplined and brave woman, but these qualities were obviously not

200

sufficient to explain her prestigious position and the intense respect and regard she enjoyed, which was usually reserved for a man. The people of Gallipoli, and particularly of the Ece-yaylasi Village, had conferred upon her such lofty human values as 'sagacity', when she only had a three-year elementary school education, 'motherhood', when she had never born children, 'valor', although she had never fought in a battle, and 'fairness', when she had never acted as a judge. More importantly, they had embraced her as something holy, a living saint. People, whose need for humane values such as justice, truthfulness, courage and foresight cannot be met by their government, devise their own solutions. Auntie Beyaz was one of their solutions. She was a virtual sage whom they could turn to, and from whose vast knowledge and insight they could benefit whenever they were in trouble. She had surmounted the social obstacle of being a woman by shunning marriage and following a diet of abstinence, she had dulled her femininity as a price. However, what lent Auntie Beyaz her respect and prominence was rather the legend of *Ghazi* Sergeant Alican. For above all she was *Ghazi* Sergeant Alican's own beloved daughter, he had raised and educated her himself. Auntie Beyaz was 'her father's daughter', and such value could only be given to a woman as the extension of a man. Therefore, Auntie Beyaz was a living legend in Gallipoli. Auntie Beyaz was a history. Auntie Beyaz was a keepsake from one of God's dearly beloved souls. And despite all the years, it seemed that no offered bribe could lead the local populace to act in a way that might cause her harm.

Until six years ago, Auntie Beyaz walked around the village with her cane, was a regular at the *kahveh* where she had tea and discussed politics and agriculture with the men (mostly berating them for their ignorance), and frequently went up to Ariburnu where she said prayers for her late father. Yet after the mighty and ruthless forest fire that ravaged Gallipoli in July 1994, she had turned her back on everything and everyo-

201

ne, and shut herself away in her house. Talat Goktepe, the fire chief who had died while fighting the flames, had been a dear friend of hers. She had been devastated not only by the rumors that the fire may have been sabotage, but also by the disappearance of the Gallipoli nightingales, along with the green plant cover. She confined herself to her house. In the years that followed, she preserved only two ties to the outside world. One was Havva, the great-granddaughter of her older brother Uzun, who provided for her food and other needs, and the other was her brother Bulut's great-grandson, the lawyer who lived in Istanbul. Still, she had not given up on following national and world events, or on reading the periodicals that her lawyer grandson from Istanbul brought along on his monthly visits. She had never given up. She was not one to give up. Auntie Beyaz was an avid TV viewer and radio listener, and she had no patience for any telephone malfunction. Auntie Beyaz had diminished, but not severed, her communication with the outside world. For it was not her habit to give up.

Because of all these reasons, Auntie Beyaz was well aware that a rabid press corps was camped outside her door, scrambling to talk to her. She only watched the summaries of the news on TV, cursed in both English and Turkish, then turned the TV off immediately. She could not stand things that she found false and exaggerated. And this time, the thing that she found false and exaggerated had to do with the one man she ever loved: her father *Ghazi* Sergeant Alican. She was determined to teach these fools a good lesson. As always, she was patiently waiting for the right moment to present itself. She was waiting to teach a good lesson. Her name was Auntie Beyaz and she had gotten everything except the one thing she ever wanted. That one thing, which her mother Meryem prevented, had been her wish to go to school and become a teacher. But Meryem paid for this mistake until the end of her life, at the hand of her own daughter. Because Meryem had not calculated that her daughter, whose education she had stopped to avert her from coming between herself and her husband, would never get married and live with her father until his dying day. The more Meryem regretted her decision the heavier her sentence became, but when she finally realized that the sentence was lifelong, she quietly accepted her fate and submitted to her daughter Beyaz. That moment of submission was Beyaz's first moment of triumph. From then on she always won. And now she needed to teach a good lesson to these cheeky journalists and reporters. It had to be a long-term punishment, the extent of which it would take them years to realize.

Thanks to Auntie Beyaz's calm effort and careful protection, Vicki managed to enjoy these special days without being quite aware of what was happening outside. The issue, as she was permitted to see it, was blithe and agreeable. There were simply a few paparazzi at the door, that was all. And they existed everywhere in the world...

The village elders warned the *Mukhtar* that the publicity created by certain journalists and reporters was disturbing Auntie Beyaz, and he in turn appealed to the gendarmerie. The ruckus and din that prevailed in the village, where the curious had also began flocking, reached a grand scale with the arrival of the gendarmes. The villagers were truly fed up with the situation and wanted to return to their tranquil life as soon as possible. But they did not want their blessed Auntie Beyaz and their favored guest Vicki to come to any harm.

That was when the lawyer from Istanbul appeared on the scene. A young lawyer who came from Istanbul at the height of the turmoil first attracted attention by successfully entering Auntie Beyaz's house. Next he put a stop to things by announcing that on April 24 Auntie Beyaz and Vicki Taylor were going to hold a press conference at the village *kahveh*. The young lawyer took care to emphasize that he was 'Ms. Beyaz's lawyer' and represented her, then explained in a very clear, calm and polite manner that 'legal steps' would be taken 'against anyone who should, before or after the press conference on April 24, stand in front of Auntie Beyaz's house and harass her'. Although some reporters and journalists were put off by having to wait two days until April 24, they nonetheless were glad to have a contact person. Besides, they liked the idea of keeping the issue hot for a few more days, and the high ratings indicated that the public was still interested in the story. Now there was also an added criminal flavor to the story. Furthermore, it seemed that arguing with this young but obviously tough lawyer would not yield much result.

The swarm of media went back home, leaving behind a few reporters and journalists. The villagers breathed a sigh of relief. The chickens and roosters began strutting leisurely around the streets. Meanwhile, a journalist who inquired after the young lawyer's name, punched the following memo into his cell phone screen:

Name of Auntie Beyaz's lawyer: Ali Osman Taylar.

The young lawyer from Istanbul was called Ali Osman Taylar.

No one had noticed this name at the time.

Vicki awoke to rooster crows and the delicious smell of *gozlemes*, which she likened to pancakes, wafting in from the kitchen. She smiled and stretched leisurely. She felt like drinking coffee. Not only that, she yearned to drink coffee. It was one of those rare moments when a person feels such great love for herself and wishes so much to spoil herself that she wants to run into the arms of special people or drown herself in the pleasure of special things that have long been missing from her life. And Vicki longed for coffee more than anything. Since arriving at Gallipoli, she had gotten by on the awful instant nescafe but she had been deprived even of that since moving into Auntie Beyaz's house. Although foreigners assumed that New Zealanders were still devoted to traditional English tea, the new generations there were now serious coffee addicts. And they knew their coffee well.

"Oh if I could only have some fresh plunger coffee, like Indonesian Java, Hawaiian Kona or the smoky, full-bodied Kenyan!" she sighed. But she was happy, and it is easier to be tolerant when one is content. Just then she heard the sharp, repeated crowing of a rooster who obviously held great confidence in his voice. The sound made her laugh. Lounging in her converted sofa bed, she began musing on the rooster who had drowned out and established dominion over all the other roosters outside. Could this possibly be the proud, albino rooster she had seen on her first day in the village? That pretty white rooster who strutted around arrogantly in the streets, not knowing that he was lacking in color? It seemed he did not have the slightest inkling that nature had neglected to add pigment to his feathers, forgotten to paint him, or perhaps even punished him somehow. Lacking that sharp blade called awareness and clueless of his color deficiency, the rooster went about merrily chasing chickens and crowing with assurance. Maybe the happiest rooster in the whole village was this white rooster with the red comb. Unaware and happy.

Vicki suddenly felt the urge to run outside, find the rooster, pick it up and pet it as if it were a cat. She actually wanted to hug and pet a rooster! The urge to pet a rooster, eh?... She smiled. She felt just as happy as the rooster. Something existed, had happened, that made her happy and here she was, a warm sensation spreading through her body like melted chocolate. She curled up like a sunwarmed cat, drew the blanket around her and smiled as though she were petting the rooster. But a voice inside her warned: 'A rooster has no consciousness!' And that is why the rooster is happy!

"Consciousness!" she cried, as though stung. "Consciousness, which informs, consciousness, which reminds, consciousness, which brings pain!"

She sighed. Her body, which had slackened like a ripe fruit, grew as taut as the stone in a fruit. She felt a tickle in her nose. She tried to sneeze, but couldn't.

"Last night…" she whispered to herself. "The things I heard last night weren't a dream. I didn't invent the things that Auntie Beyaz told last night."

She had not invented them. The things Auntie Beyaz had told the night before had come from Auntie Beyaz's lips. They were true.

"Oh my God, it was all true!"

She took a deep breath and held it in. She pulled the covers up to her nose and started thinking. The relaxed and easy expression that had appeared on her face as she thought of the albino rooster had completely vanished.

"Was it really true?"

Had the mystery that she had carried everywhere in her body and soul all her life, that she had guarded as a somewhat fantastic story and exceptional family treasure, finally been solved? Was it over and done with? Could the fantasy that had given pause to someone from each new generation of family members since Aunt Helen be revealed as completely true? Could everything have fallen into place so flawlessly?

Was it possible? Could it be? How convincing was it for an eighty-five year-old puzzle to be solved so perfectly, in a single stroke? Was it not only in movies and detective novels that such perfect denouements existed? In real life, nothing was or could be perfect.

She heaved another deep breath. She swallowed. But it didn't work. She panicked, as though she were unable to breathe. She wanted to sneeze. But that didn't work either.

"The rooster is not conscious and the rooster is happy!" she cried. She pulled the covers completely over her head and hid beneath them.

"Did you say something, *mari*? Come on, time to get up. It's morning time, Vicki *Hanim*, my girl."

Auntie Beyaz looked infinitely calm, content and beautiful as she waddled into the living room carrying steaming *gozleme*s filled with homemade cheese. Indeed, she looked beautiful.

This old woman woke at dawn every morning, performed her ablutions with cold water regardless of the season, picked up her ever present prayer beads and sat down to pray on her red prayer mat, which was embroidered with a depiction of the Blue Mosque. Vicki had learned from her that Turkish Moslems said their prayers in Arabic, which was a language foreign to them, and that when they grew old, they were permitted to pray while sitting down. She had observed that at the end of her prayer, Auntie Beyaz quietly blew the holy words into the air and dispersed a positive energy all around her. She had personally witnessed this while sitting next to her, Auntie Beyaz, her great-aunt.

"Dear God, she is my great-aunt!" trembled Vicki.

Auntie Beyaz set down the tray on the table. Besides the scrumptious *gozleme*s, the tray contained olive oil spiked with cayenne pepper and homemade tomato paste, homemade feta cheese, strawberry and rose petal jam from the garden, black olives, cracked green olives, and the tastiest tomatoes and cucumbers in the world.

"See now, you'll fancy these because they're all *organic*!" ribbed Auntie Beyaz. "When the apricots grow ripe, Havva will fix us some nice *organic* apricot jam."

Vicki did not notice the mocking tone in her voice. Her longing for coffee had grown even more powerful upon seeing the marvelously appetizing, fresh and organic breakfast. She could almost smell the coffee now.

"Oh if only we could have coffee instead of tea this morning..." she murmured.

"My late father liked to have coffee in the morning, same as you. But he liked his bitter... During the war, and during the military rule - the *Pasha*s had taken over in 1980, but you wouldn't know - coffee was mighty scarce. My mother ground chickpeas in a mortar and served it to him as coffee. Father drank that bland, scentless coffee without a word of protest. He never complained. But he didn't like it. I knew right away, I could tell with one look what father liked and didn't like…"

"Good idea, Auntie Beyaz, that's what I'll have this morning: black Turkish coffee!" Vicki exclaimed and jumped out of bed. "Just like your father…" she added and gave a meaningful laugh.

Auntie Beyaz was busy smacking her lips and adjusting her dentures, and she missed Vicki's final allusive remark. She had not worn her headscarf this morning and her snow-white hair was pinned in two braids behind her head.

"Be a dear and bring me that *marama, hele*, my girl."

Vicki had learned that '*marama*' meant a headscarf. And '*ferajeh*' was what Auntie Beyaz called slippers.

Soon they sat down to breakfast, one sipping her tea and the other enjoying her black Turkish coffee. Auntie Beyaz gave Vicki a sympathetic look and said: "Look here, my girl, we ought to get you some of that, what's it called, Nescafé or something. This Turkish coffee of ours is strong, not like your watery stuff – it'll hurt you if you drink too much."

This was the third time. Auntie Beyaz had referred to Vicki as 'my girl' for the third time. My girl: this was a warm and affectionate form of address in every culture in the world. Or, so Vicki believed. Besides, there was now an important reason for it to be true.

Vicki opened her mouth to inform Auntie Beyaz that she wanted to call Mehmet and have him bring a jar of instant coffee, but instead she found herself saying:

"Auntie Beyaz, I wonder if your father ever went to visit Ali Osman *Bey*'s family, since he saved his life after all."

She covered her mouth in surprise, but it was too late; she had unexpectedly blurted out the question, which she had be-

en planning to pose at a suitable moment, after a suitable int-
roduction. She waited anxiously, afraid that she might have offended and angered Auntie Beyaz. Meanwhile she berated herself, thinking 'oh that blasted conscious and subconscious!'

Auntie Beyaz carefully placed the *marama* on her head, took a sip of her tea and replied matter of factly:

"You bet he went to visit. He would go every year, in fact.
First he went and found Ali Osman *Bey*'s mother, Semahat *Hanimefendi*,* and his brother Salih. In the years afterwards they
hosted him in Istanbul for a week every summer. After the Re-
public was formed, they came often to Gallipoli, they became
our relatives from Istanbul. And a good sort they were, a
mighty good sort. No better than you of course…"

"Well, this is going too far!" thought Vicki angrily. "This is
simply going too far!"

Either this woman was not aware of what she was saying,
or she was a master storyteller. The first comparison that
sprang to her mind was the One Thousand and One Nights tales, which she had read while doing postgraduate studies in
psychology back home in New Zealand. She was reminded
particularly of the Arabian princess Scheherazade, who invented a new tale every night to escape execution. Scheherazade
was now posing as a woman called Auntie Beyaz in Gallipoli
and playing games with Vicki. Come to think of it, a woman of
this age could well be senile, or suffering from Alzheimer's Disease. Alzheimer patients have trouble with short-term memory, and the things that Auntie Beyaz related were clear memories left from her childhood. Right, yes, Auntie Beyaz was
suffering from Alzheimer's. Yes, that had to be it.

Yet Vicki found no relief in this explanation. She sighed with
the uneasiness of people who do not believe their own lies.

In truth, Vicki was back to where she had started from. She
grew more upset with Auntie Beyaz each time the old woman

---

*) *Hanimefendi*: Miss, but more formal than *'Hanim'*

opened her mouth to tell the very tales that she had longed to hear. Yes, she felt incensed and found the tales unacceptable. On the other hand, had she not put off her own life in order to hear these things, to receive verification for the wondrous and uniquely personal story of her dreams? Had she not, for years neglected her own life in order to track her great-grandfather's memory, hedged on her secret ambition to start a family of her own, abandoned a young man who had loved her dearly, and received an education in psychology so that she might better understand her great-grandfather? What was the true goal, the true ambition that, at almost thirty years of age, still kept her struggling to solve the mystery of her great-grandfather instead of living her own life? Why did Auntie Beyaz make her angry every time she opened her mouth and confirmed her fancies? Why? Why was Vicki upset when she should have been rejoicing?

"Because my dreams are finally coming true. Because my great-grandfather's secret is not a treasure that only belongs to me anymore. Because I have no reason to delay my life or to hide any longer. And all because of this old woman!" Vicki whispered, terrified.

Good God, was that what she really thought?

The revelation gave her goosebumps. The color left her face. She felt ill.

"What did you say, my girl? What's the matter with you? And look at how little you've eaten! Go on, have some more, or you're bound to stay skinny like that! A woman ought to have some skin on her bones, child!"

Vicki forced herself to eat a few spoonfuls of rose petal jam but when she ground her teeth on the petals, she gave that up as well.

Self-confrontation terrifies a person most of all. This is a terror so deep that even your greatest enemy cannot manage to leave deeper marks. For there is no one left to blame and no shadow left to hide behind. The only cause of the shadow

211

is a person's own body and the things that that body contains.

Here in Gallipoli, at Auntie Beyaz's house, at the age of thirty, it occurred to Vicki for the first time that her father, with whom she had lived until her university years, following her mother's untimely death, might have been telling the truth in his occasional flare-ups. Could her prejudices and obsessions have stultified her soul? Could they have, really? Perhaps it was stultified. Yes, perhaps this was stultification. Could her father have been correct? Perhaps her father really did love her and did not, as Vicki had crossly assumed all these years, derive pleasure from accusing her. Perhaps her father was right and only tried to caution his daughter because he was saddened to see her postponing her life. Perhaps the allegation that she 'avoided confronting her problems by dedicating her life to the mysterious past of a relative', was not so wrong after all... She had avoided love, relationships and life. Had she avoided them? She had evaded her father's affection and many other things in which she feared failure, she had taken refuge in her profession and in the mystery of her great-grandfather. Only psychology and her great-grandfather's secret in Gallipoli... Was it a lie? What else could explain the existence of only these two things in her life of thirty years, and the way she observed life, as a woman and a human being, from a distance? Is that what she had done? Had Vicki really done that? That... yes, that... it seemed she really had done that! And apparently she had had to travel this far, or actually this close, in order to arrive at this truth... Apparently.

A rooster crowed outside. 'The rooster and the conscious,' thought Vicki. A pang went through her heart.

"Go on and fetch me that box from inside that drawer over there!"

Vicki reluctantly walked over to the notorious archive beneath the television set. She felt like a robot. She pulled open the drawer on the stand, took out the tattered carton box and handed it to Auntie Beyaz. Auntie Beyaz put on her scotch-taped glasses and opened the box. It was filled with photographs.

"She can't very well be faking the pictures now, can she?" thought Vicki, gripped once again with terror.

"Now where did that picture go, *mari*?" Auntie Beyaz muttered as she rifled through the black and white photographs in the box. After a long while, she found what she was looking for. "Come see, my girl, come, *hele*."

Feeling like the greatest fool on earth, Vicki unwillingly took the dog-eared photograph that Auntie Beyaz held out for her and stared at it blankly. She stared and stared and could not see anything. Then suddenly her eyes popped open.

The picture was of a very beautiful middle-aged woman and two young men. The mature and elegant lady sat in the middle, wearing a close-fitting black dress in the fashion oi well-heeled European ladies circa 1900. Her dress had a deep chest décolletage, and on her head she wore a black wrap that resembled a hat, it covered her crown and part of her forehead and was tied behind her head. Her dark hair fell down to her neck from under the wrap. An embroidered shawl was draped across her shoulders. Her dark eyes were frozen in a melancholy smile. The woman looked as striking and beautiful as a movie star of the time.

A dark-haired young man, wearing a *fez* and a mustache, stood to the left of the woman. He had a vibrant, proud smile and hugged the woman tenderly with one arm. To the right of the woman stood a very fair, mustached peasant wearing a wool cap. Yes, to the right of the woman... There he was, on her right. It was he! It was Alistair John Taylor, she had memorized all of his photographs and recognized him even though he was dressed as a Turkish peasant, and wore a mustache and a wool cap!

"It's him!" whimpered Vicki. She said it in a quivering, high-pitched voice, and felt faint all over.

"Ah, yes, that's Semahat *Hanimefendi* all right!" Auntie Beyaz replied calmly. "She was fair as the moon, that lady. God rest her soul. She was a magnanimous person, did us many a favor, may she rest in peace."

"But this man is my great-grandfather Alistair John Taylor!" repeated an animated Vicki.

"Indeed... Semahat *Hanimefendi* loved my father very much. Like her own son. Before he died, Ali Osman *Bey* had managed to tell my father, in his flawless French and poor English, the name and address of his mother and willed that he visit them in Istanbul. My father was a man who held his word. He waited five years until his health and his language improved. He only reached Istanbul five years after Ali Osman *Bey* died, *mari*."

Vicki, fixated as she was on the photograph in her hand, was having difficulty following Auntie Beyaz. However impossible, she wanted the fair young man in the picture to see her, to notice her.

"Back then, our Turkey was under occupation, my girl. Those who lived then always told of how hard times were back then. The French and the Greek occupied these parts around here. Istanbul was overrun with the English, Italians and French. I was a wee little girl, I wouldn't remember, but they always told us about it. They still talk of those dark years, of the poverty, the pain, and o the cruelty..." sighed Auntie Beyaz.

Vicki had overlooked the fact that immediately after the Turks won the Gallipoli campaign, Europeans occupied this region. In truth, she had been mostly concerned with her own country's and Europe's history after Gallipoli. Could it be that Auntie Beyaz had her dates mixed up? How could the Turks have lost when they had emerged victorious from that huge war? These thoughts flitted through her mind but she was so immersed in the picture she was holding that she could not concentrate on any other subject.

"If my mother had not worked as day help on farms, we would've gone hungry, my girl. Father was ill; he might function for two days but on the third his mind would desert him, he would go into convulsion fits, run a fever and have to be put raving to bed. The country was under occupation at the time. Each household had an animal or two to its name. We sold some milk but that was all. Ah, my girl, if you only knew!... How these people suffered... May God preserve us from another occupation. May He keep enemy boots from trampling anyone's land, my girl. The occupier is always insolent, he is cruel, he is arrogant."

'The Turks were allied with the Germans, so when the Germans were defeated they were considered defeated as well... The Europeans, who had been trounced into fleeing, returned with treaties and occupied the country. But of course... I say! It must be so disheartening...' thought Vicki in a flash.

"Five years after this, Semahat *Hanimefendi*, God bless her, loses her strapping, educated, handsome elder son to the war, and mind you even his resting place is a mystery, she goes to answer the door and what does she see? Why, *Ghazi* Sergeant Alican, of course! My father. A miracle of God. What did I tell you, *mari*? There's no questioning God's work, no understanding His miracles. Yessir, indeed, and here you are: Just when this woman has given up any hope of receiving word, her son's best friend knocks on her door!"

This was exactly what irked Vicki. Since the very beginning, Auntie Beyaz had been combining fantasy with reality, and playing this dizzying game of melting characters into one another, and Vicki was sick of it, she refused to be disoriented any longer. Why was the old woman still playing these games? Was it not time for her to quit, now that she had told Vicki the truth?

"Ali Osman *Bey*'s best friend?" she protested.

"What do you think? His best friend was the man who remained by his side for two days as he died, the man who sha

215

red with him his water and biscuits, who dug his grave and prayed for him, the man who traveled penniless and mostly on foot to occupied Istanbul to carry out his will, and to provide some comfort for his suffering mother. And that man was my father, *Ghazi* Sergeant Alican! What, that's not good enough for you, Vicki *Hanim*?"

Vicki bowed her head and fell silent. She had angered Auntie Beyaz. For two young men and three characters to meld into one another - was this not a game to the old lady but instead... Did she actually believe it? She raised her head and looked at Auntie Beyaz. The woman was smiling and stroking another photograph that she held in her hand.

"Seems you never had a close friend, Vicki, my girl. One day, when you do, you will know what I mean, *mari*," she said. There was pity and compassion in her voice.

Vicki felt trapped in a lousy triangle of anger, shame and discomfort. These words once again reminded her of her father. The way her father admonished her for running away from life and for taking refuge in the past and in her work. 'Isn't it strange what similar words they use to reproach me... Auntie Beyaz and my dad,' she thought. 'My Aunt Beyaz and my dad!' she amended. 'They're both... they're both, unfortunately, they're both right!'

"When Semahat *Hanim* found my father at the door and learned that he was the friend with whom her beloved child had spent his final hours, she embraced him like her own son. And she loved him until her dying day."

They fell silent. They were both reflecting on the same people, but with different images and different perceptions. Silence fills like a balm the spaces where it is necessary. There was a long silence. A rooster could be heard outside. This surely had to be the white rooster. The White Rooster.

"Father had broken Turkish, he didn't understand it too well. Poor thing suffered from unexpected violent headaches and nausea. Often he would thrash about like knives were goring his stomach, poor man. Semahat *Hanimefendi*'s younger son Salih had become a doctor. He used to examine my father and declare, 'What you have is called melancholia.' A disease of distress, worry, anxiety, that is, something like black love... Nowadays they call it deepiression or something? Why am I telling you this anyway... Aren't you a psychologist, you'd know better than me, *mari*."

Auntie Beyaz suddenly smiled. When stern people smile unexpectedly it usually creates a dangerous excitement. Vicki was startled. But the smile was sincere, uncalculating, and much warmer than one would have expected from Auntie Beyaz. Try as she might, Vicki could not find any ill will behind the smile. It seemed Auntie Beyaz did not bear her any grudges but accepted her as she was, this 'thin, gaunt, pale, friendless, lonely psychologist tourist Zealander woman', who, at thirty, was an old maid by her standards. She accepted her. She simply did. But, then again... did she really?

Vicki smiled back. Yet it was harder for her to accept Auntie Beyaz. It took a longer time and it was painful. It was painful. Yes, it was painful. But in truth it was not the reality of Auntie Beyaz or of Gallipoli that caused her pain. What caused her pain... was not what Vicki experienced here, at a rural house in Gallipoli. No, it was not that. What pained her was confronting life with such proximity, brutality and tardiness. Being able to confront life. And of course, realizing that there were no obstacles left for living her life. But how could Auntie Beyaz know all of that?

Auntie Beyaz shifted her jaw to readjust her dentures. She blinked her blue eyes and peered at Vicki:

"Something's the matter with you today, I just hope it's for the best..." she said.

"I'm alright, Auntie Beyaz. I'm fine, don't you worry about me."

"How can I help but worry, my girl? You're entrusted to us, *mari*. Let's see, maybe we'll come up with something you like before evening and it'll bring color back to your cheeks. Maybe if we invited that rascal Mehmet over, if we found some Nescafé, you'd feel better. Did you miss your country, your parents, or your sweetheart? You're all pale, what's the matter?"

"Entrusted?"

Entrusted by whom, for what? Vicki wanted to ask but was afraid of the reply she might receive.

"Yes indeed... You're entrusted to us, my girl. It's very important around here to return safely what is entrusted to us. My mother, for example, always thought father was entrusted to her. Entrusted by God. And she cared for father above all else, until he was reunited with God. She never broke his heart, except when she stopped me from going to the teacher's college, other than that she always kept him happy. Meryem was a good wife but she was a most uncompassionate, unaffectionate mother. Ah me... Still, what can I say, God rest her soul."

'She thinks I'm entrusted to her until I return to New Zealand. That I won't stay, but go back. She wants me to leave. Of course she would – I've been nothing but trouble since I arrived. Until I got here she was an old lady who lived peacefully, with a fixed routine. An old lady. Just an old lady? Auntie Beyaz? Auntie Beyaz, just an old lady, eh? Come on! She's a unique Gallipoli woman who has managed to gain great standing in men's eyes in a country where women are so looked down on. My great-aunt. My aunt!' Vicki thought quickly.

"My father traveled on foot for days, sometimes rode on wagons with barely a penny in his pocket, and do you know what surprised him the most when he got to Istanbul, my girl?"

"What?" asked Vicki, surprised.

"I was saying that my father, *Ghazi* Sergeant Alican, arrived in Istanbul after a long and arduous trip, and he was mighty

218

surprised. You remember those British ships your great-grandfather saw at Gallipoli, and how they said "First to Constantinople and then the Harems"? Well, the truth was much different. The soldiers had described Istanbul as just past Chunuk Bair, but in truth it was a great deal farther than that... When he arrived in Istanbul, dear old father felt cheated once again. Istanbul – they used to call it Constantinople back in those days, my dad did too, but later he began calling it Istanbul – what a state Istanbul was in! The English, the French and the Italians had divided up the city between themselves. Folks who didn't have permission – what's it called, visa or something – were not allowed to move around the city, to even go from the Bosporus to a neighborhood called Anadolu Feneri... Yes, my girl, do you hear what I'm saying, can you believe what you're hearing? Having to get visa permission from the occupier so you can visit your relative in your own country... It's an outrage is what it is! May God deliver us from the same, may He deliver all peoples from the tyranny of occupation, ah my girl, how hard it was... Ah just think of it... Ah..."

Describing occupied Istanbul, Auntie Beyaz pounded her knees as though she were in pain, and tossed her head from side to side, as though she might die of sorrow. Even someone who did not understand her words might easily have grown angry at the person or situation that caused an old woman this much grief.

"Remember what I said? No matter what the nationality, once the occupying set begins its oppression, it can never get enough. Yes, indeed. In order to humiliate them, this occupying army gave the order that all Ottoman officers must salute an enemy soldier, even if he was below their rank. They just went and made it the law. A law of salutation, you see. My father used to say that so offended were the Turkish officers by this law, that great big majors and colonels took to walking around in civilian clothes, just to avoid having to salute the occupying privates. It was a very demeaning, terrible time. Youth these days don't understand, they take war and occupation to be games. Ah, my girl, what disgrace it is to be enslaved in your own land, to be subjected to another nation!"

All at once, tears began pouring from her blue eyes. The sudden flood of tears left her face drenched. She was too young to remember the occupation, but clearly, her child's heart had carried its profoundly painful and humiliating effect up to the present day. Vicki did not know what to do. Her heart, which melted at the sight of a crying man or child, was completely shattered to witness the tears of such an old woman. She went over to Auntie Beyaz and took the old lady's tiny, snow-white, finely wrinkled hands in her own. She squeezed them gently. This time, Auntie Beyaz did not push her away. For a while, the two women stayed with their sad hands interlocked. They stayed that way for a while in Gallipoli's Eceyaylasi Village.

"My father, my dear late father, used to always tell me of a terrible event he once witnessed on a ferry. He was sitting on the deck of the ferry one day, on his way to Semahat *Hanimefendi*. Right across from him sat a Turkish officer with a non-veiled Moslem lady. Father tried not to stare, but the lady was very beautiful. Just then an enemy soldier who happened to be on deck came up to them and ordered the Turkish officer to stand to attention. The Turkish officer, who was sitting with his wife, replied in fluent French and then in broken English that since his rank was higher, the occupying soldier ought to salute him first. So, the occupying officer whipped the Turkish officer in front of everyone present, but worst of all in front of his wife. You know a whip, that strap they use on animals, that's what he used to strike the higher-ranking officer. Right there, in broad daylight, among everyone present, and in the Turk's own country. Father used to say: 'That was the most humiliating day of my life. But it was also the day when I felt the most Turkish.' Although his crying and screaming wife tried to restrain him, the Turkish officer could not help but slap the occupying soldier in return. A big fight ensued, and the Turkish officer was arrested and thrown into the dungeons. Who knows what tortures they inflicted on the poor man in there.

"Whenever father told this story he would always add: 'The Turks are a very proud people. What makes the Turks strong is the fact that they have never been ruled – or, what do you call it? – colonized, yes colonized by any other nation. The Turks' greatest asset is their defiant, entrepreneurial and passionate character. Turks can never accept or endure second-class status. The triumphant spirit of the National War of Independence sprang from the passion in the hearts of these people. They will never be released of that passion's grip.' Ah me! May he rest in peace, father always loved this nation and always trusted its people, my girl."

Maybe Vicki would understand after all. Yes, maybe she would understand her great-grandfather and Auntie Beyaz. Because maybe... Who knows, maybe if she had been there, in her great-grandfather's or Auntie Beyaz's shoes, back in those days, under those conditions, suffering so much oppression and injustice at the age of twenty... Yes, why not? Maybe they were all correct: her great-grandfather, Ali Osman *Bey*, who saved him twice from death, *Ghazi* Sergeant Alican, and of course, Mother Meryem and Auntie Beyaz. Maybe she was the one being unfair, one-dimensional, and bigoted by insisting on a single, official viewpoint for everything and for history, which is a part of everything. Yes, maybe so. Yes, maybe she would start to understand. Maybe it was time for her to begin understanding the excellent lesson that two young men taught humanity, here, in Gallipoli, eighty-five years ago.

"Them Chinese, and them Africans who dress like Frenchmen, what nationality are they?"

"Excuse me?"

"I asked what nationality were them Africans who dressed like Frenchmen, *mari*."

"They must be Senegalese," Vicki offered.

"Yea, I suppose that's it. Let's see, also Indians dressed up like Englishfolk, it's said that they all used to strut arrogantly around Istanbul. Basically, those who donned their masters' clothes in turn became masters of our Istanbul. Maybe this was why father always returned from occupied Istanbul in a worse state, because this stabbed at his own wounds."

Those visits the wounded young man, the ill and foreign young man made to Istanbul during those turbulent years of occupation. Those visits he paid to the family of an enemy soldier who, as he lay dying in his arms, gave him a brand new chance at life. Who knows what brutal contradictions, what profound states of inclusion and alienation he experienced during those harrowing visits... Who knows how much strain, suffering and alienation he felt, what acute internal traumas he went through... It was hard to imagine, sitting here comfortably in Gallipoli eighty-five years later, but the thought was enough to send shudders down one's spine.

"Semahat *Hanimefendi* used to host my father at the mansion in Fatih. In those days, Fatih was occupied by the French. Father had to obtain a visa to visit Fatih. The occupiers at the passport office used to harass and denigrate father. He used to say 'Even them soldiers were sick of their job. Whereas French soldiers in other places had been discharged and had returned home, after many years of fighting, the French in Turkey were still on duty, and it drove them crazy.' And what was their duty? Why, occupying, of course! But the following year, those Moslems from *Maghreb*,* those Africans came to work at the passport office. Tell me, what were they called?"

"Moslem Africans? Well, if it was French colonies, it'd have to be Tunisia or Algeria."

---

*) *Maghreb*: north-west Africa

"Yes, that's it, bless you, my girl. The Algerians, of course. That's just what my father used to say. Well, those people worked at the passport office the following year and they gave father a Fatih visa without any trouble at all!"

'Small world,' thought Vicki.

"Now, Uskudar was occupied by the Italians. But it was easier to get visas there, and to visit the mansion at Beylerbeyi. Father used to say: 'The Italians were annoyed at the dominance of the English and the French so they went easy on the Turks.'

"At the time, Semahat *Hanimefendi*'s younger son, Salih *Bey*, was keen on joining the independence movement in Anatolia. Tell me, how can a mother's heart bear to send her younger son to Anatolia when she has lost her elder son at the Dardanelles? Her only relative, her only family left in the world, the final remembrance of her husband and her son Ali Osman? Yet Semahat *Hanimefendi* checked her sorrow and both allowed and supported Salih *Bey*'s joining the National Independence Movement. Ah, my girl, if you only knew the sacrifices this country made to end the occupation, and earn its independence! Even if I told you, you wouldn't understand..."

Vicki had let go of Auntie Beyaz's hands, but she remained close. To sit near her fennel-scented figure, to hear her tell a fairy tale in which Vicki intimately knew one of the protagonists created the sense of a live broadcast, despite the eighty-five years that had elapsed.

"I understand when you tell it, Auntie Beyaz," she said, looking straight into her eyes.

"Bah, she understands! Tell that to my hat. You young people have never known hunger or poverty, you've never known scarcity or destitution or war. You have no idea how cruel the enemy boot is!"

"True. You're right. I hope that the generations to come don't find out," nodded Vicki. Her voice contained a dejected gloom.

Auntie Beyaz sighed, at a loss for something else to say.

"God have mercy... Knows an awful lot, doesn't she..." she muttered.

Then she suddenly grew animated and added:

"Oh, in all fairness, I left something out. After Semahat *Hanimefendi* met my father, she is supposed to have said: 'From now on, I have two living sons. Salih and yourself. You will be equal in my eyes until the day I die.'"

Once more, she began rifling through the box filled with old photographs.

"Truly, Semahat *Hanimefendi*, may she rest in peace, loved my father like a son, and us like her own grandchildren. Every year father returned from Istanbul, he brought us ruffled dresses, embroidered sweaters, candies and bonbons individually wrapped in colorful cellophane, and lots of books. He would say 'Ali Osman *Bey*'s mother sent you these.' My mother would wear the dresses and store the food in the cellar without a word of protest. Semahat *Hanimefendi* also brought the first chocolate I ever tasted, when she came to pay us a visit. It was very delicious chocolate, Nestlé brand. I've eaten many a chocolate ever since but never found any that tasted like the one Semahat *Hanimefendi* brought us when I was little..."

Auntie Beyaz smacked her tongue and swallowed, as though she could still taste the chocolate. Then she adjusted her dentures with that familiar motion of her jaw. Vicki also felt her mouth water. Maybe Mehmet could bring a bar of chocolate along with the instant coffee? The good kind, though. All at once she remembered the savor of chocolates she had eaten as a child. The chocolates one ate as a child were really something entirely different. Did this have to do with a child's sense of taste or was it a nostalgic illusion caused by the innocence that childhood represented? As a psychologist, she always explained childhood tastes through psychological factors but this time she decided to contemplate the issue from a physiological standpoint. Yes, there could well be a physiological explanation why the chocolate that people consumed during childhood remained in their memory as the sweetest of tastes.

"My mother?" Auntie Beyaz forged ahead with her story. "Of course my mother did not like Semahat *Hanimefendi*. Because she did not, could not like anyone except my father, *mari*! But she was not opposed to her. Maybe because she understood from the outset that she held no sway over father on this issue. She was a smart woman, my mother!"

She resumed her search in the box of photographs. She clearly had one particular picture in mind, and she would not rest until she found it.

"You know what, Vicki, my girl?" she asked, out of the blue. "My father spoke a great deal about Semahat *Hanimefendi*'s mansion at Beylerbeyi. He used to talk admiringly of how refined and genteel the Ottomans were, but for some reason the thing I remember most clearly is the nightingale..."

"The nightingale?" echoed a startled Vicki.

"That's right, my girl, the nightingale. Although father used to say of his first visit to Semahat *Hanimefendi*'s mansion: 'I saw traces of taste and sophistication, despite those times of war and scarcity,' he spoke most magically of the moment he saw that caged nightingale. He never tired of retelling that moment, like a fairy tale, and he always had me spellbound, listening with rapt attention."

"What a coincidence, the nightingales of Gallipoli play a large part in my great-grandfather's letters as well..." remarked Vicki, with a smile.

"Nothing in life is a coincidence, Vicki *Hanim*! It's high time you opened your eyes!" Auntie Beyaz suddenly snapped.

Vicki was taken aback. She did not understand what she had said to anger Auntie Beyaz. She really did not. There was just no telling with this old woman.

"It's not like Ali Osman *Bey* did not write any other letters to his mother than the three he kept to spare her from grief! The ones he did send were those that did not contain distressing news, and among them he had mentioned the nightingales of Gallipoli. So, aiming to please her son, Semahat *Hanimefendi* had a nightingale brought in and caged while it was still young, the way he had prescribed. A mated, adult nightingale won't live in a cage, it'll die in no time, *mari*. Even a golden cage won't contain the adult nightingale. For it has gotten a taste of freedom... Freedom is like fresh air. It is necessary for everyone, at all times. Ah, my girl... Be it man or bird, any creature deprived of its freedom is bound to die gradually. Because polluted air makes a man ill, you know, cancer and all that, it's all due to pollution, you can't withstand it, you die. Pollution is dangerous. Any kind of it is mighty dangerous."

"Freedom is like fresh air. It is necessary for everyone at all times!" repeated Vicki. She liked that. This old lady was a philosopher. This old lady, Auntie Beyaz, was her own great-aunt and she was simply fantastic!

"Father started crying when he saw the nightingale. What could he do, the poor soul couldn't help himself. The nightingale must have reminded him of the war, of his friends, brother and hopes, which all perished in the war. Most of all it must have been his lost dreams, his youth, and his stolen future that hit the poor man. The nightingale was just an excuse... Semahat *Hanimefendi* panicked when she saw him cry. She began talking about the nightingale. The more she talked, the more father was relieved, the more she said, the more he felt soothed. When he returned to Gallipoli, he had brought along many books about nightingales. But the poor dear never could read them, since they were either in Ottoman or in French."

"Books about nightingales? Interesting. That means there really is something special about these birds."

"But of course, my Zealander girl! Semahat *Hanimefendi* told my father all about it. The nightingale was a most important bird in Ottoman court poetry. It was called *Divan* Literature at the time, but naturally, you wouldn't know that, how could you?"

"Ottoman Literature?" mused Vicki.

"Yes, you go right ahead and gawk, I don't know when that curtain's going to be lifted from your eyes, *mari*. Are you going to listen to me or are you just going to sit there and gawk, make up your mind, *hele*."

"Oh no, Auntie Beyaz, I just..."

"You also need to learn about the new Turkish Literature but I'm too old for all that. Someone else can inform you."

"No, please, do go on Auntie Beyaz, do. You're right, you're completely right. There is definitely a blindness at issue here. Agreed. But please, I beg you, keep telling me."

"Well, Semahat *Hanimefendi* used to talk very slowly, and even partly in French, so that father could understand. Afterwards, when father began reading modern Turkish, he brought over many books about nightingales from Istanbul, you can see them on the bookshelf in my room... But you don't understand Turkish, eh? Anyway, you go find some in your own language, what do I care?"

"Auntie Beyaz, please..."

"Oh alright... Now, this is what Semahat *Hanimefendi* said: The nightingale had a great place in Ottoman poetry. Old time poets used to compare the nightingale's song to the weeping of lovers separated from their loved ones, or to the exhilaration of lovers singing courting songs. The rose and the nightingale were considered symbols of love. There was a very strong conviction that the nightingale was in love with the rose, which, in my opinion is true. For nightingales sing their loveliest songs when they perch on the branches of rosebushes. Did you know that, *hele*? If you should ask why, well, it's God's

227

own doing, so there must be a reason. Clearly, the complex scent of the rose seduces and captivates the nightingale. And if that's not what they call love, than what is, Vicki *Hanim*? How could you call someone a lover who is not seduced by his beloved's scent?"

'You old rascal,' thought Vicki and smiled, but upon realizing that even this old, never-married woman had captured the essence of love, she felt crushed. She herself was a young woman who had run and hidden from love, and facing this fact made her weary.

"The nightingale was so in love with the rose that he cried and wailed, knowing that she was bound to wither and die, and he sang his most beautiful, most heartbreaking songs for her. And because the rosebud heard the pleading melody of the nightingale, because she heard his sleepless entreaties on behalf of his love, she would unfold into a rose come dawn. Yet every love brings with it suffering. This, beyond a doubt. The rose is lovely indeed, and yet it is filled with thorns. And the thorns pierce the nightingale's heart, and bleed him ceaselessly. That is always just how it is, my girl, so you know."

She stopped speaking, seemed to scan about for something with her eyes, then began humming in a small, childlike voice:

"Nightingale fell for a rose... She feigns shyness to unclose..."

Then, still like a child, she grew embarrassed, blushed and fell silent.

"Keep singing a bit more, Auntie Beyaz. You have a lovely voice."

"Oh, stop it! The aged wolf becomes a laughing stock for the dogs!" she grumbled.

She was upset again. But she seemed to calm down just as quickly as she flared up. Vicki waited. 'I guess every country has a different animal that becomes a laughing stock in old age,' she mulled, and smiled once more.

"What was I saying? Oh yes, when the old time poets – they were called *Divan* poets – wanted to praise the beauty of their beloved, they always chose the nightingale and spoke through his voice. As well, a person's heart, beating within his chest, was likened to a lovelorn nightingale trapped in a cage, and these poems described the vain struggles of both. See now, there's also the mystic poets, though you'd know them as *Sufis**. Semahat *Hanimefendi* often read their poetry to father on his visits."

"I know about the *Sufis*. Also, about the great poet Rumi. But he wasn't Turkish, he was Persian."

"God have mercy, see what ignorance does to people. Oh my silly girl, in Mevlana Rumi's time everyone who lived within the Empire was considered Ottoman. And everything that was Ottoman belonged to here," reproached Auntie Beyaz.

"So, you're saying that Rumi was an Ottoman?"

"Will you just listen to that question! If you want to understand the past, you must learn the rules of the past. Or you simply stand there gaping, and watch it go by... The way you're doing now."

This time Vicki did not give in to her anger. True, she was put off but she had understood that when Auntie Beyaz said "Back then, everything that was Ottoman belonged to here," she was expressing an authentic-collective concept of 'belonging'. Yes, she had begun to understand...

"Go on over to my bedroom. On the bookshelf, among the old volumes, on the second shelf from the left, I think, there should be a thin book of poetry that says 'Ahmet Hashim'. Find it and bring it over to me."

"What does it say?"

"Ah-met Ha-shim!"

"OK, I'll be right back!"

---

*) *Sufi*: adherent of a mystical group within Islam

Vicki was entering Auntie Beyaz's bedroom for the first time. She barged in excitedly. And was startled to see the books in the bookshelf by the old woman's bed. This was truly unexpected.

"Are these all your books, Auntie Beyaz?" she called out in surprise.

"Whose else? Those were left to me from my father, Semahat *Hanimefendi* and even from Ali Osman *Bey*. My Istanbulite grandson brings the new ones. My mother kept me from school but my late father always brought me books. He listened to me read the ones in Turkish. I listened to him read the ones in English. But I can't read the way I used to anymore. I grow tired, I can't see well, I can't concentrate… It's old age, my girl, what can you do?"

"I can't find it Auntie Beyaz, what did you say it was called?"

"Ahmet Hashim! Hold on, let me come see, *hele*."

She got up, dragged her feet and waddled over to the bedroom. She picked out the book immediately and returned to the living room. She was out of breath. She sat down in her armchair, put on her scotch-taped glasses, flipped open the book of poetry and this time, read out loud in Turkish.

"Egilmis arza kanar, mutassil kanar guller/ Durur alev gibi dallarda kanli bulbuller." *

"So?"

"So, nothing. That's the poem."

"Will you explain it a little, please, Auntie Beyaz?"

"Now, that's hard. You can't explain a poem… Maybe I can tell you the meaning? That's hard too, but let me try, *hele*. Now, the rose has an enchanting smell and a crimson charm, but don't forget that the same rose carries very dangerous, sharp thorns on her branches. They are so sharp, so slender that if they prick you, ah great God above! So, the poet says;

---

*) Bleeding, the roses bend toward the earth, bleeding ceaselessly/ Like flames, the bloody nightingales, perch upon the branches.

230

the rose's thorns pierce the nightingale's heart/ thus the nightingales bleed like flames upon her branches, singing the cost
of their love... Will you just listen to it: *'Egilmis arza kanar, mutassil kanar guller/ Durur alev gibi dallarda kanli bulbuller.'*
What a mighty poet, how well he puts it..."

Vicki was spellbound. She waited without speaking.

"But then again, the same poem can also be understood
this way: The roses bleed ceaselessly, meaning the roses are
blood red/ burning in the flames of desire, the blood-soaked
nightingales wait upon their branches. You savvy, *mari*? See,
the nightingales have been stained by the crimson color of the
roses, which bleed with love... You take whatever explanation, interpretation you like, that's it from me."

"Gee... It's such a striking metaphor! Blood, love, the color
red, the rose and the nightingale... A great and dangerous passion. Like the passion of the French, and also the Spanish..."

She paused and considered,

"Why, Mediterranean passion, of course," she concluded.

Without paying any attention to her, Auntie Beyaz put
down the book of poetry and resumed rifling through the photograph box, as though nothing had happened. She drew out
a picture from the box, smacked her gums to reposition her
dentures and gazed at the photograph.

"Remember what I told you, this Semahat *Hanimefendi* was
a great and fine person. She remained that way until the day
she died, she always watched over us. She took Bulut, my younger brother, to Istanbul, had him schooled there at boarding schools, "*leyli*" they used to call them at the time, raised
him in her own home, and found him a match. All of his children and grandchildren stayed in Istanbul, they became natives
of the place. And as she was dying, she entrusted us to the care of her doctor son Salih *Bey*. May God grant her abundant
peace. She was a grand woman, here, take another look at this
blessed soul."

Vicki took the black and white picture that Auntie Beyaz held out to her. This time she immediately recognized a younger Semahat *Hanimefendi*, dressed in a fine suit and reclining in the leather armchair of a photographer's studio in all her majesty and beauty. On her left stood a mischievous-looking little boy with dark eyes, who was tugging at his mother's skirt with one hand. On Semahat *Hanimefendi*'s right was a handsome young man with a gentle smile and a shy gaze, who seemed impatient to get the picture over and done with. Semahat *Hanimefendi* held this young man's arm gripped firmly in one hand. Very firmly.

"Is that him?" Vicki asked timidly.

"Yep. Who else could it be, *mari*? This here handsome young fellow is my father's closest friend Ali Osman *Bey*. Lieutenant Ali Osman *Bey*, Gallipoli war hero. He was killed three years after this picture was taken. Don't you recognize him?"

Vicki had recognized him. She had finally begun to recognize. Yes, she had begun to recognize. She was well on her way.

"It's important to recognize great and fine people, my girl. The only way a person can understand why scoundrels have not completely taken over the world is if he meets grand and wise people. But they are hard to find. Mighty and wise people don't just wander about. They wait by the sidelines until the time comes to perform their duties, then they disappear again. In order to know and recognize these people, sometimes it is necessary to come all the way here from the ends of the earth, to make the effort, my girl. My lovely, clever girl. My girl Vicki."

Auntie Beyaz's final words came and hovered before Vicki. The words hovered in the air like a stenciled sign. Vicki saw them. She saw Auntie Beyaz's words, suspended in the air. The words broke up into letters, the letters began swirling and dancing around one another. It was an inviting dance. Vic-

232

ki could not help herself, she got up and threw her arms aro-
und Auntie Beyaz's neck. This time, she did not rebuff her.
She hugged Vicki back. She hugged her. Auntie Beyaz hugged
Vicki.

She would not answer the phone immediately.

Auntie Beyaz would not answer the phone immediately. When the phone rang, she would waddle over to it and stand there, waiting. It would ring once and stop. Then, it would ring twice and stop again. On the third time, it would ring thrice. Auntie Beyaz would finally pick up the receiver on the fourth call. In the course of her weeklong residence at the house, Vicki had long figured out that this was a code.

"My darling son, apple of my eye, how are you, *mari*?"

Instead of saying 'hello' or 'who is it?', this, invariably, was how Auntie Beyaz would answer the phone. Vicki pushed and pleaded and finally learned what Auntie Beyaz was saying in

Turkish. But to whom was she saying these words? Then there was the light of bliss that came over her face as she spoke to this mysterious person. The woman actually glowed. But she would not tell her. She refused to say. The object of these enigmatic conversations remained a secret. Once she made up her mind, there was no way to get her to speak. Because she is incredibly stubborn. As stubborn as they come! Vicki thought she must have taken after her mother Meryem, but what about Aunt Helen? She was no pushover either... Now that Vicki was dying of curiosity, she would never reveal the recipient of her honeyed phrases. Also, why did she cover the receiver with her hand, as though Vicki could understand Turkish, why did she act so sneaky and mysterious?... If she were a little younger, Vicki might think she had a lover...But then again, who knows? This was Auntie Beyaz. A character unto herself. An inimitable woman!

"Vicki *Hanim*, that rascally Mehmet of yours called this morning – he bought you a jar of instant coffee and lots of chocolate. The rogue's supposed to bring them over soon. But mind you, don't open the door without first asking who it is. It could be those no-good newspapermen, and I simply have no patience for them."

Vicki laughed. This Auntie Beyaz was really something. She could be everywhere at once, she could solve anyone's problems, as well as manage everyone. Even during such a turbulent and emotionally difficult time, she had not forgotten about Vicki's coffee and chocolate.

"History, sacrifice, courage... They don't care, *mari*! Only thing they're after is charlatanism and money! See here, if you so much as say a word about my father to those newspaper and TV crews, you will not get my blessings – I will not give up my right over you and I will hound you in both worlds! Don't you forget: my father was a hero. Make sure you know that, *hele*. My father did not do anything wrong. God bless his soul!"

Yes. Her father was a true hero and Vicki had heartily embraced this as fact.

She was looking through the kitchen for the stomach pills she took every morning, and talking to Vicki over her shoulder. She stopped. She turned around and threw Vicki a measuring glance.

"I wouldn't be able to curse a girl like you though, *mari*, I wouldn't have the heart for it… Because my curses work, they would even work all the way over in Zealand. They would work all right. But no, I have foresworn it, I've sworn never to plant a curse, *mari*…"

She heard the sudden softening of her voice and it displeased her. She straightened her shrunken, hunched figure, and replaced the familiar, defiant tone into her voice.

"But you would better not say a word about my late father to anyone, you hear me?" she warned.

'To refuse to give up one's right?' Vicki wondered. Besides, what kind of right could she have on Vicki? The young woman chewed over the question in her mind, but could not find an answer. Then she began thinking about the issue of 'both worlds'.

"I will hound you in both worlds," Auntie Beyaz had said.

Two worlds: Eastern and Western civilization? Two worlds: did they represent North and South or good and evil? She could not say for sure. This had to be some sort of ethnic concept. "What are both worlds, Auntie Beyaz?"

"Eh? What did you say, *mari*? Now, where did my blasted medicine go?"

"Remember, you said 'I'll hound you in both worlds'… Which two worlds?"

"Girl, you are just too much sometimes! What're we going to do with you?" laughed Auntie Beyaz.

When she laughed, sparkles shot from her deep blue eyes; when she laughed, her uniqueness broke its mask of anonymity; when she laughed, her wrinkled face, etched with thousands of elaborate lines and white as if it were caked with dozens of layers of powder, glowed; when she laughed, Auntie Beyaz became beautiful. Auntie Beyaz turned into a beautiful old woman when she laughed.

It is hard to be a beautiful woman when you are old. It is very hard. It is the hardest. Nonetheless... it was apparently possible. Being a beautiful old woman was as difficult as carrying out an individual act of defiance against a world where many cultures considered beauty to be the sole property of young women, where they allowed it at most a twenty-year life span, and where the effects of gravity seemed only to apply to the female of the species. It was difficult, but not impossible. And here it was, in the flesh. Some women could age beautifully, and they could still remain lovely, mischievous and attractive in their later years. This is what Auntie Beyaz had taught Vicki.

As Auntie Beyaz laughed through every cell, Vicki mused on what a lovely and amazing woman she was. She observed her with tenderness, with a warm amity, with genuine admiration and a sincere feeling of empathy; she caressed her with her eyes. Vicki smiled at her. And at that instant she understood what she had meant when she said, "I will not give up my right over you." She understood suddenly, right then and there.

A spiritual claim developed between people who truly loved, protected and cared for one another, and this was simply a 'love right'. Natural and intrinsic. Yes. Although it held no mass or mention in physics or law books, such a right existed in this country. Vicki had personally and almost tangibly felt it here, toward an old woman whom she had barely known for three weeks. Perhaps only people who belonged here deserved this expression, since it was only in this culture that such a love right was allowed to exist. Because in New Zealand, the same expression, 'I will not give up my right over you', would be perceived as possessive, restrictive and a violation of per-

237

sonal space, and would be rejected immediately and never be allowed to exist. And it never had existed. But it was different here. It had been sheltered here for centuries, between the sun and the soil, without being a burden on anyone, and it conferred abundance to these people's spirits. Just like fruit and vegetables, concepts and emotions also grew and flourished in different cultural geographies. As with love and the love right... The right mentioned in 'I will not give up my right' must have been this unratified, uncodified, but humanitarian right. And that is why Auntie Beyaz had to give up her love right upon her. She absolutely had to. Vicki wanted this.

"Oh dear me, girl. God bless your soul! Hah hah ha... Making me laugh... Are you an unbeliever or something? But no, in order to be an unbeliever you must first have a religion and then disown it, right, isn't/that so? Haven't you ever heard of the next world, then?" asked Auntie Beyaz, as she continued to laugh.

'So, the next world is a religious concept, not a political one,' thought Vicki.

"You know, the world where we'll all go after we die, my girl! You know, that next world where man will not be separated as English, French, Zealander or Turk but only as good or evil before the Almighty!"

"Oh, right, that business!" sighed Vicki.

"Yes indeed, that business!" said Auntie Beyaz, rocking her head back and forth. "That very business! Oh good, here's my medicine. Look where the scoundrel hid itself. Vicki, my girl, hand me a cup of water. Get a clean cup from that dishwasher over there, but give it a rinse first. If you drink the water straight, it gets foamy, this machine doesn't rinse the cups and saucers very well. After all, it's a machine! Just a machine! My grandson from Istanbul, bless his soul, brings me these machines and tries to tell me how to use them, but they're just machines after all!"

"Your father, Auntie Beyaz," Vicki started saying.

"My father, *Ghazi* Sergeant Alican!" Auntie Beyaz interrupted after she swallowed her medicine.

"Yes, your father, Gha-zi Sergeant Ah-lee-jon," said Vicki, pronouncing his name *for the first time.*

"There you go," said Auntie Beyaz, nodding in approval.

"Was your father a religious man, Auntie Beyaz? I mean... Had the horrible war and the incredible disasters that befell him, and his second life, which was so different from his first, made him into a religious man?"

"My father was a devout man. He believed in God and thanked Him for granting him a new life and family. My father lived and died as a devout man. May he rest in peace."

"Auntie Beyaz!"

"What?"

"You know what..."

"No indeed, I do not."

"You know, but you're just being stubborn. But remember, I'm also stubborn, I take after you."

Auntie Beyaz laughed. She shook her head.

"You've turned out rather toothful, haven't you?"

"Toothful?"

Auntie Beyaz translated Turkish expressions into English literally, and it was taxing for Vicki.

"Means you are willful."

"Oh... it doesn't help, though..."

"Oh, it doesn't help, does it?... Liar... My father did not like to pray in Arabic at all. He prayed in Turkish. My mother had taught him how to perform his ablutions and prayers. But he did not visit the mosque five times a day either. 'Work is the best form of worship,' he used to tell the villagers. But sometimes, when he felt like it, he would go to the mosque, sit on the carpet, pray quietly and bare his soul to God. No one could know what it was that he wished for, or gave thanks to,

239

but they could guess. Ah, my dear old dad! He loved to count prayer beads, see these here, they used to belong to him, they are a keepsake," so saying, she lovingly stroked the agate beads that never left her clutch.

"But for some reason he was terribly fond of the prayers which preceded religious feasts. Especially the Feast of the Sacrifice... Because he hated performing the sacrifice of sheep or alike. During the Feast of the Sacrifice he would dally forever after prayers and do his best to delay coming home. And when he did come home, he would fall sick. Of course, this was in later years, when we had enough money to afford a sacrifice. So, mother would have to take up the knife and sacrifice the sheep herself. Meryem, daughter of Hasan the Circumciser!"

Vicki cringed in disgust.

"What's that face for? You don't mind eating the meatballs and hamburgers!"

She opened the refrigerator.

"Are you hungry, *hele*? Maybe you'd like some meatballs. Here, let me just give Havva a ring..."

"No, Auntie Beyaz, remember, I'm a vegetarian!"

"Oh yes, you don't eat meat. Then they can get you some fish, *mari*. You did eat that, didn't you? Hmm? If only these newspapermen would just go away, I could get some wonderful fish for you, but..."

"I'm fine, really, I'm perfectly fine. You look after me like a princess, Auntie Beyaz. Umm, no, not a princess, a sultana... Thank you. Besides, I eat plenty of fish back home, nevermind the fish... What? Why are you looking at me that way?"

"Girl, have you put on weight or something? Let me have a look at you, why, I swear you've got some color in your cheeks, and you're rounding out nicely. Good for you *mari*, you're starting to look like a woman. Whoever heard of a woman being so skinny, without any boobs or a bottom? See here, once I get done feeding you, all the menfolk will be after you..."

"Oh come off it, Auntie Beyaz, do stop pestering me. I haven't gained any weight, it's just that these *shalvar* pants make me look heavier," said Vicki, surprised to feel herself blushing.

"*Shalvar* indeed! Tell that to my hat! When you first got here that *shalvar* looked something awful, like it was covering a stick... *Shalvar* indeed! What a know-it-all *mari*!... God have mercy... Hand me another glass of water, I'm mighty thirsty. I must have eaten too much of those fried vegetables last night..."

"Oh, but Auntie Beyaz, those eggplants, and peppers, and... what else, those zucchinis and tomatoes, they were all so delicious... And that sauce of plain yogurt and garlic! Believe me, I've never eaten a tastier vegetable fry."

"My mother Meryem was not pretty," Auntie Beyaz unexpectedly began to say. "But she was a womanly woman. She had big boobs and a round, shapely bottom. She had a tiny waist. Basically, a woman who looked the part. Now, look here, a woman ought to be womanly! And a man ought to be manly. Nowadays I see on TV they have dogs the size of rats that cityfolk keep as pets in their homes. What are those things, were they produced in factories, *mari*? They've even turned the animals into fools – the poor thing barks and squeals all day, 'I wonder if I'm a dog or a rat.' The creature is confused. But a dog should be doglike, my girl! Look, nature has made a separate place for every kind of creature, that's why I say you ought to look like a woman. If creatures try to look like other creatures, it destroys nature's order, everything gets muddled up, there's no more fertility. But mind you, I have nothing to say against them that God created hunchbacks or dwarves or half or missing or backwards or different somehow. No one can say a word against them, and I'd be their greatest defender! There must be a reason for folks to be created that way... My word is against those who try to change the way they were made, *mari*, who try and act different from what they are, you understand my meaning? Because nature has made her own order and if you upset it, she won't be none too pleased! She'll give us such a punishment that, I swear, we'll rue the day we were born..."

Vicki began to laugh. Without expecting it.

"You just keep on laughing, missy. If you'd tried to look like a woman instead of a beanstalk, then you wouldn't be all the way out here tracking your great-grandfather, but back in your own country, nestled in your man's arms, suckling babes and feeling misty-eyed with happiness, like our Havva."

"What are you saying?" cried Vicki, enraged. "Is that a woman's sole purpose in life – to make love and have babies? How could you say that, a woman like you, who has based her entire life on spite for the mother who barred her from going to school, who still takes every opportunity to voice this spite for someone long dead, and who... who enjoys poetry and reads history, the way that you do? A woman has intellectual pleasures and ambitions of her own, as a human being, Auntie Beyaz! A woman is a human being first and foremost. How could a woman like you, who treasures her freedom and who has managed to establish her own order in such a macho country, reduce womanhood to solely sexuality and motherhood? Besides, look who's talking! It's not like you ever did any of those things..."

Vicki had exploded without warning and she now trembled from the livid strain of her own voice. She was not at all accustomed to these bursts of anger.

Auntie Beyaz hung her head. She spoke calmly and sadly:

"I've got nothing to say against you earning your own money and having a profession. If only Havva's father had sent her to school, if only he hadn't married her off so early, then she could have been an educated woman who drives a car, has her own money and goes and buys whatever she pleases at the market. But what I'm saying is in addition to all that.

242

These things you speak of, they should exist, they should most certainly exist... And they will... Mark my words, Havva's daughters will not live like their mother, girls nowadays are resisting their fate. Soon, no one will be able to put girls in chains. Not their fathers, their husbands, their mothers, or their governments... Those days are ending. And everywhere. But what I'm saying is this: a woman must be womanly. Let a woman be both buxom and brainy! Educated, professional women shall not give up the pleasures of motherhood, or cavorting at home with their men in order to pursue these other things! They ought not! That's what I say. That's just what I say. I say that to all of you, don't relinquish being a woman!"

She was tired. She collapsed on the chair next to the kitchen table. She sighed, readjusted her dentures with her tongue, and smacked her lips. She looked withered, shrunken somehow. Vicki felt massive guilt looking at her. She was an old woman, and Vicki had caused her grief. And unnecessary grief, at that. For, she had known exactly what Auntie Beyaz had meant, but the words had touched her own wound and she had lost her head. Whereas she was known, and sometimes accused, for being calm and collected, she had found herself frequently overwhelmed by emotion ever since coming to Gallipoli, and especially since meeting Auntie Beyaz. Her wound bled frequently, yes, it bled frequently here...

She wanted to go over to Auntie Beyaz and make it up to her but she felt too heavy to move. She could not find the strength to cover the distance of four steps. And she called herself a psychologist!

"As for me: A fine deed I did! A fine deed, indeed!!! All right, so I made a mistake, but why would you not live *your* life, o my silly girl? I'm over the hill, but you have a long life ahead of you. And what's more... what's more, I was in love with a living person, but yours has long been dead, dear heart!"

They were both angry and displeased by the things they had said. They remained in the kitchen for a time, avoiding each other's gaze. Two women, defeated but too proud to apologize, like the rueful commanders of a battle in which neither side triumphed. One of them at the start of her thirties, an urban, independent and professional woman of the 21st century, and a member of Western-Christian culture. The other in her late seventies, a rural, domestic, peasant woman of the 19th century, who belonged to an Eastern-Mediterranean and Moslem culture. Two women separated by a half century of age and two centuries of lifestyle. Two women who lacked the experience of a love to call their own, one for having been obsessed with her great-grandfather's mysterious tale, the other for having nurtured an impossible love towards her father. Two women who had never fallen in love with another man who was not their kin. One of them, Vicki Taylor of New Zealand, who concealed her own fears and deficiencies in the enigmatic Gallipoli story of her great-grandfather, Alistair John Taylor, thereby postponing her womanhood. The other, Beyaz Taylar of Turkey, who never forgave her mother but was forever condemned to secretly admire the passion and defiance with which she devoted herself to the man she loved.

Where thoughts grow dense and take on weight like solid objects, time comes to a standstill. Time came to a standstill in the kitchen of Auntie Beyaz's house, in Eceayaylasi, Gallipoli. No one knows how long time froze. When time freezes, there is no time left.

The doorbell rang. Time resumed its flow.

The doorbell rang once, and stopped. Then it rang twice, shortly, and stopped. Vicki got up from her seat and made for the door. Auntie Beyaz motioned her to wait.

"Hold on, *hele*. Wait. Don't open it yet! Let's see if it is Him. Or is it the newspapermen imitating the code?"

They waited. The doorbell rang thrice for the third time and stopped.

"Yes, that's Him. That's the apple of my eye, my darling son."

Perhaps because she had not left the house in a week, Vicki felt an odd sense of elation, without knowing who or what it was that she expected. She ran down the stairs but waited for Auntie Beyaz, who descended slowly, smiling like an eager young girl.

"Who is it?" boomed Auntie Beyaz, still wary of an unpleasant surprise from the journalists and reporters.

"Ali Osman Taylar!" boomed a man's voice from the other side.

"Ali Osman Taylar? No, this is simply too much!" cried Vicki, and crossly flung open the door.

A tall and extremely handsome young man with dark hair and brown eyes stood smiling brilliantly in the doorway. His smile froze slightly upon seeing Vicki but he recovered immediately and said, in English:

"Auntie Beyaz, you've grown so much younger since I last saw you."

All Vicki could do was utter an awestruck exclamation of:

"Wow!" in response. Then she blushed bright red.

Just then there was a burst of flashes from the massed photographers' cameras and an uproar ensued. The handsome young man who had appeared at the doorway deftly pushed Vicki inside and, dragging Mehmet the Guide in behind him, shut the door.

Auntie Beyaz gave a whoop of delight:

"Oh you little rascal, where have you been? I missed you, apple of my eye, come here, come here and let me get a whiff of you, *mari*!"

The young man practically lifted Auntie Beyaz off the ground in his hug, and the two kissed and hugged in a display of affection, to which Vicki was entirely unaccustomed. This intense affection between two people, which even warmed their surroundings, made Vicki envious; she could have cried at the drop of a hat. She truly had delayed far too many things, missed out on far too much.

"I brought you coffee and chocolate, Vicki," said Mehmet, sensing that the other two had forgotten about them.

"Oh... thank you Mehmet. Thanks for the trouble."

"Not at all. I've been of no use for days anyway, so I thought you might at least not go without coffee or chocolate..."

"Yes... You're awfully kind..."

"Tell me, are you hungry?" asked Auntie Beyaz.

"Yes, and how!" replied Mehmet, though the question was not addressed to him.

"Will you look at that scoundrel, doesn't even recognize a guest!" rebuked Auntie Beyaz.

"What guest, Auntie Beyaz, he's your grandson, I'm the real guest here. Besides, look, I washed my hair just this morning," Mehmet came back with a spoiled voice.

"Wait, wait, speak in English, I want to understand!" Vicki protested.

"She considers her own grandson a guest and not me," Mehmet explained.

"Grandson?"

"Yes indeed, Vicki *Hanim*, see, this here is my brother Bulut's great-grandson, the lawyer from Istanbul, and he is my very own grandson as well," said Auntie Beyaz proudly.

"Hello Vicki *Hanim*, I have heard a lot about you, both from our beloved media and from my Auntie Beyaz. I am Ali Osman."

Ali Osman extended his hand. Turks liked to shake hands.

"Welcome!" said Vicki, startled by the unfamiliar coyness of her own voice.

"And you, welcome to Gallipoli."

They shook hands. "Wow!" Vicki sighed once more, without even noticing.

"Wow!"

Not only was this man extremely handsome, he was also extremely attractive. Extremely! Then, baffled as to why her heart was beating like mad and why she was suddenly out of breath, she heaved a long, loud sigh.

"Hmmm!"

This made the other three turn towards her. Vicki blurted out the first thing that came into her head:

"My hair, Auntie Beyaz, I was thinking it would be good to wash my hair."

"It would be well and good, Vicki *Hanim*," laughed Auntie Beyaz. "Male or female, it doesn't matter, *mari*. Hair has got to know its place and be kept clean. That's all there is to it!"

"Parents should love their children equally. Look here, *he-le*, if a child knows that his parents extend him equal regard as his siblings, that household will have harmony, peace and abundance. The siblings in that household will love one anot-her. The opposite is an offense against God; it is a sin. Neither the parents, nor the children shall know peace."

They sat listening to Auntie Beyaz in the upstairs living ro-om, while eating the chocolates and drinking the instant cof-fee that Mehmet the Guide had brought from Eceabat and pre-pared himself. Some of the chocolates were still Nestlé brand, like Auntie Beyaz had mentioned, but Vicki also noticed Tur-kish brands such as Ulker and Mabel. What's more, some of these were truly delicious.

Young Ali Osman had taken off his tie and the coat of his smart suit, rolled up the sleeves of his white button-down shirt and sat next to Auntie Beyaz in the same cross-legged manner as her. As she spoke, Auntie Beyaz did not forget to mouth the occasional prayer and blow it in Ali Osman's direction. Vicki, who could not take her eyes off this handsome young man, was meanwhile grappling with the question of why she was so struck by him; was it as a man or as a piece, a most unexpected piece, of the Gallipoli story? But in truth, the reason did not make the slightest difference. Ali Osman inevitably exuded the stunning charm that young and dashing men cannot help but radiate toward women in their vicinity. Since Vicki had decided here in Gallipoli, at Auntie Beyaz's house and with her help, to rid herself of the powerful obsession that kept her from sensing a man's scent and which dulled her heart, she did not shrink back from perceiving this dizzying male charm and was rather disconcerted by it. Had she really made up her mind? Did she really want to divest herself of that deep evasion, that meticulous aversion and that exhausting abandonment that came from being stuck on an old family mystery, from checking her life in at the desk and from devoting herself to other people's problems? Was she prepared to confront the genuine reason behind her fear of living, which her obsession had heretofore concealed? Would she be stubborn and determined enough to carry out this confrontation? Stubborn and determined. Was she determined? That is, was it true that she had made such a decision? Had she been able to? Had she found the courage to decide and heal a very recently discovered inner wound? Would she be able to cure a spiritual injury thirty years in the making? Could a tailor mend his own torn seam, or would she find it necessary to consult another psychologist or even a psychiatrist? She did not know. Vicki could not say. But there was one thing that she did know, and strongly feel. She felt wonderful here, in Gallipoli, at Auntie Beyaz's house, right this very moment, eating chocolate and drinking coffee. Oh if only she could just wash herself and get dolled up a bit! Yes, here and now, she felt good as a human being and a woman. To feel good, very good even, as a human being and a woman, eh? Good God, what a luxury, what a blessing that is! The White Rooster must be crowing, the White Rooster must surely be crowing merrily right now on the village streets. And what a fine man this is, whose fennel perfume caresses one's skin, whose vigorous charm succeeds in seducing Vicki...

Ali Osman was either unaware of his own attractiveness or he was very used to it. There was also a third possibility but Vicki was afraid to consider it. She was afraid. Because the third possibility was 'what if Ali Osman did not find Vicki at all interesting as a woman?' 'Goodness gracious!' Vicki shuddered. She sat bolt upright and began gnawing on her lips. So, the possibility of being ignored by a man whom she found attractive was enough to upset her after all. And Vicki could accept the fact, after all.

"My father loved all three of us equally. If he brought a pair of shoes from Istanbul for one of us, he would bring a pair for all of us. If a dress was sewn for me, outfits would be sewn for my brothers as well. May God bless him! Now, to be fair, mother was the same way. Back then, everyone sat on the floor and ate dinner from a shared dish, but father had carved separate wooden bowls for each of us. Every one of us had our own bowl, plate, wooden spoon and fork, way back then. Anyhow, what I'm saying is this: mother always put equal portions into our bowls, she never slighted any of us. Mother did not love us but at least she unloved the three of us equally, *mari*!"

"Oh come on, Auntie Beyaz... Leave grandma alone... All right, she was cold, silent, and grumpy but the poor woman knew all of our names, prepared us gifts, and took wonderful care of grandpa until the very end. How many grandmas of her

age in Eceyaylasi knew and remembered each of their grandchildren's names, tell me that? And besides, she's dead and gone. It's time you let both her and yourself rest," said Ali Osman, munching handfuls of the Anafartalar almonds that Auntie Beyaz had placed before him, and enjoying being coddled.

'He's fair like Auntie Beyaz,' thought Vicki, unable to wrest
her gaze from Ali Osman.

"Would you like some more coffee, Ali Osman *ahbi*?" asked
Mehmet.

His voice contained pride in being included among the
starring cast of this much heralded story and in being privile-
ged enough to gain acceptance into a house which journalists
and reporters had for days tried to enter. One could be certain that he would tell tourists of this day for years to come.

Vicki had, at first, been put off by the use of the words '*ahbi*' and '*abla*'*, with which Turks referred to their elders. However, she had since begun to understand that this colloqu-
alism did not denote the hierarchical address of past centuries, but rather a sincere feeling of respect, and therefore it did
not disturb her to hear Mehmet call Ali Osman '*ahbi*'. Then her
eyes fell once again on Ali Osman and she felt the same urgent
need. She needed to bathe and get smartened up at once. Needed to? No, Vicki was dying to wash, clean and beautify herself. (Beautify? Whereas for years she had boasted that she
needed no other beautification than washing her face with so-
ap water.)

It is all over once a woman feels the need to get dolled up.
After that, it matters not if war should break out or the world
should come to an end. For, once a woman feels the urge to
become groomed and beautiful, this becomes her primary
concern. There are various stimulants that make a woman feel the need for beautification. The stimulant is usually, but not

---

*) *Ahbi* and *abla*: "older brother" and "older sister" respectively.

251

always an attractive (handsome/charming/young) man. Once a woman desires to feel beautiful and groomed, she must accomplish this come hell or high water. That is the way it has been since women existed upon this earth, and that is the way it will be as long as they continue to exist.

"Even so..." Auntie Beyaz went on.

"Even so, parents secretly prefer the child who is most like themselves over their other children. That is, one of the children resembles his mother or father more than the others. Now, see here, I'm not talking about hair color or height or weight!... It's the child's nature, his manner, his wit, his interests that are in common. Among the siblings there will doubtless be one who is a carbon copy of his mother or father. What can I say, it's God's own doing. You know how they say 'he's his father's son' or 'she's her mother's daughter', well, this is what they mean, *mari!*"

She nodded smugly, as though she had just revealed the greatest scientific fact known to mankind, and pursed her lips. Vicki had caught her drift. She had understood exactly what this clever, impish woman was getting at, but she did not have the strength to interrupt her and get her angry. Because the only thing on her mind was how soon she could bathe and get dolled up. She could not possibly concentrate on any other topic. She needed to get smartened up, right here and right now.

"You're absolutely right, Auntie Beyaz," Mehmet heartily lauded. "For example, my older brother studied to become an electronic engineer. I don't say this because he's my brother, but he is both extremely smart and strong. Everyone in our family is nuts about him, but my mom says that he takes after my dad. Me, for instance, I'm much more sensitive and romantic. I never forget birthdays, I'm pretty considerate toward women, etc... Anyway, you guys know me... I mean, no need to brag... Mom says 'you take after me', so I'm closer to her in

252

that way. I could say that I'm my mother's son. Congrats Auntie Beyaz, you did a bang-up job of explaining the situation! Hats off to you!"

"Enough! Stop that yelling, it's getting on my nerves! I have no patience for charlatans!" Auntie Beyaz scolded Mehmet.

Startled, Mehmet sought to understand how exactly he had tumbled into the yawning gap where people who cannot distinguish the fine line between closeness and over-familiarity frequently find themselves.

"Auntie Beyaz does not take kindly to overt praises or loud acclaim, Mehmet. You must commend her silently," said Ali Osman.

Mehmet was baffled.

"I didn't mean anything bad," he said, afraid of losing Auntie Beyaz's attention.

"I don't know if you will believe it, Mehmet, but some people truly dislike show and sensation. If you should ask how I happen to know, my reply is simple. I am the great-grandchild who most resembles Auntie Beyaz. What can I say, it's God's own doing! It's my nature, my manner... Isn't that right, Auntie Beyaz?"

"Sure it is, what did you think?" said Auntie Beyaz, softening up a little.

They were carrying on most of their conversation in English, for Vicki's benefit. Although Auntie Beyaz's elaborate, heavily accented British English, Mehmet's heavily Turkish accented English, picked up from books and tourists of various nationalities, and young Ali Osman's American-spiced English created an incredible array of sounds, what inevitably dominated the conversation was the Turkish words and phrases. Despite missing some of the details and subtle humor, Vicki understood what they were saying. Anyway, her mind was somewhere else, but she did not want to hide her presence any longer. Especially not around Ali Osman...

"You think you're not at all like your mother, that you're your father's daughter, don't you Auntie Beyaz?" she asked, summoning all her courage.

"Exactly so, I am my father's daughter!" Auntie Beyaz dismissed the matter. "I always was and I always shall be."

There was a weary and melancholic tone in her voice, which suddenly spread across the room and affected everyone present.

'Here's a true guru character. Whatever she does, whatever she feels affects her surroundings,' thought Vicki.

"Would you like to rest a little, Auntie Beyaz?" asked Ali Osman, gently stroking the old woman's back.

Having anticipated a curt and snappy refusal, Vicki was amazed to see Auntie Beyaz yield to Ali Osman with all the sweet surrender of a young maid.

"Indeed, son, I feel sleepy all of a sudden. I'd better take a little nap," said Auntie Beyaz, and, stretching out on the sofa, fell asleep quick as a baby.

"Well, I'd better go," Mehmet whispered reluctantly.

No one asked him to stay. Vicki, who accompanied him downstairs, thanked him again for the coffee and chocolates. As he was putting on his shoes, Mehmet remembered that Vicki was not his hostess but a foreign tourist who was in fact his client.

"Oh yes, Vicki, before I forget, it's not long before your return to New Zealand. I don't know what you're thinking, but if you want to extend your stay, we ought to change your reservation soon. But, as you know, it will cost you an extra $100."

"Oh dear, I had forgotten it completely! Of course, I do have a return ticket to Wellington, don't I? Well, how long before?" asked a startled Vicki.

"You have a week left. Let's get moving on it, Vicki. What do you think?"

"What? What do I think about what?"

"About your return date, of course!"

"Oh... A week? Really? Is that all? My, time really flew by here at Auntie Beyaz's house. No, no... Three weeks in Gallipoli seemed to me a lifetime."

"Yeah, you're telling me! I'm completely exhausted! I swear, the things that I've been through. This Tahsin, for instance. He's constantly following me!"

"Who's following you?" Vicki asked, taken aback.

"Who else, Tahsin. Some sort of fanatic. He catches hold of me in street corners, in deserted places, and goes on about how could your grandpa be a Turkish *ghazi*, how you should not talk too much, stuff like that...The man is obsessed with you. Crazy fanatic!"

"And why shouldn't he be a *ghazi*? Does everything have to be the way it says in the books? Besides, I wonder who wrote those books?" grumbled Vicki.

"Well, it's not that simple Vicki. Look, even your New Zealand Embassy made a statement. Basically, it seems people have nothing better to do..." Mehmet explained.

"The New Zealand Embassy?" repeated Vicki, shocked.

"People are more interested in that lovely 'great-grandpa fantasy' of yours than you could imagine, Ms. Victoria Taylor," said young Ali Osman, chuckling as he came down the stairs.

After placing a blanket over Auntie Beyaz, who had fallen asleep as fast as a baby, and staying by her side long enough to assure himself of her regular breathing, Ali Osman had joined Vicki and Mehmet downstairs.

"My great-grandfather fantasy?" Vicki echoed, crestfallen.

"Indeed. What did you expect?" replied Ali Osman in a mocking tone. "Besides, this is Turkey, we're not at all like the cool, rational New Zealanders... We're Eastern-Mediterranean, Vicki. We decide with our hearts, not with our minds, we get easily excited, easily attached and easily cooled off. We either believe a person or get mad at him immediately. What's more, no one is more expert than us at turning small frustrations into great hatreds, or minute hopes into massive fervor. In truth, most of the cultures that surround that magnificent sea called the Mediterranean are pretty much the same, but I suppose us Turks are the most mad-blooded of them all... Mad-blood. See, it's hard to explain this in English, impossible even. Because in our culture, having madness in one's blood is not an insult but rather, a commendation. Because we are both Eastern and Mediterranean. We are childish, we are passionate, and we can't seem to grow up. But that's just the way we are... A little Balkan, a little Caucasian, but most of all Eastern-Mediterranean. I don't know if it is anything to brag about, but that's just how we are! Isn't that so, Mehmet?"

Jubilated to finally find someone who understood his language, Mehmet eagerly jumped in: "Oh, God bless you, Ali Osman *ahbi*. A truer word was never said. That's exactly why folks are going crazy over Vicki's great-grandpa tale... I mean, personally, I don't see what the big deal is. What does is matter? I mean, was *Ghazi* Sergeant Alican a good man? Was he really a war hero? Was he a blessed soul, beloved by all? Well then, what does the rest matter? The man is dead anyways. What do you care about his passport? May God rest his soul, and let's get on with our business! But not everyone thinks like me, do they, Ali Osman *ahbi*?"

"Exactly right, well put Mehmet!"

"What are you saying, Ali Osman *Bey*? Have you never discussed this matter with Auntie Beyaz?" Vicki interrupted in outrage.

How could this extremely handsome, striking young man, this Ali Osman Taylar, who had reintroduced her to the long repressed thrill of feminine lust, possibly speak in such an irresponsible and superficial manner? Did she have to be so unfortunate, just when she had met someone who did not prevent her from feeling her womanhood for the first time in years? Was he a shallow person, like most other good-looking men?

"Oh come now, Vicki..." grinned Ali Osman. "My Auntie Beyaz is an old peasant grandma, approaching eighty. The only schooling she's ever had is three years of primary education. My great-grandfather apparently taught her what few English words he had learned from the Brits when he fell captive, so the poor thing assumes that her broken English amounts to something. Yes, you're right, my Auntie Beyaz is an extremely intelligent, capable and unusual woman, with a much more powerful memory than could be expected at her age. But in the end, she is just an old peasant woman. You saw how she fell asleep like a baby up there. Now tell me, how right would we be to take everything this old woman says seriously?"

Even though he had assumed the facial expression of Auntie Beyaz's mischievous grandson, Ali Osman had spoken like a lawyer defending his client. True, he *was* a lawyer.

"But what she told me was perfectly consistent, and there is nothing broken about her English, nothing at all. Furthermore, she has letters and photographs that could be considered serious proof," Vicki contested in a petulant voice.

Ali Osman approached her with a sly smile. He drew so close that Vicki staggered from the youthful masculine scent his body gave out.

"Uhh!" she moaned.

"Are you all right?" both men asked anxiously, at the same time.

"Yes, I'm fine, I'm quite all right but to be honest, I'm having trouble understanding what you're saying," replied Vicki, who could give her kingdom for a shower.

"I know exactly which pictures and letters Auntie Beyaz showed you. Ah, that old Auntie Beyaz! Once again, she couldn't help herself! When we were kids, all us grandchildren and great-grandchildren were sick of listening to those stories and looking at those pictures. We would stay away from her, just to avoid having to see those pictures again. But if she ever got a hold of us, she would never let us go, the old stubborn goat. She always had in hand some letters written by Lieutenant Ali Osman, my great-grandfather's old comrade in arms, the man they named me after, and some photographs of that family, which we loved like our own. It's been years since she has had anyone to tell these tales to, so she must have spun quite a yarn when she found you! Oh, Auntie Beyaz, oh dear, dear old Auntie Beyaz!"

Mehmet started to laugh.

"And it wasn't only Vicki, Ali Osman *ahbi*! Mighty press crews, politicians, reporters and even that Tahsin guy who followed me, everyone fell for that tale!"

"They simply leapt on a story that they thought would sell easily or earn them a few votes, that's all."

"Yeah, you're right, but they all fell for the tale, Ali Osman *ahbi*, hah hah ha!..."

"And what a story it is! Hah hah ha..."

Ali Osman and Mehmet collapsed in a fit of laughter, imitating the journalists and forgetting all about Vicki. As their laughter verged on tears, Vicki felt so angry that she could cry. No, it could not be that simple. She had been here for three weeks and the things that she had heard, seen, and experienced here were not that simple.

Mehmet, she could understand. He was a well-intentioned, naïve young man. He was one of the millions of young people who lived day to day, without getting involved in anything, without harboring any intellectual concerns or questions. And thus he would proceed to live, grow old and die, most likely without ever touching on any subject other than the stock market, soccer, entertainment and a few love affairs. But what about Ali Osman Taylar? How could he act this superficial and be satisfied with such a childish answer? How could he? That is, he shouldn't. Because he was different. Was he different? How was he different? How could he? That is, he shouldn't. Because he was an educated, intellectual lawyer from Istanbul, and he was Auntie Beyaz's favorite. What's more... What's more, what? What? What? What's more, being this handsome and charming a man... No, Vicki could not utter this last sentence. She dismissed this final reason, but already, the worm of doubt had begun gnawing at her, the question that begged 'yes, but, what if he is right?'

Yes, but...Yes, but... But what if he's right? What if Auntie Beyaz tricked Vicki with her made-up tales that exasperated everyone? Was this possible? No way. Not a chance. That was ridiculous! Besides, there were no inconsistencies of time or place in any of her stories. There weren't, were there? Were there really none? But how about the story of that circumcision? The way a young woman was supposed to have circumcised a lad without any anesthesia or sterilization, and left him unharmed? Could that be true? And how about the fact that the villagers had not found Alistair John Taylor out, even if he was in Turkish uniform? Yes, most of the old people she had met in the village were blue-eyed, but still... And how did one explain those stories of occupied Istanbul? How had a New Zealander with broken Turkish managed to infiltrate the capital of an Empire that still used the Arabic alphabet and find Semahat *Hanimefendi*'s house on the European continent, without giving himself away? True, at the time, people of over thirty-six different nationalities lived in Istanbul, and the Ottoman empire was comprised of this many different ethnicities, and yet... And yet, there was something altogether strange about this story... The worst part was thinking that she had been taken for a fool, and now the laughter of these two young men, mocking as they did the people who had believed this tale, seemed to tear at her very skin.

"Forget it, Mehmet," said Ali Osman, placing a hand on his shoulder. "Forget it, they too will soon realize how silly they've been. Anyway, they'll soon find some other sensational story, some new manufactured news item to renew the headlines. They'll forget all about this issue, it'll just fade from memory. Anyway, I'll call you. Take care of yourself."

"Take it easy, Ali Osman *ahbi*. You turned out to be a pretty cool guy. Oh yeah, Vicki, I'll call you tomorrow, we'll figure out that return ticket business, ok?"

Vicki nodded distractedly. She was very upset.

Mehmet had barely stepped out of the door when the journalists seized upon him and bombarded him with questions. Pleased at the attention, Mehmet grinned happily at the cameras.

"Oh no, not on your life! To think that a mighty Turkish *ghazi* could be a New Zealander... How can that possibly be, friends? Who would believe such a fairytale? Yes, Auntie Beyaz is an extremely intelligent, capable and unusual woman, and her memory is much more powerful than you would expect at her age, but she's just an old peasant woman, after all. She's in there sleeping like a baby, right this very moment. As for the other one, she's a very naïve tourist woman, sweet as an angel. They simply tricked her and she fell for this fairytale, that's all there is to it. No, no, I've found out the truth, you're wasting your time for no reason, friends."

Ali Osman stood by the window long enough to hear Mehmet's statement to the press. He took a deep breath. Then he turned toward Vicki.

"I apologize, Vicki. I was forced to speak that way in front of Mehmet. Thank you for handling the situation," he whispered.

His voice was serious. Gone was that inane fellow whose grating laughter, only moments prior, could only have issued from a brain that remained disproportionately undeveloped to its body.

"What do you mean?" Vicki stammered.

Dear God, what a great number of 'whats' transpired in this Gallipoli.

Ali Osman took Vicki by the hand, seated her on a cotton-print covered sofa that seemed abandoned like redundant furniture in the downstairs hallway, and, still whispering, explained:

"Auntie Beyaz could not tell me the whole story since I warned her that the phones might be tapped. But from what she implied in a few words, it seems that she has divulged you a secret that only four people in the whole world have known for eighty-five years. I immediately came over when the press got wind of the matter. Because now you also carry this critical and very precious information, which no living person knows other that Auntie Beyaz and myself. That is, you too are now responsible, Vicki."

"You knew and you tricked me!" Vicki flared.

"Well, what should I have done? Should I have allowed the matter to be announced to the press by a tourist guide who is not interested in anything other than his jeep and tourist girls?"

Only then did Vicki grasp the truth, and she raised a hand to her mouth to contain the shriek that was about to escape her lips.

"Oh my God!" she whimpered. "So you knew, as well…"

Ali Osman pursed his lips, sighed and nodded, as though they were speaking of a mixed blessing.

"So you and I… we are both… descended from…"

Ali Osman nodded once more.

Istanbulite lawyer, Ali Osman Taylar, of a family orginally from Chanakkale, and Wellingtonian psychologist, Victoria Taylor sat and stared at each other in Gallipoli's Eceyaylasi Village.

"What's going to happen now?" whispered Vicki.

"Nothing is going to happen, Vicki. We will hold a press conference. Us three. Us three bearers of this secret. You, me, and my Auntie Beyaz… our Auntie Beyaz."

He paused. Suddenly Ali Osman flashed a brilliant smile. He studied Vicki carefully. Vicki felt herself glow in the light of his handsomeness and charm. Once again she felt an unbearable urge to jump in the shower and get smartened up.

"Our Auntie Beyaz! Well, I'll be..." he mused, laughing. Then he went on calmly, as though nothing had happened:

"You two will make a statement to the press, explain that there has been a misunderstanding, that you have been mistaken, and you will issue an apology. Then everything will go back to normal."

"Absolutely not!" Vicki leapt up from the sofa. "The facts should not be concealed. At least, not anymore."

"The facts, you say?" Ali Osman asked, with total composure. "The facts, eh?"

"Yes, the facts, Ali Osman."

"Which facts, Vicki? The fact that a young man was fooled into being used as a pawn in an imperialist war only to watch his brother and his friends get murdered by his side, and to have his life ruined and his hopes shattered? Or the fact that an incredibly intelligent, well-educated young law student lost his life and his dreams while fighting against imperialism? Or would you prefer this one: The lamentable fact that one young man saved another's life with his own death, but both became victims of imperialism?"

He stopped. He looked mournful. He hung his head and waited. That was when Vicki quietly sat down next to him. She sat so close that their legs almost touched.

"There is another option. Or, another fact..." said Ali Osman, in a hurt tone. "The grave fact that a young man lived out a borrowed life in a country where he had been sent as an invader, by grasping on to a peasant girl –who he always called 'an angel'– and to the family of a law-student officer, both of whom had saved his life. The fact that by feigning death against those who had deceived him and by sentencing himself

262

into lifelong exile from his native country, a young man punished himself into a long life of pain. The fact of a lonely man who sincerely grew to love the land and the people of a country where he had been given a second chance at life. Which fact would you like to announce Vicki? Tell me!"

Ali Osman had grown angry. Vicki listened to him calmly, and waited.

"And besides, who in this day and age do you think will care about these sorrows? Who is interested in true and intimate tales of humanity, when humanity in the 21st century has assumed that rotten, shallow, consumer identity? Who? The politicians? The diplomats, the historians? Or the ignorant and destitute masses who have been blinded with nationalism and politicized religion? People will descend like vultures on our grandfathers' extraordinary tale, Vicki, they will consume it instantly and leave us nothing but blood and pain. The new millennium, the 21st century... It's all a charade! Technological advance only describes mechanic development. Technological progress does not offer us ethical progress along with it. No, people have not yet reached the level of refinement, the depth of spirit with which to appreciate this special and sacred a tale of humanity. No Vicki, if we disclose the truth now, no one will understand those two amazing youths, Ali Osman *Bey* and Alistair John Taylor. No one will be able to deduce a lesson from their lives and from their remarkable decisions. You know what would happen? In my opinion, the most magnificent historical event of the 20th century, that truth that you so want to expose, will only serve the global imperialism of the new order, that is all!"

"Are you a leftist?" Vicki mumbled.

Her voice was cool. She sounded numb. She had awakened from sleep, grown up and at the same time grown old. Ali Osman took Vicki's nearby hand in his, and gave it an amicable squeeze.

263

"Look Vicki, right now, it does not matter what my worldview is, but rather what you think about this matter. I only want you to seriously consider and make up your own mind. Now you too know the secret of my great-grandfather, I mean our great-grandfather. Obviously Auntie Beyaz truly liked and trusted you to have relayed to you this truth. Think hard; think, and if you want to, reveal the truth to the press, the politicians, the diplomats, the man on the street. But I would like you to give some very, very serious consideration to the following before you decide. If truth is to be used to benefit the wicked and oppress others, if truth has been too painfully and brutally earned to entrust to those who are undeserving of it, then should it still be disclosed? Should it be, Vicki? Considering humanity's despicable crimes of imperialism, fascism, religious prejudice and racism, which escalate as we enter the new millennium, how right would it be to offer the small but immensely significant saga of two young men to people who are incapable of reading it?"

Ali Osman fell silent. Once again, he fell silent, but he did not let go of Vicki's hand. Her head in a tumult, her heart straining to fly out of its cage, Vicki sat hand in hand with Ali Osman, wearing Auntie Beyaz's flower print *shalvar* and her t-shirt that said *'Lest We Forget -Anzac Day - Gallipoli 2000'*.

'I am wearing a t-shirt that says 'Lest We Forget – Gallipoli', there is a very handsome young man sitting next to me, holding my hand, and I am in Gallipoli, in the spring of the new millennium,' Vicki reminded herself. But this did not help her feel better. She did not feel well. All this truth had been too much for her. Far too much.

"What is truth, Vicki?" Ali Osman whispered. "Truth that has been given to us when we are unprepared, do you think that is genuinely realized truth? If you disclose the truth, the first thing they will do is demolish *Ghazi* Sergeant Alican's grave and harass Ali Osman *Bey*'s family. What's more, there will be people in New Zealand, people close to you, who will suffer, believe me, I do not exaggerate."

"Could you give me some water Ali Osman, please?"

"Vicki, are you all right? No, no, you're not. Oh God, what a fool I am! Come on, let me help you upstairs. Here, you can lean on me. That's it. Keep going. We're almost there."

They slowly ascended the stairs, arms wrapped around each other. Upstairs, Auntie Beyaz had woken and she now sat on the sofa, waiting for them.

"Son, you are far too hard on the girl. You must explain these things slowly, *mari*. She didn't learn them when she was a babe in arms, the way you did. Now, you'd better be good to my girl Vicki, or I won't have it!"

"Well, you ought to quit listening to other people's conversations, Auntie Beyaz!" Ali Osman protested.

"Well, if you hadn't shouted so much, I wouldn't have heard, *mari*! You should just be grateful that that nitwit Mehmet took the newspapermen away so they did not hear you. Now, go get this girl something to eat, the poor dear's white as a sheet. I've only just managed to put some meat on her bones, see, the poor wretch has grown prettier, looks something like a woman now. I swear, she was all skin and bone when she got here! Besides, she has been entrusted to us, don't you forget!"

"No, no, I'm fine, you don't need to worry Auntie Beyaz."

"Oh, will you just listen to that, she's mighty proud too, the little scamp, *mari*!"

"All right, ladies, I see you've become fast friends," Ali Osman smiled. "Auntie Beyaz has finally found someone else to scold to her heart's content, thank goodness I'm not alone anymore!"

"You shut up. You two are not going to fight anymore. You're practically kin!"

"We're practically kin," repeated Ali Osman, smiling at Vicki.

"But distant kin, third generation," Vicki anxiously corrected.

"There's no such thing as distant or close kin, *mari*. You're kin, that's all there is to it!"

Ali Osman raised his hands in surrender. He smiled at his Auntie Beyaz with all the contentment of people who have managed to accept the irascibilities and deficiencies of those they love. Then he brought Vicki a glass of water and sat down on the sofa beside them.

"Auntie Beyaz, as you know, the April 25, Anzac Memorial Day ceremonies will be held in two days. This year is the eighty-fifth anniversary and larger numbers of Anzac descendants always come to visit on the years that end in fives or zeroes. There are ten thousand New Zealander and Australian tourists outside. There are not enough hotels, so passenger ships are docked in the bay to provide additional board. Basically, Auntie dear, it is a packed crowd. Now, I say we hold this press conference tomorrow and get it over with th so that Vicki can attend the memorial services in peace. Besides, it's high time this tomfoolery came to an end. It's gone on far too long, what do you think?"

"I think that would be fine, son," said Auntie Beyaz, clacking her dentures.

"Do you think that's the best solution?" asked Vicki.

"Absolutely!" answered Auntie Beyaz. "My late father, your great-grandfather, entrusted his mighty secret only to me, excepting my mother of course. It was his final will. He called me to his side before he died. Dear father knew that he was going to die. He said to me: 'Beyaz, my girl, my sweet girl, the people who rule this world are cruel invaders, lying politicians and wealthy crooks. There are few good folks among the rich and the politicians, because they are not allowed to survive among them. They are never ever allowed to survive, that's the first thing you should know. Because both wealth and politics are based on ambition and power. Ambition and power corrupt a person, that's the second thing you should know. Look, my girl, I have suffered my share. But I have learned that a person's blood has no nationality. A person's blood is red and it is just as valuable anywhere in the world. A human being is always a human being, my girl. God blessed me and granted me a second chance at life, with the help of two angels. One of them appeared to me as your mother Meryem, the other one as Ali Osman *Bey*. But not everyone is so fortunate in this world.' So my father told me..."

Auntie Beyaz suddenly stopped. She smacked her gums to readjust her dentures, swallowed and waited. Vicki moved to get up and bring her a drink of water but Ali Osman motioned with his hand to wait. It seemed that he was used to Auntie Beyaz's breathers, and he knew that she did not enjoy interference. "It is my will," Auntie Beyaz went on. "Father is telling me this: 'It is my will, dear Beyaz, that you should not disclose my secret to anyone who cannot keep it. If the world is not ready for it, then let this secret rest with you until eternity... Let them not know...' Then he went to meet his Maker, my precious father, that great hero, that wise man..."

She paused again. She wiped her eyes with the tip of her headscarf. This time, Vicki waited as Ali Osman did. She too was learning.

"For years I waited. I inspected all the grandchildren, all the great-grandchildren, one by one. See that there Ali Osman, that fine young man sitting beside you, he was sharp even as a baby, he would stare like a grown man, he would speak clearly and surprise everybody. They used to call him 'man face' when he was a baby, *mari*."

Vicki scrutinized Ali Osman, trying to conjure his face as a baby. She strove to impose a baby face on Ali Osman's grown frame. Meanwhile, her own face had, for some reason, adopted a childish expression of its own and Ali Osman caught this, and gave her a wink. Vicki laughed at Ali Osman. She laughed easily, genuinely, for the first time since they had met. Laughing made her just as beautiful as if she had bathed and groomed. And for the first time Ali Osman gave her an appraising glance, and noticed her.

"Now, you two quit fooling around and listen to me. See, this boy's grandfather, my younger brother Bulut, was a teacher. Semahat *Hanimefendi*, may she rest in peace, had sent him to school. But my brother Bulut died in a car crash when he was just a lad, poor thing. When he learnt that his son, his youngest son, had preceded him to the grave, father lay sick with grief for weeks. But Bulut's son and daughter were good students. Their mother, Bulut's wife, was a nurse, and she raised her children very well. Semahat *Hanimefendi* also took care of them all. One of the children became an engineer, and the other became a teacher. Ali, the engineer, is this here Ali Osman's father. They all became Istanbulites ever since. But they come here every summer, people who are born in Gallipoli, in Chanakkale can never quite leave here, *mari*. It is something in the soil, it will not leave a person be. It does not matter where you go. You always come back here… Wait now, what was I saying? Oh yes, when Ali Osman was born, they brought him here as a baby. My mother and father were still alive at the time. Well, I knew, the minute I saw his face. I knew that this boy was going to make good. I prayed to God that he would give me life enough to see this boy grow up. They brought him here every summer. He grew up right here, with me. I was only about forty-five years old at the time. I was hardy, I would grab hold of him and take him to Chunuk Bair, to the Ariburnu-Anzac Cove. I would tell him all about the war. He was young but sharp as a whip, *mashallah*. He was mighty quick on the uptake. He always asked questions, he never tired of asking. A curious child is good, he will grow up to be someone. Even back then, this here Ali Osman was as serious as a grown man! I taught him everything I learned from my father. During the summers, this little rascal would be my own son. His mother is also an engineer,

268

the girl worked all year long, so of course, she did not mind him spending his summers here in the village, in fresh air."

"Auntie Beyaz was a very beautiful lady," Ali Osman interjected. "I was young and wouldn't know, but everyone we met on our outings stared at her. The admiration in their eyes made me fill up with pride. She was a very striking villager woman, but all the men were afraid of her. She seemed to radiate a heavenly glow, to wear an invisible halo as she walked, and her gaze seemed to emanate a particular aroma that caused others to respect her. We would visit the Ariburnu-Anzac Cove together. She would show me where the April 25 Anzac landing took place, and tell me about how a handful of Turks bravely defended their nation that morning. She would get very excited as she spoke, and her eyes would be brimming with tears. Then she would speak of how the Anzacs got trapped and killed in the hills, and she would cry for them also. Well, now... I was only five or six years old, I would become confused, and torn between both sides. Just as I was about to rejoice that the enemy had been killed and we had won, I would start to feel sorry for the Anzacs who died. Just as I entered the age of shooting games, of budding nationalism and enmity, Auntie Beyaz confounded me. Auntie Beyaz always did confound me. This unruly woman has never ceased to confound me!" said Ali Osman, laughing and shaking his head. "I never could understand. I would ask: 'Who's the enemy, Auntie Beyaz?' And she would wipe her eyes and say: 'There is no enemy, son, there is no enemy!'"

"He would start playing these 'bang! bang!' war games, there on the soil where my father and Ali Osman *Bey* had fought, but right there," Auntie Beyaz cut in. "I would watch him and think to myself, 'great God in heaven!' Here at the spot where Ali Osman *Bey* had expired and saved my father's life, here was my father's great-grandson, Ali Osman, playing war games... It caused me such a heartache. That was the reason I cried, but how was he to know, he was a wee little lad."

"Auntie Beyaz and I would gather pebbles at the Ariburnu-Anzac Cove, and sit and watch the magnificent sunsets. Some mornings she would wake me up early, and we would go to the woods to listen to the songs of nightingales. And sometimes we would sing the English songs that my great-grandfather taught us," said Ali Osman, and began to hum an old English tune.

"London Bridge is falling down, falling down, falling down/ London Bridge is falling down, my fair lady…"

Vicki and Auntie Beyaz joined in the song. The three of them: Beyaz Taylar, Victoria Taylor and Ali Osman Taylar, sat smiling at one another, in Gallipoli's Eceyaylasi Village, and sang an old English nursery rhyme, cheerful as children themselves. They laughed when the song was over. Their faces had that radiance particular only to children. A person's blood first quickens then cools at the sense of connection and warmth evoked by a childhood song. It quickens because children's songs bring back the untroubled days of childhood. It cools, because children's songs remind us of all the time that has passed since childhood. Songs of childhood are powerful painkillers that we carry within us for the entire course of our lives.

When the song was over, a brief silence settled over the living room. No one seemed to want to speak.

"I told him everything when he turned seventeen. My father had died only a few months prior. I was afraid that I did not have much longer to live myself. Ali Osman had become a strong enough youth to bear this secret. Anyhow, I had trusted him from the very beginning," Auntie Beyaz continued her story. "He listened without a bit of surprise. Not a tiny bit. You would think that a person would be a little stunned. Not this one, he is calm, he is sharp as a tack. He was, even as a child. Then he turned to me and said: 'I swear that I will keep this secret, Auntie Beyaz.'"

"Actually, I was shocked," Ali Osman explained. "I was shocked, but I did not let on."

"How long ago did you learn this fact?" Vicki inquired.

"Twenty? No, it was fifteen years ago. I was born in 1968," Ali Osman replied.

"And I was born in 1970," said Vicki, without concealing her elation.

"Means she's the same age as Semahat," Auntie Beyaz remarked.

"Semahat *Hanimefendi*?" puzzled Vicki.

"No, her great-granddaughter, Doctor Salih *Bey*'s granddaughter Semahat."

"Oh, I see..." said Vicki, reacting with a displeasure that she herself could not explain. Then she leapt up from her seat: "I must take a shower!" she cried.

"I turned on the hot water, Vicki. As you know, there's an electrical water heater in the bathroom, since we have no central heating in these parts."

"I know, I know," said Vicki, running blissfully into the bathroom as if running to heaven.

"And I'll call Havva and ask her to bring over some of her scrumptious cooking," said Ali Osman, as he walked over to the phone. Then he suddenly remembered: "Hey Vicki, us Turks always seem to think better in the bathroom, see if you New Zealanders do as well! While you're in there, consider whether we should hold this press conference tomorrow and get it over with, will you?"

"I'll see how well my New Zealander mind works in a Turkish Bath, mister lawyer!" Vicki responded, but now there was a new question occupying her mind: What kind of a person was the younger Semahat, and what kind of relationship did she have with young Ali Osman?

Vicki finally bathed.

A press conference was held in Gallipoli's Eceyaylasi Village *kahveh*, on April 24 of the year 2000, at 11 a.m. The journalists and the radio, television and internet crews from Istanbul, Ankara, Europe and Oceania once more filled the village with their noisy presence, their fancy equipment, their cameras, antenna, microphones, their laptops, their palm pilots and their cellular phones. A large number of gendarmes and men in dark suits and shades accompanied this horde, whose members included famous journalists, historians and a few translators. While some people believed these 'men in black' to be civil police, others opined that they were foreign diplomats. Additionally, the curious among the residents of Chanakkale, Eceabat, and the surrounding villages also flowed into the Eceyaylasi Village. Among them were old folks who had long meant to come visit Auntie Beyaz, to kiss her hand and receive her blessings. Also among the crowd, the careful observer was bound to notice Tahsin, who dug in his heels as he wandered about and kept an eye out for Mehmet the Guide. In the end, the village square had been turned into a veritable fairground, frightening away the White Rooster and all the chickens into hiding.

At first, there was a palpable wave of excitement in the air. One could sense a brewing scandal, a bomb waiting to explode with great impact. More correctly, one could sense the insincere and forced emotional build-up of people who fervently desired such an outcome. The sense of dissatisfaction resembles indigestion. It causes a sour and burning feeling in one's stomach. At the Eceyaylasi Village square, there was a mingled burnt and sour smell.

But things did not happen as predicted.

Those who managed to enter the village *kahveh* saw a long table placed before the Ataturk corner, where sat Vicki Taylor, Ali Osman Taylar, Auntie Beyaz and the village *Mukhtar*. Auntie Beyaz was wearing her father's Gallipoli war medal pinned to her lapel. Microphones bearing the names of various TV stations, micro-tapes and finger-length recording instruments were amassed on the table. Directly behind Auntie Beyaz hung a portrait of her father, *Ghazi* Sergeant Alican, and above that, a portrait of Ataturk. Auntie Beyaz and Ali Osman Taylar looked altogether serene, in contrast to Vicki and the *Mukthar*, who appeared rather nervous. The young Istanbulite lawyer, Ali Osman Taylor, was the first to speak.

The young lawyer first explained the reason why he was in Gallipoli. He happened to be the great-grandson of Ali Can Taylar, known as *Ghazi* Sergeant Alican, a villager of Eceyaylasi, who was a Gallipoli war hero and the subject of

273

this conference, and the grand-nephew of Beyaz Taylar, the *Ghazi*'s only surviving child. He was born in Istanbul in 1968, had graduated from the Istanbul University School of Law, had completed a two-year post-graduate program at a university in the U.S., and was a bar-association registered criminal lawyer. He was also the legal spokesperson and representative of his great-aunt, Beyaz Taylar. It was clear to everyone present that the lawyer in the gray suit, who was speaking with great confidence and composure, was a handsome and charming young man. It was so obvious that it seemed impossible that he was unaware of it.

The lawyer Ali Osman Taylar then reminded the attendees that his great-aunt, Beyaz Taylar, was a peasant woman with a grade school education, who had been born eight years after the Battle of Gallipoli, and who had never left the Gallipoli Peninsula, and he stressed that past rumors and the imminent disclosure ought to be regarded in light of these facts in order to reach a more realistic outcome.

He mentioned that Ataturk had visited Gallipoli on September 2, 1928 on the yacht Ertugrul and personally commended his great-grandfather *Ghazi* Sergeant Alican for his efforts in the literacy campaign in Gallipoli's villages following the Alphabet Reform. He added that copies of a photograph taken on this occasion, depicting Ataturk with his hand on *Ghazi* Sergeant Alican's shoulder, were available for distribution to interested parties.

After stating his belief that no one should prevent people's right to reach and know the truth, Ali Osman Taylar concluded his speech with the words: "The truth reveals only as much of itself as our intellect and courage can allow. Because the truth must be earned."

He reminded the assembly once more that people with questions could pose them after the conclusion of the statements and passed the word to Vicki.

274

When it was Vicki's turn to speak, the young woman looked considerably nervous, as she was unaccustomed to speaking in front of a crowd, especially under present conditions and in a foreign country. She had finally showered, bathed and dressed up in her own modest manner. She was wearing her jeans, boots and her blue sweater, she had left her long blonde hair loose to cascade over her shoulders and had applied some of the lipstick which, like all women, she kept stashed away somewhere among her belongings. A stranger might have easily dismissed her as one of the countless 'ordinary blonde, long-legged tourist girls' who all looked identical to the outside observer. But a closer inspection would have revealed a pinch of Maori blood in the broad arches of her eyebrows and in the flare of her nose, which she had inherited from her great-grand-mother Keri, her great-grandfather's first love, before Meryem.

Faced with the glut of cameras and microphones, Vicki struggled with the discomfort common to all who dislike the spotlight, and dreamed of getting away. She could not help but frequently turn an admiring gaze upon Ali Osman, who sat beside her wearing a fennel-scented male perfume, and she felt a kind of masochistic pleasure at reeling from his charm. As Ali Osman waited to translate Vicki's speech into Turkish, he carefully scanned the room with a pastel smile and seemed confident that he had taken stock of everything. Then he turned and looked at Vicki, once again flashed that brilliant smile and asked: "Ok, Vicki?"

'Gosh, what a smile!' thought Vicki, relaxing and turning to speak into the heap of microphones.

"I am... Victoria Taylor. I am from New Zealand, I work as a psychologist at a clinic in Wellington. I had no idea when I came here that the story I brought with me would cause so much anger and alarm. Honestly... I only came here hoping to complete an unfinished Gallipoli tale that my great-aunt Helen had told me when I was a child, and there are many such stories

275

back home. That was why I came here. Perhaps I was only after a dream, but it was my dream, nonetheless. I did not mean to disturb or harm anyone. Not at all... I do not like to draw attention to myself in general.

"I would like to state for the record that I was sincere in everything I have said and done. Ever since I was a little girl, the mystery that most intrigued me was not the identity of my great-grandfather Alistair John Taylor, but ·his sad story, which lacks even a gravesite to lend it any finality. It was simply the fantasies of a child who liked to read mystery novels and watch detective movies... What drew me was that mystery, I think that's what it was... Otherwise, I am not a person who would disturb the spirits of the dead. No, I am certainly not that kind of person.

"I was also struck by the similarity in our surnames. Naturally, since I do not know Turkish, I took this similarity as an important sign. Or at least, I was prepared to take it that way. I really was. But I've since understood that I was mistaken. I was mistaken. Yes, I admit that I was mistaken and I would like to take the opportunity here to once again respectfully honor the memory of my great-grandfather, New Zealander Alistair John Taylor, the memory of the Gallipoli war hero *Ghazi* Sergeant Alican, father of dear old Auntie Beyaz, who hosted me so graciously and taught me a very valuable history lesson, and the memory of the Sergeant's close friend in arms, Ottoman officer Ali Osman *Bey*. They were truly great people. They were great and wise people whose humanity we ourselves shall never be able to attain.

"My three weeks in Gallipoli have taught me that the term 'my heroic enemy', which was coined during the Battle of Gallipoli, is not a fantasy. It really has taught me that. If only everyone could learn the same lesson..."

"My mind is now at peace. I shall return to my country, after attending the Anzac Memorial Ceremony. But I have grown very fond of Gallipoli. I think I will return often to this wonder-ful place. Often... Yes.

"I apologize for the turmoil that I have caused. I had honestly not intended anything of the sort. Thank you for your attention."

Vicki had flushed bright red and was perspiring by the end of her speech. She hung her head and waited. Ali Osman, who had been looking ahead but listening to her with a very content expression, then glanced at the notes he had taken and translated her words into Turkish. Unfortunately, her speech failed to impress many of the journalists and reporters who had traveled a long distance to attend the press conference. People began to grumble and call out in protest. On the other hand, foreign press members and the 'men in black', whose affiliation with diplomats or the civil police was still a matter of debate, seemed highly pleased with Vicki's statement.

When he realized that the din would not settle of its own accord, the lawyer Ali Osman Taylar raised his voice and announced that his great-aunt Beyaz Taylar was going to speak last. Auntie Beyaz adjusted her dentures firmly into place, fingered her prayer beads and, narrowing her eyes, carefully scanned the assembled crowd. There was such a resolute defiance in her gaze, such confidence and startling liveliness that the hubbub inside the *kahveh* gradually faded and ceased. It seemed as though a supernatural light had been directed at the crowd, and they were at a complete loss as to how they should react. Everyone was silent. Vicki smiled, having long since learned of Auntie Beyaz's striking, charismatic presence, and of her guru-like powers of control. As for Ali Osman, he seemed rather accustomed to it all.

"You mean I'm supposed to speak now, *mari*?" Auntie Beyaz asked grouchily.

"Yes, Auntie Beyaz, it's your turn. See, these journalist and reporter ladies and gentlemen are waiting eagerly to hear what you have to say. Go ahead and tell them so everyone can rest easy," Ali Osman told her in the calm and compassionate manner of a grandson.

"I'm already at ease, son. Why on earth should I be uneasy? Let the newspapermen worry about themselves, *hele!*"

Auntie Beyaz's words, uttered in an intrepid and reproving tone, served to loosen up the crowd. People relaxed and laughed, realizing that the forbidding woman seated before them was simply a peasant grandma after all. When Vicki inquired as to the reason of the laughter, Ali Osman leaned toward her to translate Auntie Beyaz's words. Vicki noticed that Ali Osman took care not to get too close to her and to be deliberately loud enough to be overheard by others. Nevertheless, his fennel-scented perfume had touched her skin enough to set her head spinning.

"Look here, listen to me, you girls and boys from Ankara and Istanbul, and you foreign ladies and gentlemen: My father, late *Ghazi* Sergeant Alican was a great and honorable man. He was a hero. No one, and I mean no one, should even think of slighting his memory. Or, upon my word, you will rot and burn in hell!

"See, this here Vicki *Hanim*, this Zealander girl, she's my guest. And not only mine. She has come all the way to this country, so she is a guest of us all, *mari*! Now, what is it that you are having trouble sharing, *hele*? Her great-grandfather who died here, what was his name? Oh yes, Alistair John TayLOR, well, may he rest in peace. And may God also rest the souls of my father and his friend in arms, officer Ali Osman *Bey*. Leave the dead be. That's quite enough of your charlatanism! As the saying goes, a fool throws a rock down a well and a thousand smart folks waste time trying to fetch it back. Does that mean you're all smart? I sure doubt it, but nevermind... Don't you all have anything better to do, for God's sake? Is that why my father's generation saved this country from invasion, so that you could fool around like this? Is that why our strapping young lads died on the fields, so you could make money trading gossip? Did they leave this country in your hands so you could make fun of every little thing, so you could look down on everything? Eh? There's a world of work to be done! You leave the past alone, *mari*, and mind the present, the future! Let the dead be and take a look at what you yourselves are doing. Go on, then... everyone run along back to their homes, off you go!"

Although Auntie Beyaz's sharp and reproving speech had caused some people to grumble and some to titter nervously, it had above all made it crystal clear that this was the end of the discussion.

"Is that the lady they call enlightened? What a load of hooey... She's a dud, for sure!"

"Well, well! Grandma turned out to be a tough one, after all!"

"Watch out, man, we've angered Grandma Beyaz, let's get out of here before she gives us a whooping!"

"Gee, did you girls notice what a beautiful face the old lady had? Okay man, quit pulling at me..."

A few journalists cornered Vicki and subjected her to vengeful, accusative and vile questions, but she gave the same reply to them all: She was sorry, she had been mistaken, and she was being perfectly sincere.

Not wanting to return empty-handed after having spent all this time in Gallipoli, some people approached Auntie Beyaz in order to wreak from her a few general, controversial comments, but Ali Osman and the villagers had surrounded Vicki and her in a barricade. As for Auntie Beyaz, she sat beneath the Ataturk corner, calmly drinking tea with the *Mukhtar*, as though the two of them were alone at the *kahveh* and nothing unusual had transpired. The *Mukhtar* was jubilant now that Auntie Beyaz was talking to him again after years, and his prestige had been renewed. A few of the journalists planned on sticking around longer to cover the Anzac Memorial Services, which were slated to begin that evening, but most of them figured that the country had lost interest in the Battle of Gallipoli and prepared to leave in pursuit of stories that would fetch higher ratings.

Then the journalists, reporters, men in black, gendarmes, curious neighbors and security guards all packed up and left as quickly as they had arrived. The villagers heaved a deep sigh of relief and the White Rooster and chickens reappeared on the streets, to strut about freely. The clock and calendar-crazed notion of Western Time, which had been ushered in from the city, fell apart and was replaced by the languorous Eastern-Mediterranean Time. This languor was felt in the village as a smell of figs. The villagers immediately recognized the languorous scent and life resumed its very, very leisurely flow.

The village men entered the *kahveh*, sipped their tea and coffee, and began calmly surveying the weather and playing backgammon. But the joy of having Auntie Beyaz among them once again, chatting with the village men, could be read on all of their faces. Auntie Beyaz, the village sage, the guru of Gallipoli, the bounty of the Dardanelles, had finally abandoned her long grievance and returned to them. And Vicki was the name of this reconciliation. They would never again be cross with Vicki, even if she were to claim that not *Ghazi* Sergeant Alican, but their very own grandfathers had actually been enemy soldiers. Vicki had instigated a most valuable homecoming, and she now held a very special place.

The women and children of the village scattered back into the houses and the fields. The women did not have time to sit in the *kahveh* and sip tea. There was loads of work to be done in the fields and in the homes. They sighed and returned to their old ways.

Ali Osman, Vicki, Auntie Beyaz and Mehmet lingered a while longer at the *kahveh*. They had Turkish coffee and chatted about this and that, about the crops and the weather. Vicki, who now seemed peaceful and rather happy, was still reluctant to give Mehmet a definite answer about confirming her return ticket. Although she wanted to extend her stay in Gallipoli, she sensed no encouragement from Ali Osman, and thus kept her silence.

Ali Osman either pretended or genuinely failed to hear the subject, whenever she brought it up.

When Mehmet rose to depart for Eceabat, they all left the *kahveh*. Mehmet boarded his jeep and went back to the agency. Ali Osman took Auntie Beyaz's arm and, with Vicki at their side, they slowly walked towards Auntie Beyaz's house. Villagers who saw them walking arm in arm knocked on wood and murmured "God forbid she should get offended again!" and smiled heartily. It was one of those brief moments when everyone is happy.

As Auntie Beyaz had said, everyone had in fact 'run along back to their homes'. So much so that when Tahsin ran into Mehmet, on a bright and bustling street this time, he patted him on the back and said:

"Nice going, buddy! Looks like this time you taught the tourist lady how to recite her lessons properly."

"What do you mean 'recite'?" Mehmet prickled, but Tahsin soothed him in his own way:

"Yeah, sure, whatever you say, brother. The important thing is you spared us the task of twisting off the untimely rooster's head. Doesn't matter this way or that... In the end, well done, buddy! Now look, we're men of our word... We're sure to be loyal to our debt of gratitude. If you ever need us, just send the word and we'll immediately straighten out, clean and polish off your worry, okay? Oh, and tell that lawyer he's a fine, upstanding citizen!" he said.

Indeed, everyone had run along off to their homes, but there were homeless rats, as always, and they would exist forever.

"For heaven's sake, what's this story about New Zealand and yogurt, Vicki?" asked Ali Osman, laughing. "Seems you told some kind of New Zealand joke or anecdote having to do with yogurt when you first got to the Eceyaylasi Village, before you caused all that uproar."

Vicki laughed as well.

"Well, I must have made quite an impression for even you to have heard about it."

"I don't think anyone really understood, but you did manage to produce a catchphrase about New Zealanders and yogurt around these parts."

This time they laughed together.

Everyone looked happy now that the press conference and its side effects had diffused, and they were all gathered in Auntie Beyaz's backyard, among almond and rose trees, celebrating this 'liberation' by feasting on a lunch that Havva had prepared with the help of her neighbors. However, since everyone cannot ever be happy at the same time, the term 'everyone' always includes people who are pretending to be happy. Therefore, there had to be at least one person who was not actually content at the merry meal eaten among the rose and almond trees. Nonetheless, the one thing that everyone did agree upon was the deliciousness of the food.

The true reason behind the villagers' elation was naturally not some sordid tale, nor getting rid of a horde that had invaded their village in pursuit of this tale. The villagers of Eceyaylasi had believed for centuries that the blessed population of 'Heroic Gallipoli' would survive any disaster that might have befallen them. What they now celebrated was the fact that their revered Auntie Beyaz, who had shunned her compatriots and life itself for years, had finally emerged from her home and seemed possessed of her old strength. Thus was the bounty conferred upon the table, which resembled a wedding feast set beneath rose and almond trees.

Among the dishes were Gallipoli's famous '*Kachamak*'*, one of Auntie Beyaz's favorites, and Sardine *Kebab***, which they jokingly referred to as 'doodie *kebab*'. They explained that Sardine *Kebab* was best had in July, when the sardines were at their juiciest, and that since the fish were coal-roasted directly out of the water, their insides were only cleaned during the meal itself, hence the nickname. The tastiness of the dish far outweighed its moniker, and the three of them dug into the fish with great zest. The table was also laden with Gallipoli Delight, a pastry made with risen dough and plenty of oni-

---

*) *Kachamak*: a quick dish prepared with butter, flour and local cheese
**) *Kebab*: generic name for grilled dishes

ons and spinach, and *Tarak Pilaf*, a laborious dish that was prepared for the benefit of its great fan, Ali Osman. Vicki did not particularly enjoy the taste of the *pilaf*, which was made with scallops, but it amused her to watch Ali Osman munching away with childish exclamations of delight. Also on the table were a plate of salt bonitos, the inevitable *lokma* dessert, and a platter of sour apples and green almonds. Vicki stayed clear of the homemade yogurt and *ayran*, which tasted like medicine to her fruit-yogurt accustomed palette. With a great show of pity and protest, Auntie Beyaz and Ali Osman teased Vicki for drinking cola instead of *ayran*.

After the meal Auntie Beyaz retired for an afternoon nap, and Vicki and Ali Osman drove in his compact, Turkish-assembled French car to the Ariburnu-Anzac Cove, where the Anzac Memorial Services were to be held the next morning at dawn. There was an intense effort underway at the site. Officials and workers were busily preparing the area for the upcoming ceremony. Aided by the Turkish government, Australia and New Zealand had collaborated in the construction of a new Anzac Commemorative Site at the beach immediately adjacent to Ariburnu. White plastic chairs were being arranged for temporary use, paths were being cleared and grass was being mown. A mobile transmission station mounted with a giant antenna drove around looking for a place to park, since, in Gallipoli's inhospitable terrain, this was the only way to provide live broadcasting and wireless phone communication during the ceremony.

Vicki and Ali Osman watched the proceedings with interest as they strolled about among the laborers, who were all Turkish, and the officials, who were mostly employees of the Commonwealth War Graves Commission.

"It's hard to believe that the chilly and deserted cove of three weeks ago is the same sunny and crowded beach I see now," Vicki remarked.

"Don't be fooled by the sunshine. Gallipoli has a mean chill. Plus, if you call this a crowd, I'd like to see what you say tomorrow morning. By dawn, we're going to have trouble finding room to even stand. There will be at least ten thousand Anzac descendants present here," Ali Osman explained.

"I suppose most of the Anzac descendants will be Australians. We New Zealanders trail Australia in almost every subject. It starts with surface area and population and goes on from there..." said Vicki, smiling melancholically.

Ali Osman found this bitter-sweet smile very becoming on Vicki and gave her an appraising glance for the second time. Gone was the unkempt, scattered, *shalvar*-clad girl of their initial meeting, who was oddly obsessed with washing her hair. She had instead been replaced by an attractive young woman whose form-fitting jeans accentuated her tall, slim figure, whose blue sweater brought out the blue of her eyes and whose long blonde hair truly did seem worth the washing. Her lips glowed a pale pink. Ali Osman only now noticed that she had put on lipstick.

"We New Zealanders feel far flung from Europe, which is to us the center of the world, and from North America, which has perhaps become more central than even Europe in the past fifty years. As you know, we also have a commonwealth partner, Canada, in North America. Anyhow, this sense of alienation, of being left out and overlooked, causes in us a kind of melancholy. Our lively, cheerful, outgoing and athletic exteriors conceal a secret melancholy. And this is why we deem a phrase such as 'down under' to be fitting for our country," Vicki confided.

"Also, Australia, which is right next to us, is a huge island and it is more powerful than us both economically and culturally. Even though the New Zealand economy has made considerable progress in recent years, particularly in wine, beef, and wool production... I don't know, we just grow up hearing that we are little old New Zealand, the country that goes un-mentioned in many international weather reports, in favor of adjacent Australia. See, even our famous director, Jane Campion and our famous soprano, Kiri Te Kanawa have left New Zealand. I suppose you could say that we New Zealanders are a somewhat solitary, somewhat excluded, and somewhat mournful lot... I mean, some of us are, maybe not all... And naturally, these are all my own personal opinions. We don't like to generalize. Anyhow, that's the culture that produced my infamous yogurt and New Zealand joke."

"I see," Ali Osman said, thoughtfully.

He had shed his suit in favor of coffee-colored khakis and a dark blue corduroy jumper. He wore handsome loafers that matched his trousers, had once again shaved clean and put on his fennel-scented cologne.

"Perhaps this melancholy is similar to our own identity problems. Our nation's frame leans against the Eastern Mediterranean, it has one cheek in Europe and the other in Asia, its arms are stretched from the Balkans to the Caucasus, and its feet are planted in the Middle East. We too are ever struggling with an identity crisis that began with our becoming Istanbulites in 1453 and grew fiercer with the establishment of our first constitution in 1876. In Turkey, we grow up with the question: 'Are we Europeans or Asians?' We batter ourselves, and allow others to batter us with this question. On the bloody and wearying road from monarchy into democracy, Turkey's character is also one of sorrow."

"Oh, but I thought you were Eastern-Mediterraneans!" Vicki came back sharply.

Ali Osman laughed when he understood the conversation to which she was referring.

"Right you are, Vicki. But I did not give that speech only to rouse and distract Mehmet. The things I said that day were correct. Because it would be safe to say that by the end of the

286

21st century, us Turks of Turkey have assumed a completely Eastern-Mediterranean character, both culturally and genetically speaking. After continuous westward migrations, we settled in Anatolia and the Balkans. Following centuries of cultural and genetic intermingling with thirty-six different cultures, it is completely natural that today's so-called Turkish nation should share only sociologically-buried similarities with the Turks who migrated out of Central Asia a millennium ago. I once spoke to one of our internationally renowned photographers, a man who had taken pictures of Picasso, Dali and Halide Edip back in the day, and he told me that despite scouring Turkey entirely, he had still failed to discover a single true Turk's son or daughter whom he could document. Not a single one! Whatever the headhunters do, we are so intermingled that there is no 'most authentic Turk' left here. But we are all Turkish."

"What you say reminds me a little of the United States."

"True. One could well argue that the U.S. did, in a sense, model itself after the Ottoman Empire. But I would like to make a leap elsewhere at this point. 21st century Turkey could easily be likened to the New Zealand culture, which emerged from the intermingling of British immigrants with the Maoris and immigrants of other nationalities. Although non-Christian cultures such as ours may regard this new culture as roughly similar to that of Britain, I am sure that its inhabitants can write hundreds of papers on the differences between New Zealand and British cultures."

"You're right, Ali Osman, though we might be members of the British Commonwealth, New Zealand is a culture of its own. Now, I hadn't quite thought of Turkey in this way," replied Vicki, shaking her head. "How odd of my Western eyes to remain indifferent to differences in Moslem cultures, while noticing variations in Christian ones..."

"It's not odd, Vicki, it's an assertion of the system. Systems cultivate animosity or arrogance in its citizens against those who are different from them, by employing such diversionary or blinding methods as nationalism and fundamentalism. For blind citizens are easier to manipulate," said Ali Osman, with a bitter laugh.

"Are you a leftist, Ali Osman?" Vicki asked for the second time.

"Communist systems made use of the same 'blind citizen' concept, Vicki," Ali Osman replied.

"Then you're an anarchist!" Vicki concluded.

"An anarchist criminal lawyer, eh? I thought you had a more vivid imagination, Vicki."

"Well, I don't know, you keep on surprising me. Besides, I thought all lawyers were humdrum people. Money-grubbing, arrogant and humdrum people!"

Ali Osman gave a short but hearty laugh. The resulting human warmth, combined with his dashing good looks, cracked the feminine vein in Vicki, and warm feminine juices started to ooze into her body.

"And I thought all psychologists were emotionally troubled people; greasy-haired, barefoot and rebellious..."

"Not entirely false," said Vicki, feeling a little peeved.

Afraid he had hurt her feelings, Ali Osman threw an arm around Vicki and gave her a friendly squeeze.

"Oh, come on, I was just kidding. Anyway, you're not altogether wrong about humdrum lawyers. But every profession and gender has its exceptions, as you can see."

Vicki was very pleased with the arm that was wrapped around her shoulder; she reeled happily in the fennel scent that inspired in her such longing.

"Say Vicki, why don't you tell me about this New Zealand and yogurt joke," Ali Osman prompted.

"It's not really all that funny. I just thought the villagers would like me better if they saw that I could poke fun at my own culture, I thought they would make things easier, help me out... But that's not what happened."

"You mean your psychological speculation did not work?"

"How was I supposed to know that Turks made yogurt by fermenting it?"

"How do you make it?"

"Out of yogurt culture... That's the joke, even yogurt has culture but New Zealanders don't... You see, it's an extreme version of that melancholy, a self-inflicted jab... Sarcasm at its utmost!"

"But that's a good sign Vicki. It's much better than being an uptight, humorless nation incapable of poking fun at itself, one that cannot stand being made fun of and thinks it's the sole element of world culture. Thank goodness we have Nasreddin Hodja and *Laz** jokes. But there is a fervent and hypersensitive nationalism being fomented here that undermines our ability to regard ourselves critically. I hope that educated, upcoming generations will be able to overcome this weakness of ours. At least I can say that the process has begun with my generation."

He pulled his arm away from Vicki's shoulder and emphasized his words by opening his arms up in the air on either side.

"I mean the virtue of being able to see ourselves neither as pathetic and helpless, nor as the strongest and most resilient nation in the world..."

Vicki felt lonely and abandoned when he took his arm away. She was aware, through female intuition, that his arm had only touched her in a friendly manner, but she had enjoyed the feeling nevertheless.

They had strolled up to a terrace that had been especially

---

*) *Laz*: Turkish people living in the south-east of the Black Sea

289

constructed for the Anzac Memorial Services, and they now stood facing a wall inlaid with photographs. Displayed at the Gallipoli National Park, which was already an open-air museum, the eighty-five year-old pictures lent a solemn aura to the park with their mournful sepia tones.

One photograph of sick and wounded Anzac soldiers was captioned with a couplet from an anonymous Gallipoli ode: 'They lived with death/They were fed with disease.'

Another photograph, depicting a blindfolded Turkish officer crossing over to the Anzac side on May 24, 1915 to discuss the burial of Turkish casualties, was accompanied by the words of Turkish soldier Memish Bayraktar: "The dead, the dead, the dead... There are more dead here than can be counted..."

Yet another picture, of Turkish artillerymen, nestled within a larger photo of Mustafa Kemal, bore a quote from Turkish veteran Adil Shahin: "Their mission was to come and invade this land, ours was to protect it!"

Without uttering a word, Ali Osman and Vicki inspected each inlaid photograph and read the captions. Then they walked down to the beach in silence, and stood facing the now tranquil Aegean Sea. They both seemed lost in thought. Their eyes fixed upon the water, their bodies almost, but not quite touching, they stood restlessly facing the Aegean Sea, as though each had entered a profound dialogue with his and her own soul.

They remained standing there. But Gallipoli had a mean chill. They both felt an inner shiver at the wind's hardy tug. Nonetheless, they appeared insistent on standing there next to one another.

After a long while, Vicki reached out and took Ali Osman's hand. Ali Osman did not resist. They stood hand in hand at Ariburnu-Anzac Cove, without looking at each other and without saying a word. Both of them were aware of the watchful Sphinx that loomed proud and fearsome behind them, and of the dead young men who filled the Anzac cemetery.

"We're going to get cold here!" Ali Osman remembered after some time. "Let's go back to the car. We'll be here all day tomorrow anyway."

Vicki suddenly noticed that her nose was running, but she simply sniffled so as to keep holding Ali Osman's hand, and said:

"Gallipoli certainly does have a sinister chill."

Ali Osman chuckled as they walked hand in hand toward the car:

"It sure does. 'Winter is bitter in Gallipoli. It will get you, that ruthless chill. Winter is mean in Gallipoli. It is much more wicked and merciless than one would expect from the Aegean region. The howling wind tells a sinister tale, it prowls around town, roughing up people on the street.' Wait, how did the rest of it go? Oh yes: 'The quiet drizzle of early spring rain sends a tremor across your heart as if it has fully understood the wind's sinister tale. This tale moves even those visitors that don't know it, or have never heard of it before, and leaves a trace of melancholy on them. Gallipoli's wind wears you down, leaves you lonesome. Gallipoli's winter is mean and chilly. Foreigners don't understand it, they cannot believe that winter so far in the Eastern Mediterranean can be so harsh. Only locals of the Dardanelles know of the winter's bitter cold. The Gallipoli Peninsula's chill hits you hardest in early spring when the cold is the meanest.' That's what my great-grandfather *Ghazi* Sergeant Alican used to say."

"Well, he would have been one to know, don't you think?" Vicki said with a sly smile.

"Yes, he was a true Chanakkale local. It was the foreigners who did not know. See, you have learned as well."

"Right, I've learned as well," Vicki agreed absently.

When they cleared the hill where the car was parked, Ali Osman stopped Vicki, turned to face the Aegean and pointed toward the Anzac Cove.

"Did you know that the landing that took place eight-five years ago tonight was planned on Khaba Tepe but that it was mistakenly, or owing to some unfortunate circumstance, made at the Ariburnu-Anzac Cove, a mile and a half north?" he asked.

Vicki, who could not take her eyes off the lovely view below them, held back her wind-whipped hair from her face with one hand.

"I had read something of the sort. I guess it was a tragic mistake that occurred due to miscalculations of the wind and current..."

Ali Osman smiled. Seeing him smile made Vicki realize the political blunder that she had made. She understood once again that what was tragic for one could be comical for another. She tried to correct her gaffe:

"A great misfortune for our men, and a great stroke of luck for yours, naturally. Just look at that rocky beach, what an inappropriate place for a landing," she said.

"There is yet another theory pertaining to that misfortune. The English have always rejected it but it does not seem so unreasonable to me," Ali Osman remarked.

"What's the theory?"

"It's a tiny little detail having to do with a signal buoy moored near Khaba Tepe, where the Anzacs were to land at dawn of April 25, 1915. Just a detail, really..."

"Details... Do go on, Ali Osman, I'm fascinated by the signs that details conceal."

"Well, according to local legend, Turkish fishermen noticed an unfamiliar buoy moored out near Khaba Tepe and grew immediately suspicious, being already in a wartime state of mind. They reported the incident to police headquarters in Gallipoli, then, that same night, with the help of a few soldiers, moved the buoy fifteen hundred meters north to Ariburnu Cove, a most unsuitable place for a military landing. At the time, there was only one Turk who believed that the enemy might land at the Ariburnu-Anzac Cove, and that was a colonel named Mustafa Kemal. Indicating that even the Turks did not take the signal buoy very seriously at the time."

"That colonel you just mentioned, was that Ata-Turk?" Vicki asked.

"Yes, it was Ataturk. And throughout his life, he maintained that superior intelligence and common sense which he demonstrated at the Dardanelles."

At that moment Vicki grasped the admiration Ali Osman held for this man, whose visage was the one most commonly displayed on Turkey's walls. Perhaps, after returning to New Zealand, she ought to conduct a more thorough research on Ataturk. Investigate the real reasons why eighty-five years later, this man, whom Western cultures dismissed as an ordinary dictator but who seemed more than just a charismatic political leader and skilled commander, continued to exert such an influence over so many people. By now, she too was curious about the reasons. She was truly curious. What had this man called Ataturk actually done? Had he worked an illusion, a miracle, or simply established a fascist presidency, as some Westerners patronizingly claimed? Whereas all the revolutionary leaders of the early 20th century and their revolutions had disappeared by the wayside, how was it that only this man's name and revolution continued to be guarded? It was guarded. Yes, it was safeguarded. There was Auntie Beyaz, speaking of a future that would be inconceivable in any Islamic country for her rural great-granddaughters. Vicki was not sure how well she could understand this as a foreigner, but she was curious to see. Furthermore, this could be one path that would lead her to better understand Ali Osman. It could be necessary for her to understand Ataturk better, in order to get to know Ali Osman, this thrilling young man who had suddenly entered her life. She had met people who studied Rosa Luxembourg in order to better comprehend the woman they loved, or people who researched Churchill so they might become better acquainted with their father.

"So, dear Vicki, that is what Turks believe happened in what you call 'the game of fortune between our men and yours'. But, as you can guess, this theory of ours has always been met with vehement rejection. Of course, it makes a person shudder to think that a few Turkish fishermen could have foiled the plans of the mighty British Navy. But maybe it was true, who knows?"

His voice was not mocking, hurt or angry. His voice, his manner and his gaze all seemed perfectly frank. He was not sure if in fact the event he had related was true, but he was clearly curious.

"Who knows? Why not? Any opportunity can be used in the course of defense," Vicki agreed, trusting his sincerity. "In the end, our boys failed both the location of the landing and the landing itself. Your men succeeded in defense. But it was the young men on both sides who paid the..."

They fell silent. Taking care to avoid each other's eyes, they quietly shook their heads in a final gesture of regret and hid their gaze in the waters of the Aegean.

"When we were kids," Ali Osman murmured thoughtfully, "When we were kids, we used to support different soccer teams, so we would say 'your boys' in reference to Fenerbahce and 'our boys' when talking about Galatasaray. Hearing you say 'our boys' just now, suddenly made me think that you were a Galatasaray fan... As though we were still children... You and I..."

Vicki laughed and mumbled, as if to herself:

"It's so funny and childish, isn't it? Your boys and ours... How sad..."

Ali Osman turned to Vicki and smiled. That was when they looked at each other. They now looked at each other carefully, without trepidation. They saw each other. And they realized that they saw each other.

"Shall we go to Chanakkale?" asked Ali Osman, as he opened the car door. "There are cafés there that serve instant coffee, unlike our village *kahveh*," he added teasingly.

"Oh, that would be smashing, I could die for a true cup of coffee."

Ali Osman chuckled:

"Truths like that will kill you," he said, starting the car.

They spent the drive identifying trees and chatting cheerfully about the natural beauty of the Dardanelles. Ali Osman mentioned that the National Park would soon undergo a facelift and an expansion as part of a Peace Park project, but that he personally preferred it to be left the way it was. And when they stopped speaking, they shuddered to think that they were driving merrily across the land where thousands of youths had perished in blood, sweat and tears eighty-five years ago.

At Eceabat they boarded the ferry for Chanakkale. Chanakkale greeted them shyly, a city with small-town naivete. They parked the car and, as they ambled around the provincial city streets, people who recognized Vicki from the TV and newspapers, smiled and nodded at her. Vicki had not realized that she was so well known, and only then did she perceive what a great tragedy her innocent story had almost been turned into.

"Everyone is greeting me warmly," she remarked happily.

"Of course they like you, you're an innocent tourist girl who fell for a childish fairytale and apologized for her misunderstanding. They are certainly fond of you, Vicki," Ali Osman whispered through his teeth.

"I see," sighed Vicki.

They came across a patisserie that was a hangout of students from the University of March Eighteen, and resembled more a student cafeteria than a café. Upon entering inside, they discovered that a thick cloud of cigarette smoke made it nearly impossible to breathe. They ordered 'two black instant coffees' but in no time began to suffer the torture of non-smokers in an atmosphere dense with smoke. First their eyes, then their throats began to feel constricted under the almost black fog.

"Why do Turkish youth smoke so much?" asked Vicki, coughing.

"Eastern-Mediterranean ignorance..." replied Ali Osman, wincing. "Besides, if it were not for us Easterners, to which fools would smart Westerners sell cigarettes and make money?"

"Must you always bring in politics? You ought to quit practicing law and get into politics, Ali Osman."

"Who knows, maybe I will... Who knows, maybe you're foreseeing my future plans. I can't guarantee that, but what I can guarantee is the fact that, after having quit four years ago, I shall never go back to cigarettes. Come on, let's get out of here Vicki."

They paid the puzzled waiter and, leaving their coffees untouched, fled the smoke-infested café. There was a restaurant directly across the street, empty since it was before dinnertime. Ali Osman invited Vicki in there. They asked the waiter for two orders of *baklava** and coffee. Upon Ali Osman's request, the waiter had a jar of instant coffee purchased from a nearby grocery store and the restaurant, which had heretofore only served Turkish coffee, served its first instant coffee for the benefit of its foreign customer.

"My time in Gallipoli is going to be an important turning point in my life, I can already tell," Vicki confided, sipping her coffee and taking a small bite of the *baklava*, which she found too sweet. "I feel a palpable pain, like a knife wound, right here, above my stomach. I know that the pain is going to recede some day, but I will forever carry the stitches of the wound. My body shall always carry the scar I incurred in Gallipoli, Ali Osman."

"You must be a good psychologist," said Ali Osman. "If you can identify your own feelings that well, your patients must be pretty lucky..."

"I can only provide so much therapy for myself as you can

---

*) *Baklava*: layered sweet pastry

be fair to yourself," Vicki laughed bitterly. "Auntie Beyaz is the expert there. No one can surpass her. No one!"

"You're right. She's the daughter of *Ghazi* Sergeant Alican, who never lost his love or faith in humanity, and of Meryem, the queen of courage and passion. Auntie Beyaz, a sage and skillful magician. She is one in a million!" said Ali Osman with a proud and affectionate smile.

"You know that expression we like to repeat so often, the one we boast of knowing? 'Everything depends on how you look at it.' Well, Auntie Beyaz taught me the meaning of that expression the hard way. She did. Yes, that old lady taught me. I'm going to miss her tons... tons..."

"What about your house, your family, your job? Don't you miss those, Vicki?"

"Of course I do. I miss my kids, and the smell of fresh coffee in the morning, noon and evening. I miss the smell of my coffee at every hour... Gosh, do I! Let's see, I miss sailing, and eating sushi... Did I ever tell you I was a keen sailor? One who was qualified to compete for the Yachting Championship of the American Cup in the 12-metres class, no less..."

"Bravo!" enthused Ali Osman. "I've always been impressed by women who do sports."

Vicki did not hear him. She was now absorbed in thinking of the things she had left behind in New Zealand.

"I even miss my dad..." she went on. "How strange, I miss my dad, even though I've always been mad at him. Perhaps I had to leave there to realize that I missed it... Strange but true... But... On the other hand, Ali Osman, I don't feel much like a foreigner here anymore... No, I don't really feel like a foreigner here... This... Maybe this... I wonder if I've reached a stage of instinctual empathy in order to identify with my great-grandfather?"

"That's something for you to know. But since you ask, I would leave a critical situation such as this to dry in the air, so I could reevaluate it after some time. That is the best way to read the contents of a page if it gets wet. Right now, right here, everything is too new, and the stitches have not yet been removed from the knife wound on your stomach. Wait, stay calm and see."

They were silent. They sipped their coffee.

"I didn't know that you had children. In fact, I don't know anything about you, Vicki," Ali Osman confessed in an almost woeful tone.

Vicki smiled, sensing with womanly instinct that the woe in his voice indicated an interest for her.

"Oh yes, my kids! They are the kids I work with. I work with developmentally disabled children, Ali Osman. I have a group of autistic children at the clinic. They were upset with me when I told them that I would be coming to Gallipoli for a month-long unpaid vacation. But when I promised to bring them back pebbles from the Anzac Cove, they gave me permission to go. I've gathered two bags of pebbles for them. You know, I really love them. They are kind, incredibly sweet-spirited kids. I love them like they were my own children. Maybe I will adopt one of them someday... Who knows."

"So, are you telling me that a girl like you is actually unattached?" asked Ali Osman, with concern.

He waited. After some time, Vicki murmured in a faraway voice:

"There was a man. In the past, there was a man. But not anymore. Yes, I have been alone for a while. I have no one in my life except my work, my autistic kids, my great-grandfather's mystery, a bunch of cousins I haven't seen in ages, and my dad. My dad, whose love I have resisted for so long..."

She looked restless, as though she were plummeting into a deep well of fog. Not knowing what to say, Ali Osman waited for her to come back.

"I could never forgive my dad for remarrying after my mother's premature death. And yet... And yet, I loved him dearly... But I always hurt him and kept him at arm's length..."

"What about that man, that man in the past?"

"Oh, him?" remembered Vicki, breaking into a pastel smile as though her face were lit by a rosy glow. "He was a very sweet lad. He was in love with me. He was a Maori, who are passionate about love. Yes, I had a Maori sweetheart. Just like my great-grandfather... But I think I was afraid. I was afraid of falling in love with him, of becoming attached, of the responsibilities brought by love and relationships, of the responsibilities that loving someone would bring. I was terrified, so I fled. I hurt him, and made him awfully unhappy... I wrecked his life... I was terrified..."

They were silent. They became engrossed in their own sad memories, and forgot about one another. When the waiter approached them to ask if they wanted another cup of coffee, they fixed him with blank stares, as though they had forgotten who the waiter was. Ali Osman was the first one to snap back to attention. He ordered a second round of coffee, not really to drink but to lengthen their stay.

"Okay, so who is Semahat, Ali Osman?" Vicki asked out of the blue.

"Oh you women!" Ali Osman laughed quietly. "You never miss a detail, do you?"

"Is that what Semahat is, a detail?" Vicki pressed.

"No, of course not. Semahat is valuable to me. She is a very intelligent and kind girl. I can say that we almost grew up together. We were as close as siblings, and admired each other. Semahat is Doctor Salih *Bey*'s granddaughter."

"They named her after her great-grandmother, just like me," said Vicki coldly.

"I've been aware of that from the beginning, Vicki. You two have other things in common as well. In fact, you might become fast friends if you meet someday. She's a psychiatrist. You could say that their family has an inherited tradition of becoming doctors."

"But you carried on Ali Osman *Bey*'s name and his profession, which he never got to practice!" said Vicki. There was a cold and accusative tone in her voice.

Ali Osman puzzled over what he might have done to offend her. Men are inept at realizing when a woman is being jealous of them.

"Anyway, the two least compatible professions in the world are psychiatrists and psychologists!" Vicki wrote off the matter.

Then Ali Osman understood. He understood and smiled contentedly, like all men do once they realize that they are objects of a woman's jealousy. He even felt a bit spoiled.

"I'd never thought of that," he said.

He began speaking as cautiously as though he were astride an elephant in a room packed with expensive crystals.

"Look Vicki, Semahat is a close and dear friend of mine. She and I are resolved to continue our friendship, even if our paths should diverge in the future. I mean, at least that is what I hope will happen. Though our families may hope that we get married someday, we seriously do not have such a future planned. Yes, we love each other, but has there ever been a person in this world who could claim that one love would last an entire lifetime with the same name and intensity? Tell me, when does a love start or end, for God's sake?"

Vicki sighed and gave a weary smile.

"And you want to know a secret, Vicki? Semahat is one of the new generation of urban Turkish girls who don't look too kindly on marriage, who put their job first. Furthermore, who can guarantee that at this moment, right at this very moment, Semahat has not met a man that she will love better than me?"

Why had he emphasized the present by saying 'right at this very moment'? Vicki hesitated to think of the reply.

"But there is no end to that, Ali Osman."

300

"Sometimes you meet a person who makes you want to bring it to an end. It may be right or wrong, but sometimes you meet such a person," said Ali Osman.

"That must be when all those wrong marriages take place..." Vicki mocked.

"But there is no right marriage Vicki. In every human interaction, every relationship, two people come together and conflict inevitably follows. It's a law of nature that stems from the contradictions in human nature!"

"Ah laws, but of course..." said Vicki, smiling genuinely this time.

"Perhaps I'm a bit too old-fashioned for Semahat, there are many things we don't see eye to eye. But whatever the end result, Semahat is going to remain my friend, you can be sure we agree on that."

"Glad to hear it," said Vicki but did not explain what it was that she was glad to hear. And Ali Osman did not ask.

Evening had fallen. They got up and returned to the Eceyaylasi Village without speaking. It had been a long, very long and strenuous day.

Auntie Beyaz was expecting them for dinner. The three of them ate dinner and watched TV a little, as naturally and compatibly as though they had been living together at the Eceyaylasi Village, in Auntie Beyaz's house for years. Their story had fallen to last place on the TV news agenda. Then, they each retired to a different room and fell asleep.

Their sleep was jampacked with different dreams. They slept under the same roof, as relatives of the same man, in Gallipoli.

Auntie Beyaz woke Vicki up at three o'clock in the morning. It was pitch-dark, cold, and menacing outside.

"Time to get up Vicki, my girl, time for the landing, come on, up you get!"

"Time for the landing?" Vicki gave a start and jumped out of bed.

She had been having the same terrifying nightmare that had plagued her since childhood. Her great-grandfather, covered in blood and thrashing on the ground, held out his hand toward her and moaned: "You will find me Vicki, you will come to look for me, Vicki..." Her great-grandfather, Alistair John Taylor, youthful as in his final photographs in New Zealand, but with half of his face shattered, his fingers missing, and only half his body intact, was alone on a steep mountainside that resembled a lion's head, calling out to her: "Vicki, Vicki, you must find me!"

This exhausting nightmare, horrific enough for an adult, had driven her mad as a child. Just when it had finally deserted her, just when she had tasted her first ever good night's sleep here in Gallipoli, eighty-five years to the hour of the Anzac landing the nightmare was back. Vicki woke up drenched in sweat. Her heart was pounding.

"Oh dear, dear me, there's nothing to be afraid of, my girl, I was just trying to make a joke *mari*, darn my old head…" Auntie Beyaz was berating herself, having assumed that she was responsible for frightening Vicki.

"No, Auntie Beyaz, no, that's not it, I was just having a nightmare… But it's over now, see, I'm fine."

"Let's hope Providence makes it right. Nightmares are not at all auspicious, my girl. I'd better cast a few protective spells over you. You might be touched by the evil eye. Yes, that's it, just when you'd put on a little weight and started looking pretty, the evil eye comes and touches you. Just when we'd started putting some meat on your bones, *mari*, dear, dear me…"

"Oh come off it, Auntie Beyaz…You're obsessed with me being skinny… But thanks to you, the more I eat, the more weight I gain and the more I want to eat. If I ever lived here, I'd grow awfully fat from all that wonderful food!" said Vicki, yawning. She was at ease now that she had reoriented herself.

"Look here, you'd better dress warmly! Gallipoli has a mean winter, you know, else it'll get you…"

"I know, I know, that whole business about Gallipoli's infamous chill, right?" Vicki mumbled jadedly, gave several repeated yawns, and stretched like a young cat. "But only foreigners catch that chill, and I'm practically a local now, aren't I Auntie Beyaz?" she said and tittered nervously.

303

Hearing her strange laugh, Auntie Beyaz grew even more concerned. She sat down beside Vicki, stroked her back, mouthed prayers and gently caressed her hair. She was trying in her own way to protect Vicki, by warding off the evil eye indicated by the nightmare and dispelling the negative energy brought about by envious glances. Vicki, who was bitterly proud of solving her inner conflicts by herself and not allowing anyone to poke their nose into her problems, attempted out of lifelong habit to hold herself back, but did not succeed. Because a most unexpected thing had happened; the touch felt good to Vicki. It felt very good. She experienced a brief inner struggle, then gave up. After having lived in Auntie Beyaz's house for a week, Vicki no longer accused her of being a witch or a shaman, and she surrendered like a lamb to this ritual of love. She relaxed and welcomed into her body the kindness that flowed from this healing hand, which ran lovingly through her hair. It was the loveliest meditation she had ever known, and Vicki felt good. Since she had no memories of her mother, she thought of how her Aunt Helen used to stroke her hair when she was a little girl. Aunt Helen, who had been a mother to her until age ten, who had maintained a lifelong conviction that her brother Alistair John Taylor had not died at Gallipoli and who had instilled the same conviction in Vicki. Dear Aunt Helen. Aunt Helen, whose death at the age of ninety-four left Vicki once again motherless. Aunt Helen, who would have been in heaven to witness everything that was happening here. Aunt Helen, who was already in heaven.

The intense emotions summoned by Auntie Beyaz's touch washed through Vicki and made her nose tingle, and she realized at that point how much she had missed her Aunt Helen. She was about to start crying but restrained herself. Instead, she turned around and, without expecting to, wrapped Auntie Beyaz in a hug.

"Hold on, *mari*, you're going to choke me. Heavens above. See now the poor girl hasn't had a proper night's rest!" Auntie Beyaz grumbled.

Oddly enough, Vicki, who had not really hugged anyone except her Aunt Helen, had forgotten how, like herself, Auntie Beyaz was not at all fond of overt displays of affection. And when she realized that she could no longer hold herself back, she grabbed her trousers, sweater and bra and fled to the bathroom, wearing the t-shirt she used for a nightgown. She was crying without letting Auntie Beyaz know.

When she returned to the living room, her bed had been cleared, the light had been turned on and two cups of tea had been set on the table. Ali Osman was dressed and waiting for her.

"Good morning Vicki," he yawned, then teased her, "you're sure to have a good day if you've received your morning scolding from Auntie Beyaz."

His voice came out hoarse and still muffled with sleep, but he had clearly heard their conversation.

"Nah, we were just chatting…" said Vicki, lowering her head to conceal her reddened eyes.

But she did not have much of a chance to brood over her past and have self-pity. Despite having skipped the shave at three in the morning, Ali Osman was wearing his familiar fennel-scented cologne, and the scent struck Vicki forcibly. Smelling the cologne and remembering its significance was enough to jolt Vicki awake. Wide awake. She smiled with excitement. Life went on, and it was in Gallipoli that she had found the courage to taste and smell life. In Gallipoli. At the turning point of her life.

She then gave an appraising glance at the source of that smell that aroused the female within her, and found a very attractive man sitting there right beside her, dressed in casual clothes and still half asleep.

It was three in the morning but Vicki had fastidiously brushed her teeth, combed her hair, and, impervious to the hour, put on her pink lipstick. She knew she had never done anything of the sort for anyone else, but did it anyway.

She took a few sips of her tea without speaking, and waited for Ali Osman to finish his tea. Then they went downstairs. He put on his shoes and pullover while she got into her boots and coat, and they set off.

Auntie Beyaz called out to them from the window:

"Have a safe trip now, children!"

The Gallipoli National Park had been closed to motorists due to the large number of visitors expected. A few military vehicles and gendarmes were posted at the entrance to the park. The gendarmes were politely explaining to people that cars were not allowed inside due to the ceremony. Hundreds of luxury tour buses and cars were parked closely together, and the walkways of the park were jampacked with people. Travel operators were busy handing out identity badges and placards to help them keep track of their customers in the crowd. Eighty-five years after the Anzac landing, the Gallipoli Peninsula was packed to the gills with people.

Ali Osman parked his car in the first available spot. Using a flashlight that he took out of the car, he and Vicki joined the throng of people making their way toward the Ariburnu-Anzac Cove. The air was chilly and the forest was illuminated by nothing more than the occasional headlight or flashlight. It gave one a strange feeling to hear the soil crunching under the tread of hundreds of feet that walked toward the Ariburnu-Anzac Cove in the darkness. The crunch of the soil was like a song that would sadden anyone who knew its story. Perhaps it was because they had traveled thousands of miles to come to Gallipoli tonight and hear the soil's crunch that people spoke in whispers as they walked. The procession, which contained some Turks among its ranks, shared an odd sense of unity and a respectful mood, as though wary of disturbing the dead. They strode and the soil crunched under their feet. The soil of the Gallipoli Peninsula was being crunched once again, eighty-five years later. The ground crunching as they walked... The Chanakkale soil that constituted the unmarked graves of thousands of youth was crunching, and each step seemed to mourn the story of a separate lad. The soil's crunch was a hymn, those lying beneath it were a choir and those who walked above to commemorate them were a group of dancers, this is how Vicki thought of it, and when, for a moment, the vision of this tragic opera scene flashed before her eyes, she was shaken with terror. This was an extraordinary spectacle. It was an incredibly moving, frightfully searing and painful scene. So vivid and immediate was it, and so bordering on the grotesque that it made Vicki dizzy. She stumbled, unable to control herself. Ali Osman reached out for Vicki's arm, presuming that she was still too drowsy and might fall down. He took her arm and did not let go. Vicki was trembling. Ali Osman's clutch had rescued her from falling. She grasped the hand that held her arm. She held it and did not let go.

The Anzac descendants, many of them toting plastic bags filled with beer cans and carrying sleeping bags, crunched the ground as they walked. They had come prepared to drink and sing at the gravesites of their grandparents following the dawn service. Although gravesite visits that involved alcohol and noise were unusually ostentatious for Moslem cultures and seemed odd to the Turks, they tolerated it for the sake of their 'heroic' enemies' memories. Some Turks were only using the occasion as an excuse to drink on the beach and ogle the 'pretty blonde tourist girls', but the ground did not make a single sound beneath their feet. Those passing through Gallipoli, oblivious to the events that had taken place eighty-five years earlier, were people whose ears would never be sensitive enough to hear that sound anyway.

They walked a mile or so to reach the Ariburnu-Anzac Cove. But upon arriving they were met with such a crowd that it was impossible to walk any further. Lit by generators, the site might well have resembled a rock festival to someone who did not know any better. Thousands of youths wrapped in colorful sleeping bags or New Zealand and Australian flags were sprawled out on the grass, creating the atmosphere of an outdoor concert. A few Turkish and numerous foreign TV crews were immediately noticeable, wandering around with cameras and microphones in hand. At the edge of the beach, where the crowded dignitaries sat on white outdoor chairs, a podium had been constructed with its back to the sea and lit brightly with spotlights. Three poles stood next to the podium. On these, the flags of New Zealand, Australia and Turkey flew at half-mast. The space behind the flagpoles was dark. The sea waited in that darkness, eerily quiet, like the gigantic mouth of a jet-black dragon, ready to swallow into oblivion anything that approached it. The Aegean Sea waited at the Ariburnu-Anzac Cove like a wild horse that had been forced into a stable, it waited for the door to crack open and the light to shine through so it could show everyone once more that it would never ever be tamed. The Aegean Sea never forgot the thousands of young men who perished on its waters and on its shores; it remembered their sorrow as though it were yesterday. The Aegean also remembered and mourned the people who had died on its waters and shores long before Ancient Greece, but this mourning made it even fiercer. And although its gentle lapping against the shore was broadcast with microphones over the memorial grounds to pronounce the atmosphere of sorrow, the Aegean did not feel at all peaceful. The Aegean Sea railed against the mixing of its turquoise waters with the crimson blood of youth who, for thousands of years, had been sent to their death for the sake of power and ambition. The Aegean Sea remembered each shorts-clad boy who eighty-five years ago had been sent by the thousands in barges to invade this shore, and every young man wearing an *Enver* cap who waited upon the hills to stop him; the sea relived the death of every one of these young men. The Aegean Sea, restless and alone, waited like a gigantic black maw at the Ariburnu-Anzac Cove.

Vicki and Ali Osman managed with difficulty to find a place to stand. The weather was markedly chilly and everyone was wearing either a hat or a hood. Ali Osman assisted Vicki in putting on her hood and produced a baseball cap from his pocket for himself. An old and disabled New Zealander woman sat next to them in a wheelchair, her chest decorated with her father's medals, and a group of Australian youths stood behind them, cheerfully telling each other stories of their childhood.

At five a.m. a trumpet sounded on the beach. The Australian Naval Band started playing a march sad enough to move anyone within hearing distance. A symbolic troop of Anzac soldiers marched solemnly around the entire cove, and passed in front of them. The national anthems of all three countries were played. The New Zealanders and Australians who were present at the memorial grounds sang their national anthems with emotion.

"Our..." murmured Vicki, "Our national anthem, *God Defend New Zealand*, is sung in two languages, English and Maori. And it ends with '*Aotearoa*'. That means the Long White Cloud."

"Is that so?" smiled Ali Osman, with polite disinterest.

Next, the prime ministers of New Zealand and Australia mounted the podium and gave speeches. They were followed by other important people who gave other important speeches. Priests took the podium and recited prayers. Throughout all of these important speeches, three concepts flew about the Gallipoli shores: Valor, honor and victory. Everyone used these words in abundance. Everyone loved these concepts. Then the participants all sang from the booklet of prayers and

309

hymns and lit the candles that had been distributed before-hand. The ceremony went on ceremonially.

At one point during a hymn, Ali Osman noticed that Vicki had begun to weep. Taking care not to look at her directly or make her uncomfortable, he stood at her side and watched her with serene interest. Without looking at her face, but simply standing there by her side. Just then the sky began to lighten and glow pink. Dawn was breaking with colors identical to sunset.

"Look!" pointed Vicki, sniffling. "Look right behind you! There it is. Goodness, how awesome its head looks once again!"

Turning to the direction she indicated, Ali Osman saw the Ariburnu Cliff or, as the Anzacs had named it, the Sphinx. Struck by the first rays of sunlight, its mighty lion's head truly did emerge in intimidating grandeur.

"How right my great-grandfather was," Vicki said in a weary voice. "It looks so confident, so menacing. Like it can see us all, it seems to be roaring that it is the rightful owner of this place. The Sphinx is the peak of the mountain at the Anzac Cove!"

With daybreak, that dark, daunting maw turned into a gorgeous blue sea. It was as though the sun had touched it with a magic wand and produced a miracle in a matter of minutes. People who had gathered to sing hymns and national anthems on a dark and chilly knoll had suddenly found themselves in paradise; they had been transported from the restless and impenetrably gloomy location of the past hour into a fairytale setting where a crystal blue sea kissed the shores of a soft beach.

"How lovely!" Vicki whispered.

Ali Osman smiled and nodded. Now that the memorial service at the Ariburnu-Anzac Cove was over, the New Zealanders and Australians began to disperse toward separate cemeteries. They were no longer Anzacs, it was time to turn back into New Zealanders and Australians. Everyone was going to honor their own dead at their own cemeteries. Even eighty-five years after their death, the nationality of the dead was still significant.

Since the ceremony grounds were extremely congested and the tour buses arrived in turns, the dispersion took a long time. Ali Osman gazed intently at the crowd and said in a thoughtful voice:

"The Turks commemorate their Gallipoli martyrs with a ceremony on the 18th of March. But in comparison to this one, our ceremony seems awfully small and local."

"That does not surprise me," Vicki commented. "Turks hold a plain and modest commemoration of Gallipoli because theirs was the side that won the Battle of Gallipoli, and the side that was rightfully defending itself, Ali Osman."

Ali Osman gave her a bitter smile and said:

"We still have a poor awareness of our history, Vicki. And only societies that have learned the lessons of the past can have an awareness of their history. Its absence, its fragility and its inaccuracy create danger, you understand, don't you?"

"Come on, Ali Osman, quit talking politics again," said Vicki as she drew close, reached out her arm and, surprising herself most of all, hugged Ali Osman.

Her spontaneous embrace took Ali Osman completely by surprise. Nevertheless, he did not reject this display of emotion and returned the hug. Vicki was both incredulous and pleased at this outburst, but she was not sure whether Ali Osman's affection toward her was solely a sign of compassionate friendship or traditional hospitality. After all, Turks were Easterners and Mediterraneans, which meant they were warm-blooded. Besides, Ali Osman was distantly related to her. Distantly, though. Only distantly. Thrice removed… In the end, even if it was amicable or platonic, the closeness felt good to Vicki, and that terrific question was attached to the feeling: "What if it isn't?"

As they stood there embracing, a familiar face appeared in the crowd, approached and stood grinning before them.

"Good morning, lovebirds!"

311

Vicki drew back from Ali Osman in panic and, without knowing why, quickly straightened herself out.

"Good morning, Mehmet, how is it going?" Ali Osman greeted him calmly.

"Ali Osman *ahbi*, I've been looking for you guys for hours. Couldn't reach your cell phone either, it was turned off. Anyway, you found a good spot for Vicki to watch the show... No, I never would have forgiven myself if she had missed this ceremony."

"Yes, we did find a good spot," remarked Vicki.

"Did you like the ceremony, Vicki?"

"It's moving, of course."

"I'm here every year and I still get emotional. See, I honestly got goosebumps."

"If only we could also hold moving ceremonies on March 18, Mehmet. If Turks were aware of everything that happened here eighty-five years ago, we would have an opportunity to draw lessons for the future, or even evaluate the present more clearly," said Ali Osman, sighing regretfully.

"Well said, there's Ali Osman *ahbi* the lawyer for you! Hey, are you guys hungry, how about I treat you to tea and *gozlemes*? See those vendors over there, the one on the far left is a friend of mine. What do you say?"

"I love *gozleme*," said Vicki.

"Don't you want to attend the ceremony at the New Zealand cemetery, Vicki?" asked Ali Osman.

"No, no. I've been there plenty of times. Mehmet knows. This service was enough for me."

Vicki, Ali Osman and Mehmet headed toward the row of roadside stands that sold meatballs, *gozlemes*, tea and coffee. The vendors looked tired and poor. One of them recognized Ali Osman. He was a childhood friend from the Bigali Village, who worked as a guard at the Gallipoli prison but had to keep this as a second job to make ends meet. They had their tea and *gozleme*s at his stand. After a brief conversation, Ali Osman bought half of his boyhood friend's *gozleme*s, on the pretext of taking them back to Auntie Beyaz. Vicki, who believed his tale, watched in bewilderment as he piled the *gozleme*s into a plastic bag. Both of them also noticed the needy children who walked around hawking water and packets of tissue at that early hour of the morning.

Morning had dawned, the crowd had largely dissolved, and all that remained on the beach were white plastic chairs, burnt-out candles and the litter of breakfast plates. Soon Turkish workers would begin cleaning up the site. The beach was deserted, but the three flags still flew at half-mast, side by side at the Ariburnu-Anzac Cove.

"I would like to visit *Ghazi* Sergeant Alican's grave. I'm ready for it now," said Vicki, suddenly turning toward Ali Osman.

Ali Osman registered surprise, as though he had not expected to hear this. But he regained his composure in no time and turned to face Vicki. His eyes were full of compassion.

"Sure thing, we'll go look for it Vicki," Mehmet jumped in.

"I'd like to go with him, Mehmet. Because it's his great-grandfather."

Mehmet tried but failed miserably to hide the offense he took at these words. He had perceived Vicki's wish as a statement on his professional skills and thus felt hurt.

"Oh yes, Mehmet, I almost forgot to tell you. I absolutely must return to Istanbul in two days for a case, but Vicki will still be here for a few days. I'm counting on you for the remainder of her time here. Because, as you know, one can't just trust the knowledge of any old guide. This is very important business. It's imperative to be professional."

"Absolutely, Ali Osman *ahbi*, my agency conducts all sorts of interviews and orientation programs before hiring guides."

"Fine, then you can call Vicki the day after tomorrow and you two can make your own plans. Sound good?"

GHAZI SERGEANT
ALICAN TAYLAR
1897-1985

LONG-WHITE-CLOUD
↔
GALLIPOLI

FOUGHT IN
GALLIPOLI AND DIED
IN GALLIPOLI.
MAY HE REST IN PEACE

☪

LIEUTENANT
ALI OSMAN BEY
1895-1915

ISTANBUL-GALLIPOLI
FOUGHT IN THE
BATTLE OF GALLIPOLI AND
WAS MARTYRED
IN GALLIPOLI.

HE RESTS IN PEACE

☪

"OK, Ali Osman *ahbi*. See you Vicki. I'll call the day after to-morrow. Bye!"

When Mehmet started toward his jeep, Ali Osman and Vic-ki also left the Ariburnu-Anzac Cove and walked back in the di-rection they had come from. The walk they had taken a few hours earlier, through the enchanted atmosphere of a dark fo-rest, was worlds removed from the sunny, vacation-like park where they now found themselves. And the soil no longer crunched with the same song beneath the tread of passers-by.

Ali Osman drove Vicki to the cemetery at the Eceyaylasi Village. It was one of those modest, unassuming cemeteries particular to Moslems. He halted by the site of twin graves, marked by two simple headstones.

"Here they are," he said, with a gentle smile. "My great-grandfather wished to be buried alongside Ali Osman *Bey*. Se-mahat *Hanim* respected his wish and did not object, so Ali Os-man *Bey*'s remains were never taken back to the family grave-site in Istanbul. My great-grandfather moved Ali Osman *Bey*'s grave to this location and reserved the spot next to him for himself. They have never been separated since 1915."

"So, what does it say on these headstones?"

Ali Osman translated for her.

All of a sudden Vicki folded her hands together, lowered her head and began to pray. Ali Osman took a few steps back when he saw that she was praying. In a small village cemetery, two young people stood at the head of humble twin graves and paid their respects to their deceased.

When she was done praying, Vicki produced a slender earthen Maori figurine from her pocket, broke it in two and bu-ried each half into one grave. Ignoring Ali Osman's curious ga-ze, she next took out a piece of paper and read it silently abo-ve *Ghazi* Sergeant Alican's grave. Assuming that she was re-ading a prayer or a Maori hymn, Ali Osman turned his back to Vicki and waited.

315

After a long while he heard her voice:

"We can go now."

On their way to Auntie Beyaz's house they ran into the White Rooster, who was strutting about with the chickens on the street. Vicki recognized him. She told Ali Osman of how she had at first enjoyed the notion that the rooster was happy despite his color deficiency, due to his lack of awareness, but how the thought finally reminded her of human consciousness and caused her pain. They talked about consciousness for a while.

"Consciousness is painful," said Ali Osman.

"Consciousness is painful," said Vicki.

They both gazed at the White Rooster enviously, conscious that they could never again settle for being a rooster. The rooster stopped as though he had heard them, waited, then went clucking on his way. Vicki, meanwhile, had not failed to notice the kindness with which Ali Osman had lugged the dozens of *gozleme*s that he had bought from his boyhood friend all the way back to the village and handed them to Havva so she could feed them to the chickens.

Just as they drew near Auntie Beyaz's house, Ali Osman suddenly asked:

"What was on that piece of paper, Vicki? I mean, if it is all right for me to ask... What did that piece of paper say that you carried in your pocket all the way here to read at the gravesite? Was it a prayer?"

Vicki smiled, took the paper out of her pocket and handed it to Ali Osman. The page, which had been photocopied from an English language book, said the following:

"*You heroes, who shed their blood upon this country's soil, you are now in a friendly nation. May you rest in peace and repose. You are side-by-side with the* Mehmetchik.* *You, the mot-*

*) *Mehmetchik*: nickname for Turkish soldiers

316

hers, who sent their sons from distant lands, wipe away your te-ars. Your sons are in our bosom; they are and shall ever conti-nue to sleep in peace. They who perished in this land have now become our sons as well. Ataturk, 1934."

Ali Osman stopped and studied Vicki with an elated smile on his face. His eyes shone with the beauty of people who know that words cannot possibly express the joy they feel. He gazed at her without speaking.

"A person who is intelligent, fair and visionary enough to write those lines perhaps did, as you say, 'maintain througho-ut his life the superior intelligence and common sense that he displayed in Gallipoli,'" remarked Vicki.

Ali Osman nodded. He was smiling. They walked on in si-lence. When they reached Auntie Beyaz's house, Ali Osman turned to Vicki:

"Only very few things in life could have been this appropri-ate, Vicki. You read the very words that my great-grandfather *Ghazi* Sergeant Alican most needed and used to love. This was the greatest of prayers for his soul. I am grateful to you," he said.

At this point, Ali Osman was kissing Vicki with his eyes. Vicki felt this kiss on her skin. The kiss that touched her skin was clearly no longer fraternal. In the excitement of the mo-ment, Vicki began ringing Auntie Beyaz's doorbell over and over.

"See here, *hele*, don't stay away too long Ali Osman, my boy, come visit every weekend, because I do miss you an awful lot. I'll have Havva make your favorite *tarak pilaf* again... Bring Semahat along as well, I miss her too, *mari*."

"I will come visit, Auntie Beyaz, don't you worry. But I don't know about Semahat. She's got her own life, her own work schedule, her own house and friends. But I promise to visit you more often."

The time had come for Ali Osman to return to Istanbul. He had packed his few belongings and despite all his protests, had taken the plastic bag stuffed with a supply of molasses, olive oil and homemade walnut bread that Auntie Beyaz had

had prepared for him. "Really Auntie Beyaz... I'll never be able to eat all this on my own..." he muttered as he placed the bag in his car. Meanwhile, Vicki was writing down her e-mail, her New Zealand address, and phone and fax numbers for Ali Osman, and Ali Osman was showing her the cell and home phone numbers that he had added to his business card, and explaining when he was likely to be found at each number.

"Now, don't forget, there is a ten hour time difference between us. Our day begins ten hours before yours," Vicki reminded him.

"And you call us Easterners!" quipped Ali Osman.

It was almost evening and Auntie Beyaz did not at all want Ali Osman to be driving at night. All day long she had urged Ali Osman to leave early, but the young man had done everything possible to delay his return to Istanbul, or more correctly, to prolong his time in the Eceyaylasi Village. Seeing his lively and unusually cheerful mood, Auntie Beyaz had understood that there was no persuading him, so she shook her head in exasperation but did not give up entirely. She spread out her prayer mat and, sitting down, turned to her last resort. This resort was the 'travel prayer' that would protect her youngest grandson and ensure his safe trip home. In fact, she performed this prayer every time he set off on the road, but this time she was taking much longer than usual.

After peeking into Auntie Beyaz's room to make sure she had started her travel prayer, Ali Osman dropped his humorous tone and said:

"Vicki, I'd like to have a word with you."

The seriousness in his voice pricked Vicki's heart like a giant needle.

"Sure," she said, looking extremely calm and unruffled from the outside. "I'm listening, Ali Osman."

Ali Osman sat down next to Vicki. He looked deadly serious, and somewhat thoughtful.

"Look Vicki, you came here to Gallipoli, you got to know us; Auntie Beyaz, the villagers of Eceyaylasi and the Turkish press. And we got to know you. You did a good thing by coming. And you are welcome here. Come again. Make sure you come again. Acutally, I know that you will come back."

Vicki suddenly felt scared. It seemed Ali Osman had been saving some terrible news for the last minute.

"But Vicki... The real reason you came here was to prove a theory that you had in mind. Isn't that so? You had a theory based on the possibility that your great-grandfather, Alistair John Taylor, had not died fighting at the Gallipoli Front, in World War I. Am I correct?"

He knew that he was correct, but wanted Vicki to confirm it one more time. In other words, he sounded just like a lawyer. And more to the point, he had closed himself off.

Vicki was both crestfallen and surprised to hear Ali Osman bring up this topic of diminished interest, when she had been hoping that he would use his final moments to speak to her privately on an entirely different matter. She masked her surprise skillfully.

"You're right," she replied coolly.

"You are a brave woman Vicki. You are determined and resilient. You overcame all the obstacles that were thrown in your path, and held out bravely until the end. You even managed to bring to heel my Auntie Beyaz, who is stubborn as a goat, and who had shunned the outside world for years. Not only did you bring her around, but you managed to gain her acceptance and, most difficult of all, her love. My Auntie Beyaz's love is genuine. It does not depend on blood or benefit relations. Anyone who knows her can tell you that."

Vicki smiled. Auntie Beyaz's love, like all hard-won loves, bestowed a wondrous energy upon its object.

"In the end, Vicki... in the end you found a story that fit your own incomplete story perfectly, like the final piece of a puzzle, and you took it immediately. Because you had been offered the one thing that you had searching hungrily for years, and you accepted it without objection. Now you were at peace, you had solved your problem and you stopped pursuing the matter. And that was when I entered the scene. I told you that the world's cultures and humanity itself were not yet ready for such a humane and incredibly beautiful tale. You had so believed that the same man could be a hero in the same war on two opposing sides and you were so thrilled by the justification of this belief that you dutifully announced to the press the 'misunderstanding' story that I had dictated to you. Yet that press conference was your last chance. It is next to impossible that an international press conference will be held in a tiny Gallipoli village for a second time."

"Yes, so I did, Ali Osman, what of it?" asked Vicki. She sounded tense and defensive.

"Don't you see Vicki, nothing is as it looks from the outside. And perhaps even this is reason enough to think that history is not a text that should be read linearly."

"So?" asked Vicki, growing annoyed.

"So? Vicki, do you think history is simply written for the sake of interest? Can history merely be a linear text of past events? Or, do you suppose history is written without any connection to current ideology?"

"I don't understand. I don't understand what you mean. You're confusing me, Ali Osman!"

"I don't mean to confuse you Vicki, on the contrary, I'm trying to lead you to a more expansive point of view, which I think someone like yourself will appreciate."

Vicki sighed. She was starting to feel peeved.

"Look Vicki, just like you, I grew up listening to stories of the Battle of Gallipoli. But my veteran great-grandfather, and his daughter, my Auntie Beyaz, used to tell me stories that were not told to other children. My great-grandpa would frequently talk and confer with Ali Osman *Bey*, the comrade in arms who had made a vast impression on him, and whom he always referred to with great respect. As a boy I highly enjoyed this 'invisible friend' game, but looking back, it saddens me to realize my great-grandfather's loneliness. This wonderful man, whose name I am honored to bear, had not only saved my great-grandfather's life, but his past and his family had presented my great-grandfather with a brand new viewpoint."

He stopped and swallowed.

"My great-grandfather used to say: 'A human's blood is red. Nationalism cannot be found in the color of blood.' On the other hand, both he and my Auntie Beyaz were genuinely patriotic people. It was from them that I first learned what aspects of Turkish culture I could be proud of. And these aspects contained neither conquests nor heroic warfare. They did not criticize the conquests that had been made thousands of years ago, but rather turned my attention toward accomplishments regarding humanity. For example, my great-grandfather used to praise the political skill with which the Ottomans governed diverse nations for hundreds of years. They are the ones who first taught me that a true patriot is a person who contributes to the development of the country where he lives. Thus, my great-grandfather taught me to regard raucous and aggressive displays of patriotism with suspicion. My great-grandfather used to scorn coarse and showy patriotism as 'unproductive patriotism'. And history proved him right in World War II. If I should one day enter politics, as I intend to in the near future, I can confidently say that my great-grandfather's counsel will be a crucial reason for my decision."

This made Vicki smile.

"That would be very fortunate for Turkey," she said, gazing at Ali Osman with admiration.

Ali Osman dodged her gaze and continued with the same gravity:

322

"Thank you Vicki. But I would like to tell you something. I have to tell you this Vicki."

Vicki heaved another sigh.

"My great-grandfather died when I was in high school. He had been a source of living history for me, an important witness, and when he died I was left in a lurch. So I developed a keen interest in history. I studied alternative and revisionist theories as much as official history books. I used to read history while my peers read comic books. Anyhow, I finally found myself pondering the difference between writing *myth-based* culture and *scientific* history."

"Myth-based culture and scientific history?" puzzled Vicki.

"Yes. Look, have you ever considered the similarities between epic poetry and history?"

"Oh, but that's going a bit too far Ali Osman..."

"Why do you say that? Here, let's take Homer for instance. The only difference between Homer and a historian of the Middle Age who depicts history in accordance with his king's ideology, is that Homer is a poet. They both relate stories of heroism to influence future generations."

"History is not fiction, Ali Osman."

"True, history should not be fiction. But I wonder if that is the reality of the matter?"

"I don't agree, I don't agree at all!" Vicki countered crossly.

"There's a historian named Plutarch, whom Shakespeare also used to read. I have never forgotten some of his words, since I first laid eyes on them, Vicki."

Vicki, who was none too pleased to be spending the final hours of this final night conversing about history, had begun to wonder what exactly Ali Osman was getting at.

"When Plutarch says: 'A historian is the person who records the great deeds of great men,' he seems to be emphasizing a distinction similar to the one between an artists' model and his portrait. In other words, no matter what the historian

323

does, fiction is bound to become involved. Therefore, no record of history that reaches us tells the plain and unadulterated truth. It never has, Vicki."

"Hmm… I'd never looked at it that way. Yes, maybe… You might have a point there."

"Of course I do," said Ali Osman eagerly. "History depends on memory, since it is not narrated live. But history cannot be written based on memory."

Vicki sighed again, but it seemed Ali Osman was enthralled in his own words.

"Turks view the Battle of Gallipoli as a victory. The English depict it as a withdrawal on their part. For the Anzacs, Gallipoli is an event that led to the founding of their national identities. The Germans may well claim the victory as their own, since the commander of the Battle of Gallipoli was a German general. The Battle of Gallipoli is one of the most important wars of the 20th century. It was after the Turks won this war that the Russian Tzar was overthrown and the Soviet Union established, basically altering the course of history. So, once again, we have here the same war, recounted in several different versions by the histories of people who fought in that war."

Vicki could not help but listen closely to what Ali Osman was saying, though she was confused and wished that they had spent their last night more romantically.

"Besides, if you take a good look, you will see that until the 19th century, almost none of the world's cultures regarded or taught war as an objectionable thing. War was a noble pursuit for our Turkish and their European forefathers. Consider history and legends; all the nobles, the *pasha*s and the important men were warriors."

'Yes, he is speaking the truth but, damn it, I wish he was speaking of something different on a night like this,' thought Vicki with a sigh.

"No one can deny the fact that for nearly two thousand years, until the middle of the 20th century, the word 'human' stood for 'male'. This was the case. So, when people spoke of important and noble men in Christian European and Moslem Turkish histories, they always referred to our male ancestors. And this is still the case. Thus, history is a text in which male historians tell of our male ancestors, who considered war to be a noble act. Before Islam, women were also considered human in Turkish society, that is why I emphasize the religious factors, Vicki."

'They were shamanic, the Turks were shamanic,' Vicki thought in a flash.

"So it stands to reason that we know nothing about the female view of history. Women were never included in history, unless they were wives or daughters of important men. Besides, there were no women historians. There couldn't have been. That is why we have no idea what it means to exist in history as a woman. What I mean, Vicki, is that the people worth recording were noble male warriors. These were the men who killed, and who faced the danger of being killed. Once, in fact, until very recently, war was a fine and important thing. If you take a careful look at children's games today, you will see right away that the ideology of war is still being imposed upon them through these games."

"But we have entered a new century where we can now speak of a critical understanding of history, Ali Osman."

"Very good. Bravo Vicki. But in the end, history is narration and narrative, by nature, is close to fiction. It could, in other words, be said that it is open to distortion and exaggeration. And I'm afraid it will always remain open."

"But now we have films and photographs. Documentation in the 21st century is done through much easier, practical and reliable methods."

"True, but technological advances have also increased techniques of montage and simulation. In the end, whatever

325

methods may exist, history will always have a narrator. Even if the narrator is a robot's microchip brain, or artificial intelligence, its creator will nevertheless be human."

"Ah, you're too difficult, Ali Osman."

"Truth cannot be attained easily, Victoria Taylor," said Ali Osman. His voice was direct and blank. He had left all of his sense of humor in his pocket. "The path that leads to truth is always difficult. Because a misleading element called the human factor is always involved. For example, having assumed that you reached the truth, you did not even consider the possibility that I might be an agent sent by the Turkish government to convince you against spoiling written history."

"An agent? Oh my God, are you a CIA agent, Ali Osman?" cried Vicki.

"If anything, I would be an agent of MIT, the Turkish intelligence agency, Vicki."

"Are you really?" asked Vicki, covering her mouth with her hand and waiting with held breath for his response.

Ali Osman sighed and raised his eyebrows. He was irritated.

"No, no, that can't be, you can't be an agent, Ali Osman..." murmured Vicki anxiously.

They were both silent. The sound of Auntie Beyaz's unintelligible prayers and prayer beads could be heard from the next room.

"What if I asked you to reconsider everything, from this viewpoint..."

"Are you a secret agent, Ali Osman?"

"Is that so important to you? Is the possibility of me being a government agent more important than the story that you believed of how your great-grandfather defied the entire world after the war by switching sides and living as one of the people whom he had fought against? Is it more important for me to be an agent than me trying to explain to you how your great-grandfather, despite everything that you've been told in this house, could be one of the thousands of soldiers who died in Gallipoli and whose graves were never found?" shouted Ali Osman.

"My great-grandfather did not die in Gallipoli!" dismissed Vicki.

"What if he did, and what if all this was a game planned to pacify and send you home, to avoid a serious historic scandal?"

"You can't aggravate me Ali Osman! My great-grandfather named his children Long, White and Cloud, which means New Zealand, and even that is proof of the truth!" said Vicki, sounding frustrated.

"Bah, proof! If you knew the kinds of names Turkish peasants gave their children you would immediately abandon that proof and never bring up the subject again. They name them Satılmış (Sold), Durmuş (Stopped), Döne (Turn), Imdat (Help), Yeter (Enough), Kiraz (Cherry), Çilek (Strawberry), Sergen (Shelf), Miğfer (Helmet) and all other kinds of things that I would have trouble translating into English... Naturally, in light of these names, Long, White and Cloud seem perfectly innocent and meaningful. Besides... if you're so keen on people's names, why don't you think about how Meryem, who was the daughter of a Moslem peasant and who married my great-grandfather, was named after Mother Mary, and how her brother, Isa, was named after Jesus?"

Vicki began to laugh. It was more of a nervous laughter. Then she stopped unexpectedly and turned to Ali Osman:

"Are you an agent, Ali Osman?" she asked, looking straight into his eyes.

"For God's sake, Vicki, is that all you can say to me after everything I've told you?" cried Ali Osman, leaping to his feet. "Where is that intelligence of yours that I admire so much? Why are you stuck on this stupid detail, tell me!"

He was yelling and flinging his hands in the air, he was truly enraged.

"Stupid?" cried Vicki, also getting up from her seat. "Stupid, you say? I may be stupid for loving you, but if you don't tell me right this minute whether or not you are an agent, then you'd better believe that I will commit many other stupidities, Ali Osman TaylAr! Such massive stupidities that you will never forget them for the rest of your life!"

Ali Osman stood stunned. He had obviously been caught unawares. Nothing Vicki said could have surprised him more. He waited for a while, trying to collect himself, then turned to Vicki, who stood facing him, proud and powerful as a tigress. He opened his mouth to say something. But he could not speak. He was dumbstruck, like all men who find themselves confronted by a declaration of love from a woman they like. Vicki then perceived that she had won, and she relaxed.

"Yes, that is more important than anything else, Ali Osman. For I am now interested in a living man, and not what nationality my great-grandfather's passport was when he died. For the first time in my life, I have met a man who I am interested in, for my own sake. And I swear I don't care one bit what the reason is, if this man is my cousin thrice removed, or not, and if this has happened by no mere coincidence in Gallipoli! For the first time in my life I am standing on my feet and expressing my love. And if history, or my great-grandfather, is the reason for it, then fine. But if not, it's still fine!"

She stopped. She bit her lips and sat back down.

"And don't be fooled into thinking that this strength will last a long time. If you continue standing there staring at me dumbly like that, I'll soon turn back into that girl who is ashamed of her feelings."

That was when Ali Osman saw her. That was when Ali Osman saw himself; that was when he saw them together. He saw what he had overlooked for days, and he understood. He sat down gently beside Vicki and looked at her the way a man looks at a woman. He leaned toward her. Vicki did not draw back but returned his approach. And the two of them kissed. Vicki and Ali Osman kissed in this house, where *Ghazi* Sergeant Alican once used to live. They kissed. It was a lovely kiss that began shyly, but turned into a long, warm and passionate embrace.

"That's enough fighting from you," chided Auntie Beyaz, entering the living room. She stopped when she saw them kissing amorously, but expressed no surprise. Auntie Beyaz was never surprised.

"God have mercy... Can't you take that somewhere else?" she said.

Auntie Beyaz was still muttering as they withdrew from one another's lips, their eyes still locked.

"Let's see now, I'd better chant the *Mevlit** for my father's spirit in honor of this occasion. The *Mevlit* is in Turkish, we can all understand it! Yes, yes, I'd better do that. Seems that's what my father is asking for."

An hour later, as he set off jubilantly for Istanbul, Ali Osman parted from Vicki with a shorter but more familiar kiss. Auntie Beyaz poured the traditional cup of water after him, praying that he would reach home safe and sound, like water. She was still muttering to herself:

"Good, good... Now this turned out good, *mari*. There's a good in everything, anyhow. Now you will visit more often, and this girl will visit often as well! See how well it all turned out! God bless us all..."

When Ali Osman's car disappeared from sight, Vicki gave Auntie Beyaz a joyful, smothering hug. She could barely stand still. She was happy.

"Stop it, crazy girl, stop it *hele*!" said Auntie Beyaz and pushed her away.

---

*) *Mevlit*: Prophet Mohammed's nativity hymn

329

Auntie Beyaz did not at all like explicit shows of affection.

Three days later a woman smiled on a Singapore Airlines flight to Wellington via Singapore. It was Vicki, who had just read the single sentence contained in the envelope that Ali Osman had given her to open in the airplane. The smile on her face was so expansive, blissful, fennel-scented and warm that it spread through the entire cabin. The airplane was suddenly refreshed with this love-filled smile. The smile radiated a scent of happiness that touched each passenger individually, and they wandered out of their seats in search of its owner. The person they found was a young female passenger, traveling alone. She was sleeping with a smile on her face, clutching to her chest a letter made up of a single sentence. This was what the letter said:

LONG WHITE CLOUD <–> GALLIPOLI
(AOTEAROA <–> GALLIPOLI)

On sunny days, people visiting the Gallipoli Peninsula will come across an old granny who walks with a cane around the Gallipoli National Park.

This old lady has blue eyes and hundreds of fine wrinkles etched on a face so white that it seems to be covered in many layers of powder. She is thin enough to be called skinny, old enough to be a hundred and agile as a youth. She wears a flower-print *shalvar* made of cotton, a blouse made of the same fabric, and a handknit wool vest. The socks that cover her feet are also handknit. Tulip patterns are embroidered on the socks. She wears flat black leather shoes and slowly fingers the agate prayer beads that she holds in her hand. She strolls around the Gallipoli National Park, leaning on her cane.

Upon seeing her, people are struck by the enlightened beauty and acquired peace of her face, and they smile at her. The foreign tourists wave, and the local tourists salute her. She never notices the odd sense of peace and respect that she causes in those around her, and she never returns any show of affection. Because she does not see them. Sometimes she pauses and, oblivious to those around her, mutters:

"Now, *mari*, better take care of yourselves! Winter is bitter in Gallipoli, it'll get you everytime. It won't care if you're a foreigner, it's ruthless, I warn you!"

Those who recognize her consider it a blessing that Auntie Beyaz is once again out and about in Gallipoli, so they run up to kiss her hand, and leave looking dazed, as though they had just encountered the ghost of a saint. Those who don't know her find it hard to believe the speed with which this beautiful old peasant woman walks; they regard her with suspicious admiration.

Then the granny, who is eager to get to the Ariburnu-Anzac Cove and hear the nightingales sing, repeats:

"Now, *mari*, better take care of yourselves! Winter is bitter in Gallipoli, it'll get you everytime. It won't care if you're a foreigner, it's ruthless, I warn you!"

Winter is indeed bitter in Gallipoli. It will get you, that ruthless chill.

That ruthless chill will get you.

Gallipoli's chill takes no mercy.

Gallipoli's chill.

Gallipoli's.

Gallipoli.

1997-2001 Istanbul